The
Memory
Shop

Ella Griffin

ORION

First published in Great Britain in 2017
by Orion
This paperback edition published in 2018
by Orion Books,
an imprint of The Orion Publishing Group Ltd
Carmelite House, 50 Victoria Embankment
London, EC4Y 0DZ

An Hachette UK Company

1 3 5 7 9 10 8 6 4 2

A CIP catalogue record for this book
is available from the British Library.

ISBN 978 1 4091 4584 4

Typeset at The Spartan Press Ltd,
Lymington, Hants

Printed and bound in Great Britain by Clays Ltd,
St Ives plc

www.orionbooks.co.uk

For Jimmy, in memory of Silas.

And for Neil. Always.

'The most important things in the world aren't things at all.'
– Anon.

I

Vintage Chanel Compact Mirror

Nora

The photographer had already turned away and was hunched over his laptop. The make-up and hair girls were packing up their things. The model had pulled on a dressing gown and was heading for the lane at the back of the studio with her phone to her ear and a cigarette dangling from her lips.

This was the moment that always broke Nora's heart a little. When the last shot had been taken and it was time to destroy the illusion she had created.

It had taken her two days and dozens of props to create the set. A luxurious bedroom with a gilded bed and sofa, and a floor-to-ceiling window that looked out on a glittering night-time cityscape that she had improvised using a bolt of black velvet and a dozen ropes of LED lights.

She gathered her hair into a knot, climbed up a ladder and began the painstaking work of pulling it all apart, working a little faster than she liked today because she had a flight to catch.

When she had taken the backdrop down, she bubble-wrapped the crystal champagne flutes and folded the Egyptian bedlinen, then steamed the cashmere throw and the satin slip that had been draped across the sofa and packed them all back into the bags they had arrived in.

She knelt down and carefully checked the furniture for marks or scratches, then labelled them with the names of the stores they had been borrowed from. She could have done with Liv's help with all this, but she had called in with a migraine this morning, probably brought on by the fact that she would have to handle everything on her own for the next week.

Nora was going back to Dublin for the reading of her grand-mother's will and to pick up a few things from the house in Temple Terrace before it was cleared and sold. The keys of the house! Nora jammed a hand into one jeans' pocket and then the other. She got up and found her bag and rifled through it. The silver mussel shell key ring wasn't there. It must still be in the bowl on the hall table where she'd left it last night.

It was after six now but she rang her grandmother's solicitor in Ireland, hoping to arrange to pick up a spare. No reply. If Adam was at home, she could ask him to send the key over, but he had gone to Birmingham this morning. She would have to go home and get the key herself, otherwise it would be Monday before she could get into the house.

She slipped the photographer's assistant twenty pounds to finish packing up the set, dashed off an apologetic email to Liv, grabbed her case, her bag and her jacket, and ran out onto Blundell Street just in time to see a black cab coming round the corner.

'Fountain Road, off Haverstock Hill,' she gasped, dragging her case into the back. 'Then on to Belsize Park Tube.' She could change to the Piccadilly line and still just about make it to Heath-row for her flight.

There were green lights all the way and fifteen minutes later the cab pulled over outside the two-storey, red-brick Victorian house. She asked the driver to wait and ran up the steps to the front door.

Even in her hurry, she felt a rush of pleasure at the sight of the hall. The walls she had painted French grey. The console table she had stripped and gilded, the stair runner she'd had designed using scraps of Turkish rugs picked up in junk shops and at car boot sales, the gorgeous Swedish chandelier that had cost her half a month's salary.

She fished the key out of the bowl and took a moment to take it all in, and then she heard it ... The soft click of a door closing upstairs. The hairs on the back of her neck lifted. Adam had wanted to replace the original glass windows in the kitchen with double-glazing. She should have listened to him. Someone had broken in. There was a burglar up there right now. She held her breath and strained her ears but all she could hear was the thunder of her heart and the faint hum of traffic passing on the road outside.

Had she imagined the noise? She hesitated, afraid to go up the stairs to check on her own, then slid her phone out of her pocket and called Adam, hoping he was free to stay on the line while she checked the upstairs rooms. She held her breath as the call connected, then let it go in a rush of relief when she heard the sound of a mobile phone ringing upstairs.

He had been here all the time. He must have cancelled the Birmingham meeting and gone back to bed to sleep off his jet lag. She took the stairs in twos, the sneakers she wore to work making no sound and opened the bedroom door.

He was sitting up in bed, the covers pulled up to his shoulders. The curtains were drawn but it was light enough to see that he looked deathly pale.

'Hi,' he said. 'You woke me.'

'I didn't realise you were here.' Nora crossed the room, passed the pile of clothes on the rug and perched on the bed beside him. 'Are you sick?'

'Yeah,' he ran a shaking hand through the rumple of his blond hair. 'Must have been something I ate on the plane. I had to call the meeting off. What are you doing back? Shouldn't you be on the way to the airport?'

'I forgot the key to Temple Terrace. I've got a taxi waiting outside.' Nora felt torn. She had to go to Dublin but she couldn't leave him like this. 'Do you want me to call the doctor? Or go to the pharmacy?'

'No. I'll be fine. I just need to sleep it off.' He put his hand over hers and gave it a quick squeeze. 'You should go or you'll miss your flight.'

He was right. She bent over and kissed his forehead.

'Love you.'

'Love you,' he mumbled.

She was almost at the bedroom door when her heel connected with something hard. There was a sharp crack, the sound of something splintering. She stumbled and reached for the switch on the wall.

'Don't!' Adam in a voice that was almost a groan.

But the room was already flooded with light and Nora saw in a flash the details she had missed in the dark. The lacy bra lying on top of the tangle of discarded clothes on the floor. A single high-heeled shoe abandoned by the foot of the bed. The lipstick print on the wine glass on her carved bedside table.

The door to the en suite was closed but suddenly she knew, with absolute certainty that there had to be somebody in there.

Nora opened her mouth but no sound came out. Her voice was tethered to the sinking stone of her heart. She backed out onto the landing.

'Nora,' Adam was out of bed, grabbing for his clothes, shouting after her as she ran down the stairs, 'wait!'

The black cab was still at the kerb, hazard lights flashing, a plume of blue exhaust wreathing up into the still June air. The driver had been dozing; he jolted awake as Nora wrenched the door open. 'Heathrow,' she managed to whisper. 'As quick as you can.'

His dark eyes met hers in the rear view mirror. 'You want me to wait for him?'

She saw that Adam was running down the steps now, barefoot, in jeans and a shirt that flapped open over his chest.

'No,' Nora said. She heard the *thunk* as the central locking kicked in just before Adam got to the cab.

Adam tried to open the door then banged his palm against the window. 'Wait! Just wait a second!'

But the cab was already pulling away, sliding into a gap in the traffic. Adam ran alongside it on the pavement, shouting and gesticulating, almost colliding with a woman with a buggy, scattering a knot of students. He managed to keep pace as they passed the hairdresser's and the dry-cleaner's but by the time they got to the NW3 Bar on the corner, he was out of breath and he bent over, bracing his knees in cupped hands.

'He's a trier,' the driver said, softly. 'I'll say that for him.' He caught her eye in the mirror again. 'You sure you don't want to go back and give him another chance?'

Nora shook her head. Tears were spilling down her cheeks as

she upended her handbag on the seat, grappling blindly for the phone.

Liv picked up straight away. 'Hello!' She sounded tense.

'It's me. I'm sorry to call you when you have a migraine but...' Nora gulped back a sob. 'But Adam is having an affair.'

'Oh my God!' Liv gasped.

'He was supposed to be away on business but I just found him at home in bed,' she gulped back a sob, 'with someone.'

'Who was it?'

'I don't know.' Nora covered her eyes with her hand, as if she could block out the memory. 'She was hiding in the bathroom when I left. I had to get out. I couldn't stay there.'

'Are you sure?' Liv said. 'Are you certain there was someone there?'

'Liv, I saw her things! Her underwear. Her shoe! Her wine glass! And I saw the look on Adam's face!' Nora pressed the mussel shell key ring into her palm hard. 'I can't believe this is happening. I feel like I'm going crazy.'

'Take a deep breath, Nora,' Liv said levelly. 'Tell me where are you now?'

'In a cab on the way to the airport.'

'You're not still going to Dublin, are you? You don't sound like you're in any state to get on a plane.'

'I have to go.' Nora wiped her eyes with her hand. 'I promised my mum I'd do this. I have an appointment with the solicitor on Monday.'

'Fine,' Liv sighed. 'Okay. But you shouldn't be on your own. I'll fly over and stay with you.'

'Really?' Nora said, shakily. 'Are you sure? What about your migraine?'

'Fuck my migraine,' Liv said firmly.

Nora felt a rush of relief. Liv was in her corner. Liv, who had a solution to everything, 'Really? Thank you.'

'Now listen to me! No tears!' Liv ordered. 'Just try to keep it together till I get there. Maybe this is not as bad as it looks, Nora. We'll figure it out. You're going to be okay.'

If Liv said it, Nora thought, desperately, maybe it was true. She was the closest thing to an older sister that Nora had ever had and, from the day they'd met, she had looked up to her.

She had moved so often when she was young, that she had never quite developed the knack of making friends but when she moved to London, Liv had taken her under her wing. They had lived together for eight years and then ended up working together.

She was the coolest person Nora had ever met. She could be scratchy and moody, but that was what sisters were like. She was honest about her shortcomings and wickedly sarcastic about everyone else's. She believed in herself so completely that everyone else did too. And she had always believed in Nora. Told her for years, that she was wasting her talent trying to earn a living as an illustrator. And finally persuaded her to come on board her set design company. They were a good team. Nora could get on with what she loved most, dreaming up wild and wonderful ideas while Liv did what Nora could not in a million years face, easily and effortlessly.

No tears. Nora repeated Liv's words like a mantra on the flight to Dublin, in the queue at the taxi rank, on the journey across the city to the seaside town where her grandparents had lived. But she felt her eyes begin to prickle when the taxi took a sharp left into Blackrock and she saw the familiar outline of the white stucco houses on Temple Terrace.

The tall sash windows of Number 18 were tightly shuttered. The window of the empty shop front on the ground floor had been papered over with flyers and posters and tagged with graffiti. The house looked dark and unwelcoming but Nora couldn't wait to get inside. She had only lived here for a few months when she was a child, but it was the place that had always felt most like home.

She closed the door behind her and dropped her suitcase. She let her handbag slide off her shoulder and hit the floor. The tears she had been swallowing back all afternoon erupted. Her sobs echoed around her in the empty house.

Through her tears, she saw a huge, dark shape was crouched in the pool of shadow at the bottom of the stairs and a pair of steady yellow eyes was watching her, unblinking. 'Houdini,' she gasped and she made her way across a pile of junk mail and knelt down beside him and buried her face in his mane of black and gold fur the way she had when she was a child.

He was enormous, more like a bear than a Newfoundland, with a thick coat of soot- and honey-coloured fur. He had been her grandfather's pet when he was a boy. Hugh had been so heartbroken when Houdini died, that his parents had decided to have him stuffed.

His legs had been arranged at an odd angle, as if he was somehow body boarding and his mouth was set in an odd, lopsided grin. He gazed up at Nora, adoringly, with his kind, slightly crossed, yellow glass eyes.

Her phone buzzed in the pocket of her jacket. She had been screening calls from Adam all afternoon, but this was Liv's number.

'You've landed?'

'I'm at the house.'

'You can't stay there, Nora. It's gloomy and it's been empty for months.'

'It's fine.' Nora looked around the hall. The truth was, she had never seen it look so bad. Her grandmother had cleaned the house from top to bottom every other day, but she must have given up when Hugh had died. The familiar scent of beeswax polish and lemon soap had been replaced with a musty unlived in smell. Piles of post and newspapers were heaped on the marble console table. The antique Moroccan rugs that criss-crossed the polished floorboards were bunched and crooked. The Venetian glass chandelier had two blown bulbs. The carved flowers on the Balinese temple doors were blooming with dust.

'You need a fluffy robe, a hot bath and room service. Give me five minutes, I'll book you into a hotel,' Liv said.

'No.' Nora was not ready to face the world again, not yet. 'I'll be okay here, really. I'm not sure if you will, though...'

'I'm not coming to Dublin for a city break, Nora. I'm coming to look after you. My flight gets in at ten tomorrow morning. So all you have to do is get through the night. Check the bathroom cupboard, old people always keep sleeping tablets lying around. Pop a couple and get some sleep. I'll be there before you know it.'

After she hung up, Nora went upstairs on shaky legs to her grandmother's bathroom. It used to be scented with lemon cologne and rosewood, but now the air was sour with the smell of drains. There was a fur of dust on the Moroccan tiles by the sink and on the yellow velvet chaise longue in front of the small fireplace. But Liv had been right. There was a prescription bottle of Zolpidem in one of the drawers. Nora swallowed two, found clean sheets in the cabinet and carried them into the front bedroom, which she had always thought of as hers.

Everything was still exactly where it had been when she was a child: the menagerie of glass animals marching across the marble mantelpiece; the telescope set up in front of the shuttered sash window; the wire birdcage made to look like the Taj Mahal; the cut-glass globe that was so old it still showed Iran as Persia and Istanbul as Constantinople. She had been planning to bring it back to London, to put it in the alcove in the dining room in the house on Fountain Road but, right now, she couldn't imagine ever going back there.

She made up the bed and undressed and slipped beneath the cold sheets. She checked her phone and saw five more missed calls from Adam. Her screensaver was a close up of his face. Her stomach lurched as she stared at it. How he could he have done this to her? He was supposed to be her perfect man. He gazed at her from the photograph. His head slightly bent, his long lashed glittering brown eyes looking up at her from under the tangle of his dark hair, his beautiful, full lipped mouth in a half smile. She dropped her phone on the floor and pressed her face into the pillow. She couldn't stand to look at him any more.

The day they'd met, Nora had been putting finishing touches to an office set for a *Business Plus Magazine* series called 'Thirty Entrepreneurs Under Thirty'. She had been up most of the night painting an elaborate backdrop with panelling to create the illusion of a Victorian gentleman's study. She was perched on the back of the leather sofa hanging a gilt-framed oil painting when

Liv wandered past. 'Did someone here order Aidan Turner with dressing on the side?' she asked airily.

Nora looked up and there he was. Six three and lean as a rake, with a tangle of dark curly hair and a suit bag over his arm.

'God, I wish I was single,' Liv muttered as the photographer's assistant showed him to the changing room.

'No, you don't.' Liv had just moved in with a photographer called Paul King. They were talking about having kids and Nora had never seen her so happy.

'You're right. I don't! But still. Did you see those eyes?'

'Pantone one seven-five six four one.' Nora straightened the painting. 'Emerald green.' But Liv wasn't listening, she was flicking through the briefs to find his biog.

'Adam Mason. Twenty-nine. Founder and CEO of StealDealz. Blah! Blah! Blah! "Using mobile technology to create and foster a thriving online retail community." In other words, flogging cut-price memory-foam mattresses and cubic zirconium jewellery. Let's see if he's on Facebook. Photographs are private but... relationship status: None.'

'That's stalking.' Nora climbed down off the sofa and straightened some leather-bound books she was using as props for the antique desk.

'I know!' Liv said. 'I love it!'

Nora and Liv stayed late to take the set apart and pack it away, then went to join the others in the pub.

Adam was still there, the centre of an adoring circle, the make-up and hairdressing girls, the journalist who had interviewed him and the photographer's assistant who hadn't quite decided if he was straight or gay.

At the bar, Liv caught Nora looking over as they waited for their drinks. 'You should go over there and chat him up.'

'I don't think so,' Nora said. Both of them knew that hell was going to freeze over twice before she put herself on the line like that. 'He's not my type.'

But after two glasses of cold white wine had worked their magic, she was wondering if that would be such a bad thing. What was her type anyway? She thought of the three guys she'd gone out with since she'd moved to London at the age of twenty. They had all been kind and idealistic and creative and, like her, they had been determined not to get sucked into the commercial world. They had wanted to use their talents to do something meaningful. The last and best of these relationships had been with a Welsh graphic designer and graffiti artist called Denis. They'd had one blissfully happy summer going to exhibitions and galleries and walking around London photographing tags in alleys; sitting up late on the tiny, grimy roof garden of her flat drinking red wine and talking about art and movies.

They'd spoken about moving in together, too, but Denis had had his heart broken and he wanted to take things slowly. And by the time he was ready, Nora had given up on making it as an illustrator and had taken the job with Liv, styling shoots for advertisers and magazines, which was about as commercial as you could get, and they'd parted ways amicably.

Nora had been relieved and also slightly panicky. She would be thirty in two months. She didn't want to spend her life drifting from one relationship to another. She wanted someone to share her life with. A home, security, a family.

Liv went outside to take a call while Nora studied Adam's reflection in the mirror behind the bar. Why shouldn't one of *Business Plus Magazine*'s 'Thirty Entrepreneurs Under Thirty' be her type? She could change her type, couldn't she?

She was going to do it, she decided. She was going to walk over and – and what? Push his fan club out of the way? She turned around just as he looked up and he caught her looking at him and he smiled and she smiled back, then she looked away. He really did not need another woman gazing at him adoringly. A few minutes later, he appeared at the bar, beside her.

'You're the stylist from earlier, right? Can I get you something?'

She wanted to laugh. It had been this easy. But she forced herself to play it cool, to make him work a bit.

'No, I'm good, thanks.'

He turned away and she saw him frown slightly. 'The set was pretty awesome. Loved the painted panelling things.'

'Thanks!' Nora said again.

She thought he'd give up but he didn't. He stayed at the bar chatting and at closing time he asked for her number.

He rang twice the next day but Liv wouldn't let Nora call him back. Another two days went by and he texted her and asked her to meet him for dinner. She didn't kiss him that night, or on the next date. And it was six weeks before she went to bed with him.

Adam was different to any man Nora had ever met, decisive and confident, but also disarmingly needy. He got upset if she didn't pick up when he called or text him back right away and, secretly, she liked that. It gave her a feeling of certainty.

Adam was travelling back and forth to the States and Nora was working flat out. She'd drop everything to be with him when he came home and they'd dive into a romantic bubble. Those first six months, were all long hello kisses at airports and teary goodbyes. Unexpected bouquets arriving at work. Weekends away at expensive hotels, gorgeous lingerie in ribbon handled bags. Having so little time together made every moment seem charged with meaning and excitement and urgency.

They talked about renting a flat together but then, over one intense weekend, they decided it made more sense to buy a place instead. Adam had money put by for a deposit and Nora pitched in with the renovation and decoration. She threw herself into the house on Fountain Road, stripping wallpaper, painting and grouting and sanding and scouring architectural salvage yards and interiors websites and junk shops for pieces to turn it into their perfect home. With Adam travelling so much, she spent most of the last two years there alone. But by next Christmas when things were set up with his business partners in the States, he'd be based in the UK full time and then their life together could begin properly. At least, that had been the plan, Nora thought with a lurch of her heart, until she had walked into their bedroom yesterday.

A splinter of sunlight slipped its way through the closed shutters and warmed the back of Nora's neck. She stirred and turned over. Her eyes were gummed with sleep and when she opened them, there was a brief moment when her mind was blank and she felt a rush of pleasure at the sight of this room she had loved so much all her life.

Then what had happened hit her in a rush. This time yesterday she had been hurrying out of the house to the shoot and Adam had been pacing up and down the hall, talking on the phone, trying to thread cufflinks through the cuffs of his shirt.

He had waved at her as she passed and mouthed, 'Love you'. At least, that's what she had presumed he was mouthing. And she had said, 'Love you too'. She wanted to turn back time and take those words back. To grab his phone out of his hand and see who he was talking to and then to throw him out. She pushed her fist into her stomach to try to stop the pain. How long after she had gone had he waited before he opened the door to another woman?

The thunder of the door knocker broke her thoughts. She grabbed her grandmother's silk kimono off the back of the door and pulled it on as she ran down the stairs. Liv was standing on the doorstep in a tiny white shift dress, high sandals and huge sunglasses.

'Come here.' Liv was not what she called with a shudder, 'feely-touchy', but she embraced Nora now, then she stepped back and held up a blue Caffè Nero bag. 'I know it's a big cloud, but I've brought a silver lining. Chocolate croissants.'

Liv winced when she saw the state of the kitchen. 'Maybe we should go out to a café?'

'It's fine.' Nora found a tea towel and wiped dust and dried-up crumbs off two chairs and cleared a space in the piles of books and newspapers on the table.

The double-fronted glass-door cabinet that took up one wall of the kitchen was stacked with beautiful vintage china, but she wasn't up to washing cups and plates.

The combination of the sleeping-tablet fog in her head and the sight of Liv, who was part of her life in London, here in her grandparents' kitchen made Nora feel as if this was some kind of elaborate dream scene in a movie. She watched Liv unpack two takeaway cups and shake three croissants onto cardboard plates. 'I don't think I can face food.'

'Sit! Eat!' Liv commanded. 'You'll feel better.'

Nora ate one pastry mechanically and then a second. The sugar, the caffeine and the company unlocked a stream of words and Liv listened, picking the last croissant apart with her manicured nails, reducing it to a mountain of tiny flakes but eating none of it.

'It's been a horrible six months,' Nora said. 'With my grandparents dying and my mother taking off – and things with Adam have been kind of shaky, but I had no idea he was being unfaithful to me.'

'Maybe he wasn't.' Liv took a tiny sip of her coffee. 'Maybe yesterday was a one-off. A mistake.'

Nora blinked at her, trying to keep up. This was not what she'd been expecting. Liv had never really liked Adam. She'd thought he was vain and full of himself. And she had zero tolerance for mistakes.

'A mistake? To bring somebody into our house? Into our bed? How on earth could that be a mistake?' She put her paper cup down and coffee slopped out through the little hole in the plastic lid.

'Come on, Nora, this is not a fairy tale. This is real life,' Liv dabbed at the trickle of coffee that was heading for her dress with her napkin. 'He did something terrible. Nobody's perfect. If it was me, if I was in your shoes, well, I wouldn't do anything hasty until I knew all the facts. There are degrees of infidelity, right? If he was having a full-on affair, that's one thing. But if it was a one-off or a casual thing, then that's another. And,' she wiped her fingers carefully. 'If you want my advice . . .'

'Yes. I do. I do want your advice.'

'You said yourself you've had a horrible year. Adam's been trying to build the business in the States. That's a lot of pressure. It would take its toll on even the most devoted couple.'

Nora stared down at her plate, trying to make sense of this. The only truly devoted couple she had ever known were her grandparents. Hugh had put a flower on the saucer beside the teacup he brought up to Lainey in bed every morning. He'd made an hour-and-a-half round trip into town just to get her the olive oil and rosewood soap she liked. Sat up for hours most nights to read to her when she couldn't sleep.

Lainey had done her hair every morning and dressed up as if she was going to a dinner party, though actually she hardly ever left the house. It was all for him. They had been together for sixty years and then, on the day before New Year's Eve last year, Lainey had come downstairs to find Hugh collapsed in the hall, the contents of the plastic shopping bag scattered around him read like a last love letter to her. Two packets of her favourite Ginger Thins. Twenty Silk Cut. Half a dozen red tulips. A pair of lamb chops that he, a staunch vegetarian all his life, was going to cook for her lunch.

If this was how it felt to lose your partner after two years, how had poor Lainey felt?

Liv was watching her, waiting for her to speak. 'I don't know,' she said miserably. 'I can't think straight.'

'Right.' Liv stood up. 'Let's go for a walk. It'll take your mind off this for a while.'

Nora shook her head. The house was like a comfort blanket, she didn't want to leave it.

'Okay,' Liv said. 'But let's take a break. You've been going on about this place since I first met you. Come on. Give me a tour!'

Nora led Liv out into the hall with its wedding-cake plaster-work and faded Moroccan rugs spread over polished floorboards the colour of honey, and her friend walked over to look at herself in the wall of mirrors. There were at least twenty. The smaller ones were arranged around a huge gold sunburst like glittering planets.

The house and the garden were full of mirrors. Gothic and baroque and Rococo. Art Nouveau, Regency and Venetian. They shimmered at the back of display cabinets. Glittered over mantelpieces, threw back Alice in Wonderland reflections from between the espaliered fruit trees on the garden walls.

'Why are there so many, Granddad?' Nora had asked Hugh, once.

'So your grandmother can see herself in one and realise how lovely she is,' he'd replied.

Even at six, Nora had known this was unlikely. Lainey never seemed to take any pleasure in her appearance. She wore her jewellery and her bright clothes and her lipstick for Hugh, not for herself, as if it was for her some kind of duty.

'Are these genuine?' Liv was poking a finger in between the gilded, carved flowers on a pair of Indian temple doors. She backed away for a better look and stumbled against Houdini. 'What the hell is that?'

'That,' Nora said, 'is the oldest dog in the world.'

'And the kitschiest!' Liv giggled. 'He's not exactly taxidermy's finest hour, is he? But some of this stuff is kind of amazing.'

Nora watched as she inspected the turquoise crackle-glazed urn full of Lainey's umbrellas and the huge polished brass nautilus shell. The candlestick lamp made from a reindeer's antler. The upside down monkey holding a basin that was an inkwell. The boat that her grandfather had carved for Lainey from a piece of driftwood.

Liv had been right, it was a welcome distraction to take her around the house and show her the treasures that were packed into every room.

'Were your grandparents in the antiques business?' Liv asked as she followed Nora upstairs.

'My grandmother was a housewife. My grandfather worked for the Trade Board so he travelled all over the world. He brought back a lot of these things for her and the rest he bought here.'

'Well, he had a great eye!'

It hadn't been his eye that mattered, Nora thought. It had been his heart. 'I always think that everything in this house is part of a long, rambling love poem from him to her.'

'Lucky woman!' Liv said.

'Not really. Lainey was kind of lonely, I think. She lost touch with her family when she was very young. She never talked about them. And then she had that terrible falling out with my mother.'

'What about?'

17

'I don't know. I could never ask her about it and Mum wouldn't talk about it either.'

'Wow,' Liv exhaled, softly, as Nora opened the door of her grandparents' bedroom and she saw the ivory chateau-style French bed and the Murano chandelier and the blue curtains made from a bolt of silk Hugh had brought home from China.

But what caught Nora's eye were the things her grandparents had used every day. Hugh's reading glasses and his slippers, the sheepskin lining worn down at the heel. Lainey's pill bottles and her hair curlers and the pile of romance novels on the small carved table by her side of the bed.

There were hundreds of these books around the house. Hugh had bought them for Lainey and read them to her late into the night, when she couldn't sleep. It had always struck Nora as poignant that her grandmother, who was so remote, who couldn't express love herself, had an appetite for love stories and happy endings.

Liv had already opened one of the armoires. It was crammed with gorgeous evening clothes from the 1960s. Fabulous couture creations next to boutique designs in jewel colours. Nora remembered being small enough to slip between the hangers into a cave of whispering satin and silk and velvet and feathers. Liv held up a heavy cape with a fringe of jet beads and studied the label. 'This is vintage Oleg Cassini!'

'By the time I met my grandmother, she never left the house,' Nora said. 'But when she was younger, she used to go to trade receptions and dinners with Hugh. He had loved showing her off.'

She picked up the wedding photo in the silver frame to show Liv. Her grandfather, in a double-breasted suit, was beaming at the camera; her grandmother was wearing a lace Grace Kelly-style wedding gown, her dark hair half hidden by a froth tulle. She was smiling too but her dark eyes seemed sad and she was clutching Hugh's arm as if it was a lifeline.

'Jesus!' Liv said. 'That's kind of spooky. That could be you in that picture.'

'What's going to happen to all this stuff?' Liv asked, when they had climbed into the arched space beneath the rafters to look at the overspill from the house that had been packed into the attic.

'It's my mother's now but she won't want any of it, so the solicitor will sell it for her.'

'Well, I'd be happy to buy some of it. These are the kinds of things my clients are gagging for. I mean *our* clients,' she corrected herself. Until nine months ago Nora had been Liv's employee but now she was a partner.

'I was planning to bring quite a few things back home to London,' Nora said. She thought of the swan-back sofa, the Victorian bird cage, the Turkish silk prayer rug, the life-sized brass angel holding up her candelabra, Lainey's nineteenth-century Belleek china ... The list was on her laptop. 'But I don't even know if I can go back to that house.'

'Of course you can!' Liv said firmly. 'You love that house. You've poured your heart and soul into it.'

It was true. Though Adam had paid the deposit, Nora had looked after all the renovations and redecoration and she paid for every piece of furniture. It had been hard work but every moment had felt worth it. This was the house she had thought she would leave to get married, the place she'd bring home their first baby.

'Come on, Nora. Don't throw the baby out with the bath water,' Liv said, as if she had read Nora's mind. 'It was just sex. It didn't mean anything.'

Nora shook her head. 'You don't know that.'

'I do,' Liv said simply. 'I talked to him last night.'

'Why?'

'Because you wouldn't and I was so angry with him but he was even angrier with himself. He told me it was just a stupid one-night stand that got out of hand. He can't believe he let it happen and—'

'Who was it?' Nora interrupted.

'I don't know, but that's not important. What's important is that he loves you, Nora. He doesn't want to lose you!'

'What are you saying? That I should forgive him?'

'No! I think any man who does that to my best friend should

'suffer,' Liv snorted. 'But I also think that what you have with him is worth fighting for.'

Nora had never been a fighter. She hated conflict. The wiser choice had always seemed to be to walk away.

'Don't you think you owe it to yourself to give him a chance?' Liv said. 'To at least hear what he has to say?'

'I don't know.' Nora lifted her shoulders and let them drop in a defeated shrug. 'I suppose so.'

'Good,' Liv patted her shoulder. 'Can I call him and tell him you'll talk to him then?'

Nora took a deep breath. 'Okay.'

Nora showered in Lainey's bathroom then dried herself and pulled on a clean cream T-shirt dress. She peered at herself in the mirror over the sink and winced. Her eyes were puffy and bloodshot and ringed with purple shadows dark as bruises. She had never cared less what she looked like, but she didn't want Adam to see how upset she'd been, so she opened her make up bag and began to repair the damage.

'That's better!' Liv nodded approvingly when she walked into the kitchen. "I made more coffee. It's black, I'm afraid. There was no milk and FYI, there's ebola in that fridge.' She shuddered. 'So, I've set up Facetime on my laptop. Adam's expecting you.' She picked up her sunglasses and her phone. 'I'll go out for a walk and leave you to it.'

Nora put her hand out to touch Liv's arm as she passed. 'Thanks, Liv. For coming over. For being such a great friend.'

'No biggie,' Liv said, lightly. 'That's what I'm here for.'

Nora waited until she heard the front door close, then she took a deep breath and clicked on Adam's name.

He was in the living room of the house on Fountain Road. Nora felt a horrible ache of homesickness at the sight of all the beautiful things she had chosen so carefully.

'Hi,' he said. His voice was steady but he was tugging at a dark curl nervously. 'How are you, Nora?'

'You don't have the right to ask me that,' she said coldly.

'I know,' he said. 'I fucked up. I'm so sorry! It was just one time and it will never happen again. And I will spend the rest of my life trying to make up for it, if you let me.'

'That won't be necessary.'

'Listen! Wait! Just hear me out.' He raked his hair back off his face. 'This last six months I haven't felt like you were really there. It's been really difficult for me.'

'Difficult for you?' Nora stared at the screen. 'I lost both my grandparents. That's two thirds of my entire family! How do you think it felt for me? What do you think it was like when you didn't have time to come back for either of their funerals? When you did come back, you wanted to drag me out to restaurants and away for weekends and I was supposed to put on my happy face so as not to disappoint you.'

'I never asked you to do that!'

'You did, Adam. Maybe not in words. But that's what you wanted from me. Because unless I make you the centre of my world, you withdraw from me!'

It was true, she thought. She remembered the Valentine's Day after her grandfather had died. He had been away for two weeks, flown home from Boston and all she had wanted to do was curl up in a ball of grief and be held by him but he'd booked a surprise weekend at Chewton Glen. And she'd put on a pretty dress and picked him up at the airport and done her best to say the right things about their tree house suite and their claw footed bath but she was miserable and he could see it and he had spent most of the next day sulking. She had told herself it wasn't his fault that he had never lost anyone he loved, that he didn't understand that grief came in waves. But she had just been making excuses.

'Maybe there's a grain of truth in what you're saying,' Adam said, breaking her thoughts. 'And if there is, I can work on that.'

'Who was it?' Nora asked. 'What was her name?'

He flushed. 'You don't know her, Nora. It wouldn't mean anything to you.'

'How many times did you meet her?'

'I don't know,' his eyes slid to left, then to the right. 'Five or six maybe. But we only went to bed once, yesterday was the first time. Believe me. Look, this is crazy. We can't talk about this on Facetime. We should be in the same room. I'm getting on a plane, I'm coming over.'

'No!' Nora said. 'You're not.'

'Well, you come back then. This is your home, Nora. This is where you live. I'll move out for a while if you want.'

'Move out?' Her voice broke. 'I'm not sure I'd notice, Adam. You hardly live there anyway.'

'I know,' he said. 'I know. It can't go on like this. Look, I've been thinking. Making a plan.'

Nora held her hand up. 'No! You've just screwed around on me, Adam. I don't want to hear about your plans.'

'I can change my itinerary and maybe we could go to couples counselling. We could...'

The screen froze and then the connection cut and Nora's own face appeared again. She was shocked by how awful she looked. Her skin was blotched and her lipstick pale and chewed. She hated wanting to look good to Adam, but she couldn't help herself.

Liv's bag was on the floor by her chair and she leaned down and pulled out her red leather make-up purse. She was about to take out a lipstick when she saw a vintage Chanel compact and for a second she thought it was the one her grandmother had given her.

Every now and then, Lainey would slip a little treasure into Nora's school bag. A tiny cut-crystal Lalique mouse the size of her thumbnail, a scarlet lace fan, a hatpin in the shape of a flamingo. Nora had to hide all these things from her mother, who would have made her bring them straight back. The compact had been the thing she loved most. A slim disc of lustrous red enamel with a catch made of two interlocking Cs that opened with a soft, expensive click. It had disappeared years ago when Nora and Liv were sharing a flat. She thought she had lost it, but now she realised, that Liv must have taken it.

The enamel on one of the discs was cracked. As Nora opened it, the two halves fell apart and she froze. She remembered stumbling out of the bedroom in Fountain Road the previous day.

The sharp crack as her heel connected with something small and round and red on the carpet.

Adam was calling again and she jabbed the screen with her finger.

'I lost you there,' he said. 'I was just saying—'

'It was Liv, wasn't it?'

He stared at her for a few seconds, his Adam's apple jumping in his throat. 'What did she tell you? If she said it was me who started it, she was lying...'

Nora flung the compact at the screen. Adam was five hundred miles away but he was still ducking as she swept the computer off the table onto the floor.

How could she have been so stupid? Nora upturned Liv's bag on top of the laptop. How could she have been so gullible! How could she have not known that the two people closest to her had done this to her?

She picked up the delicate Wedgwood cup full of cold coffee. She was about to hurl it at the wall, but then caught herself. This was her grandmother's. It had nothing to do with Adam and Liv. She emptied the coffee over the pile of Liv's things and then got up and walked to the sink. Her hands were shaking as she rinsed the cup under the hot tap. She dried it carefully and put it away.

As she was locking the china cupboard, she heard the sound of the front door opening and, a moment later, Liv's footsteps were slow and heavy. Adam must have called her. She knew.

'Take your stuff and go!' Nora said.

'I don't know what to say!' Liv sighed. 'It shouldn't have happened. I shouldn't have let it.' She picked up her dripping laptop and shoved it into her bag. 'I didn't mean to. Nora. Believe me, the last thing in the world I wanted to do was hurt you.'

'Then why did you do it?' Nora snapped. 'Nobody made you.'

'I know. But I kind of lost the plot after I broke up with Paul. I thought I'd be pregnant by January and then he told me that he wasn't ready. And I had to keep going. That's what everyone expects of me. I'm not supposed to feel pain. I'm supposed to carry on as if nothing is wrong. But I felt like I was dying inside,

Nora. And Adam was feeling sorry for himself because you were too upset about your grandfather to throw sugar at him.'

'When?' Nora said. 'When did this start? And don't tell me it was yesterday, Liv.'

Liv stared at the floor. 'In March, when your grandmother was ill. You flew home to Dublin and he came back from the States and he called me. He said he was worried about you. And we met for a drink. That's all it was, Nora, you have my word. But, things got kind of messy. I started to have feelings for him. There was this sexual tension and it was getting worse and we thought, if we just did it, if we had sex, that would be the end of it and we could go back to normal. But we never meant to hurt you, Nora. Neither of us. We care more about you than we could ever care for each other. That's why he's so desperate to talk to you. That's why I came to Dublin to look after you.'

Nora put her hands over her face. 'You didn't come to look after me? You came to manipulate me into taking him back. Now please, will you just leave.'

Liv slung her bag over her shoulder. 'I came to try to limit the damage,' she said. 'To fix it so you didn't lose it all, Nora. Your perfect man, your perfect house, your perfect future.'

'Ah thanks Liv,' Nora shouted as she walked down the hall. 'Thanks for sleeping with my boyfriend and then making it sound like you did me a favour. And by way, thanks for stealing my grandmother's compact all those years ago.' The door slammed and Nora's last words were spoken to the empty house. 'If you hadn't, I might be an even bigger fool than you and Adam tried to make of me.'

2

Snow Globe of New York City

Will

On his last night in the apartment on Worth Street, at the bottom of a box file of old ad briefs he was just about to toss, Will found the snow globe. He shook it and watched the white flecks whirl inside the glass bubble, like a snowstorm above a miniature New York. Once, he had thought of it as a good-luck charm. But that was a long time ago, when he still believed in luck.

He finished packing, and changed into his running gear. At the last minute, he stuffed the snow globe into the pocket of his shorts, and then went outside into the humid New York summer night. His usual loop took him around Columbus Park but tonight he turned left down Lafayette Street towards the river.

He was out of breath when he got to the centre of Brooklyn Bridge and stopped to look back at Manhattan. The glittering skyline was not the same as the one in the snow globe. It dated back to the time when the Twin Towers still soared above the city.

Will felt that he should do something to mark the moment. Shake his fist at the sky, maybe, or shed a tear, but he hadn't cried for years and, besides, there were too many people walking past. So he pulled the snow globe out of his pocket, leaned over the bridge and held it out over the dark, neon-flecked water.

The next morning, Will went into automatic, as if it was just an ordinary trip. He checked that the fridge was switched off, the windows were locked, the instructions for the air conditioner, the alarm and the heating were there on the console table. He was doing fine until he got down to the foyer. Then he saw Carlos, the doorman behind the desk, and he remembered the way he always used to say Julia's name, as if it began with an 'H'.

'Alice on her way?' Carlos glanced towards the elevator.

'No,' Will cleared the lump in his throat, 'she's been on vacation with her grandmother for a couple of weeks. I'm picking her up at JFK.'

'Say *hasta luego* to her for me. I'll see you guys again, right? You're just gone for a year, right?'

'A year maybe, to start.' Will put the keys of the apartment in an envelope and gummed down the flap. 'Longer, if it works out.'

'You're kind of pale, Will. You need a glass of water or something?' Carlos's brow furrowed with concern.

'I'm good.' Will shook his hand, then took one last look around and walked out of the foyer.

His daughter and his mother-in-law were waiting at Delta domestic departures in Terminal 4. Maggie had a tan, but Alice's face was paler still beneath her already deathly pale make-up. She scowled when she saw him and turned away to give her grandmother a fierce hug.

'Love you, Grandma!' Her voice was soft but it hardened as she broke away and spoke to Will. 'Going to get a coffee. I need five dollars.'

'I'll come with you!' Will said.

She tossed her dip-dyed blonde hair with the fading pink tips and glared at him. 'I'm not a kid any more.'

'But really there isn't time. We have to change terminal,' he said reasonably. 'And get through customs and immigration. I'll get you a coffee when we've checked in.'

'I'll get it myself. Grandma gave me money.'

They watched her striding away, her fists pushed into the pockets of her tiny denim shorts. She had a ladder in the back of one leg of her tights.

'Is that a deliberate fashion statement or just a glitch?' Maggie frowned at Will.

'Don't ask me,' Will sighed.

'She's bound to be upset,' Maggie said, briskly. 'It's just nerves, Will. She'll be fine,' she straightened his lapel, 'and so will you.

Dublin is going to be great for both of you.' She put her hands on his shoulders and squeezed them, then cocked her ear at the babble of an announcement. 'I think that's my flight. I'd better go through!'

Will counted four coffee concessions in the Departures hall and he couldn't see Alice at any of them. She didn't answer when he called. He felt the sickening rush of panic that used to overtake him when she was little and slipped away from him in a store. She was fifteen now but – and she was wrong about this – she was still a kid.

He forced himself to go back and look again, and at the last place, he saw her. She was sitting cross-legged on the floor by a bank of seats, head down, flicking through a graphic novel. 'I've been looking everywhere for you! We're running late.'

She shrugged and took a tiny sip from her takeout cup. 'I need to finish my coffee.'

Don't overreact, he told himself. Keep your cool. He took her hand and dragged her, resisting, to her feet. He tried to get her moving, but she dug her heels in.

'Dad,' she said urgently, 'we don't have to do this. We don't have to go.' She looked up at him, her eyes wide, pleading. 'I won't get into trouble again. I'll be, like perfect. I promise. Can we just go back to the apartment?' Tears, like tiny diamonds, hung on the ends of her spiky black lashes. 'Please.'

'It's all arranged, Alice,' Will said softly. 'You know that.'

He'd thought he was doing okay. He'd given being a single dad everything he had. He always made Alice his first priority and she had made it easy for him. She was such a good little kid until she started middle school a year ago. And then she just changed. Overnight, almost. And the thing was, Will had seen it happen before exactly the same way with his little sister.

Maybe it had happened gradually but that wasn't how it seemed to Will. One minute Alice was sleeping with her stuffed toys and reading Harry Potter and the next she was dyeing her hair, getting a tongue piercing and painting the walls of her room black.

Okay, he thought, she's just expressing herself, that's allowed.

Nothing to worry about. Then he got a call from her teacher to say that someone had stolen an expensive watch at school and it had turned up in his daughter's locker.

Alice said she had no idea how it got there and he believed her. But at Christmas, she was arrested for shoplifting a bottle of perfume from a drugstore. Luckily, the owner took pity on her and didn't press charges. But when Will searched her room, he found hundreds of dollars' worth of clothes and video games and make-up. Almost all of it unopened and unused. What was happening?

Alice broke down and admitted she'd stolen it all and promised to stop and he grounded her. Then, the following April, she was caught with a bottle of vodka in her backpack and the school wrote to him to say that if there was another incident, they wouldn't take her back in the Fall.

Will knew he was going to have to do something drastic. He'd been talking to Maggie about moving out to Florida to be closer to her, but when the job in the Dublin office of the ad agency where he worked came up, she persuaded him to take it.

'I think Ireland might be better for her. You could sublet your apartment; give it a try for a year. You've got your sister over there and her kids. A cousin her own age. Being part of the rough and tumble of a family might be just what she needs.' His daughter, however, had vehemently disagreed.

Alice didn't speak a single word to Will on the six-hour flight from New York to Dublin. But, thirty thousand feet above Newfoundland, she fell asleep with a magazine in her lap and her head lolled against his shoulder. He sat perfectly still, as if a tiny wild bird had landed on his hand for a moment, feeling the rise and fall of her breathing, the small shell of her ear against his collarbone and he began to hope that Maggie was right and that Dublin would be a good thing for her.

For a few seconds in the Arrivals hall in Dublin airport, Will didn't recognise his sister. He still expected Gemma to dress the way she always had when she was young, as if she was perman-ently on her way to a costume party – in a pencil skirt with a stripey T-shirt and a beret, in a riding jacket and jodhpurs, or in a fringed Pocahontas dress with her hair in plaits.

But the tiny woman dancing on the spot, waving a hand-painted sign was wearing a baggy sweatshirt and jeans and her hair was short and tucked into a baseball cap. The sign was painted in wonky green letters: 'Welcome home Alice and Uncle W'. Uncle W? Gemma waved it over her head then switched it around to display the other side, which said: '– ill'. She ducked under the metal barrier and flung herself into his arms as he walked towards her. He was amazed, as he always was, at the smallness and lightness of his little sister.

'Let me look at you.' She leaned back while still hanging on to his shoulders. 'Your hair's too short!' She frowned. 'But I'm liking the greying temples. Very Patrick Dempsey-esque.'

A small blond boy with, inexplicably, a tea towel tucked into the collar of his sweater appeared beside her and looked up at Will expectantly.

'Did you see that, Froggy?' Gemma said. 'Your uncle was about to walk past me, then he saw your amazing sign.'

'Yes, you saved the day.' Will ruffled his hair. 'Good job, Batman.'

Froggy looked pleased.

'Well, where's Alice?' Gemma looked around excitedly.

'Busy pretending she's not with me,' Will exhaled.

At that moment, Alice appeared through the automatic doors, her head held high, her mouth set in a hard line that said, 'I hate this already.'

'Alice! Alice!' Gemma dodged through the crowd to get to her niece, flung her arms around her, then dragged her back to Froggy and Will. 'Group hug!'

Alice looked appalled but she was too jet-lagged to fight off Gemma's genuine enthusiasm and she put her arm around Froggy obediently. She still shrugged Will off, however, when he put his arm around her and he had to console himself with the memory of the five minutes over the Atlantic when she'd dozed happily on his shoulder.

Gemma grabbed Alice's cabin bag and marched away,

chattering over her shoulder. She had that rushed, frenetic air of soccer moms everywhere, Will thought. *Things to do. Places to go. Uncomfortable silences to fill.*

In the car park, the lock on the driver's door of her VW Polo was jammed shut so she had to get in the passenger side, then crawl across the transmission to get behind the wheel. Alice and Froggy got in the back. Will shifted a pair of muddy football boots and a hurley stick off the front passenger seat and got in beside his sister. She squeezed his knee. 'It's so good to have you home.'

Home, Will thought, watching Dublin slip past the passenger window. Gemma was taking the scenic route so that Alice could see the city. His sister talked non-stop on the forty-minute journey to Blackrock, pointing out landmarks, asking Alice if she'd seen *Black Books* and *Father Ted* or read W. B. Yeats or heard of Snow Patrol.

'That's the ugliest church in Ireland, Alice,' she waved at a breeze-block monstrosity, 'and there's fierce competition, trust me. And Will, look! There's the corner where I had my handbag robbed when I dropped you at the airport after Mum's funeral. All they got was half-eaten Snickers, an EPI pen and a box of Tampax. Crime does not pay, kids.' Will winced and shot her a warning look and she mouthed, 'Sorry!'

Will tried to see the city through Alice's eyes, as if he had never been here before, and it seemed small and flat and faded beneath the washed-out Irish summer sky. He felt faintly embarrassed by it, as if he might be personally responsible: the muddle and jumble of Drumcondra, the dingy Georgian mansions on Mountjoy Square.

'There's the sea,' Froggy announced when they got to Sandymount, but even the ocean seemed to be doing its best to disappoint his cousin. The tide was a long way out and the beach was a vast wasteland of grey sand. The water was just a tiny thread of navy, a mean ribbon on the horizon.

Gemma took a left and they drove through the maze of a suburban estate. She pulled over and parked and they got out and filed into the rental house. Magnolia walls, beige carpets, a smell of fresh paint lingering in the air. 'All your things arrived on Friday. I got the guys to stack them in the biggest bedroom upstairs.'

'Is my stuff okay?' Alice squeezed past Gemma and ran up the stairs. The others followed her.

Alice had not allowed Will to help her to pack up her bedroom in the apartment in New York. Instead, between tears and tantrums, she had deconstructed it, forensically. She had photographed it from every angle using her phone. She had separately bagged the contents of each drawer. Labelled every box of clothes. Put away her books in alphabetical order. Peeled every poster and sticker off her wall and packed them away, ready to be reapplied to a new wall three thousand miles away in exactly the same arrangement.

Alice was standing in the master bedroom staring at a dozen battered looking packing boxes piled against one wall. 'These aren't mine!' She turned around and looked at Will, accusingly. 'You promised me my things would be here when we got here.'

Froggy knelt down and peered at the dusty cardboard. 'This one has the letter "J" on it,' he said, helpfully, 'and that one.'

Will froze in the doorway. 'That's not possible.'

But he knew, even before he got to the pile stacked against one wall, what he was going to find.

Alice tugged at his sleeve as she enunciated each word again. 'Where's. All. My. Stuff?'

'I don't know,' Will said, trying to stay calm. 'I think they must have been shipped to your grandma's by mistake.

Alice gave one of the boxes a shove. 'Whose are these, then?'

Will swallowed hard. 'These? These belonged to your mom.'

He saw Gemma's eyes widen in surprise.

'You brought her things?' A flush of anger fought its way up through Alice's chalky make-up. 'And you left mine behind? That's it! I'm not staying here without my stuff. I'm going back to the airport. Right now.' She stormed down the stairs out to the car, opened the rear door and sat in the back.

Will and Gemma tried everything but Alice refused to come back into the house Will had rented for them.

Gemma made tea and sent Froggy out to her with a plate of chocolate biscuits. Will sat at the table, his head in his hands, racking his jet-lagged brain, trying to remember the day Alice and Maggie had gone on holiday. The moving van had been late and he'd been in a rush to get to work. He had told the guys that the boxes in the spare bedroom were for Florida and the boxes in the hall were for Dublin, hadn't he?

'This is not a good start,' he said, shakily.

'But it's not the end of the world. It's just a mix-up.' Gemma stood behind him and massaged his back. 'You can have everything reshipped.'

'What about the boxes upstairs?'

Gemma stopped kneading his neck. 'What's in them?'

'Just some old stuff from the apartment. I don't want to keep it here. Can I store it at your place?'

'Of course. I can have it moved over tomorrow.'

Will pleaded, reasoned and bargained with Alice one more time but still she wouldn't budge from the back seat of the car, so Gemma got in beside her and put her arm around her shoulder.

'Tell you what. Why don't you come home with me for tonight? You sleep on the blow-up bed.'

'It doesn't actually explode,' Froggy explained, with a serious expression. 'It inflates.'

'And it deflates,' Gemma sighed, 'while you're sleeping on it. But it's yours if you want it.'

Alice nodded. 'Okay.'

'Don't worry,' Gemma whispered to Will as she got out. 'She won't stay long. One night in my madhouse and she'll be begging you to bring her back here.'

Will waved but Alice didn't even look back at him as they drove away. He forced himself to go back into the kitchen to wash the mugs and the plate. He had a shower and put in a call to the new Creative Director at the Panoply New York office to check whether or not there had been any issues with the handover. But as he walked her through the plan for a campaign she was taking over from him, he kept hearing Julia's voice in his head.

'Couldn't bear to leave me behind, could you?' he felt Julia saying to him.

Except that it wasn't her voice. After fifteen years, he couldn't remember what his wife had sounded like. When he thought of her now, it was photographs, not memories that he remembered.

He ate a salad which he found in the fridge and called his sister to see how Alice was doing. She was on the sofa, Gemma said, watching a TV show with the boys. After Will hung up, he had a sudden rush of loneliness so he switched the TV on too, for company.

He must have fallen asleep, because when he woke up, the sky above the houses opposite was still a faded blue, the way it was in Ireland in mid-summer, but it was almost midnight.

He climbed the stairs and stood, for a few seconds, looking in at the pile of boxes in the master bedroom. He tried to recall, but he had no idea what was inside them.

He couldn't stand to see Julia's things in the apartment after she was gone. He had asked his mother to take whatever she wanted and then, one afternoon, when she had taken the baby to the park, he had just gone crazy. He had ransacked every room, emptying closets and drawers and shelves. Then he stuffed all of Julia's things into boxes and taped them up.

He shoved them at the back of the closet in his office and told himself that he would open them up sometime when he was ready. But he had kept putting it off. He had scattered Julia's ashes into the East River but this was where she was really buried – inside these now sagging cardboard boxes.

He flipped on the light and walked in. He put a hand on a box and felt the dust beneath his fingers. Then, without hesitating, in one swift movement, he slipped a finger under the cardboard flap, ripped it open and tipped it over.

A jumble of things spilled out onto the floor. Clothes and shoes; CD cases; a plastic bag full of toiletries; there was Julia's flannel dressing gown; a pair of her sneakers... Will pushed them to one side and picked out the CD: U2's 'All That You Can't Leave

Behind'. He ran his eye down the track list to find her favourite song, 'Beautiful Day'.

No, he thought, with a sudden rush of certainty. Her favourite song had been 'Stuck in a Moment'. It was the *video* of 'Beautiful Day' Julia had loved; all those black-and-white shots of the streets of Dublin. He'd promised her that he'd bring her here some day.

Well, he thought, with a wry smile, I finally kept my promise, Julia, here you are at last.

He knelt down and opened a plastic bag full of dog-eared paperbacks. Penny Vincenzi, Harold Robbins, Dan Browne. He laughed, softly. Julia had been a highbrow-book reader when he met her but when she was pregnant she claimed that the baby was using her brain and she read only airport blockbusters.

There was a jumble of receipts in the bag. And among subway tickets and Starbucks loyalty cards, he found a folded flyer promoting happy hour at Saint Dympna's in the East Village, the bar where Julia worked, part-time, when they'd met.

Saint Dympna was the patron saint of hopeless causes and that summer of 2000, when he was just twenty-two, Will had felt like the most hopeless of them all. He had managed to land a summer internship in the creative department of a Madison Avenue advertising agency but it had fallen through when he arrived. He'd then had to work two crappy jobs to pay off the loan he'd borrowed to get to New York and to afford the sky-high rent for his share of the matchbox-sized Brooklyn apartment he shared with three other guys from his class.

He worked five days a week in the post room of an insurance company and seven nights in a catering kitchen prepping airline meals. He might as well be back home in Dublin, he thought, for all he saw of New York. He was perpetually exhausted, too tired to party with his friends or explore the city.

Saint Dympna's served proper pints of Guinness but the female bar staff were mostly South American, couldn't pronounce the word 'Guinness', and were all ridiculously pretty. The guys who drank there gave them nicknames. Miss Brazil, Miss Argentina, Miss Colombia, Miss Mexico City. Julia was Miss Taken because she had a steady boyfriend, but that still didn't stop Will falling for her.

He'd come in for a quick beer after his shift and gaze at her from afar, admiring the twist and flick of her wrist as she sliced limes for a pitcher of margaritas; the toss of her blonde head as she reached for the tequila bottle and her T-shirt fell off one shoulder; the way she always found time to banter with the lonely older Irish guys who put up with the loud music so that they could drink something that reminded them of home.

She bantered with Will, too, sometimes, between customers, and he saved up anecdotes about his hopeless jobs just to make her laugh. The Sunday night before he flew back to Dublin, he was supposed to go to a party in New Jersey, but on his way to the subway station, he changed his mind and went back to the bar one last time, to see Julia.

'Cheer up, Will,' she teased him as she was pulling his fourth pint of Guinness. 'It might never happen.'

'I have a plane ticket that says it will,' he said. 'I'm heading back home on Tuesday.'

'That's good, though, right?' she said. 'You've don't want to be stuck here making vats of egg salad and Marie Rose sauce for the rest of your life.'

'I feel like I've wasted the whole summer. There were all these things I wanted to do and now it's too late.'

She tucked a strand of blonde hair behind one ear. 'Like what?'

Like kiss you, he thought. 'Oh, you know. All the touristy stuff. Statue of Liberty. Coney Island. The World Trade Center.'

'Really? You haven't lived until you've seen that view. Tell you what. I'll go to the top of the Twin Towers with you tomorrow morning. It has to be early, though, because I have to study.'

'Won't your boyfriend mind?' Will forced himself to ask.

'He probably would, if we were still going out together.' She wiped condensation off his glass and put it on the counter. 'So tomorrow, nine a.m., at the entrance to the South Tower?'

He nodded. She pointed at the Guinness. 'This should probably be your last one. The ride up to the observation deck is pretty hairy.'

This, Will thought, was probably not the time to tell her he was afraid of heights.

In the elevator up to the 113th floor of the South Tower, they got separated by a noisy group of French tourists, arguing over a map. Will stared at the floor, trying not to think of the fact that he was trapped inside a steel box hurtling a quarter of a mile into the sky.

Julia was right. The view was incredible. The whole city was spread out below them. The Statue of Liberty looked like a toy. Will felt as if he could lean down and pick up the tiny yellow cabs that zipped past the intersections on West Street. But he also felt like he might pass out if he looked down, so he spent most of the time up there looking at Julia.

'So!' she said, when they were back down on solid ground again. 'You've been on top of the world. You haven't completely wasted your summer.' She hiked her backpack onto her shoulder. 'And I still have four hours to write my essay.'

'Hang on!' Will left her for a minute and hurried over to where a trader was selling souvenirs. Bottle openers and key rings and lighters. He handed over five dollars for a snow globe of the Manhattan skyline and brought it back to Julia.

'Aaah!' She grinned, shook it, then watched the flakes whirl around the tall fingers of the Twin Towers. 'It's gloriously tacky! Thank you.'

'Take the afternoon off,' he said, softly.

'Can't. I have to present two chapters of my dissertation to my tutor tomorrow at three o'clock. But I could meet you after that.'

'My flight takes off at two-thirty.' Will couldn't believe this bad timing. 'If this was a movie,' he shaded his eyes to gaze up at the South Tower, 'we'd promise to meet back here a year from now.'

'Then let's do it.' She grinned. 'Will, I'll see you up there at nine-thirty a.m. on September tenth, 2002.' She turned to go.

'Maybe we could meet in the foyer instead?' He called after her. 'I don't think I could do that elevator trip on my own. I've got vertigo.'

'You just went to the top of the World Trade Center and you have vertigo?' she called back. 'You're crazy.'

'I am!' He watched her disappear into the crowd. *Crazy about you* . . .

That night, Will sat up drinking with his friends in the apartment. When, finally, they had crashed out, it was too late to bother going to bed, so he stayed up, listening to a storm blowing over the city and wondered if Julia was awake, listening to it too.

The next morning was clear and sunny, more like July than September as if New York was reminding him of all the summer he could have had with Julia and Will felt dejected as he packed up to leave for the airport. As he was slinging his bag over his shoulder, his phone rang.

It was Julia. 'A plane just flew into the World Trade Center.' She was crying. 'Turn on the TV.'

This can't be happening, Will thought, watching the footage of the blazing tower on NBC. But he could hear the sound of sirens below his window echoing from his television and as he watched the camera cut to a live feed of the Twin Towers the second plane hit.

Will couldn't remember what they said as they sat together, three miles apart, watching what seemed like the end of the world.

But he remembered that the loudest thing in his head was the sound of her breathing down the line. And how hot his phone had been against his cheek. And how they'd both whispered 'No!' as a towering thunderhead of smoke and fire tore down the side of the South Tower. Twenty-four hours ago, they had been in that building; now they watched it ripple and buckle and fall.

Will left everything and ran the thirty blocks to Julia's apartment, passing streams of people coming the opposite way, covered in dust and blood, fleeing from the city.

They sat up together all night watching rolling news, phoning everyone they knew in New York, holding one another as they cried with relief when someone else was found safe.

Finally, they turned off the TV and turned towards one another. They were the survivors. Proof that in a world that was ending in a rain of fire and burning metal and pain, something fragile and human would always be beginning.

In the morning, they walked to Brooklyn Hospital to give blood for the survivors. But as the days passed, they realised it would not be needed. They were the survivors, they realised, they and all the others who had by a twist of fate or timing, been spared. And by the time the no-fly ban was lifted, Will knew he wasn't going home. He was going to stay right here in New York and ask Julia to marry him.

Will couldn't recall a single word of his wedding speech now but he remembered how lucky he'd felt that August day in 2002, to have a lifetime of happiness ahead of him.

It must be here, Will realised, looking around the bedroom at the pile of boxes, the speech. Julia would have kept it. He stood up and rubbed the stiffness from his knees then walked over to the pile of boxes and began to rip more of them open, looking for it.

But he forgot, almost immediately, what he was searching for because he kept finding things he had forgotten about: two tickets for a film they'd both loved called *Run Lola Run* tucked into the pocket of a jacket; a vintage Blondie T-shirt she used to wear when she worked in the bar. There was a small, yellowed plastic bag that contained everything that had been stuck to the fridge door the day that Julia had died: half a dozen magnets in the shape of chillies; a card with the number of their local cab company; a sticky note with a shopping list in Julia's looping scrawl – 'Basil. Parmesan. Pasta. Blueberry ice cream. Breast pads (underlined twice)'; a menu from their favourite Vietnamese on Greenwich Street; a postcard of the blue lake in Belize from Julia's first love, a boy called Silas Kelly.

He grinned, remembering how he'd pretended to be jealous when she stuck it up on the fridge and how she'd put it right in the centre, just to wind him up.

Sixteen years was a long time and, somewhere along the line, Will had turned Julia into a cypher, a saint. But the real Julia was still here among all the bits and pieces of her life. Maybe she was the bits and pieces now.

Julia, who had once hidden a leftover croissant in the pocket of that jacket to feed stray dogs on the beach in Puerto Angel. Who had emptied that savings account to help his sister, though she hardly even knew her. Whose default password was 'incorrect', so if she ever forgot it, the screen would prompt her 'your password is incorrect'. Who had given him this truly ugly blue and yellow coffee mug on his twenty-fourth birthday. He remembered unwrapping it and reading the slogan 'Best Dad in the World' written on the side.

'But I'm not a dad,' he'd said.

'I know. But this time next year, you will be.'

The inflatable bed sprung a puncture so Gemma had made up the bed in Froggy's room and Alice flung herself on it dramatically.

'I'll get you fresh towels,' Gemma said, 'so you can have a shower.' She bumped into her eldest son Jake on the way back from the laundry room.

'Froggy will be sleeping in with you, tonight,' she said, as she was folding towels in the kitchen.

Jake muttered, tramped past her, trailing mud and clumps of grass from his football studs. 'Great. Excellent. Brilliant!' he muttered, scowling into the fridge.

'I know!' Froggy was thrilled with the idea of bunking in with his older brother. 'We can have a midnight feast.'

'Oh, goody,' Jake said. 'I'm beside myself with joy.'

Dear God, Gemma thought. Her husband was so moody lately that she already felt as if she shared her house with two teenagers. She wasn't sure she could cope with a third.

Jake glugged back a carton of milk. 'So how long is she staying here, "poor Alice"?' Jake asked, wiping his mouth and reading her mind.

'Don't call her that!' Gemma shushed him.

'It's what you call her,' Jake pointed out, reasonably.

'If she's poor,' Froggy said, 'then how come she has an iPhone Seven?'

'Believe it or not, there are more valuable things in life than an iPhone Seven!' Gemma said.

'Like what?' Froggy asked, puzzled.

'Lots of things!' Gemma picked up her pile of towels. Like a mother, she thought.

Alice wouldn't come downstairs for dinner and she didn't eat the dinner that Gemma sent up with Jake. But in the morning, Gemma found her on the sofa watching TV wearing Froggy's Thomas the Tank Engine dressing gown and eating Stephen's organic granola out of the box. Luckily, he wasn't up yet, so Gemma just about had time to run to M & S to get him some more.

'How did you sleep?' she asked Alice.

'Fine,' Alice said, quietly. Then, even more quietly, 'thank you.'

'I can run you back to your dad's house on the way to work.'

Alice set her jaw and shook her head.

At work, Gemma called Will between patients to talk about what they should do but he didn't pick up and she guessed he was sleeping his jet lag off. He still hadn't called her back by the time she was leaving work, so she drove to the rental house to bring him back to her place for dinner.

She let herself in with her spare key and shouted his name from the hall, then she climbed the stairs and walked along the landing. When she got to the master bedroom, she caught her breath in shock.

It looked as if a bomb had gone off in a charity shop. Half of the boxes had been torn open. There was stuff everywhere: CDs and books, jumbles of jewellery, clothes and shoes, stacks of ancient, yellowing college notes. Among the mess Gemma saw tangled balls of tights, a crumpled dressing gown, a tube of hand lotion. Had Will kept everything Julia had ever owned?

There were garment bags heaped on the bed. One of them was double length.

Gemma stared at it. 'It couldn't be, could it?'

She picked her way across the floor and tugged the zip. A billow of ivory froth burst out: Julia's wedding dress. The full nine yards of lace and tulle were faintly yellowed after all these years sealed in plastic.

She heard footsteps and zipped the bag up quickly.

'I didn't hear you come in.' Will was unshaven and he had smudges of shadow in the corners of his eyes.

'What have you been doing?' She gestured at the room.

'Going through Julia's stuff.'

'All night?' He nodded. 'Well, take a shower and change your clothes. This is Alice's first day in Dublin. You can't just leave her on her own.'

Will looked dazed. 'Is she okay? I sort of lost track of time.'

'She's fine,' Gemma said. 'She's hanging out with the boys. But you need to get your act together. I'll tidy this stuff up and pack it away.'

'No,' he said quickly. 'It's okay.'

'But you said you wanted to bring it over to my place.'

'I've changed my mind.'

'Will,' Gemma chewed her lip, uneasily, 'why do you still have all this stuff after all this time?'

'What was I supposed to do with it, Gems?' He folded his arms. 'Chuck it all away?'

'That's what we did with Mum and Dad's things.'

'That was different.'

'Really? How? I don't mean to give you a hard time, but, when I see all this, it kind of makes sense why you're still on your own. How can you meet a woman when you're hanging on to the past like this?'

'I've met plenty of women,' Will interrupted her. 'I've had a couple of relationships. But . . .' But none of them had lasted past eighteen months because when Will started to feel like he needed someone, his automatic instinct was to pull away.

'But what?' Gemma prompted him.

When I was twenty-four, Will thought, I believed I was the luckiest man in the world, and then I found out that there's no such thing as luck. You can feel special and chosen and blessed, you can be sure that you'll always be together. And you can lose it all in one, stupid, senseless moment. So what's the point?

43

But he couldn't say this to his sister. Other people didn't need to know that the life that seemed so solid could come tumbling down around them. So he gave her the other part of the excuse.

'It's not easy to date when you have a child. It's not just about me. I have to think is this person going to be a good mom for Alice.'

'Alice will be eighteen in three years!' Gemma cut in. 'She doesn't need a mum any more. She does need to know that her dad isn't sitting at home in a corner feeling sorry for himself. The best thing you can do for her is move on.'

Dinner at Gemma's was noisy and chaotic. Will had bought sausages and chips and the boys bickered over who was having what soda. Gemma gave up scolding them and just shouted louder so that Will could hear her. Alice agreed to sit at the table but she wouldn't speak. She ignored her plate and played Candy Crush on her phone while the rest of them ate. But when she looked up and saw that Froggy was struggling to cut up his sausage, she leaned over and chopped it into bite-sized pieces for him. Stephen arrived home late and he and Will went through a little back slapping pantomime of brotherly affection for Gemma's benefit, thought they had never liked one another.

'Alice, help your dad to clear away, will you?' Gemma asked lightly and herded the others into the living room to watch TV.

Alice began picking up plates and dumping them into the sink.

'There's a dishwasher,' Will said.

She turned her back and shoved two slices of bread into the toaster, then spooned hot chocolate into a cup, slopped in some milk and shoved it into the microwave.

'Come on, Alice.' Will sighed. 'You can't keep this up. You're going to have to speak to me.'

Nothing.

'I know you're mad at me for bringing you to Dublin. I know it seems like a punishment, but it's not meant to be. I did this because I think it will be good for you. You're the most important thing in the world to me.'

'No,' she said grimly, '*Mom* is the most important thing to you. That's why you brought all her things here and forgot mine.'

'That was a mistake...' Will began.

'You always put her above me. We had to stay in that tiny apartment because she used to live there. And all my life you've gone on and on about what an amazing person she was. How kind and funny and clever and pretty. How I should be like her.' Her voice broke. 'But I didn't even know her and I'm sick of being compared to her!'

She pushed past him and he heard her bounding upstairs, then he heard the sound of a slamming door.

'Excuse me, Will,' Froggy put his head around the door, 'is Alice staying in my room again tonight?'

Will threw his hands up helplessly. 'I wish I knew, buddy.'

He knew he should follow Alice and get her to come home with him. But he couldn't. He hadn't slept for forty-eight hours and he'd been dealing with these teenage tantrums for months now.

'I give up,' he whispered. 'I just give up.'

'Give up what?' Froggy asked.

'Nothing.' He had to get out of there. He grabbed his jacket and headed for the back door, ruffling Froggy's hair as he passed.

'Will you say goodnight to your mom for me?'

You got me so wrong, Julia, he thought as he walked back through the quiet streets to the strange house that was, for the moment, home. The only thing I know about raising a teenage daughter, is that I'm absolutely, utterly and completely shit at it.

He'd intended to go straight to bed but, instead, went back into the bedroom. He would spend five more minutes looking for the wedding speech and then he'd leave it. But when he pulled back the cardboard flaps of a new box, he saw the cream paper store bag with the faded pink ribbon handles and the Magnolia Boutique logo on the side.

Three months after Alice was born Will earned his first proper pay cheque at Panoply. He'd booked a babysitter and dinner at an Italian restaurant on West Broadway to celebrate and when Julia had complained that she looked wrecked and that none of her nice pre-baby clothes fit, he gave her two hundred dollars to buy herself something to wear.

This bag had been in the plastic sack of belongings the hospital had given him after they released her body. Will had never been able to look inside.

But now he pushed a pile of clothes out of the way, sat down and peeled off the sticker with a picture of a flower on it and opened the bag carefully. There among the rustling folds of tissue was a sleeveless, green jersey dress. A single long blonde hair was caught in the pearl-button fastening at the back.

When he saw her body laid out on a table in the morgue, everything in him fought with the fact that she was dead. She couldn't be. It wasn't possible. He told himself she was asleep. He thought he saw a tiny blue vein pulsing by her temple and the rise and fall of her chest under the sheet and he felt a surge of relief. They'd made a mistake. But, when he touched her hand, it was so cold that he couldn't pretend any longer. And he wanted to pick her up, to hold her in his arms, but he couldn't bear to. So he buried his face in her hair. It was the only part of her that hadn't changed.

Will unwound the hair from the button now and laid it carefully on top of the dress. He hadn't cried for years but his throat tightened with tears, for the two of them, for the waste of them. They had been so young, only a few years older than Alice was now. And then, like the song that he had once known by heart, the words of his wedding speech came back to him:

'Two years ago, I didn't believe in fate or chance or destiny. But we wouldn't be here now if I hadn't changed my mind on my way to a party and decided to drop into Saint Dympna's to see Julia one last time. Or if we'd waited just one day to go to the top of the Twin Towers together.

'I know now, as all of us who lived through nine/eleven do, that the future can change on a dime. For better, for worse. Forever.

'And if this is it, if the world ends right now before we cut the cake or have our first dance or go up to the honeymoon suite together, then I'd have no regrets.

'I'll still think that fate dealt me a pretty good hand. I'll feel lucky, because I got to spend even one day with Julia.'

Will looked around at the piles of her belongings scattered around the room, all the bits and pieces of her – the lovely, ordinary days they had shared.

He had been lucky, he thought. He still was. He was healthy, he was in the middle of his life. He had Alice.

What had he done, walking out and leaving her at Gemma's like that? He had to go back and get her. So what if he didn't have a clue about how to deal with a teenager. He hadn't had a clue how to deal with a baby, a three-month-old, a toddler, but he'd learned like everyone did because they had to. He could learn again.

Maybe Dublin would work out, maybe it wouldn't. But it was a fresh start, not just for Alice, but also for him.

He wrapped the dress up carefully in the tissue paper and put it back in the bag. He would sort all these things later. Most of it could go but there were a few things he wanted to keep, not for himself, but for Alice. Because one day in the future she might want to get to know her mother.

He got up, switched the light off, then closed the door and went downstairs and called Gemma to tell her he was on his way back to pick up his daughter.

3

Double-Strand Teardrop Moonstone Necklace

Nora

Nora dreamed that she had lost her key to the house on Fountain Road. She kept knocking and knocking but nobody came and then she realised that she didn't live there any more.

It was true, she thought as she walked through the tide of holidaymakers flowing from the train station to the sea. Two days ago she had wanted Adam to leave the house but now she knew that, whatever he did, she was not going back there.

She stepped to one side to let two boys carrying an inflatable crocodile past her then turned into the doorway between a bridal shop and an Indian takeaway. She passed the open door to a kitchen where two men in vests were clattering pots and climbed three flights of stairs through a cloud of curry spices to a door with a sign that said: 'Loughlin O'Leary. Solicitor.'

It was opened, immediately, by a bald man in his late sixties with tiny wire-framed glasses. She had expected him to be wearing a suit, but he was dressed like a boy scout in a blazer, crumpled beige shorts and open-toed sandals with grey knee socks.

'I'm Nora, Lainey's granddaughter.'

'Of course you are.' He nodded. 'You're the image of her! – "A girl from the side of an amphora" – that's how Hugh described her to my father, the day he met her. I was a pageboy at their wedding, you know. Sixty years ago.' He mimed flinging something into the air – rose petals or confetti, maybe – and smiled at her sadly. 'It seems like only yesterday.'

He led her across the untidy room, picking his way around boxes of files and a bag of golf clubs to get to the cluttered desk. He moved a rolled-up beach towel off one of two scuffed leather chairs and settled himself opposite her, opening a manila folder. He pulled out a single, typed page and Nora glimpsed her grandparents' signatures: Hugh's, large and tilting, taking up most of the space; her grandmother's, tiny and cramped, squeezed into the right-hand corner and she missed them both so much that she had to grip the worn arms of the chair to stop herself from crying.

'Can I get you a glass of water?' Loughlin was looking at her kindly over his glasses. She shook her head.

'Then we'll begin. It won't take long.' Loughlin tapped the will with two fingers. 'It's very straightforward. The house in Temple Terrace is to be sold and the proceeds, less any mortgages or encumbrances, go to your mother, Alanna Malone, along with any furniture, jewellery, personal effects that you, Nora Malone, do not wish to take for yourself. Your grandmother has put in a clear instruction about that – anything at all.'

Nora thought of the hours she'd spent on her list, trying to choose between the temple door and the birdcage and the antique globe. She shouldn't have bothered. 'I'm kind of between places at the moment, so I probably won't take very much. As you know, I'm really here on behalf of my mum, Alanna. She's away at the moment so I said I'd organise the house sale. How long do you think it'll take to put it on the market?'

'Well,' Loughlin said, 'I should tell you that the house was remortgaged a number of times over the years, so your grandparents retained very little equity in it. By the time the bank has its cut and taxes have been paid, your mother's inheritance from the sale will only be about forty thousand euros.'

Forty thousand? Nora stared at him. 'I don't understand,' she said. 'Why did they have to remortgage the house?'

'Hugh retired to look after your grandmother when he was still only forty-eight. They had no income except for the rental from the shop, which, unfortunately, fell empty during the recession. The house was their only asset so, basically, they lived off that. I'm sorry if this comes as a shock.'

'I just assumed that she'd inherit enough to buy somewhere back here in Dublin and come home.'

'There are a few thousand euros in savings bonds. And the contents of the house must be worth something.'

Loughlin flipped through his file. 'And I can delay on applying for probate and push the sale of the house out until the end of the year, so your mother can stay there till then.'

He didn't understand, thought Nora. Alanna hadn't been back to the house in Temple Terrace for thirty-seven years. She would rather sleep in the doorway by the café than set foot in the house again.

'It's a lot to take in,' Loughlin said, softly. 'I'll give you a minute.'

He picked up a dusty water jug and hurried out, leaving Nora alone.

Forty thousand euros. Was this what her grandmother had meant, those last few days, when Nora had sat beside her hospital bed? She had been agitated, drifting in and out of consciousness. 'I'm sorry,' she kept saying over and over. 'I did something terrible.'

The only time that Nora had seen her mum and her grandmother in the same room was on New Year's Eve, the day of her grandfather's funeral. She had hoped that on that day, of all days, they might make their peace, but they had just looked through one another.

And afterwards, her mum had gone to the pub for sandwiches with some of Hugh's friends and Lainey had refused to go so Nora had taken her back to Temple Terrace and joined her mum and her mother's boyfriend Pete in their hotel later.

It was a hostel, really, a backpacker's place on Parnell Street with three single beds and a worn carpet. There were laminated 'no smoking' signs everywhere. Pete sat on the windowsill rolling a cigarette. Nora had never met him before and he seemed nice but she wished that he would go away so that she could have a proper talk with her mother. Alanna was taking Hugh's death badly though she was trying to hide it. Nora was hoping to talk her into moving back to Dublin, after the house was sold.

'If Hugh was here, he'd quote that Kafka line,' Alanna told

Nora, 'that one about how you never really lose love. How it always comes back in another form.'

'I don't want it in another form,' Nora said tearfully. 'Hugh was the best possible form.'

'A head full of poetry. A heart full of kindness,' Alanna said. 'We were lucky to have him.'

Later, when she'd had another glass of wine, Alanna sang, 'On Raglan Road'.

'Dad loved that song,' she said when she was finished. 'But I've always hated it. It always reminds me of *her*. The bit that goes "that her dark hair would weave a snare, that I may one day rue". He certainly had a lot of things to rue about meeting my mother. She ruined his life.'

Nora let that go. 'I don't know what she'll do without him.'

'I do.' Alanna relit her cigarette. 'She'll follow him. She won't be able to live without him.'

'Don't say that!' Nora was horrified.

'It's the truth.' Her mother blinked away tears. 'Wherever he is, I hope he's having a rest before she arrives and he has to spend the rest of eternity looking after her.'

A week later, Alanna broke up with Pete and bought a one-way flight to India and since them, Nora had hardly heard from her.

Her grandmother was just as elusive. Nora had tried, over and over to arrange a trip to Dublin to visit her but both times Lainey kept putting her off. Then, one morning in early March, she got a call from a stranger, a nurse in the hospital a few miles from Blackrock, to stay that her grandmother was critically ill. She had cancelled everything and flown over to Dublin that evening.

Nora had never seen her grandmother without her signature red lipstick and her jewellery and she hardly recognised her. She was asleep, her head tilted back against the pillow, a string of amber beads clutched in one hand, but she woke up for a moment when Nora said her name.

'I'm sorry,' she muttered. 'I'm sorry. I didn't mean to do it!'

'It's okay!' Nora said softly.

'Nora!' Her grandmother's eyes swam into focus. 'You came.'

'Of course I did.' Nora leaned down and kissed her.

'What about your mother, where's Alanna?' Her grandmother's eyes darted around wildly. 'Is she coming? I need to tell her something. To explain...'

Nora had left a message at the ashram but her mother either hadn't got it or was ignoring it. 'Yes,' she lied. 'She's on her way.'

But her grandmother's eyes had closed again and she was muttering in her sleep.

Nora stroked her hair back from her face until she had settled, then gently straightened the covers and picked up the beads that had fallen from her hand. They were a luminous glossy amber but the string was old and frayed. She had thought she had known every piece of her grandmother's jewellery, but she had never seen them before.

Lainey hung on for two more days, waiting for her daughter to arrive. Every time she woke up she said her name and then frantically patted the bed covers looking for the amber beads. An hour before she died, she opened her eyes. Her voice was so weak, that Nora had to put her ear to her mouth to hear her.

'Promise me,' she whispered, 'that you'll look after Alanna.'

'I promise,' Nora said and she held her grandmother's hand so hard that when she slipped away, the amber beads had left small marks on her palm.

Loughlin was back with the water jug and he was speaking to her.

'If you like, I can organise a friend who is an auctioneer to drop over and look at the contents of the house and give you an idea of their value.'

'That would be very kind. Thank you.'

It all hung on what the auctioneer said, Nora thought, as she walked around the supermarket loading up a basket. Forty thousand would hardly buy a parking space. The contents of the house would have to make another sixty thousand euros to give her mother any chance of buying a place.

She stood in the queue behind a small girl wearing the water wings her dad was about to buy and she thought back to summers when she'd perch on the back of her mum's bike as she pedalled fearlessly along the narrow coastal road to Killiney. They'd walk down the narrow path to find a spot on the crowded rocks and before long Alanna would be talking to the people on both sides, handing out biscuits and sun-tan lotion to other people's kids, rolling cigarettes for people who had been strangers a minute ago. Nora had been so proud when her mum ran out onto the high diving board and leapt, whooping, into the sea. So proud and so terrified. Alanna always leapt before looking, sure that she would land safely. But she was fifty-one now, not seventeen; she couldn't keep doing that indefinitely. Back at the house, Nora dumped her shopping on the kitchen table and took out her phone to send a message to her.

Adam had called again, twice, while she'd been with the solicitor. What did she have to do to get him to realise that she had nothing more to say to him? She clicked through the settings and deleted his picture from her wallpaper. Then she blocked him and did the same with Liv and, for the first time in two days, she felt slightly better. She opened the fridge to put away the shopping and the smell of rotting food hit her.

Liquid lettuce. Solid milk. A tub of hummus with a covering of green fur. Nora dumped it all in the bin, then opened the cupboard where her grandmother had kept her vast collection of cleaning supplies. Half a dozen of her aprons, neatly ironed, were hanging on the back of the door. Nora put one on, then pulled on some rubber gloves. She turned the radio on loud, ran hot water into a bucket, and tackled the fridge. After two days of living in her head it was a relief to have something physical to do and after a few minutes of scrubbing and scouring, her mind was comfortably blank.

After she'd finished, she made a sandwich and ate it standing up. Then she loaded a basket full of dusters and sprays and scourers and went through the house from room to room, opening the windows to let the stale air out, polishing the mirrors, dragging the rugs out to the washing line one by one and beating the dust out of them. She rubbed beeswax into the wood and climbed up on a step ladder to dunk the crystals on each chandelier into a bowl of soapy water.

This was what her grandmother used to do. It was all she did. She'd start at the top of the house and work her way down to the bottom and then start all over again. Over and over.

Nora hadn't always known her grandfather. She'd first come to this house when she was six, when her mother had pneumonia. She had been enchanted by all the treasures and the fact that she had a real, live grandmother.

Every morning, when Lainey put on an apron over her lovely clothes and pulled on her rubber gloves, Nora trailed after her. At first, Lainey tried to shoo her back downstairs to her grandfather, then she tried to ignore her, but Nora sensed deep down that she enjoyed her company and she didn't give up. After a while, Lainey got used to her. She hardly spoke, she could get through whole days without saying more than a handful of words, but she'd give Nora a box of her jewellery to sort through or a cloth to polish the silver with and they'd work together in companionable silence.

Nora always wondered why her grandmother spent so much time cleaning and never went outside but now, as she scrubbed out the dust from between the carved flowers in the temple doors, she wondered if Lainey had simply been trying to blank her mind out too.

The house had been dusty and neglected when Nora had shown Liv around, but when Loughlin's auctioneer friend, Ed, came, to give her a valuation on the contents, it looked exactly as it had when her grandparents were alive.

Nora felt proud for them as she showed him around. He was a small man in his thirties with a thatch of red hair. He told her that his father had run the auction rooms in Blackrock and that Hugh had been his best customer. He was very slow and thorough but she could tell he was impressed as he examined hallmarks and makers' stamps and made notes on his iPad. While he was adding up his figures and checking some prices online, she made them both coffee.

Her grandfather believed that beautiful things were meant to be used every day. When Nora was at the house on Temple Terrace, she had drunk her Ribena from a Waterford crystal whiskey tumbler as intricately faceted as a diamond solitaire. Eaten her cereal from a porcelain bowl, so fine that it was almost transparent.

The plates in the flats where she lived with her mum were scratched and chipped. Drawers stuck, cupboards had dark corners where silverfish darted. The furniture was ancient and rickety. Once several hundred woodworm had hatched from their kitchen table and her mum threw it out the window into the yard below and set up cushions so they could eat their meals cross legged on the floor.

'We can play at being Bedouins,' Alanna had gamely said, covering the cracks in their lives the way she covered the stained sofas and draughty windows with sequin studded saris and second hand throws. Nora played along, though secretly she longed for the order and beauty of her grandparents' house.

She opened the cupboard now and picked out a pair of pale green Royal Doulton cups and saucers that dated back to 1890. She found two white Wedgwood plates patterned with green ferns. Poured freshly brewed coffee into a green Art Deco pot with a blue humming bird perched on the lid. Ed picked it up and examined the bottom and whistled appreciatively before he filled his cup.

'So,' Nora said. 'How much do you think it's all worth?'

'You're going the estate sale route, right?' Ed said, stirring milk into his coffee. Nora nodded. 'In that case, I think you're looking at between fifteen and twenty thousand.'

'Twenty thousand pounds!' Nora almost dropped her cup.

'Euros. It's shocking, I know,' Ed winced. 'It's not even a third of what's it's all worth. But when the bottom fell out of the property market here, it had a knock on effect. People just aren't buying beautiful things for their houses anymore. You know that carpet in the drawing room?'

Nora knew every inch of it. She used to love lying with her cheek pressed against the soft tufted red silk while Hugh told her stories about deserts and camel trains and oases.

'It's a 19th century prayer rug,' Ed said. 'Hand woven silk.

Quite rare. Worth at least two thousand euros but the most you'll get at auction is five or six hundred. Those temple doors in the hall, they're extraordinary, but you probably won't get more than three hundred. The huge stuffed dog in the hall? You might be looking at fifty euros, if you're lucky.'

Poor Houdini, Nora thought sadly, remembering how her grandfather used to automatically bend down to pat him as he went upstairs and how, when she used to her secrets into his ears.

Ed cut his pale blue eyes down to his cup, tactfully to give her time to let this sink in then he looked up at her, shyly.

'Do you mind my asking, are you under pressure to sell all this quickly? Because if you're not, if you have the time, my advice would be to forget about the estate sale and put all this incredible stuff up on eBay. It would take time to shift it, obviously, but you'd make three times more money.'

Nora didn't have time. It was Tuesday today, and she was due to go back to London on Saturday

'Sweetheart, are you there?' The voice was cracked and fuzzy. 'Damn bloody Skype! I can see myself but I can't see you!' Nora got a shock as her mother's face swam onto the screen. She was too thin and there were dark circles beneath her pale blue eyes and another few streaks of grey in her candyfloss blonde hair but after a month of 'radio silence' Nora was so relieved to see her that she almost cried. She carried the laptop out into the hall, where the signal was better.

'Oh, there you are.' Alanna beamed. 'It's lovely to see you.'

Nora's relief was quickly replaced by irritation. 'Why haven't you answered my emails? I've been really worried about you. Are you still in India?'

'No. The ashram got too busy and I needed to make some money so I bought a flight to Bangkok and took a train north. I'm on an organic farm about a hundred kilometres from Chang Mai. I'm WWoofing.'

'You're what?'

'Willing Workers On Organic Farms. You sign up and you can work anywhere around the world for a room and food. I've been helping to build an irrigation system with a bunch of students from Germany and Australia and Sweden. It's fascinating!'

It sounded, Nora thought, more like very hard work.

'Is that Houdini?' Alanna peered at the screen, her face softening. 'Give him a pat for me.'

'Don't change the subject!' Nora said.

'Guilty!' Alanna yawned. 'I was about to call you to tell you that I'd moved but then the generator packed in and then we had torrential rain, so they couldn't take it to be fixed so my phone went dead. Erica, the sweet German girl who's sharing my room, has one of those clever solar-charging yokes and she lent me her iPad so that I could check my emails and Skype you. Say hello!'

Alanna swung the iPad around and Nora glimpsed the blurred walls of a small wooden shack, two narrow beds covered with sarongs and a pile of upturned packing crates that had been turned into shelves for a jumble of clothes.

A girl of about twenty with blonde dreadlocks was standing at the open door, slipping her shoulders into the straps of a rucksack. She raised one hand in a wave, then turned and went out the door of the hut as Nora waved back.

Alanna appeared again. 'Sorry, darling, we'll have to be quick,' she whispered, 'I said I'd only be five minutes and she's counting every second. How's it going, getting the house sorted? I know it's going to be hard for you to let it all go. I hope you brought Adam over with you.'

Nora wanted to tell her mother what had happened but five minutes wasn't going to be enough to explain it all. She had read somewhere that the best way to lie was to stick to the truth as closely as possible. 'No, but Liv came over for a few days and now she's gone.'

'That was kind of her!'

The words for what Liv was fought for space on the tip of Nora's tongue but she swallowed them. 'Mmmm,' she said, then added, 'I went to the solicitor on Monday for the reading of Lainey's will.'

'That sounds so final,' Alanna sighed. She propped the iPad up and began to roll a cigarette with one hand, pinching tobacco from a pouch and sprinkling it onto a cigarette paper. She swiped at one eye, rubbed it hard. 'Listen, I've been thinking about what you said after my father's funeral about getting a place in Dublin. And I've decided you're right. It might be good to come back for a while.' She lit the cigarette and took a drag and exhaled a long sigh of smoke. 'To be honest, all this moving around is kind of exhausting.' She was smiling as she looked up but she must have seen Nora's face, and the smile faded before it reached her eyes. 'I thought you'd be pleased.'

'I am but...' Nora swallowed hard. 'There's something I have to tell you.'

Disbelief flashed across her mother's face as Nora explained what Loughlin had told her.

'Dad remortgaged the house,' Alanna repeated, softly. 'Of course. He had to keep her in the style to which she had become accustomed.'

'I've had the contents valued. There'll be another twenty thousand when everything is sold.'

'No. I told you when she died that I wouldn't take any money from the sale of her trinkets.' Alanna took a drag of her cigarette but it had gone out. 'Just thinking about all that stuff brings up bad memories for me. Sell it all and keep the money.'

'I don't want it,' Nora began.

'You might, some day. I know you love that job, but you might want to take time out, get back into making art.'

Since she'd started working for Liv, Nora hadn't picked up her sketchpad once. Styling sucked up all her creativity. She didn't have anything left at the end of the day.

'We can talk about that later.'

'Forty thousand is more than enough for me. I can live out here for years on that. I can take a break from working and do some travelling. I haven't been to Vietnam yet, or Cambodia. I met a guy who told me you can live in Pokhara in Nepal for seventeen dollars a day.'

Nora's heart sank. This was exactly what she'd been dreading.

'I'm sorry, sweetheart,' Alanna said, her voice dropping to a whisper again. 'I've got to go. I can hear our German friend breathing fire outside on the balcony.'

'Wait!' Nora said. 'I'm going to take a few small things before the estate sale. Is there anything you want?'

Alanna shook her head. 'Nothing!' she said, firmly.

What happened? Nora wanted to ask her. Why did you run away? Why did you never go back? What did Lainey do that was so bad that you never spoke to her again? But voicing these questions again would be pointless. Alanna would talk about anything except what had happened between her and her mother.

'What about Houdini?' Nora said.

Alanna laughed. 'I can't carry a stuffed dog around Asia in a rucksack.'

'Something small, then, like the moonstones or a scarf or—'

'Sweetheart,' her mother said, 'I've got everything I need right here.' She patted her heart with one hand. Her knuckles were swollen, Nora saw, and her nails were dirty. 'And so do you, Nora. Don't bother sorting through all that old junk or dragging any of it home to Haverstock Hill. Just toss the key to the solicitor and walk away. Remember, the most important things in the world—'

The connection cut before she could finish the sentence but Nora knew how it went. She had heard it hundreds of times. 'The most important things in the world are not things at all.'

If only she hadn't sunk every penny she'd made into doing up the house on Fountain Road, Nora thought, staring at the blank screen where her mother's face had been, she could have contributed secretly. She could have put in enough to help her mum to get a place and to pretend it came from the sale of the contents. But, right now, she only had eight hundred euros in her account, she didn't have a job, and she didn't have any place to live.

She had scrolled through her contacts last night, trying to make a list of possible work contacts and to find someone she could stay with in London. There were people she could ask but most of them were people she knew through Adam or part of the work world she shared with Liv. She couldn't face calling any of them, dealing with their pity and their curiosity.

Her head began to race. What was she going to do? Where was she going to go? She stood up before the panic could take hold of her and went to get her bucket and her rubber gloves, then she realised that she had done it all: there was nowhere left to clean.

Ed had told her that she should remove all her grandparents' personal things before the estate sale. She had been putting it off until now but she had to face it some time. She dug out some cardboard boxes, went into the drawing room and began to empty a shelf of Lainey's books. Her grandmother only read romantic novels. It was really just the same story over and over, Nora thought. Girl meets guy. Girl gets guy. Happy ending. Not in the real world, she thought grimly, carrying the box through the kitchen to dump it in the corridor that led to the inside door of the shop. The shop! She hadn't cleaned that yet! She dropped the box and went to look for the key.

The shop had been part of the house before Hugh bought it. It had been leased to a wedding-cake decorator and then a picture framer but it had been vacant since the recession hit six years ago. It had two doors. One from the street and one from inside the house. Nora found both keys hanging on a rust-spotted ring in the pantry.

Broken glass crunched under her feet as she stepped inside. It was bigger than she remembered – a long narrow space with a window at one end. The ceiling was high and the walls were painted dark grey and it was empty except for a broken swivel chair and a few empty picture frames.

Watery light filtered in between the flyers and notices pasted to the window outside and dust motes glittered in the air like fireflies. The air should have been stale but it smelled sweet, as if it still held the long-lost scents of wood glue and icing sugar.

As she looked around, a crazy idea floated into her mind. No, she thought, ridiculous. But still, she unlocked the other door and stepped outside to look at the shop from the street.

A faded 'To Let' sign had fallen over behind the poster-plastered window glass. The sign above it was defaced with graffiti tags but nothing could ruin the perfect proportions of the window. A deep bay, divided into three arched panels.

Her heart began to beat a little faster as she looked at it. It would take a lot of work to get it to look halfway decent. But it was empty, it was free and it was just off the main street. Hundreds of people passed by the window every day. A pop-up shop would be better than eBay. She could try to sell the contents of the house at their proper value and, if it worked, her mother might still be able to come home.

And she wouldn't have to go back to London where she would be without a job or a home. She wouldn't have to see Adam or Liv. She could stay here until Christmas. Six months to lick her wounds and gird her loins so she could go back with her head held high.

She had no idea whether six months would be enough time to clear the two floors and the attic above her and she had never sold anything in her life, but she felt she owed it to Alanna to try – and to Lainey too. To find a good home for all the things she loved and to keep the promise she had made to look after her mother.

On Saturday morning, at midday, when Nora should have been boarding her flight back to Heathrow, she got up early. The engine of Hugh's 1985 Mercedes coughed a couple of times, then turned over and died. She tried it a few more times until it started and she felt a rush of exhilaration as she pulled out onto the street, as if she was starting on an epic journey, instead of a five-minute drive to the local hardware store.

An assistant stepped forward to help her as she went inside but she sailed past him. After two years of set building, she already had an encyclopaedic knowledge of DIY and knew exactly what she was looking for.

She bought buckets of white emulsion and eggshell and varnish and undercoat. Three grades of sandpaper, two types of filler, protective masks, tape, rollers, a caulking gun, a staple gun, a power drill, long, wide wooden planks for shelving, a cheap nest of tables that might come in handy, new spotlights and a rail for the ceiling.

On the way home she drove by Loughlin's office. When she had called him to tell him her plan, he had offered to lend her a floor sander. He dug it out of the back of a cluttered cupboard in his office and carried it painfully slowly down the narrow stairs in his arms like a bride.

She ripped up the dusty, stained shop carpet and dragged it out into the garden. She started with the sanding, then moved on to the walls. They drank up two buckets of emulsion before the grey stopped showing through the white. She gave the ceiling a quick coat and then dragged the ladder outside and tackled the window, digging years of grime out of the frame and scraping off the tattered posters.

'You missed a bit!'

Nora turned to see a very small, very skinny woman in her early thirties with jaw-length feathered hair and enormous green eyes. She wore a red full-skirted dress with a crisp white lace apron and was carrying a tray holding a plate of chocolate biscuits and a plastic cup of iced coffee. She lifted her little finger, the nail painted the same red as her dress, and pointed at a streak of glue still stuck to the glass. Nora turned back to scrape it off.

'I'm Fiona from the Café LoCal on the corner. And this' – she nodded at the tray – 'is on the house. I've been watching you work out here all day; you need it.'

Nora pulled off her dust mask and climbed down the ladder. 'That's nice of you.'

'Oh, no, I'm not being nice.' Fiona laughed. 'I'm being nosy. Everyone's dying to know what you're doing with the place. My money's on a gambling den or a brothel.'

Nora took a gulp of the iced coffee. 'I'm opening a pop-up shop to clear my grandparents' house.'

'Pop-up! Very zeitgeisty. Hang on –' Fiona stared hard, and Nora realised how sweaty and dishevelled she must look to this immaculately groomed woman – 'I knew it!' She nodded slowly. 'You're Nora Malone. I sat behind you in sixth year in Westbrook.'

'Sorry.' Nora shook her head. She had only been at Wes for a few months. She remembered moving schools three times the year she was seventeen.

'I'm Fiona Cleary!' the woman said. 'Fat Fiona?' Her tone was airy. 'That's what everyone called me. Well, not you.'

And suddenly Nora saw her: a girl with a heart-shaped face and a mane of brown hair. The meaner kids in the class had called her names but she'd always appeared so confident that it hadn't seemed to bother her.

'Yep!' Fiona said, as if she could read Nora's mind. 'That really was me. I was size eighteen when I was seventeen. I'm half the person I was back then. Literally. But you haven't changed at all. You're as gorgeous as ever. Can I just –' She leaned over and picked a fleck of paint out of a corkscrew of Nora's hair. 'You went to art college, right? I always thought you might be the next Tracey Emin.'

Nora swallowed another sip of coffee. 'Turns out one is enough.'

'So you're Hugh's granddaughter. I never made the connection. I'm so sorry I didn't make it to his funeral. I had the flu and I was horribly contagious. I was mad about him. We all were. He used to come into us every Saturday with a poetry book under his arm. We'd always save him a table by the window and a plate of those carob Florentines.'

Nora looked down at the little chocolate discs studded with chunks of dried cherries, coconut, pumpkin seeds and crystallised rose petals. It was lovely to think that Hugh, who had looked after Lainey, had been looked after too.

She picked up a biscuit and bit into it. Her taste buds lit up like fireworks. 'These are good.'

Fiona smiled, smugly. 'No sugar. No fat. Fifty calories a hit. My chef's secret recipe. I'll get it out of him one of these days. So!' She tapped on the window with a diamond ring the size of a hazelnut. 'Does this pop-up shop have a name?'

Nora swallowed a mouthful of biscuit. 'The Pop-Up House Clearance Shop?'

'Ooh!' Fiona arched one lovely eyebrow. 'Catchy.'

'Well, it does exactly what it says on the tin.'

'Screw the tin,' Fiona said. 'The shop name is your first chance to sell, so it has to whet the appetite. Like Café LoCal. Local café. Low-calorie food!'

'It's only going to be a temporary thing,' Nora began. 'Six months at the most...'

'But you'll have competition!' Fiona waved a hand. 'Two charity shops. That junk shop opposite the hair salon.'

'I'm not selling junk,' Nora cried.

'Which is why you need to differentiate. You need a good name and a unique selling proposition. Trust me.'

She had trusted Liv, Nora thought, and Adam. And look where it had got her. She put her foot on the bottom rung of the ladder. 'I'll think it over. Well, thank you for the coffee and the incredible biscuits.'

'There're lots more where they came from. We shop owners have to stick together. We have a get-together in the Wolf and Goose every Wednesday night. We're supposed to talk about leveraging retail opportunities but we usually get smashed and bitch about the clampers, then fall downstairs for karaoke.'

'Sounds like fun,' Nora said, politely.

'No, it sounds like hell on earth.' Fiona grinned. 'But, somehow, it is fun.' She turned to go.

'Oh! If you're clearing the house, you'll need a hand shifting all the heavy furniture. You can borrow my chef, Adonis. And he does pretty much exactly what it says on the tin. Looks like a Greek god. Cooks like a vegan Anthony Bourdain. Pop over and borrow him any time.'

The sun moved behind the roofs of the buildings opposite and a cool breeze funnelled up from the sea as Nora began to paint the shop front. Passers-by, on their way home from the beach, joggers, swimmers and dog walkers glanced at her curiously. It was getting dark by the time she finished and folded up the ladder. She crossed the street to look at her work.

The summer sky was fading from blue to dusty lilac and a full moon was rising over the roof of Temple Terrace. The shop front was unrecognisable. With the graffiti gone and wood sanded back, the arches of the windows and the delicate scrolls of the pillars shone through.

On Sunday morning, she got up at seven to paint the window, then ran a floating shelf the length of one side wall and added more open shelves along the back wall. She replaced the rusty old spotlights with white fittings and new bulbs. She drilled holes in the ceiling and put up a rail for the backdrop for the window. Then she flipped through Ed's list, trying to work out what she should sell first. However, after ten minutes, she wasn't getting anywhere, so she went up to Hugh's study and found some paper and a pencil.

She usually did most of her styling designs on computer; it was at least two years since she'd made a sketch by hand, but it all came back. She made an outline of the layout of the shop, then began to fill in what she'd need first. A counter or a desk? The claw-footed walnut dining table would be perfect. A dressing room of some sort, so people – customers, she thought with a shiver – could try on clothes. The Chinese latticework screen from the living room would do. And she could use one of the three tall cabinets from the drawing room as display cabinets.

Now for stock: she would keep it minimal, she decided; sell only a few things at a time, make it feel like an upmarket gallery. She began to fill in her sketch quickly.

A dozen of Lainey's vases on the floating shelf – all the blue ones, maybe. And the pale-blue swan-back sofa beneath it. She could hang the opposite wall with the mirrors.

She found the bolt of leftover Chinese silk in the airing cupboard. She could cut that up and staple it to the small tables she'd bought to display smaller things: the little blue Ormolu clock, some of Lainey's costume jewellery...

She could get started on the smaller stuff, but she wouldn't be able to move the sofa or the desk or the over-mantel mirror from the house to the shop by herself.

A delicious blast of air con hit Nora as she opened the door of the café. She had been expecting something girly and flouncy, but the LoCal was cool and elegant: exposed brick, distressed boards, white tiles. Fiona was on the phone but she muted the call and shouted Adonis's name when she saw Nora. When he appeared, there was an audible sigh of appreciation from the female customers. He was tall and tanned with jet-black hair and a profile straight off an ancient coin.

'Yes, I will come,' he said in accented English. 'You will see me at three o'clock.'

And, at three o'clock exactly he arrived at the door of the shop with Ed and Loughlin in tow. Nora had forgotten about Dublin, the way everybody knew everybody.

Between them they moved the desk, the display cabinet, the screen, the over-mantel mirror and the sofa down to the shop and then insisted on shifting the boxes Nora had lined up to carry down herself.

Adonis had turned down her offer of money earlier so Nora bought him a case of beer instead. When she handed it to him, his dark eyebrows shot up in surprise. 'Thank you. No!'

'Sorry. Maybe it's not the kind you like,' Nora said.

'He likes all kinds,' Ed said, and Loughlin glared at him.

'Thank you, many times,' Adonis said stiffly. 'It is very kind.'

Was Ed laughing, Nora wondered, as they filed down the steps, or was she imagining it?

The only thing left to do now was to decide what to put in the window. The most sensible idea was to cram as much in as possible but that didn't feel right. She picked up her sketchpad and was heading upstairs to take another look around when she tripped over a box she'd filled with Lainey's old romance novels.

One fell face up and she caught a glimpse of handwriting on the flyleaf and picked it up. It was covered, back and front, in her grandmother's tiny, cramped handwriting. The nib of the pen had been pressed so hard on the paper that the writing was raised like braille:

Moonstone necklace. 1958.

One scorching August afternoon, Hugh hired a boat and
rowed me out to Dalkey Island for a picnic. Halfway across,
he put the oars down. He said he'd dive in and leave me there
if I didn't agree to marry him. He knew I couldn't swim.

I never led Hugh on. I told him he was wasting his time. I
had decided long before I met him that I would never marry,
never have a family.

I ordered him to row me back to the shore immediately, but
that man would never take 'no' for an answer. He took off
his shirt, took off his watch, took off his trousers. He was
wearing swimming trunks. He had come prepared.

The boat was leaking and the water was up to my shins
before I gave him my answer. He handed over a bucket and
told me to start baling, but there was something in the
bottom: a double string of moonstones like glittering drops
of water.

I wore them on my wedding day, eleven months later.

Nora upended the box again and began to page carefully
through the books. There were eight more handwritten notes
written on the flyleaves.

Each one was about something Hugh had given her. Some of
them were short: a scribbled line and a date.

Murano Chandelier. H shipped back from trip to Venice.
August 1980.

Brass monkey inkwell. 30th. From H for 54th b-day 1989.

But others were longer:

Angel lamp.

H brought her home on our 2nd wedding anniversary. A
life-size brass angel with her arms raised above her head

to carry a huge candelabra and a plug trailing from her polished pedestal. She was my guardian angel, he said; she'd keep an eye on me. Protect me from the dark when he was away.

Blue crackle-glazed Chinese vase. 1976.

I had to be careful what I said to H. If I let it slip that I liked something — the smell of a bar of soap, the taste of a honeycomb — it would appear. Once, he caught me admiring Bella Donna delphiniums in a magazine. Off we went on the bus to Thomas Street, where we trawled around the antique shops and found a huge crackle-glazed vase that was the same cobalt-blue colour. 'Blue to chase the blues away,' he said, Hugh, the eternal optimist. I thought that was it, but the following summer, I came down one morning and looked out the kitchen window and saw a row of belladonnas blooming at the bottom of the garden. I think he would have tethered the moon to the roof of the house if he thought it would make me happy.

Satsuma jar. 1960.

I told H once that, when I was a child, my older brother used to bring his hat home filled with oranges. That first time H went to Japan, he shipped home the fat-bellied satsuma jar with painted gold chrysanthemums. Every week, he brought oranges for me to fill it, and I did. I never told him how sad it made me feel to smell their skin on my hands and to remember home.

A *brother*, Nora thought. An older brother? Did that mean that Lainey had more than one? Her life in London was a mystery. She had never talked about it, never talked about anything personal while she was alive. Of all the things in this beautiful house, these notes were the most amazing. These tiny windows into the life her grandparents had shared.

She read each flyleaf slowly again, savouring every word, and when she got to the end of the one about the moonstones, she had the germ of an idea. She could make this memory of Lainey's part of the first window for the shop. Or even better, she grinned and she stood up quickly and hurried to find her sketch pad, she could make it the heart of it.

The couple coming home from the Wolf and Goose stopped to kiss in the rain on the corner of Temple Terrace and then again at the library.

'That's new,' the girl, said, coming up for air and pointing at a shop on the other side of the street.

'How can you think about shopping at a time like this?'

'I'm a woman, we can multi-task.' She took his hand and they crossed the street and stood side by side looking through the glass. Someone had made a whole scene inside the window, like a painting but made from real things and, somehow, it was moving.

'That is pretty cool,' he said, admiringly.

She nodded. 'Amazing.'

A piece of blue silk had been hung at the back so that it looked like a sky. A second piece was stretched out below so that it looked like the sea.

Nora had hidden a fan beneath it so that it rippled and billowed, making waves around a wooden boat made out of driftwood. A necklace of white stones trailed behind it, like bubbles.

The boy leaned over to read the note that Nora had fixed in the window:

ONE SCORCHING AUGUST AFTERNOON, HUGH HIRED A BOAT
AND ROWED ME OUT TO DALKEY ISLAND FOR A PICNIC.
HALFWAY ACROSS, HE PUT THE OARS DOWN. HE SAID HE'D DIVE
IN AND LEAVE ME THERE IF I DIDN'T AGREE TO MARRY HIM.
HE KNEW I COULDN'T SWIM.

He turned to the girl. 'It's a love story.'

'No.' She shook her head, pointing to the sign above the window that read 'The Memory Shop'. 'It's a memory.'

72

4

Freshwater Pearl Earrings

Lia

It was probably just a drunk leaning on the wrong bell, but Lia was on her feet before she was properly awake, first reaching for the outsize velour dressing gown she had worn all evening before stuffing it beneath the bed. She grabbed a short, silk robe that barely skimmed her thighs from the hook on the back of the door. It was cold against her bed-warmed skin and she shivered as she ran down the hall to answer the intercom.

There was a crackle and a face swam onto the small screen, blurred and fuzzy, like an ultrasound scan.

'It's me.'

Two words, that was all it took to rewrite a dreary Friday night.

She pressed the buzzer then dashed to the bathroom, snatching pillow cases she'd left drying on the radiator as she passed and shoving them into the airing cupboard. She switched on the strip light above the mirror. She'd had most of a bottle of wine and it showed in her puffy eyes but there was no time for mascara. She splashed water on her face, squeezed a blob of toothpaste onto a finger and rubbed it on her gums, upended her hair and spritzed it with perfume. She was back at the door when he tapped on it.

He'd been to an awards dinner. Beneath the long navy coat, she saw the flash of a white dress shirt, the crisp black edges of a bow tie. His soft dark hair was glistening with raindrops. The sight of him standing in the doorway made Lia feel as if she'd swallowed a string of fairy lights making her internal organs light up like a fairground.

'I can't stay long,' he said, brushing past her.

A few lights went out but the rest still blinked and twinkled. A minute was better than a weekend of nothing. A minute meant that he'd come *here* instead of *there*.

'Well, you'll have to take your coat off!' She folded her arms. 'Because I've never seen you in a tux.'

'You can't boss me around wearing that little dressing gown.' He made a grab for her and she stepped back out of his reach.

'Okay.' He gave her a look of mock surrender before unbuttoning the coat and shrugging it off. It fell to the floor with an expensive sigh and she wondered, briefly, whether he'd chosen it himself or whether *Gemma* had picked it out for him. Stephen extended his arms, palms up. 'Well?'

What was it about black tie that made every man look like James Bond? She could have leaned back against the wall and stared at him for hours. 'Not bad.'

'Your turn.'

She pulled the shoulder of her dressing gown down off one shoulder. 'How do I look?'

'Like nine hundred thousand, nine hundred and ninety-nine dollars. If I just get rid of this blob of toothpaste –' he wet his thumb, leaned over and rubbed gently at her lip – 'I think we can call it a round million.' He wrapped his arms around her and pulled her against the stiff fabric of his jacket. She pressed her face against his chest.

'Come to bed,' she said, talking to his heart which was beating away just beneath her cheek. 'Just for a minute.'

She felt him shaking his head.

'I can't.'

Another light dimmed in the dark cave of her heart then went out. Stephen used to be the one talking her into bed, not the other way around. She had done the resisting. She fiddled with one of the buttons on his shirt front, pushing it under her nail, into the quick.

'I hate this,' she said, and there it was in her voice, the thread of a complaint.

Stephen pulled away, held her wrists, stepped back so that he could look at her. 'I hate it too.' He looked his age when he scowled like that. On the right side of forty when they met, he was now forty-one. Sixteen months had slipped by and they were still trying to squeeze a life into snatched moments.

'Lia, I'd give anything to stay, you know that. But we have the weekend in Wicklow coming up. The last thing we need is her putting two and two together.'

And getting me, Lia thought. *Would that be such a bad thing?*

She tasted bitterness, like the wine coming back up her throat, and swallowed it down. It doused the last of the lights in her stomach. She wished now that he hadn't come. If he left now, while they were not getting on, she would be in limbo until he texted in the morning and hell if he didn't text till the afternoon.

She forced herself to smile. 'You're right.'

The tension drained out of Stephen's face. 'I could stay for a quick beer?'

In the kitchen, Lia switched on the light above the cooker hood so that the room was in half-darkness.

She pulled a beer from the fridge and handed him an opener. He flipped the lid into the sink. It landed with a clatter. They passed the bottle back and forth between them. She could feel time thundering past them, a train on the tracks, while they were stuck in the waiting room.

She leaned over and tweaked the bow tie. 'Is it one of those elastic ones?'

'Nope! It's the real McCoy.' He licked froth off his top lip, the skin above it already darkening with stubble. 'I had to watch a YouTube video twice before I could tie it.'

She leaned back against the cooker as seductively as she could with the timer knob digging into her back. 'You should have called me.'

He laughed. 'You're the Velcro generation. You wouldn't know one end of a bow tie from another.'

'Wouldn't I?' She reached over, took one end of the tie between the tips of her fingers and tugged it so that the knot unravelled slowly, then looped the ribbon around her bare throat and held his eyes while she tied it expertly.

She and Molly had practised this when they were teenagers. It was on a list in a magazine along with drinking neat Scotch and wearing matching underwear and tying a cherry stalk using only your tongue: 'Ten Things Irresistible Women Do'.

Stephen put the bottle down on the draining board. 'Come here.'

She switched off the cooker hood light, leaned away from the timer, and the fairy lights inside her came back on again, one by one.

It was always the same after he'd left – the crash, the flatlining, the way being alone turned into being lonely. The fact that she couldn't even call him to hear his voice and it might be days before she saw him again.

Lia got up, pulled her velour dressing gown out from under the bed, pulled it around her. She padded to the kitchen, opened another bottle of wine and found a tube of Pringles where she'd hidden it from herself in the oven drawer before slumping on the sofa to watch a rerun of *The Graham Norton Show* she'd watched earlier. It calmed her to know exactly what Meryl Streep was going to say to Carey Mulligan before she said it. That Graham would relent and let the owl-eyed girl in the red chair walk free while the smug guy with the gelled hair (who deserved it) would be flipped.

When she was so tired that she couldn't keep her eyes open any longer, she went into the kitchen to bin the bottle and saw his abandoned bow tie lying on the floor by the cooker. A black velvet question mark.

If you can't stand this any more, what are you going to do?

Planting a clue would be risky. It had to look like a mistake. And it had to be done this weekend, when Stephen was taking her to his family holiday house in Brittas for the night.

Lia spent the whole week agonising about what to leave. Lingerie was too sleazy. A scarf or a sweater might be overlooked. One of the cards Stephen had written her would be too personal and he might wonder why she was carrying it around.

It had to be something that would show *her*, his wife, that there was no point in putting up a fight.

The night before she had opened the shop, when she had finished making the moonstone window, Nora had walked out onto the vast, flat stretch of beach, past the dog walkers and paddlers, all the way to the tideline. She stared out at the water. Wales was just only 75 miles away and beyond it, London. The house on Fountain Road. She let herself cry a few salty tears for the life she had been so sure of, that she would never have now. Then she let the sea breeze dry her eyes and took a deep breath and turned her back on it and walked home to Temple Terrace again.

Loughlin and Ed and Fiona had put the word out and, on the first morning Nora's only customers were their friends and other shop owners. But by afternoon, the window had attracted the attention of passing holiday makers.

Nora had found three more of Lainey's notes in a pile of books shoved beneath a cabinet in the drawing room. And another two slipped inside novels she found at the back of a case of books in Hugh's study. She'd bought a packet of plain white cards, rewritten the notes and put them up around the shop, then printed a large sign to hang just inside the door:

EVERY SINGLE THING HERE WAS PART OF MY GRANDPARENTS'
SIXTY-YEAR STORY. FRAGMENTS OF THE PAST. FEEL FREE TO
LOOK AROUND. AND, EVEN IF YOU DON'T BUY, MAYBE YOU'LL
TAKE AWAY A MEMORY.

A couple eating ice-cream cones read the sign aloud and then walked around examining everything as if they were in a museum. They went away with Lainey's little blue Ormolu clock. A Dutch man bought the matching pair of aquamarine glazed vases that were, Nora noticed, the same colour as his eyes. A couple with an overheated baby in a buggy dashed in and picked up a pale pink umbrella to use as a parasol. By the afternoon, Nora had lost count of the number of customers.

Just before six, a man in his seventies came in and bought the boat in the window. His father had just died at ninety-nine years old, he told Nora. He'd missed one hundred by a whisker. The man and his brothers wanted to scatter his ashes in the sea, but the boat was a better idea. There was a hollow space beneath the sail where the ashes would fit. 'He taught all of us to sail in Dun Laoghaire Harbour when we were kids. Happy days.'

Nora thought how Hugh, the kindest man she'd ever known, would have loved the fact that the boat he had made was going to be part of this story. After the man had left, she locked the door and counted, then stared at, the money in the drawer of the desk. Three hundred euros. Not bad for her very first day.

As she walked back, that first evening after she'd closed the shop, she thought of all the times she'd walked here with her grandfather. He'd shown her the empty oyster shells with their hidden satiny linings of mother-of-pearl and explained how the pearls in Lainey's earrings had once been grains of sand.

By the time she got back to Temple Terrace, she had an idea for her next window. She found three plastic bags then went back to the beach and filled them with shells and sand.

On Thursday, with less than twenty-four hours to go, Lia was hurrying to the waxing salon in Blackrock on her lunch break when she saw the window. A tiny slice of the beach had been recreated behind the glass. A band of rippling silk for the sea. A stretch of real sand scattered with seashells. And floating at eye level, suspended somehow, was an oyster shell, half-open, revealing the gleam of a pair of beautiful pearl earrings.

When she opened the door, a cloud of lemony cologne met her. A dark-haired woman in jeans and a T-shirt was perched on top of a stepladder arranging leather books on a high shelf. She smiled down at Lia.

'Just browsing,' Lia said to ward off any sales pressure. She wished she had time to browse. There wasn't much to see but everything looked intriguing. A table of glass dishes filled with glittering jewellery. A dozen clocks of every shape and size ticked away softly on a long shelf that ran the length of one wall and a huge stuffed dog with soft, slightly crossed eyes looking up at her from under a long wooden desk.

'Actually,' Lia said, 'I was wondering, those pearl earrings in the window, how much are they?'

'Four hundred euros.'

Lia felt her mouth open slightly.

'I know it sounds like a lot, but they're a bargain.' The woman climbed down and wiped her hands on her jeans. 'They're real pearls and they're natural, not cultured.'

'What's the difference?'

'Let me show you.' The owner hauled her ladder over to the front of the shop and clambered up again. 'Can you hold this for me? I don't want to step on the sand; it took forever to do.' She leaned dangerously to one side as she untied the shell from the length of clear fishing line that made it look as if it was floating.

She climbed down the ladder again and upturned the shell. The pearls rolled onto Lia's palm. 'They feel cool, right? Real pearls are cold to the touch for the first couple of seconds and then they warm up; they absorb the heat of your skin.' Lia felt it happening as she spoke. 'Now,' the woman leaned forward, tucking her dark curls behind one ear, 'if you look closely, you'll see they're ever so slightly different? Cultured pearls are all identical, but every natural one is completely unique. That's how you know it's the real thing.'

The real thing, Lia thought. That was what Stephen called what had happened between them.

Nobody had explained, when Lia had joined Pentagon PR, that it was her job to proofread copy before it went to print. But she figured that pointing that out two months into her six-month probation would not win her any fans. So she'd taken the rap for the caption in a brochure for an artisan bakery that said:

Our dog is baked on both sides in a very hot oven so that it is soft on the inside and crispy on the outside.

She took the lecture from her boss and then she took the train to Cork, at her own expense, to personally deliver a thousand reprinted brochures and a grovelling apology to the client. He kept her waiting two hours. She sat in the reception inhaling the delicious smell of baking bread while her stomach rumbled and her chances of getting back to Dublin that afternoon receded. When eventually he appeared, he read through one brochure painstakingly slowly, stopping to query the spelling of every second word before he let Lia go. She arrived at the station just as the afternoon train was leaving and had to wait again.

The evening train had a party atmosphere, which lightened her spirits. The carriages were packed with groups of twenty-somethings heading up to Dublin for the weekend. She had to squeeze through three carriages before she found a seat. Then, as she was about to take her coat off, she glanced at the blond, curly haired guy in the seat opposite, scrolling through his phone, and, for a split second, she thought it was Dara.

She dragged her case all the way to the end of the train, the automatic doors hissing open and closed, as if it was really him. As if he was really here and not in Sydney, about as far away from her as he could possibly get.

The last carriage was packed with older people, trying to escape the rowdy crowd. She hiked her case up onto the rack above and sank gratefully into the window seat opposite a man in a business suit. She put in her earphones and played a Lana Del Ray album she had been avoiding since the break-up. Swooping love songs with shimmering crescendos that had been the soundtrack to last summer. She felt sorry for herself. It had been a shitty day. It had been a shitty year.

Houses flashed past. A line of cars, headlights like round car-toon eyes, waiting at a level crossing. A village came and went, swallowed up into the night. The man opposite glanced up and their eyes met and he gave her a quick, searching look, then he went back to his laptop.

She had been trying so hard to hide her upset and now, in this unguarded moment, the music had found its way through her armour and this stranger had seen through it. She studied his reflection for a while in the mirror of the glass. He was old but not *old*. A lean face, with starbursts of lines around his eyes. Soft dark hair that curled over the white collar of his shirt. Long fingers tapping away on his keyboard, a wedding ring on the left hand.

Until her sister's wedding, a month ago, Lia and Molly had shared a flat on Mount Street, a low-ceiling attic at the top of four flights of stairs where they'd lived in happy clutter, sharing clothes and make-up and secrets, climbing into one another's beds late at night to dissect their love lives and plan their futures.

Lia lived in an apartment in Milltown now. She still couldn't get used to the emptiness of the kitchen when she sat at the breakfast bar, eating her cereal. The silence that gathered around her when she switched off the hairdryer or the shower. The fear that thundered through her when she heard a noise in the middle of the night.

The train was slowing up to pull into a station when, with no warning, the man opposite suddenly lunged at her and grabbed a handful of her hair. Lia was about to scream when he leaned back and opened his fist and showed her the moth. It was the biggest one she had ever seen. A twisted, hairy body the thickness of her little finger, squirming between two brown speckled wings.

The man slid the window open, held his hand out and tossed the moth out into the darkness. Then he brushed his hands on his trousers and sat back down again.

'Are you okay?'

Lia's scalp was fizzing with revulsion, as if imagining what would have happened if that creature had become tangled in her hair. She nodded.

A woman in a crumpled blue uniform that was several sizes too big for her appeared, pushing a trolley. She jolted it to a stop at their table in a jangle of rattling glass bottles.

'Tea-coffee-sandwich-drink?' she parroted, without even looking at them.

'A white wine,' the man opposite said. 'And a beer.'

He put the wine, a small screw-top bottle, and a plastic glass in front of Lia.

'You look like you need that.'

She opened it, poured it and took a gulp. She felt her stomach muscles begin to unclench.

'Thank you. It's stupid to be so scared.' She gripped the plastic glass. 'It's just a moth.'

'I'm the same with dogs.' He took a sip from his beer can.

She smiled gratefully. 'I'm fine with dogs. So if one flies into your hair...'

He pretended to duck and covered his head with his hands. 'They can fly now?'

He worked in PR, too. An online betting company, the one that was always getting into trouble for its outrageous TV ads.

'That sounds like fun,' Lia said.

'It is.' His brown eyes were amused. 'If your idea of fun is pacifying Outraged of Oughterard and Ballistic of Blackrock. We've had campaigns banned before the glue was even dry on the posters.'

'But,' Lia smiled, 'that's the whole point, isn't it?'

'Scccch!' He pretended to frown. 'Nobody's supposed to know that. I'll pay you to keep my secret.' He picked up her empty wine bottle, shook it, and stood up. 'How about another tiny bottle of wine?'

'I should be buying you a drink.' But she barely had the bus fare to get back to the flat.

'It's on me. I need another one, after all that talk of flying dogs. I'm Stephen.'

'Lia.'

When he had gone to the dining carriage, she turned her phone to selfie mode then touched up her eyes and dabbed on some lip-gloss. A woman on the other side of the carriage shot her a knowing look. *It's not like that!* Lia wanted to say. It hadn't been. Not then. Not at the start.

Stephen couldn't keep a straight face when she told him about the typo but he stopped laughing when she admitted that she'd taken the blame for it.

'Why did you do that?'

She dipped her finger in a drop of spilled wine on the Formica table and traced a figure of eight.

'It was my manager's mistake.' Helena was supposed to have

given Lia a job description but she'd never got around to it. 'I didn't want to get her into trouble.'

Stephen shook his head and sighed. 'And now you're paying the price of nice, right?'

'I suppose.'

'You're way too bright to have to do that.'

'I don't know about that.'

'I do. You got our marketing strategy in five seconds flat. So, from now on, you're going to stop looking out for other people and start looking out for yourself. Deal?'

She laughed. 'Deal.'

The journey, which had dragged all day, seemed to flash past and soon, too soon, the train slowed to pull into Heuston Station.

Stephen shut his laptop with a very final-sounding click and slid it, together with a pile of papers, into his briefcase.

Lia had a flash of them sitting on stools in that dark bar on Parkgate Street – a different ending to the evening to going back to an empty flat.

They both got off the train, crossed the long concourse, together but not together, and stopped outside the door of the station. The tide of passengers from the train split to flow around them, hurrying across to the bus and tram stops, buttoning themselves up against an icy breeze that was funnelling up the river. They did not move.

'This is going to sound like a cliché but,' Stephen said, eventually, looking at her then looking away, the wind lifting the end of his scarf as he wound it around his neck. 'The world is your oyster.'

'Well, it will be my first one.'

'Really?' He looked back at her, his eyes dark, a little twist to his mouth. 'I wish –'

What, she thought, with a twinge of longing, what do you wish?

He put his hand on her arm and gave it a quick squeeze. 'I wish you the very best, Lia.'

He turned towards the taxi rank and strode off while she crossed the road and began the walk up the quays. The blond, curly haired guy she had seen earlier on the train brushed past her and she realised that she hadn't thought about Dara for hours.

Lia held the pearls up to her ears and looked at herself in the tall, gilt-framed mirror. The pearls glowed softly against her skin. They looked luxurious and grown up. But four hundred euros?

'I don't know . . .' she said. 'I love them, but it's a lot.'

'I know. I can put them on hold for you if you like,' the shop owner said. 'You go away and have a think about it.'

It was a lot, Lia thought but it was cheaper than the price of a hotel room for two nights, of letting things drag on, of waiting for Stephen to keep his word and end his marriage.

'No. I'll take them now,' she said.

The day after the trip to Cork, Lia took her manager aside and, with a hammering heart, she reminded her that she hadn't been given a job description. Helena sulked for a few hours then sent one over by email, along with a note saying that Lia would be reimbursed for the taxi fares and train tickets.

Lia felt exhilarated, as if she'd been let into a secret club. She wished she could tell Stephen that she had kept her promise, but she didn't know his second name so there was no way to track him down.

She thought about him, though. She pictured him sitting opposite her at the breakfast bar in the kitchen. Imagined him calling her from the living room when she came back to the empty flat. It was just a harmless fantasy. Even if she could find him, nothing would happen. She would never get involved with a married man.

Then, one Friday when she was having a drink in the pub next to the office, she saw a familiar figure sitting at the bar, his dark head bent, once more, over his mobile phone.

'Hi.' He seemed to struggle for her name when she rapped him on the shoulder.

'Lia.'

'Lee-ah,' he repeated, 'of course.' His voice was deeper than she remembered.

There was an awkward moment as she wondered whether she should kiss his cheek or shake his hand. Then the crowd jostled her, pushing her closer to him and he patted the empty stool beside him. 'Sit down.'

She glanced back at the knot of her co-workers, sitting huddled around a table of drinks, getting smashed.

'I'm with people from work.'

'Ah.' He looked disappointed. 'I just popped in for a quick one.' He put down an empty glass. 'Bad day. Didn't feel like going home but –' He stood up.

'Look,' the words were out of her mouth before she could stop them, 'can't I buy you a drink at least? To thank you for the moth and the wine and the pep talk?'

'I shouldn't, really, on an empty stomach.'

'Dinner, then.'

His face brightened. He looked five years younger when he smiled. 'You sure you don't have something better to do?'

She had thought she might call by her sister's flat on the way home from the pub, spend another Friday night playing gooseberry with Molly and Colm.

'No. Not really.'

She took him to her favourite Japanese restaurant, a tiny, shabby place on Capel Street with wooden benches and sacks of rice piled up by the counter and Asian waitresses running to and from a curtained-off area at the back of the restaurant, which concealed the kitchen.

They both squashed in at one end of a long table of rowdy Italians who were celebrating something, cheering, taking pictures on their mobiles, talking incessantly and good-naturedly.

'You're going to have to order for me,' Stephen said looking helplessly at the menu. 'I don't know my teriyaki from my tempura.'

He was delighted with what she chose and praised everything as if she'd made it herself. They tucked into steamed pork dumplings and deep-fried tofu, edamame beans, seaweed salad. Drank cups of steaming miso and hot sake.

He was as easy to talk to as she remembered. They talked

about work and weird colleagues and high-maintenance clients and then, as they relaxed more, she told him about her family, about growing up in Galway and moving to Dublin for college and he reminisced about growing up in Brittas Bay with his two brothers and about his parents, both dead now. He didn't mention his other family. She avoided looking at the ring on his left hand, would not let herself think about his wife, who was probably wondering where he was right now.

The Italians had left and the dishes were cleared away by the time Lia realised that the waitresses were cashing up by the door and the evening was nearly over.

Stephen looked at his watch. 'Midnight. Any second now the bells will chime and you'll disappear into the arms of some infatuated boyfriend.'

She shook her head.

'Fiancé?'

'I had one of those once,' she said, lightly. 'But we broke up a month before the wedding.'

'That was brave.'

She shook her head. Dara had dumped her, then quit the country to go to Sydney and had left her to face the fallout alone. Then, at Christmas, Molly and Colm had got engaged and everyone had tiptoed around her, treating her as if she would break. As if she hadn't already broken.

Stephen tapped his finger against his sake cup, his lips tight. 'I got married when I was twenty-three. I thought I was doing the right thing. I thought it was love but I think I was playing the hero. She was an addict, before I met her. She'd only been sober for a few months and she was so fragile. It made me feel like a man,' he smiled wryly into his cup, 'the idea that she needed me so much. But people change, you know? She certainly doesn't need me any more, she doesn't need anyone. Half the time, I don't even know why we're even together.'

Lia was afraid that if she said anything, the relief she felt on hearing that his marriage was fizzling out might leak through, so she nodded, sympathetically.

'Oh well.' Stephen sighed. 'You make your bed, you lie in it.

You make two beautiful sons and then you move into separate rooms. That's how it goes.' He ran his fingers through his hair.

'I didn't know,' Lia swallowed hard, 'I didn't realise you had kids.'

'Two. Jake's twelve. Fergus – we call him Froggy – is six. You'd love them.'

'I'm sure I would,' Lia said, wishing they didn't exist, wishing that the most handsome, interesting, open man she'd ever met in her life was single and childless.

When the waitress came over with the bill on a saucer Lia put her hand on it.

'No!' Stephen pulled the saucer away from her.

'It's my treat.' Lia wrestled it back. 'You bought all that wine on the train.' Paying was what friends did and that's all they would be. She held on to the saucer and fished her debit card out of her pocket.

'You're so sweet,' Stephen said, looking at her in a way that was more than just friendly. 'Do you know that?'

They fell into step as they walked up Henry Street and the longer neither of them spoke, the harder it was for Lia to think of a way to break the silence. And maybe that was better, to just listen to their footsteps ringing on the pavement. To walk beneath the dazzle and glitter of the Christmas lights, to pretend, for a few more minutes, that they were going somewhere together.

They crossed O'Connell Street and joined the queue at the taxi rank. When they reached the top, when the next car was his or hers, Stephen turned to her.

'You can say no, please say no if you want to, but can I do something? So I don't have to spend the rest of my life knowing what I'm missing?'

She fell into the kiss like a skydiver. Alive and exhilarated and afraid of what would happen when it ended. Her eyes were closed, but she felt the queue shuffle past, leaving them behind.

Two days later, he sent her a message on Facebook to say he couldn't stop thinking about her. He asked her to meet him in a hotel on Kildare Street. She sat in her empty flat, asking the wall what she should do, but she didn't pick up the phone and ask Molly. She knew what her sister would say.

She very nearly didn't go. She never wanted to leave.

Lia told herself she wasn't a marriage breaker. You couldn't break something that was already broken and Stephen's marriage was a sham. His words, not hers, and this was the real thing – this rush and passion and heat that she felt when they were together, the need for him that consumed her, that woke her up in the night and made her reach for her mobile phone, check her texts again in case he'd sent one while she slept, hold the phone in her hand in case he was awake thinking of her.

They talked on the phone when he was driving to work and driving home and they met as often as they could: in a greasy spoon in the flower market, in a burger bar in the Ilac Centre, at the hotel for the first couple of weeks and then at her apartment. She wanted to give him Molly's key but he wouldn't take it.

'We have to be careful how we do this,' he said as they lay in her bed, the lit fountain in the courtyard throwing spangles onto the ceiling. 'We need an exit strategy.'

Gemma was unstable, he admitted to Lia. She hadn't had a drink in fifteen years but alcoholism was a disease. Anything could trigger it.

'This could push her over the edge, you know? And if she had a drink, anything could happen. She could show up at your office and shout the place down.'

Lia had a horrible image of her manager's face. Of herself cowering in a toilet cubicle, while a mad woman she'd never met kicked the doors open one by one.

'And I want to make this easy for Jake and Froggy.' Stephen turned towards her, his closeness, the dark head, the dark eyes, filling her with a happiness that pushed her fear away. 'I want them to love you the way I do.' He ran his finger down the side of her face.

'But you will leave her?'

He caught her hand, laced their fingers together, squeezed hard. 'I'll be out of there by the spring. I promise you.'

For a person with a terrible poker face, Lia turned out to be a surprisingly good liar. If there was a chance of seeing Stephen, all she had to do was open her mouth and the perfect excuse slipped out. She couldn't meet her mother in Kildare to go Christmas shopping/go to a wreath-making workshop with Molly/make the office party because she was getting a cold/doing a Bikram yoga class/working late.

'Holy crap!' Molly said, opening a drawer in Lia's flat looking for a pair of spare wool gloves for a Saturday afternoon walk on the pier and finding it full of lacy knickers and balconette bras. 'What's all this for?'

'I bought it for the honeymoon,' Lia said, with a little quiver in her voice that was so convincing she almost believed herself.

Molly bit her lip.

'Don't worry about it.'

'I'm not worried.' Molly slammed the drawer closed. 'Because he's out there somewhere. The real love of your life. And if he knew your top drawer looked like a concession for Agent Provocateur, he'd be banging on the door right now.'

Lia was afraid to look up in case she smiled. The love of her life was, at this moment, at a research group in Smithfield. If he could get away early, she was going to tell Molly she was too tired to go to the movies after the walk and he would be banging on the door in just a few short hours.

It made her feel queasy how easy it was to fool her sister. They had always told one another the truth about everything. Molly had slept beside Lia the night that Dara had dumped her, wrapped her arms around her, physically restraining her from getting out of bed and driving to his house and begging him to go ahead with the wedding.

And the lying wouldn't end when Stephen moved in. They'd have to pretend they'd just met, or Molly would look back and count the times she'd been fooled.

Lia went home to her parents' farm in Galway for Christmas. Stephen had told her he couldn't get away from his family until the New Year, but, on Christmas night, he texted to say he could meet her on the afternoon of Boxing Day. 'I have to see you!' he wrote. 'I miss you. I love you.'

Lia had to force herself not to grin like a lunatic as she watched TV and ate chocolates and played charades. There was nothing she wanted more for Christmas than this.

She woke up far too early. Snow had fallen in the night and turned her father's fields white. She sent Stephen a blank text and, a moment later, he sent her a blank text back. Their code for saying, 'I'm thinking of you.' She showered, packed and dressed and sat at the kitchen window drinking cup after cup of coffee, waiting impatiently for everyone to wake up so that she could go.

It was nearly eleven by the time they were all gathered in the kitchen, everyone making a different breakfast. Colm scrambling eggs in one pan, her dad frying Christmas pudding in another, Molly making a spinach smoothie, her mother assembling a plate of cheese.

'I have to go back to Dublin.'

The blender stopped. The kitchen fell silent. Four pairs of eyes looked at her in disbelief.

'But it's Boxing Day!' Molly said.

Lia tried to look miserable but her happiness was like a beach ball she was struggling to keep underwater.

'Amelia,' her mother was holding a cracker in one hand and a cheese knife in the other, 'there's a blizzard coming. Surely they won't expect you to risk your life driving to Dublin in that?'

'I'll drive her.' Lia's father turned off the gas ring and smacked his palms together.

'I'll do it.' Colm stood up. 'I could stay with my parents tonight and drive back down in the morning.'

Molly grabbed his arm. 'Well, you're not going on your own. I'm coming with you.'

'Please!' Lia had to shout to be heard over the noise. 'I'm not putting anyone through a five-hour round trip. I'm perfectly capable of driving myself.'

'What's so bloody important that they have to drag you away from home at Christmas?' Molly frowned at her.

'It's a campaign. For an online betting company,' Lia said.

'I don't care if it's an address to the United Nations,' her mother said, disgustedly, hacking blindly at the Stilton as if she was trying to murder it and dispose of the corpse. 'Everyone belongs at home at Christmas.'

Lia went upstairs and changed quickly out of her jeans and sweater and into her green velvet dress with the gold-beaded collar. She could do her make-up at the petrol station on the Longmile Road. The snow was steadily falling again and she had to get on the road.

There was a tap on the door and she turned away and pulled her coat on so that Molly wouldn't see her dress.

'Can we talk?' Her sister sat on the bed.

She put her hands behind her and gripped the dressing table.

'I wasn't going to tell anyone till New Year's Day,' Molly covered her mouth with her knuckles; she was smiling but her eyes were brimming with tears, 'but I'm up the Hilary.'

Lia stared at her. 'The what?'

'The duff, Lia. I'm pregnant. I'm going to have a baby.' Molly gnawed on a fingernail. 'I'm sorry. It's okay if you're upset about it. You're the one who is supposed to be pregnant by now, not me. I feel like I'm stealing your bloody life.'

Lia took Molly's small hand. Her fingertips were cold, the way they always were. Cold hands, warm heart.

'You're not stealing my life. You're living yours. That makes me happy. I swear!' The grin she'd been holding back since Stephen's call that morning now burst onto her face. 'That and the fact that you're going to get so fat!'

'Revoltingly fat!' Molly said happily. She wrapped her arms around Lia and the two sisters leaned into one another, listening to the sounds from downstairs – their parents' voices from the kitchen, Colm whistling 'Lucky' out of tune, over the sound of the shower pump. And Lia felt lucky, for the new life that was beginning beneath the fleece of Molly's Christmas-pudding onesie and for the new life that she couldn't tell her sister about yet. She and Stephen had talked about having children.

'We won't wait too long,' he'd said. 'I don't want to be an old dad.'

Her mother filled a hot-water bottle and a flask, made a small mountain of sandwiches that she wrapped twice, in greaseproof paper and tinfoil. Her father syphoned petrol from the Land Rover, even though she had half a tank in her ancient Polo. He reeled around a bit afterwards and when he kissed her goodbye, she could smell it on his breath.

They all waved her off, wearing Christmas cracker party hats, slightly crumpled and rakish. For a moment, Lia, with her velvet dress hidden under her parka, her high-heeled shoes stuffed under the passenger seat, felt like she didn't belong. But this time next year, she and Stephen would be out in the open. They would both be part of this picture.

The hot-water bottle was cold before she got to Athlone. The motorway was deserted but icy so she had to go slowly. It took so long to get to Dublin, that, in the end, she only had three hours with Stephen before he had to go back to pick the boys up. But it was worth it. The rightness of being with him made all the rest of it fade.

After he'd gone, she slept for a while and when she woke up, the apartment was dark. There was nothing in the flat except a can of baked beans and two crusts of stale bread, which she toasted and ate with the beans while she watched bad TV movies.

Back home in Galway, the Christmas trees in the kitchen and living rooms would be twinkling. There would be blazing fires in every room and candles on the dinner table. They'd be eating her mother's infamous turkey curry. Molly would be pretending that she wasn't drinking because she had a cold. Colm would be hiding hunks of her mother's dry turkey and watery sprouts in his napkin. Her dad would be assuring her mum that there wasn't too much cinnamon in the sauce. And, afterwards, they'd play Trivial Pursuit and charades, her parents bickering over who got the lucky blue plastic pie, her father drinking single malt and flinging Quality Street at anyone who said 'sounds like' because it 'compromised the integrity of the game'.

Stephen couldn't leave home in February because Jake broke his collarbone falling off a trampoline. It was Froggy's birthday in April, so he had to stay around for that. In June, he went on a family holiday to Tuscany. The villa had been booked the previous summer so he couldn't cancel it. His brothers and their kids were going too. He texted her from art galleries and restaurants and beaches. He loved her. He would tell Gemma when he got home. Definitely.

But while they were away, Gemma found a lump in her breast and there were weeks of waiting before it was diagnosed as a benign cyst.

Lia knew that she should feel some pity for this woman who might have cancer, whose husband was cheating on her, who had probably never even loved her, but she didn't. She hated her. She hated the whole family, all of them, for finding excuses for pulling Stephen back into their orbit.

In August, Lia's niece was born and it made her sad in a way she'd never been sad that the man she loved wasn't there with her, around Molly's hospital bed, drinking sneaked-in champagne in Styrofoam cups and suggesting daft names for the baby: 'Apricot', 'Audio', 'Ocean' and 'Vodka'.

Lia told Stephen that she needed a date. A solid date she could count on. That she couldn't build her life around vague possibilities and endless promises. He broke down and told her how awful it had been at home.

'Please, tell me you'll wait,' he said, pushing his thumbs into his eyes, as if he was trying to force the tears back in. 'Tell me I haven't lost you.'

Her heart softened. 'Of course you haven't.'

'Once the boys have settled down, I'm out of there, Lia.'

But another Christmas came and he was still living at home. They swapped gifts in the restaurant where they'd had their first dinner. Stephen gave her a beribboned box from Brown Thomas with Myla underwear slipped between the layers of tissue paper. She gave him a cashmere dressing gown, then brought it back to the flat and hung it on the back of her bedroom door. The following morning, she got into her car alone and drove west again to spend Christmas with her family.

Her phone was like an itch she had to constantly scratch. She checked it every few minutes, pretending she was taking pictures just for an excuse to look at her screen.

Afterwards, her photo stream was full of random shots, of the tablecloth and the half-eaten dinners. Of her mum with battery-operated fairy lights in her hair, the dog looking embarrassed, in antlers. Of the plum pudding on fire, the sprig of holly burning dangerously, but mostly, she had pictures of Lia's baby Flo being passed around at the table like a parcel, or gazing at the camera sternly, as if she knew exactly what Lia was up to.

The shop owner polished the pearl earrings carefully with a soft cloth.

'I used to play dress up with these when I was a little girl,' she said wistfully. 'But I never heard the story about them until after my grandmother died. You think you know a person, then they turn out to be someone completely different.' She opened a drawer in the desk. 'They don't have a box but I think I have one that'll fit.'

'It's okay, I don't need one—' Lia stopped as the owner pulled a slim black leather box out of a drawer. It opened with a satisfying click and the pearls slotted in, one by one, glowing like moonlight against the dark blue velvet lining.

On Friday evening, Lia went home from work, showered, then got dressed for her trip. She slipped the earrings into her ears, then loaded the car and joined the traffic on the N11.

She glanced in the rear-view mirror every now and then, admiring the soft sheen of the pearls. It almost seemed like a crime to separate them. Stephen's wife was hardly going to hand the earring back after she found it. But Lia felt that she would get something far more valuable than a pearl. She'd get the man she loved, for life.

She followed her Sat Nav past the turn-off for Brittas, then turned right and right again before pulling the car over outside the house where Stephen had grown up. It was nothing like the farmhouse in Galway, which was really only a glorified bungalow. It was a little bit apart from the neighbours on either side; soft grey brick with a faded red-pitch roof and big bay windows that reflected the golden flare of the late summer sunset.

He had shown her a photograph once. 'Sometimes,' he'd said, looking at the screen, 'I used to feel like I was two people: the person I was when I was growing up and the one I became when I met Gemma. When I can be with you all the time, I feel like I'm my younger self again... if that makes sense.'

It did make sense to Lia. She missed her younger self too.

The girl who had sat opposite him on the train could not have dreamed about the double life she led now. It scared her how easily she had deceived everyone and how ready she was now to deceive Stephen. But when she left this house tomorrow evening, the deception would be over. They could start all over again, out in the open.

The front door opened. Stephen came out to the car to meet her and she felt a rush of pleasure and anticipation. This was what it would be like to come home to him.

'You found it.' He opened the back door to take out her case and a gust of soft country air blew in. The smell of wet hedges and turf smoke, a salty tang that must be coming from the sea. She got out and turned around, her heels sinking into the gravel, trying to guess which way the dunes were, but Stephen was already at the door, waiting for her.

'It's lovely,' she said, looking around the small hall. The white wood panelling was scuffed and dusty and two bulbs in the chandelier were missing but there were some small seascapes on one wall and wind chimes made from scraps of sea glass clinked softly over their heads.

He put her case down. Usually, the first thing he did when they met was kiss her. But he folded his arms and she saw that his mouth was set in a sullen line. He had tried to cancel the weekend that morning, said that Gemma was all over the place because her niece had come to stay. But Lia had insisted. If she didn't plant the clue now, she knew she never would.

She put a conciliatory hand on his arm. 'Can we look around?'

'It's pretty musty.' He turned away and began opening doors, moving on before Lia could get a proper look at what was behind them.

She glimpsed a living room with faded red-velvet curtains and a jumble of mismatched armchairs. A smaller den with a leather sofa, a flat screen and bookshelves stuffed with tattered paperbacks. Plastic crates of old board games, jigsaws and video-game consoles sprouting tangles of wires.

The downstairs toilet was covered in cobwebs. A pair of surfboards were propped against the sink and a washing machine was wedged into a corner next to a lovely antique wooden sideboard.

She followed him down some shallow steps.

'I would have opened a few windows,' he said, opening the door of the kitchen, 'but it's too bloody cold.'

'We can light a fire.'

'I tried.'

He crossed the tiles to the fireplace and began poking at a pile of smoking turf. Lia looked around.

It was a lovely space but the mahogany dining table with carved feet was too big for it. The range was crusted with old grease. There was a line of dead pot plants on the windowsill.

Everything was neglected and uncared for, just like Stephen. It had been taken for granted for years. It needed love.

Stephen threw the poker down. 'It's gone out!' He glared at her over his shoulder. 'Let's get out of here. We can go to Wexford and book into a decent hotel.'

He looked so stern that Lia almost gave in. Then she reached up and touched one of the pearls in her ears. It had warmed next to her skin, just like the shop owner had said it would.

It had started out as an ugly grain of sand but it had turned into this beautiful precious thing. What they would become, she and Stephen, felt like it was hanging on this moment, the way the pearl was hanging from her ear.

She looked around for something, anything, to change his mind, then pointed at a cluster of small seascapes that hung between the range and the back door. 'I saw some more of these in the hall,' she said. 'Who painted them?'

'They're just stuff I did in school.' Stephen wiped his sooty hands on his jeans.

'Really?' She walked over to look at them.

'Mam had them framed.' Stephen's voice softened. 'She loved the sea.'

Lia wanted to like them. From a few feet away, the water looked convincing but, up close, the paint was applied too thickly – blobs of green and purple and lavender flecking the blue. Lia swallowed a chunk of shame. 'She must have been so proud of you,' she said.

'That was a long time ago.' He came over and looked over her shoulder. 'I wouldn't be able to paint like that now.'

She turned and put her hands on the lapels of his jacket. 'Of course you would,' she said, kindly. 'Talent like that doesn't go away.'

That was all it took to change the temperature. There was warmth in Stephen's eyes and there was another painting upstairs.

She could feel him watching her as she went up ahead of him. She opened the first door on the landing.

'That's just my old room,' he said.

Lia smiled at the ghosts of a poster, left on the wall. 'Do I sense the ghost of Pamela Anderson?' she said.

'Come on!' he laughed. 'I'm not that old! Try Sarah Michelle Geller.'

'Buffy!' she said. 'Very classy!'

She looked around at the empty bookcase, the dark open mouth of an old-fashioned wardrobe.

'I thought we'd stay in my parents' old room. I made up the bed. I had to stop and buy bed linen on the way. I nearly forgot it.'

'What reminded you?'

'I don't know.' He shrugged but his dark eyes were warm. 'Come on. I'll show you.'

Lia lay back on the big brass bed on the rough, too new sheets and tried not to think that this was where *she* must sleep when they came here on holiday. Instead she imagined what she'd do if this house was hers.

For a start, she'd get rid of that cheap popcorn finish on the ceiling. She'd put up new blinds and change the carpets, and she'd cover the ugly chairs and sofas with proper throws, clean the cobwebs and the windows, turn it back into the home it had been when Stephen was a child.

They could live here, she thought with a rush of delight. It was only an hour from Dublin. They could both commute. Stephen's boys could come down at the weekend and she could invite her parents and Molly and Colm and Flo to stay. She closed her eyes and imagined the hall lined with candles in storm lanterns, music on the stereo, the big mahogany table moved to the living room and covered with a linen cloth, vases of flowers picked from the tangled garden.

'I'll go down and try to get that fire to play ball,' Stephen said, when he woke up. He kissed her forehead. 'And open the wine. Is it in the boot?'

Lia had a sudden flashback to the two bottles, a Sancerre and a Borolo, sitting in a bag on her kitchen table. 'Damn! I forgot the wine. Is there a local pub I can go to?'

'Yeah, but' – he shook his head – 'they wouldn't have anything drinkable. There's an off-licence in Arklow. I can be there and back in twenty minutes.'

His headlights swept across the bedroom like a searchlight as he left and the car turned on a spray of gravel and was gone. Lia ran downstairs naked and slipped on her coat. She opened the front door and went outside to her own car.

It was properly dark now, the dark sky glittering with stars, a sickle moon hanging crookedly above the tall trees that shielded the house from the road. She carried the bag of shopping into the kitchen and unpacked it.

A spatchcock chicken, rosemary potatoes, sprouted broccoli and molten chocolate soufflé from M & S. She'd also brought tea lights and two scented candles from her flat, and a heat log which she'd picked up at a petrol station when she'd stopped to ask for directions. She dumped it into the grate and it smouldered for a moment, then burst into flames. She took a picture and texted it to Stephen. 'Hurry back!' she wrote. Then she changed 'back' to 'home'.

She opened every cupboard looking for an oven tray, then

tried what looked like a pantry, but found that it was locked. She turned the handle over and over before she gave up and found a Pyrex dish in the drawer beneath the oven. She washed it, then tipped the chicken and potatoes in. She opened a drawer looking for tinfoil and saw a key, hanging on a grubby white ribbon.

There was indeed a pantry behind the locked door. It was lined with deep shelves packed with pots and pans, tins of tomatoes and beans, boxes of cereal, packets of soup. And in the space beneath the shelves, a jumble of things that had been hurriedly shoved in: a red down coat with a fur collar; a pair of Wellingtons with a daisy pattern; an armful of clothes, cardigans and dresses on hangers; a tatty old flower print toilet bag. *Her* things.

Lia lined her foot in its cage sandal up against the Wellingtons. Gemma had big feet, at least two sizes bigger than hers. She slipped her hand into one of the pockets of the red jacket and pulled out a trolley token and Kit Kat wrapper.

Lia had to fight an unexpected wave of pity for this woman she didn't know, whom Stephen had so easily and completely erased.

By the time he got back, Lia had set the table and lit the candles, Ellie Goulding was playing from her portable speaker, the fire was blazing and the kitchen smelled of roasting food.

He dumped a pair of clinking plastic bags on the floor and pulled out a bouquet of roses. Fat, velvety pink roses that hadn't come from a petrol station.

He handed them to her and kissed her. 'Sorry. I was off earlier. It felt strange having you here.'

'But it's okay now, isn't it?'

He shook his head. 'It's amazing.'

They sat for hours over dinner. Stephen telling stories of long-ago Christmases and orchard raids and skinny dipping, girls using his father's rotten ladder to climb in his brothers' bedroom windows.

He carried her drunkenly up the stairs, bumping her knees against the bannisters, walking sideways to navigate the long, narrow landing, and they fell asleep, their arms wrapped round one another.

Stephen woke her up with breakfast. Coffee, scrambled eggs, toast, one of her roses in a water glass.

It reminded Lia of the hotel breakfast on their first morning together. How he'd tugged the belt of her robe afterwards and pulled her back into bed. But then she noticed that there was only one setting on the tray.

'What about you?'

'I'm spoiling you this morning.' He set the tray down. 'You eat, have a shower, I'll go back down and clear up. If we get on the road by eleven, we can go back to your place for lunch before I have to go. Okay?'

Another few hours with him before the empty Saturday afternoon began. She smiled up at him. 'Okay.'

She propped herself up but she was too nervous to eat. She drank the coffee he had brought her and stripped the petals off the rose. She looked at her reflection in the dressing table mirror. Her face was pale, her mouth tight with anxiety. If she didn't do this now, she might not get a chance again.

When she came back from her shower, Stephen had stripped the bed and covered the mattress with a pilled grey wool throw. She folded last night's dress and packed it away in her small suitcase, slipped on jeans and a soft sweatshirt with sneakers.

There was nothing else to do now. She slipped one pearl out of her ear and looked around for the right place to drop it. She hooked it onto the grey wool throw and stood back. Too obvious. She unhooked it and bent down and put it carefully on the floor by the side of the bed. It gleamed like a tiny white light bulb on the threadbare red carpet.

She imagined Gemma glancing down and seeing it as she pulled back the covers to get into bed. Or better still, feeling it beneath her heel, stooping to pick it up, looking at it and knowing, before she even called Stephen to demand an explanation, that whatever this was, it was the real thing.

She heard the crunch of footsteps on the gravel below and went over to the window. Stephen was walking past below, carrying a black sack of rubbish and a smaller plastic carrier bag with the wine bottles. She smiled to herself. She had never seen the domestic side of him.

He walked round the side of the house to the two plastic wheelie bins, lifted the lid on one and then stopped. He looked around, almost furtively, then closed the bin lid and went over to his car and put the bag in the boot instead. She stood watching him, curiously, as he went back into the house. A moment later he came out again with another black plastic bag. This one was stuffed with bed linen and towels. She could see the corner of the white duvet cover poking out of the top. He had hidden every trace of his wife from her, and now he was hiding every trace of her from his wife. Every trace, she thought, except one.

'You've got everything?' She looked up and saw that Stephen was standing in the doorway of the bedroom now. She nodded

'Right, well, I'll carry these down for you.' He picked up her bag and stood at the door, waiting for her. 'We really should get going.' He was like a bouncer, she thought, waiting to escort her off the premises, but she had to let him go first, in case he saw the earring.

'I'll be right down. I just need to use the loo.'

She bent down as she passed the bed and planted the gold post more firmly in the carpet. Her heart was hammering as she crossed the room and closed the door behind her. It was done. She went into the bathroom and stood there for a few seconds, then flushed the loo. As she turned to go, she saw that the bathroom cabinet was open. It had been empty last night but now the toilet bag she'd seen in the pantry was on the bottom shelf. Stephen must have replaced while she was asleep.

She took it out and unzipped it. There was an empty tube of cheap moisturiser, a rusty Venus razor, a hairbrush, half a dozen scrunchies, a few loose Tampax. And at the very bottom was a pink-and-white box of two Clearblue First Response Pregnancy tests. Lia's hand was shaking as she opened it. The flap had been torn open and one was missing. The room felt as if it was tilting. Separate rooms, she thought, that's what he'd told her.

*

Stephen was waiting for her in the kitchen. There must be a neighbour, she realised at that moment. Someone he didn't want to see her. That was why he had hurried her into the house last night.

He kissed her and they walked out to their cars together.

'You can follow me,' he said.

Lia couldn't look at him. She opened her car door.

'Hey,' he said before she could get in. 'Don't be sad.' He put a finger under her chin and turned her head so she was facing him. 'Gemma and the boys will be down here from Friday, so we'll have a weekend in Dublin.'

He lifted a strand of hair that had caught under her collar, then noticed her earrings. She had changed her mind about leaving one behind. She was wearing both of them now.

'Pearls,' he said. 'Very nice.'

She shrugged him away

'Did someone give them to you?' He raised an eyebrow.

'I bought them for myself.'

'Because you're worth it.' He smiled as she got into the car.

She looked up at him for a long moment. 'Yeah,' she said. 'I am.'

His BMW broke down just past Silver Strand. He had pulled over on the side of the road and opened the bonnet. He waved at her frantically as she drove past him.

She saw his face in the rear-view mirror. A look of disbelief and then anger. Her phone buzzed with incoming texts all the way back to Dublin. She didn't read any of them and when she got back home, she sent him a text message. Two words: 'It's over.' Then she deleted his number from her phone, erasing him as easily as he had erased her.

5

Hand-knotted, Silk Moroccan prayer rug

Caroline

When Caroline looked up from the TV, Mac was standing between the end of the sofa and the piano gazing at her, sideways, with his good eye. He took a step forward, trying to look nonchalant.

'Out!' she said. He dropped his head as if he'd been shot then reversed, at speed, back out into the hall, manoeuvring past two side tables and a footstool, careful not to knock anything over or tangle his legs in the flex of the lamp. He was surprisingly graceful for a dog the length of an ironing board.

Caroline unmuted the TV but she could still hear him sighing tragically over the sound of *Countdown*. She might as well get the bloody walk over with.

She took Liam's old anorak off the coat stand. It had holes in both pockets and a zip that had lost its loop and could only be pulled up using a paperclip. Everything about it was depressing, most of all, the fact that she hadn't thrown it away. How was she ever going to let go of her marriage when she couldn't part with her husband's tatty cast-offs?

It was thirty-seven days since Liam had left, the door slamming so hard that the saucepans in the kitchen cupboards rattled. Mac had cowered at the bottom of the stairs, his ears turning to follow the crunch and scatter of the gravel as the car roared out of the driveway.

He would kill someone, Caroline thought with perverse satisfaction. Mow down a child or an old person. He would be arrested and hauled off to jail. Then maybe he would understand how his carelessness hurt other people.

Liam didn't come back for three days and when he did, she

was out. She came back to a drawer emptied out; a hand's width of empty space in the wardrobe, two dried-up clumps of mud and grass from where he'd dragged his golf bag through the hall. Another mess for her to clean up. What a surprise.

Lucy called her from New York for the first time in weeks. 'Dad says he's living at a hotel.' She sounded worried. 'What happened?'

'It's complicated.' What had happened was actually very simple. She had flipped. After another weekend of silence and mono-syllabic replies to her questions, she had woken to the sound of the TV on Monday morning, stormed downstairs, and snatched the remote control from Liam.

'We never go anywhere. We never do anything. We have nothing together,' she'd shouted. 'What are we actually doing here?'

'Well,' he folded his arms and looked at her with an expression of maddening calm, 'I'm trying to watch CNN News,' he said. 'And you're wandering around the house naked.'

She *was* naked, she realised. She hadn't noticed. He usually didn't notice either, but now he was looking briefly at her, his eyes disinterested.

'Can I have the remote control?'

'Sure.' It missed his head by a good six inches and smashed on the windowsill, sending bits of plastic and batteries skittering onto the laminate floor. 'You can take it with you when you leave!' she had shouted, so loudly that she was surprised that Lucy hadn't heard her from the other side of the Atlantic.

'Mum,' her daughter sounded exasperated now. 'The whole point of the two of you retiring early was so that you could spend time together. It makes no sense to split up now. Can you please talk to one another and sort this out?'

If they could talk to one another, Caroline thought, this wouldn't be happening. 'If your father has anything to say to me,' she said tightly, 'he knows where I am.'

Apparently, he didn't. A week went by, then another one. When, finally, he called, it was to tell her he wasn't coming back.

'I've rented an apartment for a couple of months.'

'So this is it,' she said bitterly. 'This is how forty-one years of marriage ends. Not with a bang or whimper, but with a phone call.'

'I don't know if it's over,' he sounded hesitant, 'I just think maybe we need some time apart.'

'You don't even sound upset!'

'Neither do you!' Liam said. 'You sound angry. I could rant and rage and break things too, but what good would that do?'

'So what am I supposed to do when you move into this bachelor pad? Rattle around a bloody four-bedroomed semi-detached with a bloody dog I never wanted in the first place?'

'Caroline, you can do what you like.'

After he'd hung up, she tried to think of a single thing she liked, but she couldn't. She could think of plenty of things she didn't like.

She didn't like the fact that Lucy and Cal both lived thousands of miles away. She didn't like the fact that she had left her job in HR to retire, at sixty, with Liam and her friends had told her it was a mistake; she'd done it anyway. She didn't like the fact that she had given more than half her life to a man who wanted to look at the television more than he wanted to look at her body. She didn't like her body, the way that her hair was thinning and her waist was thickening. There was nothing she could do about any of these things but she could do something about this house and all the hideous junk they'd filled it with since they moved in. She went online and downloaded a book on de-cluttering.

The book was ninety-two pages long but the central idea could have been written on the back of an envelope. You were supposed to take every single thing out of every cupboard and hold it in your hands or your arms and close your eyes and ask yourself if it made you truly happy. If the answer was 'no', then it had to go.

Does this make me happy? It was a simple question but it wobbled in Caroline's mind like a soap bubble, then burst beneath the weight of other, more difficult questions.

What if she got rid of the wonky old gas heater and there was a power cut? What if she threw away this huge saucepan and the children got married and had their own children and brought them back for Christmas and she had to cook a ham?

What if Liam decided to come back and wanted to brew beer using the unopened kit she'd given him for his fiftieth birthday? Or suddenly had the urge to make love to her in the scratchy red lace nightdress he had given her the previous century?

Caroline held each thing and then she folded it or washed it or dusted it and put it back again exactly where it had been. She tried not to think of the most difficult question of all.

What was happiness? And why couldn't she feel it?

Caroline put Mac's lead on and opened the door. The rain came at them sideways, spitefully, hard little drops that stung her face. The dog didn't seem to notice. He plunged his huge head into the hedge and emerged dripping with a look of euphoria as if he had just won the canine lottery.

The children had been in their teens when Liam had acquired the dog. He insisted that a dog would turn them into the kind of family that went for hikes on Sunday afternoons instead of watching TV and playing video games.

The fluffy puppy was supposed to be a terrier, but it grew into a rangy monstrosity. No matter how much Mac ate – his appetite was enormous and indiscriminate – his ribcage still showed through his wispy black fur. His bad eye, clouded with a cataract, gave him a disreputable look. His back had a hyena hunch. He slunk rather than trotted. People dragged their dogs and children across the road to avoid him, which was a shame, because Mac loved other dogs and people, especially children.

Her own children had played with him for a few weeks, then gone back to their X-Boxes. Liam was lumped with walking him, which served him right. But he didn't seem to mind. He went out early before work and last thing at night. Caroline never seemed to be in bed and awake at the same time as her husband, but he didn't seem to mind that either.

Mac followed the route that Liam must have taken for the past twelve years. Taking a right at the end of the estate, crossing two sets of traffic lights, then turning onto the slip road to the sea. The waves were tossing and frothing around the crooked granite finger of the pier. The yachts in the marina rose and fell, their masts clanging. The wind tore the hood of Caroline's anorak off and she didn't bother putting it up. Mac wanted to stop and sniff every lamp post on the seafront. Caroline put her head down grimly and dragged him along through the lashing rain.

It had been threatening to rain the day she met Liam. There was an open-air concert on the campus. She was sitting on the damp grass by the Arts Block with her friend Linda, both of them in flimsy cheesecloth dresses, headbands and sunglasses, though the sky was overcast and grey. They were waiting for Damian. They seemed to have spent the last six months waiting for him.

The first band was tuning up on the stage, the sharp whine of a guitar ripping the air, the bass kicking in, a low, vibrating chord which she felt like excitement in the pit of her stomach. It was the last day of her second year at college and the summer was about to begin. Freedom, as well as rain, was in the air.

Someone sat down behind her and she turned to look over her shoulder. Everything about the boy was uncool. His hair was too short, his jeans were not flared. He was wearing a Paddington Bear duffle coat. The coat was the least cool thing of all, but at least he was dressed for the weather.

Caroline hugged her goose-bumped arms to her chest.

The boy leaned forward. 'Want to borrow my coat?'

'What? Oh.' She shook her head. 'No. It's okay.'

Linda shot a scornful glance at him then her face brightened. Damian was weaving his way back through the sprawling figures on the grass, a hat perched on his wild Afro, a blue plastic bag swinging from his hand.

'We have ignition,' he said. He knelt down and produced a bottle of tequila from the bag and began to section four lemons with a Swiss Army penknife. He tipped a little mountain of salt onto Linda's and Caroline's hands and handed them each a piece of lemon.

The oily burn of the tequila mixing with the sharp lemon and the crust of salt made Caroline want to gag. She turned to the boy behind and held out the bottle, a belated thanks for his offer of his coat. 'You want some?'

'No thanks.'

'Who's that guy?' Damian scowled at Linda and she fluttered her eyelashes.

'Oh he's not *my* man,' she said, 'he's Caroline's.'

'He isn't,' Caroline hissed but it was too late. The boy shuffled forward to sit beside her.

His name was Liam and he was a second-year Engineering student. The rain and the band began at the same time and he shrugged off his coat and put it over her shoulders.

Without knowing it, he settled the unspoken tussle between the girls. Today was the last day of term. Damian would finally have to decide which one of them he wanted. The boy had made his mind up for him.

When Caroline looked around, Damian and Linda had gone, taking the tequila and leaving a little pile of lemon rinds on the grass. Beneath the sting of disappointment, she felt relief. She wasn't sure she had what it took to keep a guy like Damian anyway. She glanced at the boy from under the hood of the duffle coat. His drenched hair was plastered to his forehead. He was not bad-looking, she thought. He might even be attractive, without those clothes.

Later that night she sat on the single bed in the box room of his house-share, hoping he didn't think she was a slut, drying her hair with a towel and reading the spines of his shelf of books while he cooked scrambled eggs.

He came back bare-chested, in his jeans, beaming in a way that Damian never would have, as if nothing could make him happier than the sight of her on his bed. And he was attractive, without those clothes. Long and lean and beautifully made.

'You have a lot of travel books.'

'Yeah,' he passed her a plate with two neat triangles of toast topped with egg, 'there are a lot of places I want to go.'

'Me too.' She had only been abroad once, to Barcelona on a school trip. But even then, in an age of travel agents and package holidays, Caroline wanted to go everywhere. She had a part-time job typing theses for post-graduate students and she was saving every penny so that she could spend next year travelling when she graduated.

Liam climbed into the bed beside her and balanced his plate on his knees. 'So where will we start?'

'San Francisco,' she said through a mouthful of toast.

'Paris.' He handed her a mug of tea.

'Madagascar.'

'Brazil.'

Caroline smiled and leaned back against his pillows, imagining rice terraces and carved temples, rain forests and tropical beaches. She wondered, shyly, if the two of them would travel together.

What she didn't know then was that there would be three of them. That last night of the summer term they had made a tiny dark-eyed girl with a halo of blonde hair.

By next summer, they were living in a semi-detached at the end of the bus line, miles outside Dublin. Liam had given up his science degree to work in an insurance company and Caroline was at home, minding Lucy, already pregnant again, this time with Cal.

Her friends with their long hair and their hippy clothes frightened the neighbours and they, in turn, seemed frightened by the clutter of plastic toys and the baby clothes drying over the radiators. They passed Lucy quickly from one to the other, as if having a child might be contagious.

Half her class had J1 Visas for the States. Linda was going to San Francisco for the summer. Damian, naturally, was heading off to live in a commune in the Mojave Desert. And Caroline's twenty-one-year-old life had run into a cul-de-sac in a maze of suburban houses. But by then she was in love with Liam and besotted with her daughter, so it didn't matter. There was nowhere else in the world she would rather be.

Caroline trudged through Monkstown, past Salthill and on to Blackrock through sheets of rain. They were almost at the main street when Mac turned abruptly and walked straight into the doorway of an antique shop. He put his nose to the bottom of the door and began to sniff.

Caroline wiped her eyes with a drenched hand and looked in the window and saw what she thought at first was a huge painting hanging on the wall at the back of the shop. A glorious, muted blaze of crimsons and reds and deep pinks. Soft squares that blurred into one another the colours of ballet slippers, rose petals and ripe raspberries.

She hesitated, then opened the door and went inside. Antique shops were usually choked with dusty clutter, but there were only a couple of dozen things for sale. Was it even a shop, she wondered?

A tall blue-and-green Chinese jar filled with oranges stood on a table by the door. A china dinner service was arranged in ascending order of size on a long white shelf that ran the length of one wall, starting with a dozen delicate egg cups and ending with a tureen.

The other wall had a washing line hung with silk scarves, turning in a breeze. There was a gilt chair upholstered in pale-blue velvet, a stone lion that must have been a garden ornament and a large oak dining table with carved feet.

All of these lovely things would have been intriguing if it were not for the painting on the back wall that glowed softly like a fire. It was all Caroline could look at. And it wasn't a painting, Caroline saw now, it was a rug.

She started towards it but Mac hung back behind her drenched legs and began to whine. Then she noticed the other dog. He was even bigger than Mac and solid, like a great black bear with golden markings round his eyes and on his snout. He was lying beneath the table desk, perfectly still, staring at them.

'Oh, don't mind Houdini.' A dark-haired girl, who looked about her daughter's age, appeared through a side doorway. 'He's almost five hundred years old... in dog years! Hey,' she clicked her tongue at Mac. 'Come and say hello, boy.' Mac advanced, slowly and cautiously, leaving a trail of wet paw prints behind him. He sniffed the stuffed Rottweiler with a bewildered look.

'I'm sorry, he's ruined your floor!' Caroline said, looking at the trail of paw prints.

'It's just a bit of rain.' Nora knelt down to rub Mac's wet ears.

'What is he? A greyhound? Lurcher? Borzoi?' Mac rolled over onto his side and put his huge paws in the air and the girl grinned and patted his ribcage.

'He's a liability,' Caroline said, but she wasn't looking at Nora any more. She was staring past her at the rug.

Everyone who came into the shop had fallen in love with the rug. Nora had fallen in love with it herself, the first time she had seen it. She had been six and she and her mum had been living in the house-share on Leeson Street, a huge high-ceilinged room with bare boards and drafty windows and a kitchen built into a corner with a cooker and a fridge. One morning, her mum would not get out of bed. Her eyes were open but her hair was wet and her face was hot and nothing she said made sense. Nora called her grandfather and he told her to help get her dressed and downstairs and into a taxi to the hospital.

Her mum was wheeled away immediately and Nora was left sitting on a plastic chair at the nurse's station. When Hugh arrived, he scooped her up in his arms and explained that her mum had to stay for a while, but that she was going home with him.

Nora had never been to Temple Road before. She hadn't even known it existed. He carried her around the house in his arms that morning, distracting her by showing her all the treasures.

He brought Houdini in from the hall and put him on the red and pink silk rug and settled Nora beside him. He fed her hot chocolate and gingerbread biscuits on a lacquered tray which had carved lizards for handles.

And he told her the story about buying the rug in a souk in Marrakech. He filled her mind with images of snake charmers and camels and men in robes sitting cross-legged on cushions drinking mint tea.

Nora had heard a noise in the hall and had looked up. There was a tall, thin woman, with very dark eyes and very red lipstick, at the door. She had an apron over a beautiful red velvet dress and she was wearing sparkly earrings and rubber gloves, which Nora thought was a very interesting combination.

'Hello!' she said.

The woman bit her lips nervously. 'Hello!' she said quietly. 'Who are you?'

The woman hesitated for a moment. 'I'm your grandmother.'

And maybe it was because she recognised herself in those dark eyes, or maybe it was because, despite the bright lipstick and the sparkly earrings and the bright dress, Nora could sense that this woman was sad, but she stood up from the rug and walked over and hugged her.

'Where is it from, the rug?' the woman in the dripping anorak cut across Nora's thoughts.

'Morocco.' She pointed at the card she had pinned to the note on the wall.

Caroline bent her head to read the words on the card:

Moroccan Prayer rug (circa 1850). Hand-knotted. Silk.

In 1961, my grandfather took my grandmother to Morocco on their honeymoon. He slipped out of the hotel in Marrakech one afternoon while she was asleep and bought this rug and had it shipped home for her.

She wiped her hand on the anorak, and then laid her palm against a square of deep, soft pink. The threads were dense, softly tufted, velvety. The colour was so intense that it felt like it was soaking through her skin.

Caroline laid her palm against another square of silk, the same deep red as the heart of a red rose. *Morocco*, she thought wistfully.

When they were first married, *when having two children under three was overwhelming*, she and Liam used to recite the names of places they would go when they were free.

He had started it when he was changing one of Cal's legendary, terrifying nappies.

'Bali,' he'd said, shoving the nappy into a plastic bag.

'Brazil,' she'd said, holding her nose as she handed him a fresh one.

'Turkey.' He reached for the baby wipes.

'Burma.' She passed him the baby powder.

'Sri Lanka.'

'Mexico.'

They could go on for hours. It kept them going through hourly night feeds and three-in-the morning hospital visits. Through Lucy's eating disorder and Cal's dyslexia. When had they stopped? Caroline couldn't remember.

Caroline and the dog were both drenched when they got back to the house. She wrapped herself in a towel and found another one for Mac. She rubbed him down and he closed his eyes and shivered with pleasure. When she was finished, he shook himself, then licked one of her wet elbows as if he was returning the favour.

She filled his bowl with food and then, when he looked at it sadly, she opened a can of tuna and dumped it on top, then she opened a bottle of cheap red and put a Tesco Lasagne in the microwave.

She took her plate into the living room. She had Sellotaped the broken remote control back together but it took five minutes of fiddling to get it to switch on the TV. There seemed to be news on every channel. Disaster after disaster, unfolding across the world. She was one of the fortunate ones, she knew that. Why couldn't she feel it? Why couldn't she feel *anything*?

She stared down at the carpet, a hardwearing oatmeal nylon picked so that it wouldn't show the stains. But there they were. A faint purple circle from where two-year-old Cal had dropped a glass of Ribena. A smear of orange from an accident Lucy had had with a tube of fake tan.

She leaned down and touched the carpet and a tiny spark shot at her fingertip. She put her finger in her mouth and remembered how the tufted silk rug had felt under her hand and wondered how it would feel to walk on it in bare feet. A line from a poem she'd learned at school came floating back: *I have spread my dreams under your feet. Tread softly, because you tread on my dreams.*

The rug cost two thousand euros. She couldn't buy it but she could go back and look at it, couldn't she?

She visited the shop every day that week, stopping by for ten minutes on her walks with the dog. The owner, Nora, didn't seem to mind that she was just a browser. She was always pleased to see Caroline and she had started saving her sandwich crusts for Mac, making a fuss of him while Caroline stood, staring at the rug.

On Friday, Liam texted her the forwarding address for his post – another sharp little nail in the coffin of their marriage. She found her laptop and tapped in the details and an estate agent's listing came up. She stared at the pictures of the shiny galley kitchen, the tastefully neutral magnolia living room, the bedroom with the floor-to-ceiling window where her husband would sleep alone tonight. He wouldn't be alone for long, she thought; he'd find someone else. Men always did. This was *his* reward for treading on their dreams. He got to start again. She slammed the laptop closed. What about *her*? What was her reward?

'I want to buy it,' Caroline said on Saturday, spinning on her heel and turning to look at Nora, her face flushed with excitement.

Nora stopped patting Mac and stared up at her, surprised. The rug had been admired by dozens of people since she'd put it up, but nobody loved it the way Caroline did. Nobody, except maybe Nora herself.

Before she came to Dublin, she had imagined bringing it back to the house on Fountain Road. She'd pictured how it would glow against the French grey-painted floorboards in the bedroom, imagined the feel of the tufted silk beneath her bare feet as she got up on a sunny morning to brew coffee to bring back to bed for Adam.

But now the thought of that house that she had loved and of the man she had trusted turned her stomach.

If anyone had to have it, then it should be this woman, who really, really loved it. But she didn't look as if she had a lot of money.

'Are you sure?' she asked slowly.

'Two thousand euros.' Caroline looked her straight in the eye. 'I have it in cash.' She dug her hand into the pocket of Liam's old anorak and pulled out an envelope. Fifteen hundred she had withdrawn from the bank that morning, plus the five hundred the second-hand jewellery shop had paid her for her wedding and engagement rings. Her fingers felt oddly bare without them, but her heart felt lighter.

The next morning, Nora turned up in a battered Mercedes Estate with the rug in the back rolled up and tied with a fat satin ribbon. Hemp side outwards, it looked dingy and faded and Caroline's mouth dried up. She could hear Liam's voice in her head. 'You spent two thousand euros on a piece of old carpet?' But he had spent at least that on his rent and deposit. And he had told her to do what she liked.

She picked up one end of the rug and helped Nora to carry it into the house. The hall was stuffed with furniture: a bulky coat-stand swaddled with jackets; an ugly console table shoehorned in beside an IKEA open-shelved unit stuffed with scuffed boots and shoes which Cal and Lucy had discarded years ago.

'We'll put it in the living room,' Caroline panted. But there was no room in there either, so they laid the rolled-up rug on its side on the stairs and Nora helped her to move two brown velvet lazy-boy armchairs from the living room into the dining room.

Caroline felt a surge of energy at the sight of the space they left. 'Would you be able to help me to clear the rest?'

'Of course. This is pretty much what I do all day when I'm not at the shop. Clear furniture. I'm getting my grandmother's house ready to be sold.'

'Are you sure? Are you sure you won't ruin your clothes?' She looked at Nora's pale yellow 1960s dress. 'You always wear such lovely things.'

'Thank you!' Nora pushed a corkscrew curl out of her eyes. 'They're not actually mine. They belonged to my grandmother.'

Her own clothes, the ones she'd brought over from London, were reminders of her life there. Things she'd worn when she'd lived with Adam and worked with Liv. Wearing them brought back too many memories, so she had bundled them all up, shoved them into her carry-on bag, and carried it up into the attic. She'd dumped it up there in the darkness, where she didn't have to see it.

Nora and Caroline hauled out a laminated sideboard, four occasional tables, three lamps, a broken chess table, an ancient DVD player, the sofa, the TV on its fat, grey plastic legs, and a laundry basket into which Caroline tossed the ornaments, cushions and dusty old magazines.

Nora went out to the car to get a pair of pliers and they pulled up the tack strip and lifted the edge of the old nylon carpet. It came away from the floor with a ripping sound and a cloud of dust. They rolled it up and dragged it out into the back garden.

Next, they carried the rug into the empty room, Nora undid the ribbon, and it opened up like a flower as it unrolled across the bare floor.

Caroline exhaled. 'I love it!'

'I know,' Nora bent down and rested her palm against the tufted silk, then she patted it and stood up. 'I'm so glad it was you that bought it. It would have been hard to let it go to anyone else.'

Caroline waited until the front door closed, then she pulled off her boots and socks, her jeans and sweatshirt, then her underwear, and lay down on the rug. She was naked in the middle of the afternoon with the curtains open. If one of the neighbours went out to put something in the wheelie bins, they'd see her, but she didn't think about that. She thought about how good the silk felt on every inch of her skin and how good it felt to give yourself the thing you wanted most in the world.

Now that Caroline knew what made her happy, it was easier to know what didn't. She opened the kitchen cupboards she had reorganised just a few days ago. Sixteen mugs, most of them chipped. Eighteen mismatched dinner plates. Chipped vases, scratched bowls. A rusting toaster. A dusty food mixer. A blackened set of baking tins older than her own son.

She filled six black plastic bags and dragged the lot out to the shed. Everything in there could go, she decided, peering into its dusty cobwebby depths. But why stop there? The shed itself – its timbers greyed by rain, its roof sagging – could go! It blocked her view of the only nice tree in the garden, an orange blossom. She broke off a branch and brought it into the house. The scent of the leaves reminded her of that long-ago school trip to Barcelona.

She hadn't kept a single mug, so she drank her coffee from a thick tumbler, like the café manchada she'd ordered in her schoolgirl Spanish every morning in the café around the corner from the hotel. It had been thick and frothy and came with a crusty rope of doughnut. She remembered that, on the second day, two boys had shot past on a rattling moped and one of them had shouted 'Guapa!'. She'd worn that thrown-away word looped around her heart for years: *Pretty*.

She remembered a flamenco show they had gone to in the Plaza Real. The ripple of sniggers from some of her classmates when the lead performers came out on stage – a portly man in a tight shirt with long black hair and a woman with a wonky, greying bun and a ruffled red dress that clung to her round figure. They were *old* but that didn't matter once the music began. They danced as if they were possessed. Circling and stamping, their hands clapping, their feet stamping. Everything powerful and passionate and alive seemed to be pouring through them. Caroline had felt it pouring through her too, filling her heart until she thought it was going to burst.

She went and got her laptop and searched for 'flamenco', clicking on the first video she found. The music was dark and wild, the voices howled – angry and sad and defiant. They sent Mac skittering on his claws out into the hall but it was the perfect soundtrack for Caroline.

It wailed through the house while she pulled clothes out of the closet and wardrobe. This time, she held each thing for only a moment and asked herself, 'Does this make me happy?' The answers came as fast as the clicking castanets. 'No!', 'No!', 'No!'

She kept two T-shirts, one pair of jeans, a cream sweater, a green velvet jacket she had bought in a sale and forgotten, a red cotton halter-neck she'd had for years and a navy crêpe dress which Lucy had posted her from New York last Christmas for her thirtieth anniversary party. She dumped all her shoes except the sparkly flip-flops and the ankle boots.

Not a single pair of her knickers made her happy, not even the ones she was wearing, so they all went too.

The next morning, pleased with her progress, she tackled the bathrooms, the small study, the airing cupboard, the attic. Mac was used to the music now. He slept on the landing, his long legs jerking, his huge paws twitching in time to the clapping and stamping.

She got rid of most of the threadbare old bed linen and the towels. She filled bags with half-empty cans of hairspray and shaving foam, bottles of ancient conditioner, cracked eye-shadow pallets, dried-up foundation.

She threw away all of her books except the half-dozen she knew she would definitely read again. She kept a box of mementoes she found in the attic: Mother's Day cards the children had made with wonky hearts and writing that got smaller and smaller as it headed for the bottom of the page; essays they'd written; school reports and graduation certs; postcards they'd sent from Ibiza and Croatia, Sydney, Mumbai and Bangkok. She studied their faded writing on the back, the snatches of their days which they'd scribbled. Lucy had drunk a pineapple juice made from two (underlined) whole pineapples in Hanoi. Cal had stood where he'd drawn the 'X' on the picture of Angkor Wat as the sun was coming up.

Caroline had never thought of this before but a part of her and Liam had lived out those old dreams of travel through their children.

She loaded the car. Mac was waiting hopefully in the hall so she let him squeeze into the back on top of piles of bags. He stood up as she drove, his mouth open in a snaggle-toothed grin, leaning into every corner as if he was on the back of a motorbike.

Caroline hadn't been hungry since Liam had left. But as she drove home from the recycling centre in the empty car, she was suddenly aware of an emptiness in her stomach. She pulled over outside the pretty little vegan café in Blackrock. The handsomest man she had ever seen in her life was behind the counter. He asked her in a heavy accent what she'd like.

She looked back at him blankly. 'I have absolutely no idea,' she said.

He grinned as if this was the best possible answer and delved into the chill cabinet and came up with tiny samples for her to try. Fat green olives stuffed with almonds, fried green plantains with char-roasted peppers. Homemade focaccia and a rhubarb bavarois that melted in her mouth like ice cream.

If Mac had ever been off the leash on the beach, he'd entirely forgotten the experience. He capered around her in circles, stopping suddenly and inexplicably to dig holes. Caroline sat in the soft grey dusk, trying to remember when she had last gone to the beach. It must have been around the time the kids got too big to make sandcastles. She sat on Liam's folded-up anorak and ate her food and drank the pineapple and mango smoothie that Adonis (that was actually his name!) had made for her. She was five miles from her front door, but she felt as if she was in a foreign country.

The rug was like the first point on a map. Caroline had no idea where it would take her but she knew it was somewhere she wanted to go.

She cancelled the subscription to Sky and bought a rosewood-scented candle, a red lipstick in a slim gold case and a pale yellow dress like the one Nora had worn when she delivered the rug. She stopped buying the microwave meals and biscuits she'd been lived on since Liam left and ate what she liked, which was good coffee, fresh fruit, brown bread and smoked salmon. Toast spread with butter and lemon curd.

Cal phoned one evening from Sydney. This was a first. She was always the one who called him.

'Everything okay, Mum?' She almost laughed. What a silly question to ask someone whose forty-one-year marriage was sinking like the *Titanic*.

'Everything's good.'

'Lucy said you and Dad were . . .' she heard him swallow – 'are not living together.' He had been such a sweet little boy, always smoothing things over, trying to make all of them get on. 'Are you going to get a divorce?'

She wanted to say 'ask your father.' She wanted to say it was in his court. She wanted to badmouth Liam. To cast herself as the victim but even as the words were forming in her mind, she knew that this wasn't true.

'Your father isn't ready to make those decisions yet and neither am I, so we're not in touch at the moment. We're taking some time out.'

'I could fly over and help you to resolve this,' Cal said. 'I could mediate. I did a conflict resolution course for work...'

Caroline wanted to put her arms around him. 'It's okay, sweetheart. It's not your job to look after us. It's our job to look after you. And you know, if you need us, we'll always be here. You know, whatever happens, we both love you.'

There was a pause. 'You know –' Another pause. 'You know I love you too.'

She had squeezed those words out of him so many times. Saying, 'I love you' with a question mark, every morning when she drove him to school, at the end of every phone call. Asking for what she was owed. Never satisfied with the muttered answer. But this time was different. These words, she would hold on to.

'Is there someone there with you?' Cal asked. 'I can hear a man's voice.'

'Oh, that's just Paco di Lucia.'

'Who?' He sounded worried, as if he thought she had replaced Liam already.

'He's a flamenco singer. You should Google him. He's very good.'

Just looking at the children had made her happy when they were small: her son's dreamy newborn eyes, the tiny pink seashell of her daughter's ear peeking through the yellow silk of her hair. But she was perplexed and confused by the people they were now, by the fact that they didn't need her any more.

She had wanted them to fill the space between her and Liam but they had left, one after the other. Liam started working late and at the weekends. He watched the news over her shoulder at the dinner table. He stopped looking up from his book while she was undressing.

And every time he hurt her, she made sure that she hurt him too. She made snide comments about his weight. She was rude to his family. She pretended to be asleep on the nights that he did reach out to touch her. And, two years ago, she'd refused to dance with him at Lucy's wedding reception.

He had stood up and tried to lead her out onto the floor but she had dug in her heels, her too-high mother-of-the-bride shoes. She had humiliated him in front of their American in-laws and everyone at the top table.

'We're not teenagers,' she'd hissed.

But the truth was, she had believed that, deep down, they still were. That when they retired, the people they'd become over the past three decades – their weary, resentful, irritable grown-up selves – would simply disappear. And the nineteen-year-olds they'd been when they'd first met would wake up and step out, ready to live out all their dreams, just as they'd always said they would.

Instead, they were left with who they'd become. Two strangers who didn't seem to like one another. Liam took the dog for longer walks and spent more time on the golf course. She hid behind the newspaper or the laptop, joined a book club and a gym, moved into the spare room to get away from his snoring.

Why on earth would they go to Asia or South America or Australia together when they couldn't stand to be in the same room?

Caroline borrowed a sledgehammer and tackled the garden shed. It buckled then came apart with a groan that almost sounded human. When she had cleared away the broken planks and splinters, there was a raw brown gash beside the lawn and a fat blister on her index finger. She bought herself a small, carved Moroccan table and four fat red velvet cushions in a charity shop as a reward.

Happiness was complicated but she was getting the hang of it.

A glass of wine made her feel happy. A bottle made her maudlin. So she bought the decent kind and limited herself to two glasses.

Feeding the birds made her happy but having them shit on her new Egyptian cotton sheets hanging on the line did not. They would have to cater for themselves.

Mac made her happy, but all the years she had ignored him made her sad. She made it up to him by letting him sit on the rug and sleep at her feet, so they were even.

The most surprising thing about feeling happy was that it made her feel sad too. As if both feelings were related; fraternal twins.

She closed the doors of the children's rooms. They could clear them when they were next home. But when there was nothing left to sort, she tackled Liam's things.

He had only taken one suitcase and his wardrobe and drawers were still stuffed with his clothes. She weeded out all things that were shabby or didn't fit him any more and bagged them up. Then she folded his good jumpers, shirt, jeans and jackets and suits and paired his odd socks. Had he loved these things, she wondered. If he held them in his arms would he hold onto them or let them go?

She found his old travel guides in an old suitcase in the attic, dog-eared and slightly damp. This was where their dreams had been hiding all these years. She held each one in her hand and let the tears come, then packed them away in a box with his collection of Penguin paperbacks. She sent him a text, telling him that his things were ready to be picked up but there was no rush.

When Liam arrived, he looked like a different man. He had lost weight, his hair was longer. He wasn't wearing his glasses.

'Did you drive?' she said, falling back into her familiar old habit of having a go at him.

He lifted a defensive shoulder. 'I got lenses.'

The snide remark came into her mind in a flash. 'At your age?' Instead, she said, 'Good for you.'

She wondered if she looked different to him. If he noticed her newly cut hair, her red lipstick, the soft cream sweater she had bought to go with her old jeans.

She had left Mac in the kitchen, but when he heard Liam's footsteps, he hurled himself against the door and burst into the hall in a blur of legs and fur. He leapt at Liam, howling as mournfully as Paco di Lucia. He planted his paws on Liam's chest and his chin, he nibbled his ear lobes, then dropped to the floor and rolled onto his back and writhed with joy.

'He missed me,' Liam said softly. And he sounded so surprised that Caroline almost felt sorry for him.

'Your things are upstairs,' she said quickly. 'In the bedroom. Take whatever you like. I can get rid of the rest.'

She held on to the dog and watched her husband take the stairs in twos in that boyish way he always had.

She went into the kitchen and looked out at the garden, focusing on the orange tree, trying not to see the ragged scar the shed had left in the ground.

She was opening a bottle of wine when Liam came back downstairs. She looked up to see him in the doorway, the box of paperbacks and travel books in his arms. Behind him, another two boxes were stacked by the front door.

'Is that all you're taking?'

He nodded. 'I don't have much room. I'd take Mac off your hands too, but I can't. I'm sorry. I know you didn't want him.'

'It's okay,' she said. 'I like having him around.'

'Well,' Liam looked around the empty kitchen and tightened his hold on the box, his lips twisting a little, as if he was trying to keep them steady, 'I should make a move.' He turned to go.

This might be the last time he saw this kitchen, she thought, this house. 'Would you like some wine?'

He hesitated. 'Maybe just a glass.'

'Go and sit down,' she said. 'I'll bring it in.'

She put the bottle of Shiraz back into the wine rack and took out an expensive Borolo she had bought herself in the Dalkey deli. She set out some green olives in a small blue dish. *The Last Supper*, she thought, and remembered that night at the beginning. The scrambled eggs he had brought her in bed. She tilted her head back to stop the tears falling. *This is not the end*, she told herself, firmly, *the end came a long time ago.*

Liam was standing in the empty living room still holding the box in his arms. 'This is all new,' he said.

'The rug is old.' She put the tray on the low table, sitting down on one of the fat cushions. 'A hundred and forty years old. It cost a lot.'

She waited for him to ask how much, but he didn't. Instead, he put the box down and heeled his shoes off, then sat down, cross-legged, on the rug opposite her.

She handed him a glass of wine. Why couldn't they have been like this before? she thought bitterly; two people facing one another, sharing a bottle of wine.

He took a sip and his face softened with pleasure. 'This is good. And that,' he looked down at the rug, 'that is extraordinary. Where is it from?'

'Morocco.'

'Morocco.' He echoed. He looked down into his glass and a long awkward silence opened up between them. But this wasn't like the silences before. This was different. It felt as if he was thinking about her, not ignoring her. And, after a minute, he looked up. And there he was again, behind the thinning hair, the starbursts of wrinkles, the softening chin, the old Liam, or rather, the young one. The boy with the floppy fringe and duffle coat who had started it all.

'Thailand,' he said, very quietly looking at her with the same dark, hopeful eyes.

He was playing their game again. Caroline wanted to tell him that was too little, too late, but instead, she said, 'Brazil.'

He smiled at her, the way he had that first night. 'Ethiopia.' He reached for her hand.

She hesitated a moment then she took it. 'Vietnam.'

6

Art Nouveau Silver Tiffany Hairbrush

Gemma

'What superpower would you pick?' Froggy asked Gemma as she was filling a pitcher with orange juice, plugging in the iron and stirring a spoonful of sugar into the Bolognese sauce, all at the same time. Stephen hadn't been at home on a Friday night for months. She'd decided they'd have something proper for once, instead of just pizza on the sofa.

Froggy wrapped his arms around her legs. 'I'd have super strength, so I could lift you up.'

'I'd have X-ray eyes,' Jake said without looking up from his laptop. 'So I could see through walls.'

Of girls' houses, probably, Gemma thought, wryly. Jake had discovered the opposite sex this summer. He now spent more time on his appearance than she did, emerging from the bathroom every morning with carefully gelled hair in a cloud of Lynx.

Froggy tilted his head back so far that she could see his adenoids. 'What about you, Mama?'

'I'd choose indivisibility!' If she was indivisible, she could do one thing at a time and do it properly. Check the ingredients before deciding to make Bolognese instead of winging it. Get the boys' clothes organised for their summer camp so that the next morning wouldn't be bedlam. Change out of her manky work uniform before Stephen got back.

She checked the clock. No time. He'd appear in ten minutes. His car had broken down on the way back from a business trip last week and it was still at the garage. He'd been home early every single night this week. He'd actually helped Jake with his calculus homework on Tuesday and had read Froggy a story last night.

She was supposed to pick the car up tomorrow after she took Alice shopping, but, honestly, she felt like leaving it there. It was kind of nice to have her husband around the place for a change.

She was out of oregano so she sprinkled some pimento on the top of the bubbling sauce and tasted it again. A glug of wine and it would be just about passable. But there was no wine. Stephen had a thing about not keeping it around the house. Gemma had been sober for sixteen years, but he still didn't trust her around alcohol and she wasn't sure she quite trusted herself. She had been on edge so long, that sometimes she thought that one more thing was all it would take to pull her loose from this ordinary life and propel her into a relapse.

I am fine, she told herself. Everything. Is. Fine.

She squeezed a dollop of Heinz ketchup into the sauce and slapped the lid on. She was doing her best and it would have to do. There was a frozen baguette at the back of the freezer and just about enough time to make garlic bread. She detached Froggy from her legs and banished the boys to the hall.

When Stephen opened the front door, they were parked on the bottom step of the stairs. His eldest, with his newly square jaw and broadening shoulders, and his youngest, who was still a baby really, were sitting in a litter of markers and colouring pencils, their heads bent together over a drawing.

Unexpected tears welled up behind Stephen's eyes at the sight of them, at the thought of just how close he had come to losing them. This time last week, he'd been on his way to Wexford to meet Lia, but now, the person he'd been then seemed like a madman.

'Hey, Dad!' Froggy beamed up at him. 'Want to see a 'rupting volcano?'

'An *erupting* volcano,' Jake said with an older-brother eye roll. 'Sure!'

Stephen had been incensed with anger when Lia just left him on the side of the road on the way back to Dublin. Not just because the BMW had clapped out and he had no way of getting home, but because he had actually believed that he couldn't live without her.

But over the last six days, as it sank in that she was not going to return his calls, that it was over, he realised he had dodged a bullet.

What he really couldn't live without was right here. His boys, his home, his family. He felt it lodge in his throat, a hard lump of relief, as he bent over to kiss the top of Froggy's head and ruffle Jake's stiff-gelled hair before he had a chance to duck away. 'That's deadly!'

'It's a natural disaster,' Froggy said, proudly. 'It's supposed to be deadly.'

'Where's your mum?'

'She's in the kitchen,' Jake said. 'Cooking something.'

'Seriously?' Friday night was pizza night. Most nights were pizza nights or fish-and-chips nights, or ready-meal nights. But as he opened the kitchen door, a rich, fragrant garlicky smell wafted out to greet him.

'Hey,' Gemma said, without looking up. Her white uniform was spattered with splashes of sauce and she had a smear of butter on her cheek.

He walked over and put his arm on her shoulder. He was so out of the habit of touching her casually that it felt like an awkward gesture. 'Something smells good.'

'It's not me,' she said defensively. 'Long day, and I haven't had a chance to change.' He felt her tense, but he didn't move away.

'I just thought we'd eat in the dining room tonight,' she said. 'Have a family meal for once.'

'Good idea.'

'Oh shit! The garlic bread!' She broke away, grabbed a tea towel and opened the oven. She pulled out a smoking tray. She plonked it onto the cooker. She peered at the charred crusts, her shoulders hunched defensively. 'It's completely ruined!'

'Come on!' Stephen said, rolling up his sleeves. 'It's fine. We can cut the burnt bits off. We can save this!'

*

'Alice had another meltdown, last night,' Will hissed when he opened the front door to Gemma the next morning. 'I'm at my wits' end. Will you just try to explain where she was heading with all that stuff in New York, Gems? I'm getting seriously worried about her.'

'I already said I would,' Gemma whispered back. She had to stop herself telling him that she was seriously worried about him. He hadn't shaved and he looked as if he hadn't slept either. Without the routine of his ordered New York life, her clean-cut, crisply dressed, workaholic brother seemed to be morphing into a rumpled slacker.

'Have you sorted out Julia's stuff yet?' She tried to sound casual.

His eyes slid away. 'I'm getting there.'

Either Alice had overheard her dad or she had picked up on the hidden agenda for the day out. Outside, by the car, she had a sullen, uncooperative look and edged as far away from Gemma as she could, her shoulder pressed against the passenger-seat door, her knees drawn up defensively under her chin.

Gemma felt as if they were not side by side in her decrepit VW, but on a narrow ledge a hundred feet up in the air. One wrong word, one clumsy move, was all it would take to send her into freefall.

She and Will had been on a similar ledge twenty years ago. Only, then, he was the one who was trying to haul her back in. And it hadn't worked. She had wound up at twenty-one with six lost years, a serious addiction, a tattoo she didn't remember getting and a sense of self-aversion and shame that never left her. It ran her life. She constantly had to stay one step ahead of it by proving what a perfect mother/wife/worker/friend/sister she was. And now she had to add 'aunt' to that long list.

She had stayed awake long after Stephen had dozed off, rehearsing what she was going to say to Alice: an update on the lecture she regularly gave Jake about the dangers of drink and drugs and delinquency. But Jake, for all his teenager attitude, was still a kid. Alice was a tougher audience. Her niece didn't say a single word on the journey into town, but her body language said it all: *Save your breath. I barely know you. Whatever you have to say, I'm not going to buy it.*

Gemma had been just the same when she was fifteen and the little pep talk she had prepared would not have got under her radar. The truth was, there wasn't a thing an adult could have said back then that would have jolted her off the path she was on. Or, she thought, turning left onto Drury Street, was there?

'You know, Alice, we don't have to go shopping.' She waited a beat. 'We can go shoplifting, instead, if you want. I've heard you're pretty good at it.'

Alice swivelled her head to look at her. There was a spark of curiosity behind those Teflon eyes and her mouth had opened slightly. Gemma fiddled with the indicator. 'What's your M.O.?'

'My what?'

'Your modus operandi,' Gemma said lightly as she took another left into the multi-storey car park. 'You know, your technique. Do you use a coat with big pockets? A backpack? Or do you slip stuff beneath a dress?'

'I don't wear dresses.' Alice tugged the hem of her extra-large T-shirt down over her extra-tiny shorts.

'Oh, you should,' Gemma said. 'It was crazy how much stuff I used to be able to get under there.' Alice turned to look at her, her blue eyes widening. Gemma's fifteen-year-old self would not have caved in so easily, she thought.

She forced herself to stay silent and not to say another word as she searched for a free parking spot, and it was Alice who finally broke the silence as they were reversing into a space on the top floor.

'You shoplifted?' she said, sounding unconvinced. 'You, like, stole things?'

'Oh yeah,' Gemma said, calmly. She could leave it there. Say she did it once. That it was wrong. Segue right back into the pre-planned lecture. But she felt the slippery ledge beneath the rubber pad of the clutch pedal. 'I didn't want most of the stuff I took. I just needed the money for drink. And drugs. You wouldn't believe what a quarter ounce of grass used to cost in Dublin. And don't even get me started on coke.' She unbuckled her seatbelt and got out, Alice was scrabbling out of the car after her. She looked astonished.

'Mostly, I shoplifted to order,' Gemma said, still keeping her tone calm and offhand. 'People would tell me what they wanted, I'd nick it and they'd pay me. CDs. Cosmetics. Clothes.' She hit the central-locking button twice, but it didn't work. She had to crawl back into the car and lock each door individually.

'Once I stole a Waterford Crystal decanter and a set of six glasses from the top floor of a department store,' she said over her shoulder. 'I had to cram this huge box up under my school uniform. I walked right past the doorman, my hand on the bump, as if I was pregnant.' She crawled back out of the car again and pushed down the button to lock the driver's door before she closed it. 'But that was in the days before CCTV and security, so you might need to give me a refresher course.' She looked at Alice expectantly. 'Any tips?'

Her niece was staring at her in horror.

'No? Well, maybe we should just shop the normal way, today. Your dad gave me two hundred euros to kit you out until your own things arrive.' Alice's carry-on case had contained make-up, video games, an ancient stuffed penguin and at least twenty graphic novels.

Most teenage girls would have done a happy dance at the chance of retail therapy, but Alice just kicked at the oil-stained floor of the car park with the rubber tip of her sneaker. 'Whatever.'

Gemma ignored her and walked towards the exit sign and, after a moment, Alice fell into step beside her.

'I know what you're doing,' Alice said suddenly when they reached the lift. 'You're, like, telling me all this because you want me to trust you.' She studied the pink ends of her dip-dyed hair. 'Then I'll tell you stuff and you'll spill it all to my dad.'

The lift doors opened and Alice stepped forward but Gemma put her hands on her shoulders, stopping her. 'Listen!' Her niece was far taller than she was, but Gemma could feel the bird bones of her and, in them, a little tremble of cold or anger or fear. 'I do want you to trust me,' she said, softly. 'But I will never tell Will anything you say to me in confidence. Because if I did, you'd never trust me again.'

The lift doors closed and they stood there for a moment, face to face in the underwater light. Alice shrugged Gemma off, but her eyes were pleading.

'Can we just go back to your place?' she asked quietly. 'I don't want new stuff. I want my own stuff.'

'I know,' Gemma said. 'But it won't be here for another five days. You can't keep wearing the same thing every day.'

'Why? You do!'

Gemma used to be the queen of dressing up. Now she had two uniforms. Jeans and a sweatshirt for home and the white coat she was required to wear at her job in the dental practice. Not that she had to do anything remotely medical. She made appointments and answered the phone and picked up her boss's suits from the dry cleaners'.

'I'm thirty-seven.' Gemma jabbed the lift button again. 'Nobody cares what I wear.'

Alice stuffed her fists into the pockets of her shorts. 'I'm just not very good at shopping,' she said in a small voice.

'Well, I am,' Gemma said, firmly. She had been the queen of shopping too.

A deafening wall of Rihanna rolled over them as they walked through the doors of Topshop. When Jake was playing music this loud, Gemma would yell at him to turn it down, but the thump of the bass snapped her awake like a shot of double espresso and her shopping mojo came back from wherever it had been hiding.

She strutted ahead, plucking jeans and tops off rails. Alice trailed behind, biting her cuticles and casting anxious, awestruck looks at the teenage assistants with their face piercings and sleeve tattoos, their vertiginous shoes and their carefully constructed carapaces of cool.

'Behind all that ink and hair gel, they're all just as terrified as you are,' Gemma wanted to tell her niece. But what was the point? Alice would never believe her.

The fitting room smelled of musky teenage sweat and lemon air freshener. Gemma dumped the pile of clothes on a bench and left Alice to it. Then she went back down two flights to the ground floor for a proper scour.

She flicked through the rails, pulling out anything she thought was a possibility. A black off-the-shoulder top, a pair of heavy denim dungarees, a T-shirt with a red-sequinned skull, a pair of Doc Martens with red soles. She dragged herself back up the stairs, her arms aching under the weight of her haul. 'Overdoing it again, Gemma!' she said to her reflection, as she passed a wall of mirrors. She still got a fright, sometimes, when she saw herself. Before she had Froggy, her hair had been her calling card. Thick ripples of elbow-length blonde curls. Catwalk hair, that's what they called it in salons now. When she was young, she used to brush it a hundred times every night but it was kind of hard to do that after she started drinking. Most nights, she was so smashed that she couldn't count to ten properly and the glossy curls turned to frizz.

She had wanted to be a hairdresser. She'd actually started training in a salon at the weekends, but the owner caught her stealing from the till and fired her. However, some of it had stuck. When she got sober and, when she began to learn about self-care again, she bought professional scissors to trim her own split ends and splashed out on decent conditioner.

Stephen had told her that her hair was the first thing he'd noticed about her. She had been so shocked when he asked her out. She thought it was some kind of trick. She couldn't understand what a normal, strait-laced guy like him could see in her.

She had kept her hair long all through her twenties. But seven years ago, when Froggy was only a baby, he had screamed for ten days solid and it was Stephen who had finally found out why. A two-foot long hair had twisted tight and almost invisibly around one of his toes. Another day, the doctor told them, and the circulation would have been cut off altogether and he would have lost it. She had felt like the world's worst mother.

She had cut her hair short that night and had kept it short ever since, though she hated it. She told herself that she'd grow it out when the boys were older, but she knew she'd never have the time to manage it. And it wasn't like Stephen would have noticed. He'd been working all hours. He was hardly ever home and even when he was there, he was too distracted to notice her.

Alice didn't like anything she tried on except a pair of denim shorts slightly darker and slightly briefer than the pair she was wearing, and a tattoo sleeve that Will was going to hate – but it was a start. She rejected everything in Zara and H&M but things picked up a little in Miss Selfridge. After half an hour, she edged nervously out of the fitting room in a grey fake-leather bomber jacket, a pale pink T-shirt and skinny black jeans. She was all elbows and turned-in knees and she looked so lovely and vulnerable and self-conscious that Gemma wondered what it would be like to have a daughter.

She had secretly stopped taking the pill at Christmas. Stephen had been cranky all through the holidays, like a caged bear, and she'd had a crazy idea. Maybe, if they had another baby, it would re-set the clock on their marriage. Take them back to happier times. At Easter, when they took the kids down to Wexford, her period had been a week late and she had been half excited, half terrified that it had happened. She'd even bought a pregnancy test but it was a false alarm. It was probably just as well. She wasn't sure how Stephen would have taken it. He was under so much pressure at work.

Alice frowned at her reflection and Gemma remembered that awful, awkward place between fifteen and eighteen when you felt that it was your job to pick out any flaw in yourself before anyone else could do it for you.

'You look amazing,' she said.

Alice lifted her shoulders up to her ears and hunched them together. 'The jacket's okay but the T-shirt's way too girly.'

'Don't move!' Gemma hurried over to a shoe rack and came back with a pair of fake-leather biker boots, winter stock reduced to twenty euros. They were a game changer. Alice hugged them to her chest all the way to the till and Gemma had to nudge her to put them on the counter so that the assistant could scan them.

Gemma was on a roll now. Chasing the same high she used to find at the bottom of a bottle of vodka. Even if she'd wanted to, she couldn't stop herself. She marched Alice in and out of all the shops on Grafton Street and then down to Temple Bar.

They had been getting worse in the last couple of years, her compulsions. If Froggy had a headache, she'd take his temperature every ten minutes in case it was meningitis. If she couldn't get hold of a patient the first time she rang, she'd call back over and over, sometimes as much as twenty times, until she got through. When Stephen worked late, she'd sit up with her laptop singeing her knees waiting for him, bingeing on Netflix.

She had stopped going to AA meetings years ago, but she'd been often enough to know what she was doing. She was medicating her anxiety. Trying to distract herself from the fear that she had screwed up somehow. That she had done something, or not done something, and that was why Stephen was so distant, why everything felt so shaky.

But Stephen had been really sweet last night and he was at home right now assembling a flat-pack bookshelf that had been lying around for a year. He'd offered to take them all out for pizza tonight. So why did she still feel so edgy?

She was flagging now and so was Alice. They both needed a rest, but Gemma still marched them around Urban Outfitters twice. And as they were leaving, they hit the jackpot. Alice stopped at a rail and picked out a flower-print dress. The dress was black and the print was small, but it was pretty and feminine and summery. Gemma felt like Jesus Christ and Nelson Mandela and Angelina Jolie rolled into one. Two hours ago, Alice had insisted that she didn't wear dresses, yet, here she was, inspecting this one.

'It's a hundred euros,' she said, wistfully. 'I don't think we have enough left.'

'I'll buy it for you!' Gemma snatched it before she could change her mind. 'My treat.'

'Shouldn't I try it on?'

'We can bring it back if it doesn't fit.' Gemma was already pulling out her credit card, the worry that it would be maxed out when she had to pay for Stephen's car was swept away by the relief. She had done a good job. She could have lunch now.

Alice had eaten half a bacon sandwich two days ago and had picked all the pepperoni off Froggy's pizza last night, but as they walked to the nearest burger joint, she suddenly announced that she was a vegan.

Gemma was starving and the thought of lentils and Quorn made her want to weep but she whipped out her iPhone to check options. The best vegan restaurant in Dublin was back in Blackrock, of course, half an hour's drive away.

The Café LoCal had that pretentious hipster look she hated on sight. Exposed brick and white walls and deliberately mismatched china. A waitress in a yellow prom dress and a white frilly apron led them to a table by the window. Gemma caught herself looking at her enviously the way Alice had looked at the assistants in at Topshop. This was how she used to dress back in the day.

Alice slid into the booth and settled her shopping bags carefully on the seat beside her. She bent her head over the menu and tucked her hair behind her ear like a child, then as if she was reminding herself to play the part of what she actually was, a moody teenager, she mumbled, 'I'm not really hungry.'

'Well, I am!' Gemma said, grimly. She would have eaten a vegan shoe if that was all there was on the menu. Instead, she ordered a tofu steak burger with a cauliflower bun and sweet potato fries. 'Make it two!' she held a hand up to stop Alice's protests. 'I'll eat yours if you can't. And can we have two Cokes?'

The waitress shook her head. 'We don't do sugar but we can whip you up a guava and star-fruit energy smoothie. Or I could bring you the organic wine menu.'

Gemma tried to hide a grimace. 'Two smoothies please.'

Alice frowned down at the table. 'You can have a drink in front of me, you know. I'm not going to, like, finish it when you're not looking.'

'No I can't,' Gemma said tiredly.

'Why not?'

'Because,' she had started telling the truth, she might as well continue. 'Because I'm an alcoholic.'

Alice looked up at her, fascinated. 'So what would happen if you had one glass of wine?'

Gemma shrugged. It was a good question. 'I don't know. Maybe I'd leave it at that. Maybe I'd get completely wasted. I'm not really in a hurry to find out.'

The waitress came back with a loaded tray. She put down their plates and a bowl of sweet potato fries, then lined up two frosted jam jars of smoothie and gave Gemma a look that said, 'I dare you not to like it!'

Alice lifted one slice of cauliflower and poked at the golden, crispy tofu steak beneath it suspiciously.

Gemma took a tiny bite of her burger. It was incredible. Salsa and guacamole leaked out the sides and she licked it off her fingers. 'How is your dad? How's he doing? Is it just me or is he acting a bit...' she licked her fingers – 'weird?'

'He's acting really weird!' Alice was dipping fries into pink Himalayan salt and posting them into her mouth. 'He's not doing any exercise or working out and he stays in his room, like, nearly all the time. Sometimes I can hear him walking around in there, talking to himself.'

That didn't sound good, Gemma thought. 'Did he do that back in New York?' she asked worriedly. 'Talk to himself?'

'I don't know,' Alice said through a mouthful of food.

'What did he do to relax?'

'Museums. The gym. Squash. Tennis. Jogging.'

'Does he have' – Gemma tried to sound casual – 'friends?'

'Sure. He has work friends and he hangs out with the parents from school.'

'What about, you know, women friends?'

'Sometimes he goes on dates and, a couple of times, he's had a girlfriend but I only know that because I hear him on the phone.' She crushed salt crystals with a black painted thumbnail. 'He never tells me anything.'

'Maybe he thinks it might upset you.'

'He doesn't care what I think,' Alice said, bitterly. 'If he did, I wouldn't be here. I'd be in New York at my old school with my old friends!'

Gemma didn't have to imagine the loneliness of losing everything and everyone she'd known. She'd had to give it all up when
she got sober. She'd had to cut ties with every friend, lose every
phone number, move back in with her mother, start over.

Poor Alice, she thought. She leaned over and grabbed her
niece's hand and squeezed. 'I know coming here feels like the
end of your life, but it's not.' She turned Alice's hand over and
pointed at her palm. 'Look, you have an incredibly long lifeline!
You'll have plenty of time to decide where you want to live and
what you want to do.'

Alice snatched her hand back. 'What about my mom? Did her
lifeline end in the middle of her hand?'

Gemma felt ashamed. That was glib, what she'd said. 'Honestly,
I don't remember.'

Alice was watching her when she looked up. 'But you knew
her, right?'

Gemma nodded. 'I lived with her and Will for a few months
when I was twenty.'

Alice bent her head over her plate, avoiding her eyes. 'What
was she like?' She had Julia's pale skin and wide, blue eyes but
she had Will's nose and his ears poking through her dyed hair.

Gemma took a sip of her smoothie. It was a virulent orange,
like Froggy's cough medicine, but it tasted of sunshine and sweet,
pulped fruit. 'She was lovely.' You couldn't bitch about dead
people. They were all saints, though, in fairness, Julia had been
pretty saintly while she was alive too. That was what had made
her so very irritating.

She had snooped through Julia's things when she was at work,
hoping to find some dirty little secret, but she was always disappointed. The tasteful clothes hanging in her closet were clean
and ironed and arranged by colour. Cashmere sweaters, corduroy
skirts, faded Levis, summer dresses. Her underwear was pretty
and feminine, sweet, rather than sexy. The bottle of white wine
in the fridge had been corked after one glass. There were no pill
bottles among the expensive jars of creams and lotions in the
medicine cabinet.

Gemma could feel Alice staring at her, waiting to hear more.

Platitudes gathered on her tongue. Beautiful. Generous. Kind. Lovely.

She sighed and put her smoothie down. 'To be honest, she was incredibly annoying. She was one of those people who always knew the right thing to say and do and wear and . . .' She shook her head. 'She was just perfect and I always felt completely inadequate compared to her.'

Shit! she thought. This was not what you were supposed to say to a dead woman's child. But when she looked up, Alice was nodding slowly. She understood, Gemma realised. She must have grown up comparing herself to Julia too.

But the truth was, Gemma had felt inadequate long before she met Julia, even when she was a small child, and it got worse when she was a teenager. Everyone else seemed so bright and shiny and sure of themselves. So it was such a relief the first time she had a drink. It was like she'd found the cure. A can of beer or a couple of swigs of vodka and, abracadabra, she felt better about herself. Funnier and wilder and braver. In a few months, she went from being the quietest kid in her class to being the most popular. Then she started hanging around with the kids in the years above her. The cool girls, who pilfered cigarettes and Xanax from their mothers' handbags. The boys who always had a stash of weed and knew where to score ecstasy.

She had found her tribe. The misfits, the dropouts, the dreamers, the stoners. They skipped school, congregated at free houses. Her parents had no idea how to cope. Will, three years older, tried to rein her in but in the summer of 2001, he went to New York and met Julia and never came home and everything went south for Gemma after that.

The guy she was seeing started dealing coke and she started taking it. Her intake of booze doubled and she began to drink first thing in the morning. Her mother found a stash of drugs and money in her bedroom. She actually wanted to go to the police but Gemma had managed to blame the whole thing on the people she was hanging around with. Then they did what Will had just done with Alice – in reverse. They shipped her off to the States to stay with her sensible big brother.

A whole summer, rent-free in New York. Gemma felt like she had won the lottery, not like she was being punished. She was supposed to be looking for a part-time job, but instead, she trawled around the bars in Alphabet City, flirting with strangers, playing up the Irish accent so that they bought her drinks.

But a week after she arrived, she woke up in the back of a police car, her hair clogged with vomit. She had been beaten up and had been found passed out in a toilet in a bar in Brooklyn. She didn't even know where Brooklyn was.

It was Julia who took a cab down to the 9th Precinct to pick her up. She took her to the hospital to have a medical examination to confirm that she hadn't been sexually assaulted. It was Will who delivered the ultimatum: she had to clean up or go home. But it was also Julia who paid for the month-long stint in rehab.

It was not like 'Girl Interrupted'. Most of the other residents were ancient. There was Lois, a woman in her forties who had crashed her car while drunk and had killed her eight-year-old daughter. There was Dean, a guy in his sixties who had stolen his granddaughter's mobile to buy booze. And Carol, who had been a high-school teacher and then, within a year, had ended up living homeless.

These people, these fucked-up grown-ups, were Gemma's crew now, her tribe. She knew in her heart that she had nobody to blame but herself but, instead of blaming herself, she blamed Julia.

Two weeks into her rehab, Will came in for a group family meeting.

'She's not my family,' she hissed, when Julia left her room to go and get coffees from the vending machine. 'I don't want her here.'

'I didn't bring her for you,' Will said, looking her straight in the eye. 'I brought her for me.'

He held on to Julia's hand while he told a roomful of strangers about Gemma's drinking. All the nights he'd lain awake worrying where she was and all the ways he'd hidden her drinking from their parents. The times he'd slept on the floor of her room in case she got sick and choked on her own vomit. The morning she'd been on her way to school and he'd found her passed out in the bus shelter.

Gemma had wanted to die of shame. Not just because of what she'd done to her brother, but because even if she got better, which she probably wouldn't, smug, saintly Julia would know all these shitty things about her. Forever and ever.

Except that there hadn't been a forever. Julia, who had never done anything shitty in her entire life, had been killed two years later. She had been hit by a cab running a light as she crossed West Broadway on her way home to her husband and her three-month-old daughter. Gemma had always blamed her sister-in-law for stealing her brother and kick starting her own descent into full-blown addiction, when really, she should have thanked her. It was Julia who had paid for the rehab that had saved her. She owed her, Gemma thought. She owed her big time and this was her chance to repay her, this chance to look after the beautiful, troubled teenage girl sitting opposite her.

'What?' Alice touched her lip, brushing away a few grains of salt. 'Why are you staring at me like that?'

'Listen,' Gemma said. 'You don't know where you're going yet, but I do. I've been there, I'm still wearing the T-shirt. And it says "Loser" in great big block capitals.'

'Shhh!' Alice said, glancing at the couple at the next table. 'Everyone will hear you.'

'I drank. I flunked my exams.' Gemma ticked off her fingers. 'I didn't go to college. I got married to the first normal person who liked me because I was terrified that no other normal person would ever like me.'

Alice's wariness changed to horrified fascination.

Gemma looked down into the crumple of her napkin. A single piece of cauliflower sat like a small flower on her lap. 'I can't wish I did it differently, because I have my boys and I love my boys.' She looked up again. 'But you can do it differently. You have choices!'

Alice shook her head, slowly. 'I don't. I don't get to choose.'

Gemma thought she was going to talk about Will dragging her to Ireland again but instead she took a deep breath.

'It's not like I want to do stuff, like get wasted, or steal. I don't choose to do that. It's like it chooses me and I can't stop myself.'

'Yes, I know!' Gemma said. 'I know exactly what you mean. But I promise you, just noticing that, just being self-aware, is a choice. It might not stop you doing that stuff straight away, but keep doing it and it will. You're doing great, I promise you.'

Alice looked surprised and then pleased.

'What about you?'

'What about me?' Gemma pulled out her credit card again.

'Your choices?'

Gemma zipped up her bag, caught the waitress's eye and scribbled in the air for the bill. 'Don't worry about me. I might not have been to college, but I have a PhD in muddling through.'

As they walked back to the car from the café, Alice stopped to look in a shop window. It contained one gorgeous diamanté brooch that seemed to be floating in the air, and dozens of popping soap bubbles.

'Wow!' Alice said. 'That is like, so cool!'

Gemma glanced over her shoulder. The parking ticket was about to run out and Blackrock was notorious for clampers but Alice was intrigued. 'You want to take a look inside?'

Nora had always loved Lainey's vanity set, a heavy silver backed mirror engraved with flowers and a matching brush with soft pale yellow bristles. Once, when she was helping her grandmother to dust her dressing table, she had picked that brush up and tried to pull it through her own tangle of hair and then, when that didn't work, she had pulled Lainey over to the stool and made her sit down. And before her grandmother could stop her, she had climbed into her lap and unpinned her grandmother's long, braid while Lainey had closed her eyes tight and sat completely still, hardly breathing, her shoulders hunched, her mouth trembling, while Nora carefully re-braided her hair.

Nora smiled at the memory now as she arranged the brush and its matching mirror on a low table near her desk. Then she looked up as the door opened and a woman and a teenage girl with pink tipped hair came in.

'How did you, like, get all those bubbles blowing in your window?' the girl asked.

Nora put the brush and mirror down. 'Here, I'll show you.'

She brought Alice over to the window and Gemma looked around. It was a shame they were in a rush, she'd have loved to browse. The shop was full of gorgeous bits and pieces. Antique furniture and vintage china. She looked at a rail of gorgeous clothes and then past it at a Japanese kimono that was pinned to the wall. Pale pink silk embroidered with cherry blossom. If she'd seen this ten years ago, she would have pounced on it. She'd have accessorised it with platform flip-flops, thin white socks and one of those pastel umbrellas that were hanging from the ceiling. She'd have backcombed her hair into a high bun and turned herself into a blonde Madame Butterfly.

'Do you want to try it on?' The shop owner was looking at her.

'Oh no!' Gemma began but Alice was nodding. 'You should!'

The owner unpinned it from the wall and handed it over. Gemma slipped it on obediently. It was a whisper of a thing, the silk so light that it felt like air. For a moment, she felt like her old self. Then she remembered that she actually *was* old. Way too old for fancy dress.

'It's cute! You should so buy it!' Alice said.

'Maybe I would,' Gemma took the kimono off, 'if I still had long hair.'

'You could, like, buy it and then grow your hair,' Alice pointed out.

'You're sweet,' Gemma said, 'but I don't even own a brush any more.'

'Oh, no!' the owner said suddenly, peering out of the window. 'That's the third person who's been clamped today.'

Over her shoulder, Gemma spotted a man in a Hi Vis jacket slapping a sticker onto the windscreen of her car.

'Shit!' Gemma threw the kimono at Alice and sprinted for the door but it was too late. The car was already clamped.

The shop owner came out into the street to try to reason with the clamper.

'Come on,' she said, 'the ticket's only five minutes over.' But he refused to budge.

'A hundred and twenty-euro fine!' Gemma rummaged for her phone to call the de-clamping service. 'That's probably more than the car is actually worth.'

'I'll pay half of it,' the owner said. 'If I hadn't persuaded you to try on the kimono—'

'No,' Gemma said, 'thanks for offering, but it's my own fault.'

She tried not to do the maths as she read her credit card number out over the phone to get the car released. She was almost certainly maxed out now.

She drove Alice home, and got out and helped her to unload her bags.

'I enjoyed that,' she said and she meant it. Despite the exhaustion and the soul baring and the clamping, she had loved her day with her niece.

Alice wriggled out of her hug and headed towards the front door in the biker boots she'd changed into in the car. Then as Gemma was getting back into the car she came hurrying back.

'I got you a present,' she mumbled, 'hang on, I just have to wrap it.' She turned away and pulled some tissue paper out of one of her shopping bags, then handed the clumsily wrapped package to Gemma.

'Alice, you didn't have to buy me anything.' Gemma pulled off the tissue paper. It was an antique hairbrush. The bristles were thick and soft and the silver back was embossed with a delicate pattern of fleurs-de-lis and roses. It was the loveliest thing anyone had given her in years. 'Oh my God!' she whispered. 'It's lovely. It's beautiful.' She looked at the hallmark. 'It's Tiffany!'

'I didn't, like, spend my own money!' Alice shrugged. 'Dad gave me a hundred euros to buy you something.'

'That's so kind of him and so kind of you!' Gemma held the brush to her chest. 'Thank you!'

*

Des the mechanic was pulling the shutters down as Gemma parked in front of the garage.

'The late Gemma Kennedy,' he tapped his wrist and rocked back on his heels, 'I was supposed to close at four.'

'Sorry! I thought it was five.'

He had swapped his usual oil-stained overalls for a soft blue plaid shirt and jeans. He smelt of some kind of warm, spicy aftershave.

'Sorry, I got clamped in Blackrock.'

Des smiled. 'Sure you did. You always had the best excuses for showing up last. Just as well you're worth waiting for.'

'Right!' she said, going heavy on the irony but pleased all the same.

Des had been in a twelve-step group she'd gone to when she'd first got out of rehab. She used to bum cigarettes from him and swap war stories while they smoked them after the meeting. She'd liked him but there was a rule in AA that you weren't allowed to date anyone from the programme until you'd been sober for a full year. And by that time, she had stopped going to meetings and she was seeing Stephen.

Des was doing okay, she thought, watching him pulling the shutters back up again before going inside to get the BMW. There were a few threads of grey in his hair, a few lines around his eyes, but he still had the shambling grace he'd had when he was twenty. And if the calm and order of the office was a reflection of his state of mind, he was in a good place. She wondered whether he was single. Whether he'd been about to go on a date and she'd made him late.

She locked her car and followed him inside and he unlocked a glass-fronted box, took a key off the row of hooks, and handed it to her.

'Do you mind if I leave the VW here for the weekend?' she asked him. 'I can pick it up on Monday after work.'

'Sure I can't persuade you to leave it here permanently?' Des raised his eyebrows. 'It's on its last legs, Gemma. I can sort you out with a reliable little runaround for a couple of hundred euros any time, just say the word.'

'The word,' Gemma handed her card over, 'is "overdrawn".'

'Ah!' Des nodded sagely as he fed her card into the machine.

She tapped in her pin and held her breath, waiting for the card to be declined but miraculously it spat out a curl of paper.

Des ripped it off and handed it to her. 'Getting away with murder again!' He grinned.

'Just don't tell anyone where I hid the bodies!'

They walked over to the BMW together. 'I gave it a little valet,' Des said. 'I just left the rubbish in the boot but I can bin it for you, if you like.'

Gemma popped the boot open. There were two green plastic rubbish bags inside. She opened one. It was half full of discarded food packaging from an M & S meal for two. There were three empty bottles at the bottom of the bag: one red, one white, one dessert wine. She laughed to herself. Whoever had enjoyed all this had had quite a night.

'This must belong to someone else,' she said to Des, 'I don't know how it got in here.' But he didn't answer and she realised that he had gone back inside to lock up.

She opened the other bag, curious to see what she'd find. It was half full of crumpled bed linen and towels, the packaging it had come in was thrown in on top of them.

Gemma stared at them for a long moment. Her mind was racing too far ahead for her to understand but her stomach was queasy with intuition. She opened the first bag again and scrabbled around in the bottom until she found two receipts.

One was for bed linen from the Dunne's Stores near Stephen's office in Dublin. The other was from Coyne's off licence in Blackwater. Ten miles away from the holiday house in Curracloe.

'No!' she said out loud. 'No! There must be another explanation!' She checked the last four digits of the credit-card number. It was Stephen's.

She put her hand to her mouth, as the pieces fell into place.

He'd said that the car had broken down on the way back from the meeting in Cork. But he hadn't been in Cork or at a meeting. He had been in Wexford, at their holiday house, and he hadn't been alone. They had brought the kids to that house every summer. Froggy had been conceived there.

'Gemma, are you okay? You're as white as a sheet.' Des was standing beside her. 'Are you feeling sick? Do you want to sit down for a minute?'

'No! I'm fine.' She closed the boot and shoved the receipts into her jeans pocket. 'But I'm going to take my own car. If that's okay.'

'Sure but—'

'Please, Des!' Her voice was breaking. 'Don't. I can't.' The words ran out and she wrenched open the door of her car. For once, it opened and she jumped in and drove away.

Stephen and the boys would be waiting for her. The pizza restaurant was booked for six, but she drove past the turn-off for home and kept going until she got to Kiely's in Donnybrook. The pub where she'd ordered her first underage drink.

It was noisy and busy with an after-match crowd. Groups of drunken mates shouting over the sound of the TV. Peals of hilarious laughter erupting around her as she pushed her way to the bar.

She slung her bag over the back of a stool. A barman with a shaved head and a beard came over.

Gemma scanned the ingredients of the cocktails.

'Long Island Iced Tea,' she said. If she was going to have a drink, she might as well make it a strong one.

He took his time making it. Measuring the vodka and gin. Crushing the ice. Cutting a lemon into fiddly slices and shaking his stupid shaker for so long, that Gemma wanted to scream.

She had waited seventeen years for this cocktail. She had stayed away from trouble. She had sat through parties watching everyone around her get smashed while she sipped fizzy water. She had been a responsible mother. She had been the designated driver. She had married a nice, safe, reliable man who would never let her down. But he had let her down. She deserved this.

Finally, the barman put a low, frosted tumbler in front of her. 'Nine euros.'

Gemma shook her head. She could have bought a bottle of

gin and a bottle of vodka for that in 1995. She slid her credit card over and picked up her glass. It felt familiar, like shaking hands with an old, cold friend she hadn't seen in years. She put it to her lips.

'Sorry!' The barman, the stupid, annoying barman, was there again. 'The contact-less payment didn't go through. D'you want to try the pin?'

He seemed even more embarrassed than she was when her card was declined.

'I can pay you later,' she said, holding on to the glass. 'I can come back with the money...'

But he had his hand on the glass too. She wanted it badly. Just not badly enough to fight him for it.

The driver's door of the Polo refused to open this time, so Gemma had to unlock the passenger door and crawl across to the seats. The strap of her bag caught on the gearstick as she crawled and it upturned and all her things spilled out around her. She sat sobbing in the detritus. A couple of used tissues. A blister pack of antihistamine for Stephen's hay fever. Froggy's nit comb. Jake's spare inhaler. A dog-eared diary full of orthodontist's appointments and soccer practices and PT meetings and violin lessons. A pile of dog-eared Lidl and Aldi discount vouchers. And in the middle of all of it there was one lovely thing. The hairbrush that Alice had given her.

Gemma picked it up and held it against her heart as if it was a living thing. She hugged it and she hugged herself and rocked and sobbed. There was no coming back from this, she thought. Her marriage was over.

She cried until her voice cracked and there wasn't another tear left inside her. She flipped down the sun visor.

Her face was blotchy and her eyes were swollen but she was sober. She hadn't screwed up and she wasn't going to. She had her boys and Alice too. She owed that to Julia.

She'd find the strength to go home. She'd take the kids over to a neighbour's house to sleep over and then she'd tell Stephen to pack his bags.

She'd get through it all, one day at a time, one minute at a time, starting now.

She wiped her eyes with a tissue and blew her nose. Then she began to run the brush through her cropped hair. 'One... two... three...' she counted.

7

Ammonite Fossil Marble Table

Nora

Nora brought her coffee outside and drank it at the door of the shop. The sun was hidden behind a sea of fog that had draped tendrils of mist on the roof of the library opposite. She took a breath of damp, salty air and listened. It was eerily quiet. She ached for the soothing hum of London, the throb and thrum of flowing traffic and distant trains that reminded her, when Adam was away and she woke up in Fountain Road, that she wasn't alone. Was he away now, in Boston or Philadelphia? Or was he at home in their bed? A month ago, she would have known, but now she couldn't remember.

She swallowed a mouthful of cooling coffee and a lump of longing for him and for her old life in London.

All those weekends she'd spent obsessing about the house, ordering fabric samples, testing out paint colours, browsing junk shops for antique mirrors and lamps, scavenging in architectural salvage yards for the perfect Belfast Sink and claw-footed bath... She had spent the two years making a home, she thought sadly, and now she was taking another one apart.

She had thought that she might cry the day she sold the seven small red lacquer boxes that fitted together, like secrets, one hidden inside the other. She had learned every hinge, every click of those boxes when she was a child. She had burned with possessiveness when one of her customers, a man in his thirties, had turned his back and spent ten minutes pulling them apart and putting them back together.

Eventually, she couldn't stand it any more. She'd addressed his back. 'Can I help you?'

When he turned around, his face was flushed. 'Yes. I don't know, maybe.' He cleared his throat. He stuffed a hand into the pocket of his jacket and extracted a small black leather box. Carefully, as if he was performing open-heart surgery, he opened it and removed a glittering diamond solitaire. 'I'm just trying to figure out if this might fit inside the smallest box.' His red face turned crimson.

Nora had put her book down. 'Let's see,' she said softly. When he left the shop, she had watched him go with the boxes tucked under his arm, wondering what part they would play in a stranger's destiny.

Everything she put into the window sold quickly and every few days she had to create a new display. She looked forward to it in the way she used to look forward to her art projects at college. Every one was a blank sheet of paper, a chance to let her imagination run away with her.

It was the thing she enjoyed most, taking out the little cache of Lainey's notes, rereading them until one sparked an idea, then working out how to use the window to tell the story.

Temple Doors. 1960.

I never travelled with Hugh. Never saw France or Japan or India. But he brought all these places back to me. When the Indian temple doors arrived, packed in a crate the size of a skip, I rolled my eyes and said, 'What's this monstrosity? Have you brought me back an elephant?' But his enthusiasm wasn't dented. As he brushed the sawdust from between the carved flowers, he told me about the night he'd been to a Hindu festival. And now, nearly sixty years later, I feel as if I was there too. I can feel the heat in the air and smell the incense and see the stars and the fireflies and the bright colours of the women's saris. He didn't just give me things. He gave me memories.

Adonis and Ed had helped Nora to anchor the doors in the centre of the window. She'd dyed two sheets dark blue and pinned Christmas lights between them for stars and criss-crossed fine-wire LED lights in front of the doors for fireflies.

She'd already sold them to an interior designer for two hundred and fifty euros. It was only after the woman had paid her, in cash, that Nora had wondered if maybe they were worth more. Pricing Lainey's things had been the hardest part for her.

Money was coming in but it was going out too and she was running behind the monthly target she'd set for her mother's house fund.

It wasn't just that she was charging too little. There were costs she hadn't anticipated. Loughlin had advised her that she needed public liability. She'd also had to pay for car insurance and a service so the Merc would pass its NCT.

As Nora finished her coffee she heard footsteps of a lone runner coming towards her from the corner. A tiny, familiar figure appeared out of the mist, jogging towards her in black Lycra and luminous pink trainers. Nora backed into the doorway of the shop before Fiona could see her.

Fiona had decided that Nora needed her help. She had added her to an extensive list of people she looked after. Nora knew about the list because Adonis had told her. Fiona had given him a job when he was living in a homeless shelter. She had helped his friend Nikos to write his CV. She gave OAPs and unemployed people fifty per cent off between three and five every day when the café was quiet. She made nutrition plans for lots of her regular customers and she was Blackrock's official parking angel. If she saw the clampers prowling in their van, she'd text every shopkeeper in the village and she was not above running out onto the street to try to stop them clamping a car.

Nora slipped into the shop and closed the door. A moment later, it opened again.

'Hi!' Fiona said. 'I'm on the way back from my five K, and I just thought I'd drop this over.' She handed Nora a LoCal takeaway bag.

'You shouldn't have!' Nora opened the bag, expecting to find some of Adonis's addictive date-and-peanut breakfast bars or an almond milk frappé. She felt slightly disappointed when she saw a sheaf of papers. She pulled it out. It was a neat spreadsheet that listed the contents of Temple Terrace.

Fiona unscrewed her water bottle and took a gulp. 'I've started an inventory of prices for you. There's a memory stick in there too so you can put it straight onto your computer.'

'But...' Nora stammered. Fiona had never been inside the house. Unless she'd broken in when Nora was asleep. She wouldn't put it past her.

'I hope you don't mind,' Fiona said. 'I was helping Ed with a nutrition plan for his Iron Man and he mentioned he'd done a list of the house contents, so we put our heads together and did some Googling. We checked out the prices for a few things on eBay and a couple of online vintage shops. You can fill in the rest yourself between customers.'

Nora clenched her jaw. 'It's very kind of you...' It was bloody intrusive actually. 'But I don't need—' As she was about to hand the papers back she noticed a price listed in the box opposite the temple doors. Six hundred euros. 'That's seems a bit high.' It was over twice what she had charged.

'It's the going rate on the Internet,' Fiona looked over her shoulder, 'plus twenty per cent for overheads and staff.'

'But I don't have overheads,' Nora said. 'Or staff.'

'Yes, you do!' Fiona said firmly. 'This shop didn't decorate itself. That window didn't make itself. And lovely as they are, these things aren't going to sell themselves. You need to put a proper value on what you have here.'

Nora chewed her lip and scanned the top page again. 'Do you really think people would be prepared to pay these kinds of prices?' she asked nervously.

Fiona nodded. 'Absolutely. And if you invest a couple of hundred in packaging – nice bags, ribbons, tissue paper, you can add five per cent more. I've put the number for the place that does my stuff. Mention my name and they'll give you a discount.'

After she had gone, Nora sat down with her cold coffee and loaded the spreadsheet onto her computer. She started with the first thing on page two. The beautiful lacquered globe drinks cabinet. She had planned to sell it for a hundred euros. There was a slightly smaller one on eBay for four hundred and fifty euros.

She felt a surge of relief. She had been running behind her target for her mother's house fund, but if she did what Fiona had suggested, she could make it. It would not be easy to get Alanna to accept the money, but she could cross that bridge when she came to it.

Later that day, Nora was sorting through Lainey's drawers full of scarves. A rainbow of plain squares and bold Sixties prints. Crimsons and turquoises, emerald greens, soft greys, pale yellows, petal pinks. A Lanvin. A Hermes. Two Zandra Rhodes. An Yves Saint Laurent.

As she put her hand back into the pool of silk to pull out another one, her fingers touched something solid. She moved the scarves aside and pulled out a paperback book with a cover that showed a house silhouetted against a star studded sky. Nora opened it on the flyleaf, hardly daring to hope and then caught her breath when she saw that it was covered in her grandmother's dense writing.

Marble table with ammonite fossils. 1959.

I told Hugh why I couldn't sleep. I told him about the nightmares. I told him everything after that proposal. I thought I'd take what had happened to my deathbed, but I had no choice. I had to knock myself off the pedestal he'd put me on. To make him realise that I wasn't the kind of woman he wanted to marry. I expected him to walk away but instead, he arrived at the rooming house on Grantham Street where I was living with the tea chest strapped to the back of his motorbike.

'This will help you sleep,' he announced, when he had unpacked the little ammonite table. How? I stared at it. Was I supposed to bang my head against it?

No! I was supposed to look at it! The past was part of me, he said, the way the fossilised snails were part of the marble.

But the past wasn't who I was, any more than those snails were the marble.

For six years, nearly seven, he almost made me believe that was true. But no man, not even one as determined and devoted as Hugh, could change what had happened or my part in it. I couldn't escape my past, no matter how much he wanted me to.

Nora sat back on her heels. What did her grandmother mean? What was in the past that she couldn't escape? Was she talking about the war? About being separated from her parents and losing touch with them? What did she mean 'her part in it'?

Her grandparents looked down at her from the photograph on the dressing table. She wondered what Lainey had done that was so bad that she thought that if Hugh knew, he wouldn't marry her.

It was a Saturday evening, way past time to close the shop, but Nora had been putting off going up to get started on more clearing and sorting. She hung on, rearranging the stock that was left after a busy week, making notes of what she might need for when she opened on Monday: some more of the bone-handled cutlery she had been selling in sets, tied with ribbons; mirrors – she'd sold four this week and was starting to run out of replacements. She might put up some paintings in the blank spaces. She had decided to put the little ammonite table in the window but she would need some bigger pieces for the shop. The blue velvet love seat. The stone lion from the garden. The little lacquered card table Hugh had shipped home from Italy.

When Adonis arrived at seven, he brought Fiona with him. She made herself useful, clacking up and down stairs on vertiginous sandals, carrying armfuls of leather-bound encyclopaedias that Nora had decided she'd sell this week, polishing cabinets, stringing ribbons around cutlery.

'Do you need help with any other thing?' Adonis asked when he had carried everything down to the shop. His accent always made the most ordinary thing sound courtly and formal.

'No, thank you,' Nora said. 'But why don't you stay?'

'He's meeting *friends*.' Fiona brushed a few flecks of mustard-coloured lichen off his T-shirt.

'Please, Adonis,' Nora reached for her bag, 'will you let me pay you this time?'

'No!' he said, nodding. 'This is my pleasure to help you.'

Nora pulled out a twenty-euro note. 'At least let me stand you a drink.'

'Thank you, no,' he said, sounding flustered. He backed towards the door.

Fiona swallowed a smirk. 'No getting plastered now!' she called after him. 'We've got a new menu to plan! Seven a.m. start tomorrow.'

He said something in Greek and picked up a tea towel and tossed it at her.

'You missed!' Fiona laughed. She turned to Nora. 'Probably not best to offer him booze when he's on his way to a meeting.'

'You said he was meeting friends!'

'He is. Ed and Loughlin. They're all "friends of Bill".' She wiggled her eyebrows. 'Do I have to spell it out? They're *alcoholics*, that's how they know one another.'

'Oh God.' Nora's jaw fell open. 'I gave them beer, the first time they came around to help!'

'You're kidding me!'

'No! I bought them a whole case!'

Fiona dissolved into fits of laughter and Nora started laughing too. Every time one of them managed to stop, the other sent her into fits of helpless giggles again.

'A whole case.' Fiona clutched her side. 'I wish I'd been there to see their faces!'

'They did look pretty horrified.' Tears were running down Nora's face.

'Oh well! They're big boys,' Fiona said, finally catching her breath. 'Well, Adonis is. Loughlin is on the small side and Ed is vertically challenged, but you know what I mean!'

Fiona had brought dinner. Cauliflower risotto with hazelnut

butter and quinoa salad dressed with mint and lime juice. A bottle of cold white wine.

They ate in the kitchen with the French doors wide open to let out the heat and to let in the scent of roses and peonies from the garden. Nora was sweating. She had changed into a pair of shorts and one of Hugh's old shirts to move the things down to the shop. She felt dusty and dishevelled sitting opposite Fiona, who looked fresh and cool in a floaty red halter-neck dress that left her shoulders bare. She looked as if she was dressed up to eat in a five-star restaurant. What was she doing here in Nora's grandparents' kitchen on a Saturday night? Surely she had better places to be?

'Are you sure you don't have plans?' Nora asked, carefully.

'Absolutely.' Fiona grinned. 'If I wasn't here, I'd still be working. If Adonis hadn't physically ejected me from the café. That's the downside of being married to your business.' She flicked a feather of hair out of her eyes. 'But there are upsides. I don't have to share my bed with it or worry it's going to run off with someone younger or skinnier.'

Nora laughed. 'I'm sure that would never happen to you.'

'Not if I can help it! God,' Fiona pushed her plate away, though it was half full. 'I know that makes me sound like a man hater but I'm not. I was engaged for three years.' She touched the huge diamond on her finger. 'I gave back the ring he'd given me. This was a little present from the café.'

There was a long silence. Nora waited for Fiona to fill it but she didn't. She didn't want to swap confidences so she felt like a cheat when she said, finally, 'What happened?'

'I don't know.' Fiona shrugged. 'Pressure of running a business together. We kept putting the wedding on the long finger. That and my secret affair with croque monsieurs and crème brûlée. The café was a French brasserie back then. Everything had cream and cheese and butter and sugar. Usually all four.' She pushed her plate away. 'He just stopped fancying me, I think. It was an awful mess. I had to buy him out of the business. And the funny thing is,' she tucked her hair behind her ears and smiled up at Nora, 'within a year, I'd changed the name and the menu and

I was a size ten. Adonis arrived and everything changed. The name over the door. The menu. My BMI.' She tilted her chin up and grinned. 'Revenge is a dish best served cold, containing two hundred and fifty calories or less and prepped by a chef who looks like a Greek god.'

Adonis had left Athens after the banking crisis, she told Nora, and come to Dublin to work in an up-market vegan restaurant owned by a distant cousin. But he was lonely in Dublin and he started drinking heavily. He lost his job and then his apartment and he was living in a hostel when Fiona took him on. 'I live in dread of the day he'll meet someone and leave me!' she said worriedly. 'You should see the way the yummy mummies and yoga bunnies throw themselves at him. It's only a matter of time.' She sighed. 'I'll just have to make sure I write down all his recipes.'

She looked up at Nora, her wide green eyes sparkling with curiosity. 'What about you? Is there someone back in London?'

Nora felt her shoulders lock, her face tighten. 'No, I'm single,' she said. It was the first time she'd said it out loud since June. It shocked her to hear it but it was the truth. She had better get used to it. 'But I'm not looking to change that,' she said quickly before Fiona got any ideas about setting her up with one of her customers. 'It's going to be a full-time job getting the house cleared before January.'

'Well, you're doing a great job with the shop,' Fiona said, picking up Nora's discomfort and changing the subject. 'The entire Dun Laoghaire–Rathdown business community has come down with a bad case of window-envy. You must have a background in display?'

'Not really.' Nora shrugged. 'I was an illustrator and then a set designer but I loved shop windows when I was small.'

It used to drive her mum crazy the way that Nora could stand for ten minutes gazing at the display in the window of a fruit and vegetable shop or a chemist or a boutique. Her favourites were the department stores with entire rooms set out behind the glass. Empty sofas beneath glittering chandeliers. Comfortable chairs arranged around tables set for dinner. Bedrooms complete with rugs and reading lights. Her mother would shift from foot to foot and mutter darkly about how people thought they owned things but things actually owned them. And Nora wished she could step through the glass and live inside one of those calm, comfortable worlds.

Alanna was always on the move. Changing jobs. Moving flat. Trying out a new town. The muddle and the chaos never quite got sorted before they had to pack it all up and start again. It gave Nora a queasy feeling to wake up in a different room every couple of months. To have to get used to strangers' faces on the stairs in a different house share. To have to start at a new school and try to break into new circles of established friends. She fantasised about living in the same place for her whole life, like her grandparents had, and filling it with beautiful things.

'Well, they say that if you do what you love, it's not really like work, don't they?' Fiona cut across her thoughts. 'And speaking of work, I know this is a bit cheeky, but do you think you could design a window for me?'

The windows for The Memory Shop had all been sparked by Lainey's things. Nora didn't have the first idea what do with food. But Fiona had been so generous that she couldn't refuse.

For the café window, Nora hung a table with a chequered cloth from the ceiling and laid it with plates piled with glued-on cakes and latte glasses filled with frothy coffees made from modelling clay. Fiona's customers loved it and so did the other shopkeepers. Nora began to make windows for them too.

A display for the hardware store with a lit chandelier made of a dozen cheese graters with solar light bulbs that lit up at night. One for the bridal boutique owner with a wedding dress at the centre of a blizzard of fake rose petals created by the cross draught of two desk fans. A life size wire sculpture of a ballgown from wire coat hangers for the dry cleaners. It took Nora over a hundred coathangers and two evenings to complete it but she enjoyed every moment of it. It felt exhilarating to be making something without a tight brief or a difficult client or Liv pestering her about going over budget on time.

Megan the owner was so delighted that she had insisted on

giving Nora three months unlimited dry cleaning in return, which was coming in very useful for Lainey's clothes.

But much as she loved doing windows for other people, it was the windows for The Memory Shop that Nora looked forward to most. The next one was going to be the most dramatic. The glass would be completely blacked out except for one tiny, tantalising circular hole. Behind it, illuminated by a spotlight, she was going to put Lainey's marvellous ammonite table on its side so that passers-by could see the tiny grey fossils of sea creatures floating beneath the polished marble. She was going to paint a question onto the glass. 'What do you see when you look into the past?'

Adonis had carried the table down into the shop as if it was a feather but Nora was regretting now that she hadn't asked him to move it into the window for her. It might, she thought, as she pushed as hard as she could to try to nudge it across the floor, weigh a ton. She had only move it a few inches when she heard a voice.

'Are those fossils?'

There was a boy at her elbow. White blond curls and very bright blue eyes behind small round glasses. He reminded Nora of someone, but she couldn't think who.

'They are fossils, but they used to be snails.' She moved out of his way and he squatted down to look at them.

A man with the same white blond hair in a sweatshirt and jeans poked his head around the shop door. 'Christopher! There you are! Come on. We're in a hurry!'

'I just need a minute,' the boy pleaded.

His dad, it had to be his dad with that hair, sighed. 'Well, make it a quick one.'

'It can't be quick.' Christopher pushed his glasses up his nose. 'It's always the same length. Sixty seconds!'

'Fifty-nine,' his dad said. 'Fifty-eight.'

The boy turned back to the table. He put his nose so close to it that his breath steamed up the marble. 'Is it okay if I touch it?' he asked her. Nora nodded and he traced the shapes of the tiny ridged shells that seemed to float below the surface. 'How old are they?' He squinted up at her.

'Guess.'

He blinked hard as if he was calculating. 'A million years?'

She shook her head. 'More like two hundred and forty million.'

'Whoooooah!' he gasped, clutching the edge of the table as if he was on a roller coaster.

'Thirty seconds, Christopher!' His father tapped his watch. 'Sorry,' he said to Nora. 'It's his birthday and I'm going to buy him a –' he paused, dramatically – 'a what? Chris?' he prompted.

'An X-Box three sixty,' the boy said looking back down at the fossils. 'What are they called?' he asked Nora.

'Orthoceras.' Hugh had taught her the word when she was about eight and it was still there, like a fossil itself, laid down in the back of her mind. 'They're part of the Cephalopoda family. Hang on.' She went behind the desk and rummaged in a box of Hugh's leather-bound encyclopaedias and came back with Volume C.

He peered over her shoulder as she flipped through the tissue-thin, gilt-edged pages until she found the right one. 'Cephalopoda. These marine molluscs lived in the sea two hundred and forty to sixty-five million years ago and became extinct during the Cretaceous period, at the same time as the dinosaurs.'

The boy's face lit up with excitement. 'Did you hear that, Dad? These snails are as old as dinosaurs!'

'Great.' His father grinned. 'Now come on! Let's go.'

Ten minutes later the grin was well and truly gone. 'Come on, buddy, you're just being silly.' He glared at his son, then shot Nora a resentful look. She didn't blame him. This was her fault. She had got carried away.

'But it's my birthday,' Christopher said stubbornly. 'And this is what I want.'

Nora knew now who he reminded her of. It was Hugh. What was it Lainey had said in her note about the moonstones? 'That man never took "no" for an answer.'

The boy's father rolled his eyes. 'But you said you wanted

the X-Box three sixty, with the TB Console and two controllers and . . .'

The boy shook his head. 'That's what you said I wanted,' he said quietly.

'Well, yeah,' his father shrugged, 'sure. I might have suggested it, but . . .' He saw Nora looking at him and he looked away, sheepishly. 'But I was just thinking of you. Of the fun we'd – I mean you'd – have playing games and—'

'How much is it?' Christopher asked Nora. She thought of the eight hundred she had just this morning filled in, in the little box on Fiona's neatly typed inventory. She tried to remember the cost of the X-Box she'd given Adam last Christmas. The one he hadn't had time to take out of the box. 'It's four hundred euros.'

'That's a hundred euros cheaper than the X-Box!' Christopher said, breathlessly.

'Fine.' The man shook his head. 'Great.' He dug his wallet out of his back pocket. 'But I'm telling you, you'll probably be bored with it in a week.'

The boy shook his head. 'I won't,' he mouthed.

Nora wrote out a receipt. 'This says that if you change your mind and decide you want the X-Box, you can have your money back. If the shop is gone, don't worry, just email me, I've put my address here.'

'How long is that valid for?' The man frowned.

'Two hundred and forty million years for a refund,' Nora handed Christopher the receipt, 'two hundred and fifty million for an exchange.'

Will had arranged the contents of the boxes he had unpacked around the room. Julia's books in piles in alphabetical order, the way she had liked them, her CDs in two high towers, organised according to genre. The double bed was piled with a mountain of her clothes. Sweaters, dresses, coats, skirts, shorts. And her shoes, nineteen pairs, were lined up in two rows along one wall. Trainers and low heels and high heels and worn brown leather summer sandals that still held a few grains of sand and the shadow of her heel and five tiny imprints of her toes.

Will was sorting them into pairs when he heard the thunder of small footsteps on the stairs outside and the sound of hammering on the door.

'Will! Will!' The voice was high and breathless. Neither of Gemma's boys called him uncle, which was fair enough. He had only been in Ireland twice since they were born. He hadn't exactly played an avuncular role in their lives. Still, it was odd to be addressed so informally by a seven-year-old.

'What is it, Froggy?'

'Alice wants to ask you something.'

When Will got downstairs Alice was sitting cross-legged on the living-room floor using a brand-new bath towel to dry an enormous, astonishingly ugly and very wet dog that Will had never seen before.

'He's been standing outside the house next door in the rain for hours,' she said. 'But nobody lives there.'

The dog leapt to his feet and greeted Will joyfully. It was like one of those YouTube videos where animals are reunited with their owners.

'Maybe he's a stray,' Alice said, hopefully, hauling him off. 'If he is, can we keep him?'

She looked so wistful that Will's heart melted. 'We'll see.'

The dog wasn't a stray, of course. He had lived next door until two weeks ago but the couple who owned him had gone travelling and had left the dog with a friend to look after, but it kept vaulting the wall of her garden and making the two-mile journey home to Blackrock to stand outside the empty house.

Will had driven it back last night after the kids had gone to bed. He was on his way up the stairs when he ran into Gemma in her dressing gown, on the landing.

'Thanks for letting us stay, Will,' she whispered. 'And thank you for this.' She held up an antique silver hairbrush. 'It means the world to me.'

Will shook his head. 'I don't know what you mean.'

'Alice bought it for me when we were shopping, the day I found out about Stephen. She said you gave her the money to buy me something.'

Will waited for her door to close, then tapped on Alice's door. His daughter was reading a graphic novel. She didn't look up when he opened the door; she was still sulking because he had insisted on driving the dog home.

'Alice, did you shoplift a hairbrush?' Will asked.

Alice looked up from her book, her eyes wide and blue, Julia's eyes, behind the thick lines of kohl. 'I wanted to get something for Gemma,' she said. 'And it wasn't like actual shoplifting. I mean, it's just a piece of junk. It's only worth, like, two dollars.'

'It's an antique!' Will said patiently. 'It's probably worth fifty times that! But that's not the point, the point is you stole it.'

Alice stood up and yawned theatrically. 'Well, you stole my entire life!' she said. 'My school, my friends, my home ... So I guess that crappy hairbrush just makes us even.'

She walked past him and, a moment later, he heard the door of the bathroom slam.

The dog looked up at Will reproachfully, as if it had expected more of him.

When he came down this morning, the dog was back and Alice, who was an on-off vegetarian, was cooking the dog some bacon.

'Dad! Please!' She had tugged Will's sleeve as he looped a length of washing line through the dog's collar. 'I want to give him something to eat before he goes.'

'Just because you want something,' Will had said levelly, 'it doesn't mean you can have it. He's not yours, Alice. And neither is the antique hairbrush you stole. So you're coming with me now to return both of them to their owners.'

But she didn't come, of course. By the time he'd finished his sentence, she had fled upstairs and slammed her door.

Stephen's BMW was parked a few doors away from Will's house. The electric window rolled down as the dog dragged Will past.

'Will! Mate!' he said in a loud whisper.

Don't call me mate, Will thought, anger smouldering in his belly, as he turned. *I'm not your mate.*

'I don't want the kids to see me. I don't want to upset them. I just wondered if you've had a chance to talk to Gemma, like

I asked you?' Stephen was gripping the edge of the car window, his knuckles white. Will nodded.

'Did you tell her we need to talk? I don't want to lose my marriage, Will; I don't want to lose my boys.'

Stephen should have thought of that, Will thought, before he screwed around on her. 'She doesn't want to talk to you.' Stephen's face crumbled. For a moment, he looked as if he was going to cry. 'Give him her some time. Maybe she'll change her mind.'

'She will change her mind, won't she?' Stephen's voice was reedy with hope.

'I don't know,' Will said. Though privately he thought the chances of it happening were zero.

When Gemma told him that she'd caught Stephen having an affair, he'd expected her to fall apart, maybe even to start drinking again, but she had been incredibly together. When Stephen refused to leave their house, she just packed the boys into her car, drove around to Will's house and moved in. He had two free bedrooms. He'd told her to stay as long as she liked. He thought it would be for a few nights but she'd told him yesterday that she had called a lawyer to discuss a divorce.

'Go home, Stephen,' he said. 'Or go to work.' Then he turned in the direction of the green, the dog stopping suddenly, every couple of yards, so that the carrier bag on Will's arm slammed uncomfortably against his thigh.

'Shit!' he said as metal connected painfully with his hip for the fourth time. The dog, as if it was following his instruction, squatted on the grass and did exactly that. A woman playing frisbee with two small boys turned to glare at him.

'Sorry,' he muttered, scooping up the disgusting mess in a plastic bag and holding it at arm's length to knot it.

He was sorry. Sorry that he wasn't sitting in his corner office on Lexington Avenue coming up with ideas for a TV spot for a soda drink instead of trudging around a dreary suburban estate in Dublin with a bag of shit belonging to a dog he didn't own. Sorry that he had been so stupid that he'd thought bringing Alice back to Dublin would fix anything.

*

Nora bubble-wrapped the ammonite table and copied the definition of 'Cephalopoda' from the encyclopaedia onto a white card and wrote 'Happy Birthday, Christopher!' That was the end of her dramatic window display, she realised. She was going to need something to carry her over while she decided what to put in there next.

It must have been the snail fossils that reminded her of the antique Belleek Tridacna tea set. She went up to the kitchen, took a cup off the china cabinet and held it up to the light. The porcelain was ridged and fluted, like a clam shell. The cup had a pair of feet shaped like sea snails.

She put them on a tray and carried them carefully back down to the shop. She hung the 'back in five' sign on the door, dashed to the florist and came back with six helium-filled balloons dancing on pale-green ribbons. She attached a ribbon to the handle of each cup then switched on her two fans at the lowest speed and let the cups drift and float up behind the glass.

Movement stopped people in their tracks, she'd noticed. People paused to look in the window and then drifted in to browse. Two sisters bought one another diamanté necklaces. An art teacher bought the queen conch shells that Hugh had brought Lainey from Hawaii. A pair of five-year-old twin boys with shaved heads played *Star Wars* with two of Hugh's walking sticks while their mother admired a pair of embroidered French linen sheets, still in their packaging. The woman wrestled the sticks away from the grumbling twins and put them back in the stand and turned to go, then came back to the desk. 'You know what that pair gave us for our wedding anniversary?' She nodded at the boys. 'Head lice. We had to cancel a romantic dinner to fight a long and horrible battle with nits and we won! So I'd like to buy those sheets. We deserve a bit of a reward.'

Nora tried to imagine Adam cancelling a meal out to comb through a child's scalp for nits and she suppressed a grim laugh. It would never have happened. He would have hired someone to do it. Or more likely, left her to it.

She was setting out a new set of sheets in the display cabinet, scattering them with sprigs of lavender, when a man came into the shop.

'Feel free to browse,' she said, over her shoulder. 'Let me know if you need any help.'

'I do need help, actually,' he sounded defensive.

Uhoh, she thought. Fiona had said she'd send Adonis over to sort out any trouble but her phone was on her desk, too far away to reach. He was in his late thirties with thick black hair that was beginning to grey and an interesting face – all hollow cheekbones and dark eyebrows and dark shadows beneath tired looking blue eyes. He had a huge dog tied to the end of a piece of washing line and a plastic bag which he put onto the desk now.

'I think this might be yours.'

Nora squared her shoulders, marched over and opened the bag and there, to her delight, was Lainey's silver-backed Tiffany hairbrush that had disappeared the previous week. 'I've been looking for this everywhere! I thought it had been stolen.'

'It was stolen,' he looked embarrassed, then ashamed, then desperate. 'But maybe it wouldn't have been if you had some kind of, I don't know, security system in here.'

'Sorry?' Nora stared at him, confused. Was he selling security systems? Was that what this was about?

'I don't mean to be critical, truly,' he frowned, 'but this place is an open invitation for shop lifters. You didn't even turn around to look at me when I came in. I could have walked out with your phone.' He nodded at the bubble-wrapped ammonite table. 'I could have hauled that off and you wouldn't have even noticed.'

I'd like to see you try to pick it up, Nora thought. Then she noticed the muscles in his arms and the breadth of his shoulders beneath his black T-shirt. He was a fraction under six feet, but he looked as if he worked out a lot. She forced herself to focus. 'I'm a bit lost here. Are you saying you stole that hairbrush from my shop? And that it's my fault?'

'No! Of course not!' He puffed out his cheeks with air and then let it out slowly. 'My daughter stole it,' he said apologetically. 'It's just, maybe she wouldn't have taken it if you were a bit more, I don't know, vigilant.'

'Vigilant?' Nora's voice was tight. The dog, sensing a row, scuttled over to Houdini and lay down. 'Right. Well, thank you for the advice.'

'You're welcome. Maybe it will stop things disappearing, you know? And I'm sorry and embarrassed, obviously, and I hope you'll accept my apology.' Had he made an apology? Nora wondered. If he had, she hadn't heard it. He pulled a wallet out of the back pocket of his jeans. 'What do I owe you?'

'Nothing,' Nora said. 'I'm just glad to get it back.'

'You don't understand, I don't want to return it,' he said very slowly, 'I want to buy it.'

'I do understand,' Nora said even more slowly. 'But it's not for sale.' Whether he had apologised or not, she didn't want him to have it.

'Fine. Okay.' He sighed wearily and he put his hands up as if he was surrendering. 'Well, I'm sorry to have disturbed you. Have a nice day!' He turned around and strode back to the door.

'Don't!' Nora yelled, but it was too late. He had already slammed it behind him sending a gust of air into the window. There was a moment's silence, then the smash and a tinkling sound.

Nora winced. She went over to the window and rolled up the backdrop. Three of the teacups were still bobbing in the air. All that was left of the others were the handles, still attached to the ribbons. Nora covered her face with her hands. Those cups had survived 120 years until this afternoon.

The door swung open. 'Don't worry!' It was the man again. 'I'll be out of your hair in two seconds, I just forgot the dog.' He frowned down at the pile of shards on the floor. 'What happened here?'

'You slammed the door,' she said flatly. 'But it's my fault.' It had been a stupid idea to tie delicate porcelain cups to balloons. She bent down and began picking up slivers of china.

'Stop! You'll cut yourself.' He looked around. 'Do you have a broom?'

'I can do this myself.' He didn't move, so she sighed and pointed at the back of the shop. He came back with the brush and handed it to her and stood, watching as she began to sweep the pieces up. 'I'm paying for those cups.'

'It's not about the money,' Nora made a pile of the splinters. He bent over, suddenly, and picked something out of the scatter of broken pieces. It was one of the tiny porcelain shell feet. Amazingly, it was still intact. Nora put out her hand and he handed it to her.

'So what is it about?'

Lainey had trusted Nora so much that she had let her play with her precious Belleek china. Nora remembered pouring imaginary tea into these cups. Hugh would add invisible lumps of sugar solemnly, then crook his little finger delicately and pretend to sip his tea daintily but her grandmother never had time to play. She was always too busy dusting or polishing or washing or sorting. But she would glance over and watch their game wistfully, as if she wanted to join in.

'It's about the memory,' she said, brushing the last pieces of the cups onto the dustpan and standing up. 'These belonged to my grandmother. She died in March.'

'Oh,' he said. 'I'm so sorry.' He looked around at the shelves of encyclopaedias, the pair of celandine-yellow velvet chairs, the globe cocktail cabinet, the stone garden lion with lichen on his mane. 'All of this was hers? The hairbrush too?'

Nora nodded.

'Oh God,' he sighed defeatedly. 'Talk about a bull in the china shop. I feel terrible. Can we start again?' He put out his hand. 'I'm Will Moran.'

Nora hesitated, then wiped her hand on her dress. 'Nora,' she said. 'Nora Malone.'

They shook hands quickly. She felt the fine grit of china dust between his thumb and her palm, the past, clinging to their fingertips like pollen.

'Listen, about before,' he said, after she had taken her hand back. 'I'm the one who should have been vigilant. It's not the first time my daughter has stolen things. She's been having a few problems lately. She took the brush as a gift to my sister and I wanted her to keep it because she just found that her husband is having an affair. Sorry,' he rubbed his hair with the flat of his hand, 'I think this is sounding a bit like a soap opera.'

It sounded horribly familiar to Nora.

She wouldn't let him pay for the cups but she sold him the brush and the matching mirror for his sister and she wrapped them in silver tissue paper and put them in a ribbon-handled bag.

'It's been nice meeting you, well, not nice, but,' he smiled ruefully. 'Interesting.' He turned to go.

'Don't forget your dog!' she called, as he opened the door carefully.

'He's not mine.' Will came back and picked up the length of washing line. 'He belongs to the people who live next to the house I'm renting but they're travelling and the friend who is supposed to be minding him can't manage him. My daughter took him in last night. He's the first thing she seems to actually like about this city.'

'Why don't you hold on to him, then?' Nora said. 'If their friend can't manage him. If your daughter's acting up, a dog might be best thing for her.'

Will looked at her, thoughtfully. 'Maybe you're right.' He looked at her and swallowed hard. 'Listen, you're going to think this is crazy but hear me out. You know what would be really good for Alice, my daughter? If you'd let her work here with you a couple of times.'

'I don't think...' Nora began.

'Unpaid, of course.' He cut across her. His face changed when he was enthusiastic. He didn't look so tired, his deep set blue eyes sparkled with enthusiasm. 'She's got every weekend free. It could be her way of making up for stealing from you and maybe if she was on the other side of the counter she'd realise that shoplifting was wrong. She's a nice kid, you know. She's just lost her way a bit. It's not her fault, it's hard being the child of a single parent and—' He stopped suddenly. 'Sorry. This is not your problem. I should be thanking you for not prosecuting her, not asking you to give her a job. I shouldn't have asked.'

He looked so completely dejected, that Nora softened.

'It's okay,' she said. 'It's not a bad idea actually. I could use a bit of help. Saturdays are getting really busy.'

The café was packed but Fiona spotted Nora and started making her a decaff latte.

'Those ancient snails on your grandmother's table are taking their time!' she yelled over the hissing and gurgling of the coffee machine. 'When are they going make it into the window?'

'I sold the table before I could put it in,' Nora yelled back.

The machine stopped. Fiona narrowed her green eyes. 'Did you get full price?'

Nora winced. 'Not exactly. But it went to a good home.'

'Which makes zero financial sense!' Fiona had appointed herself as Nora's unofficial accountant. She tapped the paper cup sharply on the counter to get rid of bubbles and topped it up with steaming milk. 'You can't lose sight of your targets.'

'It's okay! I'm actually ahead of my projections this week.' It was true. After an uneven start, Nora's fund for her mum was growing steadily. 'Plus I just got an offer of a free helper!'

Fiona stared at her as if she'd gone mad as she explained. 'You're hiring someone who stole from your shop?' she gasped. 'Who is basically a kleptomaniac? Good idea, Nora! Does she have a friend? A chef who nicks stock? A light-fingered waitress, maybe?'

'Everybody deserves the second chance,' Adonis said quietly. He was tossing handfuls of nuts and seeds into a giant mixing bowl, measuring everything by eye, the way he always did.

'You big softie!' Fiona gave him a dig with her elbow as she edged past him with Nora's takeaway soy latte.

'No! With this situation, everybody is the winner. Nora has someone to help,' he drizzled a spoonful of honey into the mix. 'This girl has a sense of responsibility.'

'That's what her father said.' Nora remembered the way Will's eyes had lit up when she said she'd give Alice a try. He had looked like a different person when he smiled.

'Well, you tell her I'll be watching her like a hawk!' Fiona handed over her coffee. 'Have you met her yet?'

'He brought her around to meet me yesterday.'

Nora had recognised Alice from the previous week, the day she must have taken the brush. A tall, thin, awkward-looking girl with dip-dyed blonde hair, the ends a bleached-out pink. A rash of spots on her chin. One arm covered with a tattoo sleeve. She'd held on tightly to the dog's washing-line leash and had scowled in a way that was probably supposed to be intimidating. 'Sorry about taking the brush,' she'd muttered.

'Apology accepted,' Nora had said, bending to stroke Mac. She recognised him too, now that she saw him again. The rangy body, the patchy coat, the paws with toes the size of peanuts. He belonged to Caroline who had bought the Moroccan prayer rug. He recognised her too. He'd buried his nose under her arm and swung his long skinny tufted tail like a pendulum, then strained on his leash to get over to Houdini. Alice had jerked him away and glared at Nora. Poor thing, Nora thought. This must be a teenager's worst nightmare, being dragged here to apologise to a stranger. 'We'll have fun,' she said cheerfully, sounding, she realised, just like her mother. 'See you Saturday.'

She had watched them cross the road afterwards: Will was talking to Alice, Alice was walking as far away from him as she could. Only the dog had looked back, turning his head almost 180 degrees to look at her over his shoulder to give Nora a conspiratorial look.

'What's he like?' Fiona handed Nora her coffee and waved her money away. 'The dad?'

Nora shrugged. 'He seems okay.' But he hadn't seemed okay really. It wasn't just the way he'd lost it over the brush. 'A bit stressed maybe.' And kind of vulnerable, she thought. It wasn't just her. Everyone had baggage, some hurt they were trying to get over.

Nora had scoured Temple Terrace hoping to find more of Lainey's notes. She had searched every bookcase, cleared out drawers, checked beneath beds and at the backs of cupboards. She had tracked down every romance novel in the house – there were hundreds – and paged through them carefully, afraid she would miss a few words scrawled in a margin, but none of them had been written on.

Then, one evening, Adonis, who had shifted the carved French Provincial chest, handed her two crumpled balls of paper he'd found in the bottom drawer.

'Maybe letters,' he said enigmatically, 'I don't know.'

Two more notes. This time, they were scribbled on the ripped-out flyleaves of two of Hugh's poetry books. The first was about the green silk scarf with the border of tiny elephants.

Lanvin scarf. 1960.

I lost the first two babies at ten weeks, one after another. I was convinced that it was a sign that I wasn't meant to have a child and I was too heartbroken to try again. For nearly three years, Hugh and I didn't talk about it. Then, the Christmas before I got pregnant with Alanna, Hugh gave me the green Lanvin scarf with the baby elephants on the border. Elephants never forget and neither did Hugh. It was his way of reminding me that I still had a chance to be a mother.

Two miscarriages! Poor Lainey! Nora bit her lip. She must have wanted a child so much.

She smoothed out the second note. It was written in the same blue biro, on both sides of the ripped-out page. There was no date on the top. Just two words in blue biro:

Gold Locket.

We called her 'Alanna', the Irish word for 'darling child'. The baby I thought I could never have.

She was all Hugh, from the moment she was born. Pale and fair and sunny. She had nothing of me in her. I felt like a fraud when she looked at me with those wide, trusting eyes. I was sure that if she knew the truth, she'd reject me.

I loved her so much but I was terrified that I'd hurt her. Even when she was feeding peacefully in my arms, my mind raced, as I imagined what would happen if I dropped her, if she slipped when I was bathing her. If I rolled over when she was sleeping and crushed her.

Hugh thought I was doing a great job but it wasn't me. It was Alanna. She was a perfect baby, calm and loving and sunny, even when she was teething. She'd suck happily on my old locket; she cut her two front teeth on it.

But the fear got worse. And after a year, I was so anxious that I just couldn't look after her any more and Hugh had to take over. I was ashamed but I was relieved too. I knew that she would be safer with him. I wasn't a fit mother.

Poor Lainey, Nora thought. She had lost two babies before they were born and then had given up her daughter. And poor Alanna. She believed that her mother never loved her.

The locket wasn't in any of her grandmother's jewellery boxes but Nora found it wrapped in a linen handkerchief and stuffed at the back of a small drawer in the dressing table. The chain was blackened and broken and the locket was tarnished but there they were, the tiny dents of her mother's teeth marks.

Alanna had made Nora promise that she would not send her any of Lainey's things, but the locket and the note about it were missing pieces of her story and no promise was going to stop Nora from sending them to her.

Gemma, Will's sister, dropped Alice off the first Saturday. This must be the woman who had just found out that her husband was having an affair, Nora realised, watching her curiously. She wondered if she had flashbacks to the moment she found out too, if she lay awake sometimes, wondering how she could have been taken in so easily that she hadn't even suspected anything.

But if Gemma lay awake at all, she was hiding it well. She was wearing full make up and a 1950s prom dress, bright red lipstick and a yellow headscarf, tied Grace Kelly style under her chin.

'Thank you for taking Alice on!' she whispered to Nora when Alice was putting her jacket away. 'You're an absolute lifesaver. I've been trying to keep her occupied at the weekends to keep her out of Will's hair. They're not getting on. Long story! But from now on, I'm going to be working on Saturdays. I'm retraining to be a hairdresser.'

'Wow! Good for you!' Nora said.

'It's hard going but I'm loving every moment of it!' Gemma sighed happily. 'It doesn't feel like work, when you're doing something you're passionate about, does it?'

She was floundering but Gemma grinned. 'I hope you're right!'

There was a long, awkward pause after she'd left. She'd let Alice break it, Nora decided. If she was going to serve customers, she'd have to get over her shyness and her hostility. The silence dragged on and on, but eventually, the girl wandered over and stood peering down at Houdini. 'How long has he been, like, dead?'

'At least seventy years,' Nora smiled. 'He was my grandfather's and they were pretty much the same age, although obviously, Houdini is older if you factor in dog years.'

Alice slow-blinked her mascara-caked lashes and clicked her tongue stud, then bent down and patted Houdini gently. 'What's he stuffed with?'

'Memories, mostly,' Nora said, not wanting to think about what else might be under Houdini's smooth coat. 'You want to get started?'

Alice shrugged and managed to summon up a scowl. 'I guess.'

Nora had scribbled a list of things for her to do. If she was going to be here every Saturday for the rest of the summer, she might as well make herself useful.

She chewed her hair and sighed a lot but as the day wore on, she seemed to forget her mood and she hummed along, out of tune, to whatever was playing into her headphones as she polished glasses and untangled necklaces and dusted and sorted four packs of original art deco playing cards into order.

The Italian screen that Nora had been using as a changing room sold during the week, so the following Saturday, Nora sent Alice to the hardware store for fishing wire and they put up a rail for a curtained-off area together. She seemed to enjoy doing practical things, anything that didn't involve talking to a customer.

It was now almost September and all the schools were holding their Debs balls. Nora had put out a rail of Lainey's evening dresses and pegged three of the loveliest ones to a washing line in the window, then set her fans to top speed. It was a simple idea but it looked absolutely magical. The silk and satin dresses billowing and dancing, as if they were caught in a summer breeze.

The window worked its magic and they were run off their feet all morning. Well, Nora was run off her feet, while Alice sat on a stool behind the desk, looking bored and doing the wrapping.

Nora helped a mother zip her daughter into an apricot chiffon shift dress with tiny gold rose sequins. It hung on her narrow body like a shimmering waterfall.

'I've got some evening gloves the very colour, if you want to try them?' she suggested.

The girl nodded slowly without taking her eyes off her reflection in the mirror.

'Oh my God! You look so beautiful,' her mother put her hand to her mouth. 'I think I might be going to cry!'

Nora and her Mum had gone shopping for her Debs dress when she was eighteen. Alanna had been horrified by the whole notion of a coming out dance and she had muttered darkly about the oppression of patriarchy and the anachronism of debutantes in the 21st century. Then she had spent far more than she could afford on a boned, navy satin and told Nora that it made her look like a 1950s Italian movie star. 'Not that I approve of movie stars.' she'd said. 'Or the way women were treated in the 1950s.' Nora smiled to herself remembering it.

'Alice, can you run up to the hall and bring down the box of bags and gloves I left at the bottom of the stairs?'

Alice didn't seem to hear her. She was staring at the mother and daughter wistfully. Poor thing, Nora thought, going upstairs herself to find the gloves. Beneath all that make up and that attitude, she was as insecure and vulnerable as any fifteen year old. She needed looking after.

Alice ignored her salad and sat picking purple nail varnish off her fingers while Nora ate.

'If you don't want to eat that, I can run over to the café again and get you something else,' Nora said.

Alice shrugged. 'It just feels kind of weird eating in here,' she looked around the shop, 'surrounded by dead people's stuff. I can't even go into my dad's room at home. He's got all these boxes of my mom's stuff. It's creepy.'

'Oh!' Nora let her words sink in. 'I didn't realise your mum was dead, Alice. I'm so sorry.'

'It's okay.' Alice pushed her sandwich away and sniffed. 'I was, like, three months old when she died. I didn't even know her.'

Nora nodded. 'I didn't know my father either.'

'Really?' Alice looked up at her. 'Is he, like, dead too?'

'I have no idea. My mother only met him once. I wasn't exactly planned.'

'You were not a mistake, though,' Alanna had told her. 'You were the best thing that ever happened to me.'

Nora lined up the edamame beans on her paper plate. 'They met at a music festival. She tried to find him to tell him but—'

'Maybe he didn't want to be found,' Alice said tartly.

'Maybe,' Nora said, smoothly. 'But I know what you mean, about not missing someone you never knew. My mother was incredible, though I didn't always think so at the time. Every time we settled somewhere, she got restless. I think I lived in a dozen places before I was eight.'

'My dad's the opposite,' Alice snorted. 'We lived in this one tiny apartment but we could never move anywhere because of my mom.'

'I'm sorry,' Nora said softly. 'That must have been so hard for you.'

'Not really.' Alice lifted one shoulder in a small shrug. 'I don't even remember her. But my dad is, like, obsessed with her. You know, when we moved to Ireland, he brought all her stuff instead of mine. It was, like, weird.'

It wasn't weird, Nora thought, it was sad. She wanted to ask more. To find out when Will's wife had died and how, but she forced herself not to ask.

She gave Alice a box of costume jewellery to sort through then took the gold locket out of the drawer and Lainey's note about it. She pulled out a card and wrote it quickly then copied the post restante address she had for her mother in Bali onto a jiffy bag.

'Could you run out and post this?' she asked Alice.

Alice put down a diamanté bracelet and turned her head to read the address.

'Is Alanna Malone your sister?'

'No. My mother.'

'Is she on holiday?'

'No, she's working on a farm.'

'Really?' Alice clicked her tongue ring. 'Isn't she, like, really old?'

'Yep!' Nora handed over ten euros. 'Now scoot!' She wanted this done before she could change her mind.

Fiona had said never to trust Alice with money and never to leave Alice alone in the shop, but later that afternoon, on impulse, Nora turned to her.

'Could you look after the shop for an hour?'

'You mean, like, sell things?' Alice said. 'Serve customers?' Nora nodded. Alice would have refused three weeks ago, but now she sniffed. 'I guess so.'

Nora set a timer on her phone and forced herself to stay upstairs for sixty minutes, trying not to wonder if Alice was stealing something.

When she came back Alice was giddy with excitement. 'You were ages! Where were you?' She gabbled through the list of things she had sold: three glass decanters in a tantalus; a diamanté brooch; the hummingbird tureen...

'That's wonderful!' Nora grinned. 'Well done.'

Alice opened the drawer they used for cash. 'The money is all there. You can count it if, you like.'

'No.' Nora closed it firmly. 'I don't need to. I trust you.'

*

Nora had sent Alice to the stationery shop for a roll of glue dots. The shop was quiet, so she opened her laptop to check the prices for some new things she had brought down. Somewhere between eBay and 1stdibs, she decided to check Facebook. And at the top of her timeline was one of those Facebook Memory shots. A photograph of her and Adam, exactly a year ago.

It had been taken by a waiter in a restaurant in Ibiza, where they'd gone for a weekend to celebrate Adam's birthday. Nora had spent two uncomfortable hours having fake lashes applied one by one, and half an hour being waxed within an inch of her life and a hundred pounds on a very tight white Reiss bodycon dress which had felt, in the heat, like a corset. She looked uncomfortable, she thought. Adam looked as he always did, beautiful and effortlessly at ease, that half smile aimed directly at the camera. She stared at the picture and she felt as if she was looking at a couple of strangers.

The door opened suddenly and Fiona burst in, tottering slightly in her trademark heels, with a cardboard tray of takeaway coffees in one hand and a paper bag in the other. 'I got the bastard!' she said with satisfaction. 'The clamper! I saw him ticketing Laura's Micra and I chased him halfway along Idrone Terrace, scared the living daylights out of him! But I got myself too.' She twisted her mouth into a sad clown smile. 'I think I've ruined my dress.'

Nora saw the dark spreading stain of coffee on the pale-blue skirt. 'Hang on!' She hurried up to the kitchen and came back with a basin of ice cubes. She grabbed a pink-and-black prom-style cocktail dress off a hanger and handed it to Fiona. 'If we're quick, we might be able to save it!'

Fiona passed the coffee-stained dress out of the changing area and Nora began to rub the skirt with ice cubes. A moment later, Fiona emerged holding out the full skirts of Lainey's dress. She did a pirouette. 'Why did sweetheart necklines go out of fashion? This is so flattering.' But actually Nora thought it wasn't flattering at all. Fiona was on a punishing diet-and-exercise plan for a wedding she was going to in October. Her clavicle bones were like crossed blades.

Fiona pulled up a chair beside Houdini. 'So where's the Artful Dodger?'

'Alice? I sent her to pick up some stationery.'

Fiona snorted. 'Well, I hope she's going to pay for it.'

She upended the paper bag. A half-dozen tiny brownies dusted with icing sugar fell out onto the plate. She rearranged them, like dominos.

'Adonis's latest drug. Beetroot instead of chocolate. Medjool dates instead of sugar, sixty calories a pop. Like class A drugs. Have one, if you can. Most people don't stop till they've had five.'

Nora shook her head. 'I'm not having one unless you do.'

'You're condemning me to another thirty minutes on the treadmill but... what the hell!' Fiona picked one up and broke off a tiny corner.

Nora slotted a whole square into her mouth. The dusting was hazelnut powder, not sugar. It was so delicious that she picked up another one immediately.

'So,' Fiona's green eyes were glittering with mischief, 'who's the hot guy?'

Nora's mouth was too full to reply so she raised an eyebrow and shrugged.

'The handsome one you're stalking on Facebook! You left your laptop open and I just happened to look. Very nice!'

Nora's throat closed around a lump of brownie. Her breath caught behind it. She felt her face flush.

'Ah! The old "my mouth is full and I can't speak" trick!' Fiona grinned. 'Well, I can sit here all day, if I have to!' The grin faded. 'Are you okay, Nora? Are you choking?' She pulled a tissue out of her pocket. 'Here! Spit it out!'

Nora shook her head but the chocolatey mess was coming back up. She grabbed the tissue and let it out. Her nose and her eyes were streaming and hazelnut drool was running down her chin. She dropped her head and put her hands over her face.

'Oh Nora.' Fiona came around the desk and crouched beside her, slid an arm around her back. 'What is it?' The kindness in her voice just made Nora cry harder. Slowly, as the sobs died down, the whole story came out.

Fiona's face was flushed with anger by the time Nora was finished. 'How could they do that to you? I'm so sorry, Nora!' Fiona ducked her head so that she could look into Nora's face. 'And so proud of you! They left you with nothing! No job. No home and look at you now! Look at what you've done! You are amazing! Absolutely amazing.'

Nora cut her off. 'No. I'm not. I'm stupid and gullible. I loved him, Fiona. I thought he was the one. How can I ever trust myself again?'

'Bullshit.' Fiona lifted Nora's chin gently so that they were eye to eye. 'You trusted your instincts and set up this beautiful shop to help your mother. You trust Adonis and Ed and Loughlin with all your grandmother's precious things. You trust me to give you advice, which I admit,' she wiped a smear of chocolate off Nora's chin, 'has been a job of work! You even trust bloody Alice who is probably robbing your change right now! Oh!' She looked over Nora's shoulder. 'Oh, hello, Alice!' The girl had slipped in from the doorway that led to the house. Fiona stood up and Nora wiped her eyes quickly with the soggy tissue. 'How long have you been standing there?'

Alice ignored her and dumped two carrier bags on the floor with a clatter. Tinny rap music, like a trapped wasp, poured from one of her dangling ear buds.

'She can't hear you!' Nora said.

If Alice couldn't hear her, Fiona thought, then why was she looking at her as if she'd like to murder her?

Nora was going to put out the two rococo over-mantel mirrors and paint the question she'd asked her grandfather onto the glass. 'Why are there so many mirrors, Granddad?'

After she had finished filling in the letters, she decided to gild them, which turned out to be incredibly fiddly. 'Look at me,' she grumbled to Houdini, 'stuck in a hot sweaty window on a gorgeous Sunday afternoon, gilding the bloody lily, literally.' But the truth was, she was enjoying herself hugely. Making a window was the thing that made her happiest and she was humming to herself when a knock on the window made her jump. She looked up to see a man's face, inches from her own. Her brush slipped, leaving a slash of gold on the glass.

It was just Will, she realised. He was all in black, dark jeans, dark T-shirt, sunglasses that he took off as she looked up. She wiped her hands on her shirt and opened the door. Mac gave her a joyful sideways look and a flying lick and shot past her to Houdini. He greeted him as if they were long-lost friends, sniffing and whinnying and wagging his tail so hard that it upset a tray she'd balanced on a stool. A dozen tiny pots of model-maker's paint rolled away to the four corners of the shop.

'Mac! You idiot!' Will dashed around retrieving the pots, pulling out his T-shirt and making it into a well to gather them into.

'It's okay, they're empty,' Nora caught a flash of his tanned stomach above the waistband of his jeans and she looked away quickly and noticed that the shirt of Hugh's she was wearing barely covered her thighs and that her legs were bare and paint spattered.

'Sorry, I didn't mean to crash in on you.' Will dropped the pots onto the desk. 'Gemma took Alice and the boys to Brittas Bay for the day and I needed a walk and –' he hesitated – 'there's something I have to ask you.' He sighed. He pulled a small glittering chain out of his pocket and held it out. 'Did Alice steal this?' Nora stepped closer, wishing she'd had a shower earlier. On his palm was one of Lainey's loveliest necklaces. A fine gold chain with a blue enamel kingfisher that had a tiny chip of sapphire for an eye. She hadn't even noticed that it was missing. She wasn't sure what to say, but she didn't have time to hesitate.

'No,' she lied. 'I gave it to her to thank her for all the hard work she's been doing.

'Thank you!' Will looked up at the ceiling and exhaled deeply. 'I saw it and I thought, oh here we go again. You've made my day!' He perched on the edge of the desk and smiled at her. He seemed in no hurry to go.

Nora waited a minute then she picked up her paint pot. 'Do you mind if I just get the window finished? I'm on the last letter. If it dries when it's half done, I'll have to do the whole word again.'

'Sure!'

Nora squeezed back into the window and climbed onto the bottom rung of the ladder, pulling the hem of the shirt down as far as she could, aware of those blue eyes, watching her.

'What are you writing?' he asked, trying to read the words backwards.

She told him about the question she had asked her grandfather and what he'd replied.

'Wow! Sounds like your grandparents were soulmates,' he said.

Nora caught a drip of gold paint with her fingernail and wiped it on her shirt. She thought about the sadness and the darkness between the lines of Lainey's notes. 'I don't know. They definitely loved one another but I think it was complicated. I had no idea how complicated until I started clearing the house.' Why was she telling him this? She barely knew him. 'Can you hand me those?' She pointed at a box of Q-tips. 'I thought I was finished but I just realised that the whole window is covered in my fingerprints.'

He handed her the box, then took one and stepped up to the glass.

'Oh no!' she said, afraid he'd smudge a letter. 'Don't! Please!'

'Trust me!' he said in a gravelly voice, only a note deeper than his own. 'I'm an art director.'

She asked him what he'd done in New York as they cleaned. He told her about the three hundred-person creative department he'd run, the accounts they handled.

'It sounds like a lot of pressure,' Nora said.

He nodded. 'It's the kind of pressure I like.' He rubbed at a tiny fleck of paint until the glass squeaked. 'I'm lost without the routine of work. I've got a spot as Creative Director in the Dublin office starting in September. But honestly, I don't know if I'll be able to take it. It all hangs on whether Alice settles at school. If she doesn't, I'll have to take her back to the States.' He sighed. 'What about you? What made you decide to leave London, if that's not a personal question?'

'No,' Nora said without looking at him. 'No, it's not personal at all.' She didn't want to talk about Adam and Liv. She didn't want to think about them. So she told him she'd come back to clear the house because her mother was travelling. 'Once every-thing is sold and the house is gone, the shop will be closed so I'll probably have to go back to London. There's nothing for me here anymore.' It was true, she realised with a twinge of panic. All her work contacts were in the UK. She suppressed a twinge of panic. She couldn't face the thought of going back now, but she might feel different in three months. She reached for a tissue to wipe her hands. 'I think we're done.'

'Good job,' Will said, craning his head back and forth, inspect-ing the glass. 'So do you need a hand with anything else?' He scratched a paint spot off one wrist and looked at her hopefully.

'You might regret it!' Nora said.

He grinned. 'Try me!'

Will held the delicate carved, gilded frames while Nora unscrewed them from the wall, then they carried them carefully down the narrow corridor to the shop. He held them again as she screwed them carefully to the heavy wooden struts she'd made, then they went outside to take a look.

The gilded letters glinted in the early evening sunshine. Nora had angled the mirrors so they reflected the high gilded clouds above the roof of the library.

'We did good!' Will said. 'We did pretty amazing, actually,' he grinned at her. 'I think we deserve a beer.'

Nora tugged at her sweaty, paint-stained shirt. 'I'm not really dressed for a bar.'

He looked her up and down quickly. 'I think you look pretty cool but, tell you what, why don't we grab a couple to take out?'

The thought of a cold beer after her long, hot afternoon in the window was too tempting to turn down. She nodded.

Mac walked ahead of them along the sun-baked, sleepy street and Nora waited outside the off-licence with him while Will bought two bottles of Rolling Rock.

A breeze blowing up from the beach dried the sweat on the back of Nora's shirt as they walked along the terrace to the shop. She could smell the fragrance of gorse blowing down from Killiney Hill. She imagined London baking in the last flare of

August heat. Parched parks. Hot pavements. Air heavy with the smell of diesel. She didn't miss it, not today. She was glad to be beside the sea.

They sat on the floor near the open door of the shop, their backs to the wall. Will levered the caps off the bottles with a coin and passed one to Nora.

'Cheers!' They clinked.

Nora took the first cooling sip. It was delicious against the back of her parched throat.

'So,' Will tilted his head back and nodded at the ceiling. 'This is quite a house. Does it belong to your family?'

Nora rested the bottle against her collarbone as she told him about her grandparents and about sorting through their things before the house was sold. He asked her where she got the ideas for her windows.

She smiled. 'They just come into my head fully formed. Though most of them are sparked by notes my grandmother left behind.'

'You do know that they're pretty incredible, don't you? I mean I've seem some pretty amazing window displays in New York but yours are something else again.'

'Thank you!' Nora said, pleased. 'That means a lot.'

'What were the notes about?' Will asked.

It seemed too intimate to talk about with a stranger. 'They're memories, fragments of her life. They're kind of like a disjointed diary with a lot of gaps. Sometimes I think maybe she left them for me to find. And sometimes, I wonder if I'm even supposed to be reading the notes at all. They're pretty intimate and she was such a private person.'

'I don't know. I think sometimes diaries are meant to be read,' Will said. 'I wouldn't dream of reading Alice's now, but I used to read it when she was little. I wanted to make sure she was doing okay, you know? I thought I could fix anything that went wrong but now –' He shook his head. 'Well, let's just say, I don't have to read her diary to know that she hates me.'

'She's a teenager.' Nora wriggled down a bit to get more comfortable. 'All teenagers hate their parents. Didn't you hate yours?'

Will shrugged. 'Not really. I felt kind of sorry for them, actually.

They were just lost really, trying to deal with my younger sister, Gemma was pretty wild in her teens. What about you? Did you rebel against yours?'

'It was just my mum and me and no,' Nora smiled ruefully. 'My mother was the one who acted like a teenager. I was little Miss Sensible, always trying to protect her. But I look back now and I'm in awe of her. Single parents don't have it easy.'

He nodded, a sigh escaping. 'That's the truth. So, did you and your mom live here, in this house with your grandparents?'

'God! No! We lived pretty much everywhere else. London, Limerick, Cork, Clare, Galway, Mayo. A dozen places in Dublin.'

He whistled. 'That's a lot of moving around. Which place did you like most?'

Nora sifted through the memories of the cramped flats above rows of shops, the smell of takeaway food and the noise of the traffic drifting up from the street below. The house-shares with strangers, kitchens where everyone's food had labels. The commune in Clare where she had been home-schooled for a while. The borrowed cottage by the sea in Mayo with a single stove that her mum kept going somehow all through one Baltic winter.

'If I had to pick one, it would be the flat opposite the cinema in Rathmines. My mum made friends with the ushers, she kind of befriended everybody. And they'd sneak us in to watch a movie whenever we wanted.'

Her childhood hadn't been conventional. The places they had lived had been shabby and they had always been broke. Alanna hadn't been able to give her stability, she thought, but she'd given her so much variety. Those afternoons they'd spent in the popcorn scented dark, watching the same film over and over were some of her happiest memories

Will watched Nora from the corner of his eye as she talked. Her beer bottle was empty now and she was picking the label off carefully, with a gold-spattered thumbnail. He should probably go soon, let her get on with her work. Walk the dog then go back to the empty house. He had promised Gemma that he'd move into the box room, so that the boys could have the larger bedroom. But he wished he'd bought four beers instead of two now so he could stay here sitting on the floor drinking cold beer, talking to this softly spoken woman, breathing in the smell of the sea air wafting in the door.

Nora wondered what Adam would think if he could see her sitting here having a beer with this man. She wished he could see her. He had always hated it when she paid attention to a barman or a waiter or a client. Even though he was the one who had been unfaithful, he would hate to think of her enjoying the company of anyone else.

Maybe it was that, or maybe it was the fact that she'd been holed up in the shop all day. But when Will said he was taking Mac for a walk to Dun Laoghaire, she asked him to hang on and went upstairs and changed into a clean dress of Lainey's, and then she went along too.

Alice and Mac were inseparable until it was time for the dog to have a walk, then she disappeared off to her bedroom and left Will to it, which was fine with him. He hadn't signed up for a new gym yet and he needed the exercise. Plus, it gave him an excuse to hang out with Nora.

He'd drop in at around the time she was closing the shop and they'd walk the pier in Dun Laoghaire or take the path that ran by the train tracks overlooking the sea or they'd walk inland, cutting through the mazes of suburban estates in Monkstown and Killiney, where the air was smoky with the smell of barbecues and gangs of kids lay sprawled in the long grass on the green, eking out the last few days of their summer holidays.

Will was usually guarded around women. He had dreaded dating back in the States. The posturing, the props, the expensive dinners where two people pretended to be relaxed while they basically interviewed. He had hated the mutual admissions about romantic history. The inevitable questions about Alice's mother and the moment of disclosure when he had to put it out there that he was a widower. The way it defined him made him an object of pity.

But with Nora, on those walks, conversations meandered pleasantly. He'd talk about advertising, she'd tell him about an idea she'd had for a window. They'd chat about films or books or childhood memories. She didn't talk about her past or ask about his and he felt his armour loosen and then, melt away. It helped, maybe, that he was too grateful to Nora for giving Alice a chance to be guarded around her.

Saturdays at the shop were the highlight of his daughter's week, not that she told him that, but he'd overhear her telling Gemma and the boys about serving a customer or helping Nora with a display and listening to the pride in her voice made him feel ridiculously happy.

Nora insisted that Alice was the one who was doing her a favour, but that was just like her. She thought nothing of helping a stranger or giving up her glamorous career in London to make money for her mother.

Sometimes, on the way back from their walks, Will and Nora would drop into the Café LoCal on the way back for something to eat or a glass of wine. Will caught the owner, Fiona, giving him that warning look that said, 'Don't mess with my friend'. But he looked right back at her. He didn't have anything to hide. He and Nora had found themselves back in Dublin, after years of being away, neither of them had any friends in the city, they were in the same boat, but it was completely platonic. It wasn't that Nora wasn't attractive, because she was. She was gorgeous obviously. With all that dark hair and her brown eyes and her olive skin, she looked more Italian than Irish. But he sensed that she wasn't looking for a relationship and neither was he.

He had to focus on finding his feet back in Dublin, looking after his sister and her kids and most importantly, getting his daughter settled in, which wasn't easy. After another blazing row with Alice about going back to New York, or a couple of days of being sent to Coventry after she finally agreed to get fitted for a school uniform, Will was grateful to be able to take time out and enjoy Nora's company. At least that's what he told himself, until the night of Nora's surprise party.

Will had enrolled Alice in the school Jake attended, but she flat out refused to go. Then suddenly, at the end of August, a few days before term started, she caved in and agreed to give it a try and Gemma said she'd bring her into town to shop for a uniform.

Will dropped them at the Dart and then went to the Café LoCal to celebrate with a double espresso.

'What are you doing Friday night, Will?' Fiona asked him as she filled his takeaway cup.

'Um.' Will looked at her wide, unblinking green eyes and felt his eyebrow go up involuntarily.

'Jesus! God! No!' she babbled. It was the first time Will had seen her flustered. She was usually completely unflappable but now she was blushing. 'I'm not asking you out! I'm checking to see if you can come to Nora's party.'

'I don't know.' Will felt relieved and then offended. He and Nora were friends, weren't they? So if she was having a party, why hadn't she invited him?

'It's a surprise, for her 33rd birthday.' Fiona turned away to slide a cinnamon and carob Danish into a bag and by the time she turned back, she was back to herself. 'So you can't say a word! Are you in?'

'Sure,' Will said, 'I guess.'

Fiona flashed her dazzling smile and passed him his pastry and his coffee. 'I thought you might be,' she said, meaningfully.

Julia used to laugh at Will's poker face. He had always been terrible at keeping secrets. He was afraid that, if he saw Nora, he'd blurt something out about the party, so he stayed away from the shop for the rest of the week. He missed their walks and, by the time he got the café on Friday, he couldn't wait to see her.

The place was already filling up with people. There was a contagious air of excitement and complicity. Fiona had invented a catering awards ceremony and Nora had reluctantly agreed to get dressed up and go along with her. At the last minute, they were going to swing by the café and there they'd all be, waiting for her. Will hadn't had an evening out since he left New York and he found he was enjoying himself as he drank Mojito Punch and waited for her to appear.

Everyone was friendly. Adonis, the chef, gave him the name of a good local gym. Nora's solicitor, an elderly man called Loughlin, invited him to join him for a swim in Sandycove the following Sunday. When Will mentioned that he might be house hunting soon, a young guy called Ed started filling him in on the state of the Irish property market.

For a minute or two, Will forgot to watch the door and then suddenly, there were cheers and there was Nora, in a yellow dress with a sunflower print, her hair loose and a look of absolute shock on her face. Will had an urge to hurry over and put his arm around her to comfort her, but before he could, the others surrounded her and he had to stand back, waiting for his turn to talk to her.

Finally, they were face-to-face. He wanted to kiss her cheek, the way everyone else had but for some reason he couldn't explain to himself, or maybe didn't want to, that seemed wrong.

'Hi!' he said, woodenly.

'Hi.' Nora's eyes flitted away and she tucked a springy curl behind one ear.

They stood there awkwardly. Will had chatted easily to her for hours on their evening walks but now, he couldn't seem to find any words. He was aware, suddenly of the lemony smell of her perfume and the length of her eyelashes and the tiny dip in the centre of her full top lip. These things must have always been there, but he was only now noticing them.

Nora cleared her throat and tugged at a curl. 'So how's your week been?'

'Oh,' he rocked back on his heels, like a tongue-tied teenager, unable to meet her eyes. 'You know, busy.'

'Me too,' she said, awkwardly.

Another long silence. This one was so thick that if Will had leaned across the counter and picked up one of Adonis's knives, he could have cut it. He was beginning to think that he couldn't take the tension for another second, when Fiona rescued him.

'Monopolising the party girl!' she scolded. 'That's not allowed, she's supposed to mingle.'

She dragged Nora off to meet a couple who had just arrived and Will, who felt as if he had been holding his breath for about an hour, exhaled. Jesus, he thought, watching the woman who owned the flower shop giving Nora a bouquet. What had just happened there? Whatever it was, he hoped it wasn't going to happen again. He and Nora were friends, the last thing he wanted to do was complicate that.

Will started his new job at the Dublin agency the week after the party. There was a mountain of work to get through – clients to meet, the creative team to meet, politics to negotiate. This was what he was good at, the reason he'd risen so high, so quickly back in New York. The reason they'd wanted him to come to Dublin. But, infuriatingly, he couldn't focus. Sitting in a meeting or reviewing a creative presentation, he would think of her name. Nora Malone, and have to suppress the urge to say it out loud, just to hear the sound of it.

By Tuesday afternoon, he knew he was starting to wonder if he was losing his mind. The only way to deal with this, he decided was to face her, to try to get things back to normal after the weirdness of the party. He left the office and drove home and picked up Mac and got to Nora's as she was closing up.

'Hey,' she said, brightly, looking up from her desk, 'you left the party early on Friday.'

He let go of Mac's leash so the dog could curl up beside Houdini. 'Big day on Monday.'

'I forgot, how did it go?'

'Good! Great!' he said. In fact it had been hell. What was good, what was great, was that the tension of Friday seemed to have disappeared completely. 'You want to come for a walk?'

'Love to,' she said lightly. 'But I'll need to get something warmer to wear.'

Nora bounded up the stairs to her room and closed the door and leaned against it. Talk about being caught off guard, it had gone okay, she thought, checking her face in the last remaining mirror on the wall, hadn't it? She hadn't blushed, she hadn't been tongue-tied, she'd kept it light and friendly and so had he.

She had thought something was wrong last week when Will hadn't shown up at the shop and then, at the party he'd acted so bored and then he left without even saying goodbye and she'd had to put on a bright face and pretend that she wasn't disappointed. She'd woken up on Saturday morning with a mojito hangover and the realisation that, at some stage in the last few weeks, she'd started to have feelings for him. She had spent the whole weekend talking sense to herself. Will wasn't interested in anything more than friendship, and that was a good thing. She had come a long way, but she was still getting over Adam's affair, the last thing she needed was to have her heart broken again.

She grabbed a pale grey cardigan with tiny pearl buttons from the wardrobe and picked up her sketchpad so she could show Will some drawings she'd made of one of Lainey's brooches, then she hurried downstairs again to join him.

Nora decided it would be good for Alice to be left on her own the following Saturday so she went upstairs for an hour to get a start on clearing Hugh's study. When she came back down Alice's eyes were glittering with excitement.

'Oh my God! It was, like, *so* busy when you were gone!' she gabbled. 'An old lady bought the brass hat stand. She tried to get a discount but she looked really rich so I said no. And some really small kids came in with their dad and he bought them that gold and turquoise necklace. And another lady wanted to put a deposit on six of the pink-and-white plates. I wasn't sure how much to ask for so I said fifty. She'll come back with the rest on Monday, if that's okay.'

'It's not okay,' Nora laughed. 'It's brilliant! You're amazing! What would I do without you?'

Alice shrugged, nonchalantly. 'It was no big deal really.'

After they'd closed up, when Alice was leaving, Nora called her back. 'I was wondering if you'd like to help me to design the next window?'

'Are you serious?' Alice's eyes widened in delight. 'I'd love to!'

When she was gone, Nora locked up and walked to the café. Laura was serving tables. Fiona and Adonis were behind the counter, doing something complicated to a watermelon with cheese wire.

'Will was just in,' Fiona said. 'You missed him.'

'Really?' Nora said trying to keep the disappointment out of her voice. Will probably had better things to do on a Saturday night than hang out with her, though truthfully, she could have done with the company. 'What are you up to tonight?' she asked Fiona.

'Late night shopping. I have nothing to wear for this wedding in October.'

Fiona had more clothes than anyone Nora had ever met, except, maybe, Lainey. 'You need help?'

Fiona looked up, surprised. 'That's sweet but no. I go into military-operation mode when I shop. You'd cramp my style.'

'No problem!' Nora shrugged, not very convincingly. 'I need to get on with clearing the study anyway.'

She picked up some miso-glazed aubergine and a wholemeal doughnut with raw chilli chocolate for dinner and walked back to Temple Terrace the long way, by the sea. A super-moon was hanging on the horizon and people had stopped to lean their elbows on the wall and admire it. Everyone seemed to be in twos and Nora didn't want to stop, afraid that she'd look as lonely as she felt. She had Will's number, he had given it to her in case there was a problem with Alice, but they had kept it casual so far. No calling, no texting. It would break some unwritten rule of their friendship if she asked him to meet her and he might think it meant something. But it didn't mean anything, she told herself, as she opened the door of the house, except that she was dreading tackling Hugh's study.

She had started sifting through the study a week ago and had abandoned it because she'd been in a rush. She needed to do this thoroughly. She was hoping she might find the pages Lainey had torn out of Hugh's books, but instead she found a collection of old receipts, bank statements, tax returns, chequebooks, Trade Board memos on yellowed paper, flimsy faxes whose print had all but disappeared, travel itineraries, old-fashioned airline tickets, books with silky covers and multicoloured carbon copies. There was also a stack of gilt-edged invitations to receptions dating back to 1953. Hugh's working life had been reduced to these piles of paper which she would have to throw away.

She was on the last drawer of the filing cabinet, stacking up a thick pile of spiral-bound reports, when she found a plastic folder. She opened it, expecting more memos, but instead she found a bundle of passports, held together with a rubber band.

She opened them one by one, smiling at photographs of Hugh. Tiny windows that showed him at twenty, thirty, forty, fifty. She flicked through them to read the coloured stamps and stapled-in visas: China, Turkey, Brazil, Japan, Indonesia, the US.

When she came to the last passport in the bundle, she stopped. This was different. The others had the Irish harp stamped onto faded green-linen covers. This was just four pages of yellowed paper held together with rusty staples. The print on the front was in a language and an alphabet that Nora didn't recognise, Greek maybe, but she knew the face in the faded black and white photograph immediately.

The café had closed for the night but the light was on and Fiona came to the door when Nora knocked.

'I took a rain check on the shopping trip,' she said. 'We have just invented the most incredible watermelon sorbet with frozen geranium-leaf tuiles. It's absolutely mind-blowing. I'll get you some from the freezer.'

'Adonis,' Nora put the stapled pages on the counter. 'Is this Greek?'

He dried his hands carefully on a piece of kitchen paper and walked over slowly and bent over to examine them. 'Yes.' He picked up the pages and studied them. 'These are travel papers for a person called Eleni Demetriou. Born in Kriti – Crete,' he corrected himself, 'in 1933.'

That was the year Lainey had been born, but she had been born in London, not Crete, Nora thought, hadn't she?

Adonis pointed at the photograph. 'She is very like you, this Eleni Demetriou.'

Nora nodded slowly. 'She's my grandmother.'

8

Silver-Grey Marabou Feather Shrug

Fiona

Carl had come back into Fiona's life on an unexpectedly cold, wet summer morning, appearing, like a sexy, denim-clad genie, from a pile of bills. She was standing at the till, flipping through them, keeping an eye on Laura, who was taking orders and Adonis, who was behind the counter, flattening balls of cauliflower pizza bases with his fist, oblivious to the trio of besotted businesswomen who seemed to have forgotten the agenda for their breakfast meeting.

The Lo-Cal was packed with holiday makers sheltering from the weather. They wiped the rain off their sunglasses with napkins and stashed their buckets and spades beneath the tables and ordered cinnamon soy lattes and egg-white omelettes and hot spelt scones as if they had trudged through Arctic wastes to get there.

They had already polished off most of the hazelnut butter shortbread, Fiona noticed, as she slipped a finger under the gummed flap of a heavy cream envelope. Adonis should really get another batch into the oven before the eleven o'clock crowd arrived.

She pulled out the tasteful, gilt-edged invitation and grinned. Andrea, one of her suppliers, was getting married. It had been a whirlwind romance, just two months from meeting to proposal. Proof that these things happen, Fiona thought, even if they only ever happened to other people. Her eye skipped down to the name of the groom and her smile froze. Darren Cross. There could only be one. Fifteen years ago, he had been the king of sixth-year cool, the boy who had called her 'Fat Fiona' or 'Double F' for short.

They'd all be there, she thought, Carl would probably be the best man. She crushed the card into a ball in her fist. When she looked up, Adonis was watching her, his huge hands expertly tossing a ball of dough, stretching it into a whirling, wobbling wheel that he would bake to a light crisp for Fiona's legendary two hundred-calorie pizza.

'What is it?' his dark eyes asked. After two years working side by side in the tiny kitchen of the café, he had developed the knack of reading her mind.

Fiona shoved the crushed invitation into the pocket of her frilled apron and pointed at the almost empty tray of shortbread. 'We're running out!' she mouthed. One of Adonis's spectacular eyebrows lifted a fraction. He knew she was fobbing him off but he still brought the pizza base down to earth with a flop. One of the businesswomen gave a flirty little 'yay', which he ignored. He wiped his floury hands on his black apron and strode off to the storeroom to get a new batch started.

Fiona tossed the invitation into the recycling box. She'd RSVP with an excuse and send over a lovely gift later. But she kept thinking about the invitation all day. And when she had closed the café, when Adonis and Laura had left, she retrieved it from the box.

She stared at it and then turned to examine her reflection in the window. It was still a surprise to realise that this was what she looked like. This slim, petite woman with the cap of feather-cut hair and the wasp-waisted navy dress. She was at least three pounds over her ideal weight and her hair needed highlighting, and she didn't have a plus-one, but the wedding wasn't until October. She'd have plenty of time to get all that sorted, wouldn't she? She would bloody well go, she thought, if only to see the looks on their faces when they saw what she had transformed into.

By the end of September, Fiona was down to seven and half stone. She'd had two chemical peels, a course of micro-dermabrasion, and a round of injectables. She had bought and returned four dresses and she was still looking.

The plus-one was proving to be as elusive as the dress. Tinder had been a disaster so she paid five hundred euros to join an exclusive dating website instead. So far she'd met six men. That was six dates more than she'd had in the last two years.

And if she had been looking for someone to actually go out with for the longer term, instead of wear on her arm to the wedding, there were a few guys she might have seen again. The primary school teacher who had screen grabs of his favourite kids' essays on his phone. The single dad who looked at her all evening as if he'd won the Lotto. The only real possibility was the incredibly buff personal trainer, but he'd let her know that he was away on the day of the wedding so she was back to square one.

She was also on her third make-up trial. Her waitress, Laura, did beauty treatments at night to pay for childcare and the upkeep of her chameleons, Ricky and Martin. They watched Fiona through their perspex tank as Laura blended four shades of contour cream onto Fiona's face with a tiny sponge, changing colour themselves from time to time as if they were trying to keep up with her.

'You don't *need* a plus-one, you know. You would so rule that wedding if you simply went on your own.' She leaned back to look at her handiwork and sighed. 'Oh my God. You are a dream to work on. You are so gorgeous.'

Fiona felt the compliment strike her and slide off, like coconut oil off Teflon.

'Weddings are sexy places.' Laura dabbed a dot of glue on her hand and began to apply individual lashes to the corners of Fiona's eyes. 'You might meet the love of your life.'

But Fiona *was* going to meet the love of her life. That was the whole point of all this. The six a.m. boot camps, the three hundred-euro highlights, the dress she had finally found that cost almost as much as a second-hand car. She had found it on the second floor of Brown Thomas. A sheath of the palest pink crêpe that skimmed her body. A soft grey leather belt, narrow as her little fingernail, to cinch in her waist. The assistant had followed her to the fitting room and then stood there while she stripped to her underwear, an experience that triggered a tsunami of body shame that Fiona covered up with meaningless chatter while the assistant eased the dress over her head and zipped it up.

'It looks incredible on you but we're going to have to alter it. We don't have time to order it in a six.'

She was a size six! Fiona stared at her reflection in disbelief. She had been size eighteen when Carl had seen her last.

Ten days before the wedding she got another match from the dating website. A ridiculously handsome investment banker called Andy who had just come home to Ireland after five years in Asia.

They met for Japanese food and before they had even ordered their meal, he had already said the words 'servants' and 'swimming pool' so many times that she'd lost count.

'Oh, God,' he waved the glass of the Chablis he'd spent a full minute swilling around his mouth before allowing the poor waiter to pour, 'am I sounding a bit smug?'

'No.' She smiled. He sounded like a huge amount of smug. Like a series of Facebook updates from a place called 'Success'. Cocktails at Raffles Hotel in Singapore. Weekends in Hong Kong. Diving trips to Tioman Island in Malaysia which was, 'once you got away from the honeymoon pits, a total paradise'.

He was perfect, she thought. And he was hired – if he was around in October.

After he had polished off most of the Chablis, he put his glass down, leaned back in his chair, and sighed with pleasure.

'Well, this is a first,' he shook his head, 'a date with a woman who's actually hotter than her profile picture.'

'Thank you. That's so kind,' she said awkwardly, her confidence deserting her, as it always did, when a man seemed to like her.

'It's not kind, it's true. At least half of my matches have turned out to be, let's say,' he smirked and made little quote marks with his fingers, 'larger than advertised.'

The smirk faded when Fiona turned down a second date.

They said that inside every fat person was a thin person waiting to get out, but, for Fiona, it was the other way around. The plus-size teenager she'd been had not gone away, she had just retreated inside.

Residual shame, that's what her counsellor had called it. Sandy was a specialist in body image. She was a small, loud, cheerful woman in her forties with dark roots showing through her dyed blond hair and a BMI, Fiona calculated at the first appointment, of at least thirty. She wore bright wrap dresses that clung to every bulge and curve like cling film and she clearly did not give a hoot about it.

She was an old friend now, one of the people Fiona trusted most in the world, but that first day, sitting in one of the two cream leather chairs in the tiny consultation room, she had felt as if it was her job to fix Sandy, not the other way around. Was it wrong for a body-image specialist to be overweight, she wondered? Would it be an idea to hand her some of the café flyers she kept in her bag now? Or should she wait until the end of the session?

'So,' Sandy had folded her arms in her ample lap, looking at Fiona kindly across the low glass coffee table that separated them, 'tell me why you're here.'

And Fiona, who could shout an order to Adonis over the hundred-decibel din of the lunchtime crowd and read the riot act to any supplier who gave her less than a hundred per cent, squirmed in the leather chair and her voice, when she finally managed to speak, sounded girlish and apologetic as she explained that, between the ages of fifteen and twenty-eight, she had been overweight.

'Well, obese really. Let's call a spade a ... a ...' she felt a lump rise in her throat – 'shovel. Anyway, I thought when I got thin, everything would be okay. And it is. I have a great business and good friends but I have problems with, you know –' the word stuck in her throat like a crumb – 'intimacy. Relationships. That kind of thing. I was engaged for three years. Me and my ex set up the café together, but he said that I treated him more like a friend and he was right. I see other people getting married, having kids, and it's like they're from another planet. I don't get it. I don't get how you do that...' Fiona ran out of words and she never ran out of words.

Sandy pushed the cheerful pink-and-black zebra-print box of tissues across the table. Fiona pushed it back again.

'I'm not going to cry! I'm not a crier,' she said, taking a deep breath. 'And I'm not stupid. I know I'm not unattractive. I know it up here!' She tapped her forehead, then put her hand on her heart. 'But I just can't seem to get the message to here.' She plucked a tissue from the box and balled it up in her hand.

She used to eat tissues when she was fifteen. She'd lock herself in the loo at school and swallow a wad of them before lunch, hoping they'd block that gaping hole that no amount of food ever seemed to fill.

The memory caught and a whole trail of other memories came up, like a line of ugly bunting. The chocolate wrappers she'd hide at the bottom of her schoolbag and share out between different bins on the way home. The packets of biscuits she kept in a shoebox at the bottom of her wardrobe.

She had tried to brazen it out. She'd stalk past the knot of fifth-year boys who hung around outside the assembly hall with a smart put-down ready to ward off the snickers and the jeers. She pretended not to hear the whispers and giggles in the gym changing room when she changed from her uniform skirt into her shorts and T-shirt.

She blew her nose hard on the tissue now. 'Why can't I get over this crap?' she asked Sandy. 'What is wrong with me?'

'Nothing,' Sandy said, firmly. 'When you lose a lot of weight, you don't always lose the negative self-image that came with it.'

She pointed at the box of tissues. 'If I threw that at you a couple of times, sooner or later, you'd duck every time I picked it up, right? You'd want to protect yourself from getting hit. It's the same with rejection. If the people around you are constantly judging you, you develop ways to cope – strategies. And a pretty good one is to second-guess rejection. To ditch someone before they can ditch you.'

Fiona flushed. That was what had happened with her ex-fiancé. When the first rush of falling into bed with one another had worn off, she had found it hard to believe that Bruce really wanted her. How could he? So she had fallen back on her old defences, making jokes about her size, hoping that he'd reassure her, but he'd just looked confused. He'd never seen her before. She had withdrawn to protect herself and when he had withdrawn too, she had accused him of not fancying her.

Sandy leaned over and patted her arm. 'I've been in that chair. I know how it goes. Now,' she picked up a spiral-bound notebook with a cover that matched the tissue box, 'can you remember when the negative feelings you have about yourself began?'

Fiona had never really thought much about food until she was fourteen, the year her dad had his accident. He'd been hit by a forklift truck at the factory where he worked and had spent six months in hospital. Her mother had been too frantic running in and out to visit him to make proper meals and Fiona had had to look after herself. Chips and chocolate and biscuits didn't make her anxiety about her father go away, but they covered it over under a blanket of fat and sugar. By the time he went back to work she had put on three stone and she didn't know how to stop comfort eating.

The bigger she got, the louder and funnier she had to be to compensate. She shrugged off her classmates' taunts and shot back smart-ass put-downs. She made sure that they never knew just how much they hurt her but the scars were there and they were deep. And even though she'd lost the weight and reinvented herself, the old insecurity refused to budge.

She hadn't told Sandy about the wedding. Sandy was all about 'safe spaces'. She might persuade Fiona not to go. She hadn't told anyone else either, not even Nora, who had been to the same school, who probably remembered Dazzler and Carl.

'I've found the dress,' Fiona announced as she and Adonis and Laura grabbed a quick coffee by the till after the breakfast bedlam had died down a bit.

'Yay!' Laura raised her cup for a 'cheers'. 'What about the hot banker?'

'Total tosser!' Fiona put her cup down with a clatter. 'I hate men,' she said darkly. 'Present company excepted, obviously!'

'You're not a man, Adonis !' Laura said. 'You're a god.'

His parents must have had a premonition before they named him because he looked as though he should be in a gilded pantheon in the sky, not knocking back an espresso in a suburban Dublin café. Fiona still thanked all the other gods that he had walked through the door three years ago. There wouldn't be a Café LoCal at all, if it wasn't for him.

He'd intimidated her at first, but he was so grateful for the chance she had given him, so serious about his job, and so clearly not a player, that she had relaxed completely around him. Most of the time, she didn't even notice what he looked like. But there were times, like this moment, as she watched him rinse out the Lilliputian espresso cup, turning it carefully in his huge hands, when she thought, Oh my God, he's so beautiful.

Suddenly, she grabbed her sunglasses. 'I'm just running across the road to Nora,' she said as she headed for the door.

The Memory Shop had a new window display. A pale-grey marabou shrug suspended in mid-air, the feathers shifting and stirring as if it was about to take flight.

There was a definition painted on the window: TO SHRUG OFF – TO DISREGARD, TO DISMISS, TO IGNORE, TO MAKE LIGHT OF.

'Best window yet!' Fiona said as she opened the door.

Nora was at the back of the shop, stacking crystal dessert dishes in a pyramid on a low table. 'You like it?'

Fiona grinned. 'I love it!' She watched Nora add another glass dish to her pyramid, to create a new tier. 'Careful, you'll break it!'

'You sound like my grandmother!'

There was a slam from upstairs and the crystal glasses sang as they picked up the vibration.

'It's okay, Lainey!' Nora called out. 'I'm using Blu-Tack to stick your precious glasses together. Actually, I'm running out of Blu-Tack. Can you grab another packet from the drawer in the desk, Fiona?'

Fiona stepped carefully around the stuffed Rottweiler and rummaged around until she found the packet. She pulled it open and began to roll the sticky gum against her palms.

'Eight days!' she groaned. 'I have eight days left to find someone to bring to this bloody wedding. You don't have any gorgeous single male customers, do you?'

'There's Will?' Nora said. 'Not that I think he's gorgeous, obviously, but, you know,' she stammered, 'but he's single.'

Fiona had to stifle a laugh. It would be obvious from outer space that Nora and Will were attracted to one another. The sexual chemistry between them at the party had been almost indecent. But for some reason, they were both pretending it didn't exist. 'No,' she said. 'Will is lovely, but it's not really *my* type.'

'Right. Okay.' Nora looked relieved. 'Have you thought about asking Adonis?'

Fiona groaned. 'I don't know. It's tricky. I'm his boss. He might feel he had to say yes.' He might feel sorry for her, she thought. He had seen her at her worst. She had been pushing size twenty when he had first come to work for her. That was how he would probably always see her. 'And he's usually pretty busy at weekends. He does extra catering jobs so he can send money back to his family in Greece.'

'I wish he'd take money from me, but he always refuses. I'm going to pick something of Hugh's to give him.' Nora stepped back, reached over, and flicked the switch. She had threaded fairy lights through the tiers of dishes and they sparked against the facets of the cut crystal and tiny rainbows danced in the air like fireflies. 'Is there anything you think he'd like?'

Fiona and Adonis had spent hundreds of hours working together side by side. She could have written a book about all the things he liked – the farm near Thessaloniki where he had grown up; his four older sisters, whose names he said as if he was speaking about flowers; his younger brother, whose college fees he was paying; his country.

He liked food, but not in the way Fiona once had. He liked the fun and the adventure of it. He liked throwing six random ingredients onto the counter and letting magic happen. He was the real reason the café had succeeded. She was working on getting him to accept a 30 per cent stake in the business, but so far he'd refused.

Nora was still waiting for an answer.

'Oh I don't know,' Fiona said eventually. 'Adonis is not really into *things*.' She shrugged. 'What he'd really like is for veganism to be mandatory, for AEK Athens to win the Champions League. Oh, and for Greece to burn the bond holders and end austerity.'

'Right.' Nora nodded. 'I was thinking of giving him Hugh's old camera, but I'll have a word with Lainey,' she flicked her eyes heavenward, 'see if she can arrange any of that with the powers that be.'

'While she's at it, ask her to send a presentable man my way before the wedding on Saturday week? He doesn't have to speak. In fact, not speaking would be an advantage as long as he looks the part.'

'Fiona, I don't want to pry,' Nora looked at her carefully, 'but why is this wedding such a big deal? I mean, you don't even know the bride really, do you?'

'I know the groom.' Fiona cleared her throat. 'And so do you.'

'Who?'

'Darren Cross, from Westbrook? Remember him?'

'Vaguely, I think.'

'Half of the guys from sixth year in Westbrook will probably be there.'

'God, I hated that place!' Nora made a face. 'Who's going?'

'Evie Vaughan. It's Evie Casey now. She married Carl. Remember him?'

'The gorgeous Carl Casey!' Nora shook her head. 'Well, he was never going to get away from her, was he? Do you remember the time she wrote his name fifty times down the leg of the desk in the science lab?'

'It was eighty-two times and,' Fiona swallowed hard; she had never admitted this before, 'and it was me who did that, not her. It's so embarrassing.' She wished she could take the words back now that they were out. 'I had such a terrible crush on him.'

'So did I,' Nora said, 'though I don't think he ever actually spoke to me.'

He hadn't spoken to Fiona either until the evening he caught up with her on the school driveway.

'How's it going?' he'd said to her, casually, as if they chatted regularly.

'Spiritually? Psychologically? Socio-economically?' she'd replied. If this was a wind-up, she might as well hit the ground running.

He shrugged. 'Just generally.'

'Fine. You?'

'I'm screwed,' he sighed. 'If I flunk one more maths exam, I won't be allowed to do the honours course and my dad will kill me. I'm not kidding.' He stepped ahead and walked backwards in front of her, so that she had to look at him. 'He will actually –' he put his hands around his neck and pretended to strangle himself, making his eyes bulge, letting his tongue loll out – 'murder me. So I was wondering,' he gave her a long look, 'if maybe you'd give me a hand. You know, explain it all to me.'

'What did you say?' Nora asked, as if all of this had happened yesterday, not seventeen years ago.

'I told him I didn't think that Evie would be very happy about that and he said they'd broken up. I was such an idiot. I felt like I'd won the lottery.' Fiona rolled her eyes. 'I squeezed into this really old pair of size-sixteen jeans the first time I went round to his place. I had to lie on the floor and pull the zip up with a coat hanger. I really thought in some deluded part of my head, that it was an excuse to see me. That he really, you know, *fancied* me.' She snorted contemptuously.

'Of course you did!' Nora smiled. 'So, what happened?'

'What happened was that he went from being a D– to a B– in maths and he made a complete fool out of me.'

Fiona had ached for him on those Saturday afternoons sitting beside him on his narrow bed. Every week, their heads, bent over the text book, they seemed to get closer. She stopped buying chocolate and spent her pocket money on eyelash curlers and spot concealer and mint chewing gum. She rehearsed witty one liners the night before just to crack him up: 'The parabola or a weapon of maths destruction, as we can call it' and 'It's not just you, Carl. Three out of two people have trouble with fractions.'

She couldn't remember what she'd said to make him laugh so hard that he fell back onto the bed, gasping for breath, but she could remember how light her heart felt as she lay down beside him. How she'd thought, 'This is it' and swallowed her chewing gum quickly so that it wouldn't get in the way when she leaned over and kissed him.

'Jesus!' He leapt away from her as if he'd been electrocuted and wiped his mouth with the back of his hand.

Fiona could still feel the burn of humiliation as she saw Carl's look of incredulity. How could she have been so stupid? How could she have thought, for even a second, that he wanted her, when he could have anyone?

'You weren't stupid.' Nora was outraged. 'He led you on! And he would have been lucky to have you. Anybody would be. What an awful thing to go through.'

The weeks following her humiliation were worse. Fiona lived in fear that he would tell somebody what had happened. The last six months of school were torture. She thought it would never end. She relived the humiliation of that moment every time she saw Carl. She thought she'd escaped when she finished her exams.

'Follow your passion', that's what the career guidance teacher had always said, and that's what she had done. She was the star of her class at catering college and then she was snapped up by an upmarket restaurant. Bruce was already working there and they'd cooked up a plan to set up their own brasserie and somewhere along the line, they'd gone to bed together and one night, a year later, after a three course meal and a bottle of good wine, he'd proposed and she had accepted, but she had never believed that it was her that he wanted. Every time a pretty girl walked into the brasserie, she thought, here we go. This is where he takes a good look at me and leaves me but when he did leave her, it wasn't because of anyone else, it was because she couldn't trust him. It wasn't personal. She didn't trust herself. She had misread the signals all those years ago, she was terrified of doing it again.

'Oh God,' Fiona groaned. 'Listen to me wittering on! I came

over to tell you about my fabulous dress, not dump all this on you. Just tell me to shut up next time.'

'Never!' Nora said. 'I'm here for you anytime. I mean that.' And she did. Liv hadn't ever opened up to her like this, she had kept up her image of impenetrable cool, even after Paul had walked out on her. It seemed strange to Nora now, that they had been friends at all.

She gave Fiona's narrow shoulders a squeeze. 'Good for you, for going to that wedding and showing Carl Casey what he missed out on. I would love to be there to see his face when you walk in.'

'Be careful what you wish for.' Fiona managed a hollow laugh. 'If I can't find anyone by Saturday week, you might end up as my plus-one.'

When Fiona got back to the café, Adonis was pulling a large circular baking tray from the drawer beneath the counter. He held it up like a ceremonial shield. He looked as if he was about to go into battle instead of making a batch of sugar-free French macaroons.

He would look incredible in a tuxedo, Fiona thought, slipping on her apron and tying it in a double knot. All those horrible little cows from Westbrook would fall at his knees. Go on, she told herself, ask him. But what if he thought she was coming on to him? She remembered, with horrible clarity, the time she had nearly kissed him.

He had stayed behind on Christmas Eve to help scrub the kitchen and clear out the fridges before the holiday. Fiona had turned off the soundtrack of carols that had driven them all mad since November and put on an Abba album and they'd half danced as they worked side by side. Adonis sipping mineral water; Fiona polishing off a jug of powerful leftover vegan eggnog.

When they were finished, she turned out all the lights and locked the door and Adonis pulled down the heavy metal shutter as if it weighed no more than a feather before he helped her to carry the bags out to her car.

She was going home to her parents' house for the night. She

had bought a cashmere dressing gown for her mother and a horrendously expensive bottle of thirty-year-old single malt for her father, because she couldn't give them what they really wanted – a clatter of grandchildren who would rampage through their neat house and swing out of their carefully decorated Christmas tree. Her brother's kids were thousands of miles away in Melbourne. They would chat on Skype in the morning but it was not the same thing.

Her parents believed that a meal without meat was like a day without sunshine, but tomorrow they would be forced to politely munch their way through Fiona's vegan nut roast, and her mother would come up with a statistic about the impact of the meat-production industry on the ozone layer which she had researched carefully for the occasion.

Her father would make Fiona pull every single cracker in the box and she would have to engineer it so that he got the novelty every time because he got so downcast when he lost. Afterwards, when he was loading the dishwasher, her mother would fill her glass and say something in a contrived casual voice like, 'Have you ever tried that Grinder thing, Fiona?' And she'd have to resist explaining the difference between Grinder and Tinder and say that she was really too busy with the café to see anybody. And her mother would look even more disappointed with that answer than she had been with the nut roast.

And then the three of them would settle down to watch the Christmas movie. Her father would fall asleep and she and her mother would 'oooh' and 'aaah' at the stunts in *Raiders of the Lost Ark* or choke back their tears at *Toy Story 3*, and it would be lovely. It would probably still be lovely when she was a childless spinster in her sixties and they were heading for ninety.

Adonis had a cousin and a couple of Greek friends in Dublin and then he had his AA buddies. He probably had half a dozen invitations for Christmas.

Maybe it was the Abba songs or the alcohol in the eggnog radiating warmth through her body beneath her tightly belted coat but the thought that she wouldn't see him until the New Year made Fiona feel sentimental.

After he closed the boot of her car, she reached up and took his ridiculously handsome face between her hands and pulled it down to her level, which meant that he practically had to bend double. She was just about to kiss him when she realised what she was doing.

'Oh my God!' she said. 'That eggnog was stronger than I thought. I think I'm drunk!' She pulled away and fanned the air between them theatrically as if a whiff of alcohol might send him running for the nearest pub.

He said nothing, then insisted on unloading her boot and putting her in a taxi. She cursed herself all the way back to her parents' house. She'd thought about texting him to explain, to apologise, but in the end, she just left it. What could she say? And when the café reopened in the New Year, neither of them mentioned it.

But this was different, Fiona told herself. She was sober. And maybe she could avoid any confusion by keeping it on a professional footing. That was it! She wouldn't ask him to come as her plus-one; she'd pay him overtime to come.

She waited until Laura was serving a customer to corner him.

'Adonis,' she said, casually, lifting the lid on an enormous pot of courgette noodles on the stove, 'I'm going to need you next Saturday, if that's okay.'

Adonis did everything slowly and thoughtfully and he never did two things at once. He finished shaping a spoonful of pale-pink macaroon mix and dropped it carefully onto the tray before putting the spoon into a jug of hot water. He wiped his hands, which looked as if they should be hurling thunderbolts, not whipping up tiny pastries that tasted like clouds, then looked at her. 'Saturday?' he said in his serious deep voice that made him sound like Morgan Freeman playing God in a movie.

'As you know, the café is closed,' she said, breezily, 'because I have this wedding to go to and for various reasons I don't want to go on my own. So I want to, well, employ you to come with me. I'll pay you, obviously. The church service starts at one and the dinner is at six, so you'd be free by nine o'clock, ten at the latest, just in case you had anything planned for that night. Does that sound okay?'

Adonis looked at her for a long moment then he shook his head. 'I am so sorry, but this is not possible —'

'No!' Fiona cut across him. 'No. I understand. It's okay. Forget I asked.'

'But—'

'Really! It was a mistake!' She turned and dashed into the stockroom with her cheeks burning. She didn't need Adonis to take her to the wedding, she told herself as she reorganised her already perfectly organised shelves. She didn't need anyone. She could do this all on her own.

'Have you thought about a hat or a fascinator?' the shop assistant asked, as she was zipping Fiona into the altered dress.

'Thanks, but no thanks.' Fiona raised her arms so the girl could buckle the narrow, grey leather belt. 'I just want to keep it simple. Classy.'

She lowered her arms and turned to check her profile in the shimmering pink sheath, then she stopped dead.

'Fuck!' she whispered 'What are those?'

There were fat sickle moons of flesh bulging beneath each armpit. She gave the dress a sharp jerk but they didn't move.

'It's just a little bit of armpit skin,' the assistant said, lightly. 'Nobody will even notice it.'

'That's not skin!' Fiona gasped. 'It's fat.'

'Everybody has them. Here!' The assistant pinched one of the little bulges between her fingers then tucked it deftly back under the fabric of the dress. Fiona watched as it oozed out again. A disgusting little sausage of flab.

Two women were flicking through the rails of Lainey's evening dresses. A man and a woman were trying to decide between the cherry-wood coffee table or the little card table with the mother-of-pearl inlay. Two students were trying on Hugh's hats which Nora had lined up on the floating shelf this morning. For once, she wasn't paying attention to the customers, she was Googling

Crete. Moving her cursor over the map, saying the names of places out loud in her head: Falassarna, Sitia, Rethymnon, Paleocastro. Wondering which province her grandmother had come from. She had searched through every piece of paperwork twice now. But she had found nothing that tied Lainey to Greece. She had asked Loughlin if he knew anything but he was as bewildered about it as she was.

'Hugh knew,' he told her. 'He must have.'

'Why do you think that?'

'Because of what he used to call her, of course.' Loughlin smiled. 'The girl from the side of an amphora.'

The two women left and the couple chose the card table. After much deliberation and several selfies one of the boys chose a green silk-lined trilby and the other settled on a soft oyster-coloured fedora. Nora had to smile as she watched them go, their brims tilted low, an extra swagger in their step. They almost collided with Fiona as she burst through the door.

'Come and get drunk with me,' Fiona dumped the beribboned bag that contained the useless dress onto the floor and sank down onto a chair by the desk. 'I need to be hooked up to an IV of chocolate Martinis.'

Nora was marking the two hats as 'sold' on the spreadsheet. 'Actual chocolate? I thought your body was a temple!'

'Tonight,' Fiona said, grimly, 'it's a motorway café.'

Nora grinned and looked up, then she saw Fiona's expression. 'What?'

'The dress. It's a disaster.' Fiona gave the bag a spiteful kick and it fell open, a wide yawn of dark rose tissue paper.

'But you said it was perfect!'

'It is perfect,' Fiona's voice was bright. 'Unfortunately, however, I'm not.' She waved one arm over her head with a manic smile. 'Full house!' she shouted. Nora stared at her, confused. 'Bingo wings!'

'You do not have bingo wings.' Nora shook the dress out from its folds of tissue paper and caught her breath as the silk slipped through her hands. She propelled Fiona, protesting, behind the red lacquer screen she was using as a dressing room. Then she helped her out of her top and skirt and into the dress and led her back out to the gilt-framed mirror. Fiona closed her eyes tight and wouldn't look.

'Fiona,' Nora said, 'you look beautiful.'

'Don't say that.' Fiona's voice cracked. 'And please, don't give me that whole sisterly "love your lumps and bumps" crap, please. This is not about how I see myself. This is about how other people will see me.'

Nora locked the door and led Fiona over to Lainey's yellow velvet chaise longue sofa that already had a 'sold' sticker. 'By other people, I'm guessing you mean Carl.'

'And Evie. And Darren. The whole lot of them.' Fiona tugged miserably at the hem of the dress. 'I know it's petty and childish, but I just wanted them to see how much I'd changed but I haven't changed really. Fat Fiona is still in here,' she prodded a finger viciously at the soft fold of her underarm, 'and no matter how much weight I lose or how good I look, she's won't go away.' She covered her eyes with her hands. 'Jesus Christ! What is wrong with me? Why does what some bunch of teenagers thought of me in the past still have the power to hurt me?'

Nora remembered once, asking her grandfather about why her mother and her grandmother couldn't put the past behind them and he had quoted a line from a poem. 'When it comes to hurt, the heart doesn't follow a calendar,' and it had maddened her at the time, because she wanted a straight answer, but he had been right.

Look at Fiona, struggling with a rejection that had happened when she was seventeen. Look at her. She had chosen not to see the cracks in the perfect life she was trying to make with Adam because she was scared of having the kind of rootless, insecure life she'd had as a child. Look at her mother, in her fifties now, but still running away from home.

Fiona stood up suddenly and reached behind her back to unzip the dress but Nora put a hand up to stop her.

'Wait! Close your eyes,' she said. 'And don't move until I come back.'

Fiona wanted to tear the dress off, to grab the delicate silk in both hands and pull the seams apart but she waited with gritted teeth until Nora came back. She felt something slip over her shoulders, the slip of silk, the tickle of something softer.

Nora made small adjustments. 'You can open your eyes now.'

Fiona looked down and saw that her shoulders were covered in feathers. At least a dozen layers, silver grey to the purest white, each one with its own pearlescent sheen.

'Nora,' she said, crossly, 'you've ruined your window for nothing because—'

But she broke off as she saw her reflection. The shrug was cape-length so it covered her arms to the elbow. It was ridiculously opulent and it would have been too much for most dresses, but the pale-pink sheath was so pared back that it worked. She lifted her shoulders and the delicate barbs of each feather shifted and settled against her skin, as if each one held the memory of wings.

Darren was already at the top of the aisle, looking nervous, when Fiona arrived at the church. She had been expecting a skinny, swaggering seventeen-year-old with a slight sneer, not a balding man on the fast-track to middle age with a belly that was straining the buttons of his grey morning suit.

Would Carl have changed? she wondered, slipping into a pew. She had never allowed herself to Google him or track him down on Facebook. She had been so focused on how she would look to him that she hadn't thought about how he would look to *her*.

She looked over her shoulder and scanned the crowd nervously; there were a dozen people who looked familiar. She registered a few turning heads, approving glances from the men, darting looks from the women, but she could tell that nobody recognised her. A string quartet began to play the 'Wedding March' and the bride swept up the aisle.

Fiona forced herself to forget Carl and to focus on the ceremony. On Andrea's beaming face. On the music and the readings and the long sermon about what love was and wasn't. She felt the way she always did at weddings: happy for the couple but confused too. She had no idea how they had done it, got all the way from 'hello' to 'I do'.

Darren's voice shook with emotion as he said his vows. Maybe he had changed, Fiona thought. Maybe life had knocked the streak of casual cruelty out of him. Maybe he'd be a model husband. Kind and caring and gentle. She hoped so.

As Fiona filed down the aisle afterwards, a pregnant woman with long red hair and pale-blue eyes tapped her on the shoulder. 'Fiona?' It was Dee Jacobs, Evie's best friend. 'I thought it was you. That dress is incredible. And the feathers. You look amazing!'

'Thank you,' Fiona said, lightly. 'So do you.'

'In my dreams.' Dee fanned herself with the order of service. 'Have you ever tried finding anything decent to wear when you're the size of a bloody whale?'

There was a beat, a small silence, and Dee's pale face flushed a deep crimson.

'Yes, I have,' Fiona said.

Dee laughed nervously and her eyes darted away. 'This is crazy, isn't it! Everyone together again like this. I feel like I'm at school assembly!'

'Did Evie and Carl make it?' Fiona tried to sound casual.

'They missed their flight. They're coming straight from the airport.'

The crowd shuffled forward, separating them, and Fiona felt a hand on her back. She turned to see a tall, handsome man in sunglasses.

'Fiona? It's Brian Cosgrove.' He flipped his sunglasses up so that she could see his eyes. 'Cozzie!'

'Sorry?' She shook her head, though she knew who he was. He had slipped a carton of milk onto her seat in chemistry class once, an experiment, he said, in weight and mass. It had exploded and she'd had to be a good sport and laugh with everyone else and sit for the rest of the day in her soaked, sour-smelling skirt.

'Third wedding I've been to this summer.' Brian gave her an eyebrow flash. 'It's like a contagious disease. Have you caught it yet?'

She shrugged and felt the grey feathers lift and settle. 'I think I might be immune.'

He grinned. 'Me too. Maybe we can catch up later?'

The crowd was funnelling through the door now and Fiona was aware of a ripple of curiosity around her.

She congratulated the bride, told her how lovely she looked, then crossed the churchyard to the car park. If she left before everyone else, she could get to the hotel first. She wanted to see Carl before he saw her.

She was almost at her car when she heard a voice – husky, petulant, familiar.

'You should have let me drive, then. At least I have a sense of bloody direction. I don't know where your tie is. Try the carry-on bag. Daisy, stop whining and get out of the car or it'll be too late to throw your confetti at all.'

A moment later, Evie was coming towards her, a faded version of her seventeen-year-old self, her lovely face slightly haggard beneath her fake tan. She was wearing a stop-the-traffic-lights yellow lace halter neck and holding the hand of a small, weeping girl in a matching yellow tulle tutu.

She stalked past and, a moment later, a man unfolded himself into the space between two lines of cars, a tie in one hand. He saw Fiona and froze.

His jaw was leaner and his face was longer. There were creases at the corners of his eyes, but she would have known his hair anywhere. The thick thatch of blond and, beneath it, those inky-blue eyes, framed by those long lashes.

'The parabola. A weapon of maths destruction!' His voice was like a pin pulled from a grenade. 'That still makes me laugh.'

He remembered her, she thought with an unexpected surge of pride. 'Hello, Carl.'

He leaned back against the car and shook his head. 'Long time no see. How are you?' He grinned. 'Spiritually? Psychologically? Socio-economically?'

She shrugged, and the feathers rose and fell. 'Oh generally, I'm pretty good.'

'I can see that. Did you open that restaurant?'

'I did. I run a health food café. How about you?'

'Still in London. Human Resources. I just about qualify for the "human" part. But I flunk the "resourceful" bit.'

He looked at her hopefully, waiting for her to laugh. She saw that he wanted her approval.

'Tell me something.' He folded his arms. 'Was it you who wrote my name eighty-two times on that bench in fourth year?'

'What bench?'

'It was in the science lab. Evie took the hit for it but I always thought that maybe you'd done it.'

Fiona laughed. 'If I was going to write your name multiple times, I'd pick a prime number.'

'Course you would.' He flushed. 'Sorry. I was just—'

'Carl?' Evie's voice rang across the car park. 'Carl!'

'Duty calls.' He looked at her, regretfully. An ordinary-looking man with thinning too-bright hair and a stain on the yellow tie that matched his wife's dress.

What had she been expecting? Why had she spent the last six months policing every bite she put into her mouth? Why had she ever cared what he thought of her?

'Maybe we could find a quiet corner later on, catch up on' – his eye met hers – 'old times.'

'Yeah,' Fiona lied. 'Maybe.'

Fiona was stuck at a table on the very edge of the ballroom with two of Andrea's other clients, their partners, and a single gay man and an elderly lady. Carl was three tables away. Fiona could almost have forgotten that he was there but every time she looked up, he was staring over at her meaningfully.

'Oops!' the old lady gave her a nudge after the speeches. 'You've got a little spot of wine on your lovely dress.'

Fiona soaked a paper towel with water and locked herself into a cubicle in the ladies. She took off the feather shrug and began to scrub at the stain on the front of her dress. It was just beginning to fade when she heard the door open and the tip tap of three pairs of heels on the tiles outside.

'Oh. My. God! Did you see Fat Fiona?' a woman said. Fiona froze.

'See her?' It was Evie. 'She nearly knocked me over in the car park! What a way to go, mowed down by a whale.'

'She's hardly a whale any more!' This was Dee. 'That pink dress is just to die for.'

Fiona heard the snap of a compact. 'I nearly pissed myself laughing when I saw that feathery jacket thing,' came Evie's voice, again. 'Because of Carl's nickname for her at school.'

Fiona held her breath. Had Evie known that Carl called her Miss Q? Had he told her?

'He used to call her Big Bird.' There was a sound of running water. 'She was crazy about him. You know, when we were in fourth year, she used to show up at his house at the weekends offering to help him with maths. She pinned him down to the bed once and kissed him. He had to fight her off...' Evie stopped in mid-sentence as the cubicle door opened.

Fiona sashayed past the three women to the line of basins. She saw the shocked little 'oh' of Evie's mouth in the mirror and the widened eyes of the other two women. She could sense that they wanted to flee, but they stayed, frozen to the spot while Fiona washed her hands slowly and dried them on a paper towel. Seventeen years ago, her bravado would have been an act and beneath it, she would have been cringing with shame. But now, she found she was enjoying herself. Their discomfort and embarrassment was like a delicious dish that she had waited seventeen years and she wasn't going to eat it all in one go. She was going to relish it.

'Sorry,' she said. 'I didn't mean to interrupt your conversation. Please, carry on!' She examined her face in the mirror and opened her bag and slowly, carefully, precisely, re-applied her lipstick.

'Gosh,' Dee tittered nervously, 'this is awkward. I'm really sorry, Fiona. I had no idea you were in there.'

Evie pretended to adjust the strap of her dress. 'Well, I'm not sorry,' she said airily, though her face was flushed red. 'If you eavesdrop like that, you're just asking to have your feelings hurt.'

Fiona's feelings weren't hurt, she realised. The only feeling she had right now was pity for this brittle, insecure woman trying to feel better about herself by putting someone else down. Her classmates were still the people they'd been when they were seventeen, not very nice people, but that was their problem not hers.

A dozen smart ass put downs flashed through her mind as she turned to face the three women, but she let them go. She had nothing to prove to them anymore. She remembered the definition on Nora's window: TO SHRUG OFF – TO DISREGARD, TO DISMISS, TO IGNORE, TO MAKE LIGHT OF.

So she lifted her shoulders, dropped them, then, as the feathers settled into place again, she turned on her heels and walked out and left them there. She passed the door to the ballroom without a backwards look. The band began to play as she went down the sweep of steps and out into the crisp October air.

She took a deep breath and kicked off the sandals that had been cutting off her circulation all day and then took the short cut around the side of the hotel to the car park.

As she passed the open door to a kitchen, she heard someone calling her name. She turned, hoping that it wasn't Carl, and saw a familiar figure. His dark hair was pulled into a chef's hairnet. His white jacket was rumpled and his chequered trousers were stained with some kind of red sauce but Adonis looked, as he always looked, as if he had just fallen from heaven.

'You were working here tonight?'

'Yes.' He nodded. 'Of course, for my friend who is the chef of the wedding. I tried to say this to you, but—' But she had cut him off, Fiona remembered. 'I can come with you now if you like. I am finished my shift.'

Fiona could hear the sound of the band in the distance. They were playing an Abba song now. 'This song always reminds me of Christmas!' she said.

'Yes,' he smiled down at her from his great height. 'It reminds me of Christmas also.'

'Do you want to dance?'

'Here?'

'No.' Fiona nodded at the hotel. 'In there. At the wedding.'

'Yes!' he nodded. 'Of course, but' – he gestured down at his chef's overalls – 'is this okay? What I'm wearing?'

'Yes,' Fiona said, firmly. 'Well, maybe lose the hairnet.'

He pulled it off, put out his hand, and she took it.

'Wait!' she said, as he led her back, just before they got to the dance floor.

She let his hand go and slipped off the shrug and threw it on a chair. It was beautiful, but she didn't need it, she had nothing to hide now. A feather came loose and floated before them as she followed him out onto the crowded dance floor.

9

Vintage Green Silk Pierre Cardin Scarf

Michelle

Someone had been making magic in the window of the closed-down gallery on Temple Road. A floating flash of green caught Michelle's eye as she drove past. She turned to see what looked like an iridescent butterfly rise and dive behind the glass.

Luke slammed the flat of his hand on the dashboard and she jammed on the brake, squealing to a halt as the traffic light turned red.

He turned to her. 'What the—?' The loud blare of a horn cut him off.

They both turned to look over their shoulders in time to see a man in a yellow Yaris behind them shake his head in a pantomime of disbelief.

'What's your problem?' Luke yelled. His mouth was so close to Michelle's cheekbone that she could feel the vibration of his voice along the bone.

'It's okay,' she said quickly. 'It was my fault!' But the man in the Yaris was mouthing something back.

'Right,' Luke said grimly, 'if that's the way you want it.'

Fear flipped open a trapdoor in Michelle's stomach and the sunny Sunday, the brunch with friends, teetered on the edge, ready to slip through. 'We're going to be late.' She leaned across him and put her hand on the door handle to stop him opening it. 'Can't we just forget about this?'

Luke flung her hand away, opened the door and strode back to the Yaris. She put her hand to her mouth and looked in the rear-view mirror. She saw the other driver's face crumple as Luke, tall and solid, fists balled, bore down on his car. She looked away, staring at the window of the old gallery instead.

It was not a butterfly behind the glass, she could see that now. It was a piece of material, a scarf, floating up, then drifting down again. She shut out the shouting and watched it turning and whirling, rising and falling, dancing in a hidden updraught of air.

'The world has gone mad.' Brian squinted gloomily up at the chalkboard of specials, shaking his head. 'What kind of ape threatens women in broad daylight?'

'He didn't actually threaten me,' Michelle began.

'Only you,' Luke looked at her affectionately, 'would say that a man shouting at the top of his voice wasn't threatening.'

'Well, I did stop suddenly... it was probably just a normal reaction.'

'The scary thing,' Brian cleaned his glasses on his napkin, 'is how normal a person can look until –' he clicked his fingers – 'they snap. You must have been pretty scared, Michelle.'

'With Luke there to protect her?' Liz scoffed. She took a bread roll out of the basket and prodded at the ramekin of butter with her knife. 'Hardly. I'd say he changed his tune when he saw you getting out of the car.'

'Let's say, he toned the road rage down a bit.' Luke smiled. 'And I don't think he'll pick on another woman in a hurry.' He closed his menu with a snap. 'I see thugs like that guy on every shift. The last thing they're expecting is someone who'll stand up to them.'

The waitress arrived to pour the wine. *Thug*, Michelle thought. The word didn't match the round-faced, balding man in the Yaris. He looked like someone's chubby dad.

But by the time the main course arrived, the wine was softening the sharp edges of the shock and she wondered if she was wrong. Maybe the other driver *had* been threatening. Looks could be deceptive. She knew that from experience.

'A paramedic?' Liz had pretended to swoon when Michelle told her about Luke. 'That's practically a fireman. Where did you meet him? You never go out! Please, don't tell me he just strolled into the shop. That's like a plot from one of your books.'

They had been thrown together by accident, literally, after Hugh, one of Michelle's favourite customers, had had a fall.

He was in his 80s, tall and leggy as a heron, with lovely manners and a mischievous twinkle and a halo of white hair that reminded Michelle of a dandelion clock. He was a regular at Moby Dickens. He'd come in once or twice a week to browse through poetry and science but he only ever bought romance novels.

That Saturday, three years ago, he'd taken a turn. One minute, he was standing at the counter paying Michelle for three Nora Roberts books, the next, he was tilting like a falling tree, his temple just missing the sharp corner of the counter.

By the time Michelle had sprinted around the corner, he was flat on his back between Self Help and Spirituality. He blinked up at her, confused. 'How did you get up there?'

'You had a fall.' She'd knelt down quickly and pulled off her cardigan. She rolled it up and put it under his head. 'You need to stay where you are for a minute. You might have concussion.'

One of the other customers was already on her mobile, calling an ambulance, and another was running out into the street to get help. A moment later, she hurried back in with a man in running gear.

'I'm an off-duty EMT,' he said, softly, crouching beside Michelle. He was built like a rugby player but his face was surprisingly mild. Gentle grey eyes and a boyish scatter of freckles beneath a thatch of brown hair peppered with grey. 'Who do we have here?'

'This is Hugh.'

'Hello Hugh, I'm Luke.' He put two fingers on the old man's wrist and Michelle's eyes went automatically to the other hand, looking for a wedding ring. *Oh my God*, she thought, *how shallow am I? Wondering about a stranger's marital status when this poor man could be about to die.*

'Tell me, Hugh,' he said, 'do you feel dizzy or confused at all?'

'Once you hit eighty, you feel dizzy and confused most of the time,' Hugh said. 'I'm fine. I'd be back on my feet but this young lady won't let me stand up.'

'Your daughter's right.' Luke gently unbuttoned Hugh's coat. 'You need to take it easy for a few minutes.'

'Daughter? No, Michelle's my wife.' Hugh had smiled conspiratorially up at Michelle. 'She married me for my money but I don't mind. Who would?'

Luke glanced up at Michelle and she wished she had bothered with mascara that morning and blow-dried her hair, instead of shoving it up into a tangled bun. He nodded and then looked back down at Hugh. 'You're a lucky man.' He looked down at Hugh. 'Can you lift your arms above your head? Both of them? Good. Now, can you give me a smile?'

'Which one of us are you asking?' Hugh managed a shaky grin.

'Well, your sense of humour is intact. How about your chest and arms? Any pain? Any numbness?'

'Just a few pins and needles in my pride. How's my heart rate?'

'Slightly elevated,' Luke said calmly. 'But it's probably the shock and the books.' Luke nodded at the three novels that had fallen out of their paper bag. 'All these love stories would raise anyone's blood pressure.'

'Oh,' Hugh looked embarrassed, 'they're not for me. My wife, my real wife, not Michelle here, has insomnia. It's my job to read her back to sleep.'

Michelle pictured Hugh sitting up in bed with a white-haired woman, her eyes drifting closed as she listened to his voice, a lifetime of affection and kindness gathered into the pool of lamplight between them.

'Lainey!' A flash of panic crossed Hugh's face. 'I need to tell her what's happened.' He tried to sit up but he wasn't strong enough and he sank back down to the floor. The corners of his mouth began to tremble. 'What *has* happened?' He was trying to keep his voice steady. 'Is it something bad?'

'I don't think so.' Luke patted his hand and then took it in his own, held it tightly. 'You have a slight weakness on the left side and my best guess is that you've had a mini stroke, which sounds bad, but is actually a great sign. A warning light that you need to change your diet and start taking medication. They'll run some tests at the hospital but I think you'll be back reading to your wife in a day or two.'

Michelle wanted to hug him.

'Thank you.' Hugh gripped his hand. 'Thank you. I'm supposed to stay around until Lainey's gone. She'd kill me if I died first.'

Luke grinned at Michelle and she grinned back and she could have stayed there all afternoon, looking into his kind grey eyes, but she heard a siren wailing as it turned the corner into the street and the blue light of the ambulance hopped around the shelves like a poltergeist and the spell was broken.

Looking back, it seemed to Michelle that she had been sleep-walking through her twenties. Drifting through a succession of relationships that went nowhere. By the time she was thirty, she was the only one of her friends who was still single.

Delia plagued her with links to Salsa Singles classes and Speed Dating evenings she never went to. David spent an evening com-posing a Tinder profile she never posted. Liz dragged her out to bars and clubs, but she felt like a fraud perching on a bar stool in borrowed stilettos. She had forgotten how to fake the bright confidence it took to talk to strangers, how to bump and grind on the dance floor, as if nobody was looking, when somebody looking was the whole point.

So she had spent the last three years hiding behind books and box sets, pouring all her energy into her job, telling herself and everyone else that if there was someone out there for her, he would find her.

And now here he was, this tall, gentle stranger dusting off his knees and asking her for her phone number so that he could let her know how Hugh got on in hospital.

Luke called on Monday to say that Hugh had been discharged. 'The stroke was tiny and it's probably a one-off. If he attends the outpatient clinic and takes the meds, he's going to be fine.'

'That's great news.' Michelle beamed at the thought of Hugh

going home. 'You were amazing on Saturday. I feel so lucky that you just happened to be passing by.'

'I feel pretty lucky too.' There was an awkward silence. 'I mean, he's quite a character and that's a lovely shop you have. I pass it every other day on my run but I've never been in before.'

'Well, come in next time,' she winced at the eagerness in her voice.

Two days later, when she came out of the stockroom, he was standing in the Self Help section, his head tilted, scanning the spines of the books. He had his back to her but she recognised him, that strong muscled neck, the broad shoulders, the thick hair with just a sprinkle of grey.

She was glad it was midweek and she was alone in the shop. 'Can I help you?'

'I hope so,' he said without looking around. 'Do you have anything on the rules of dating beautiful blonde bookshop managers? The thing is, I'm a bit rusty at the whole romance thing and I don't want to scare her off.'

Luke wasn't rusty at all, he was perfect. If she had written a checklist, he would have checked every box. Romantic. Sexy. Kind. And, somehow, absolutely crazy about her. Nobody had ever listened to her as intently as he did. Or turned up to drive her home when she was working late. Or told her friends that she was one in a million. Or picked her up as if she was as light as a paperback and carried her up the stairs of her apartment, past her surprised and disapproving cats, Tuxedo and Bowtie.

That first Christmas, he gave her a diamond solitaire on a fine gold chain and by Valentine's Day they were living together.

'He's so gorgeous.' Her friends had swooned when they met him. 'Does he have any friends?'

The strange thing was, Luke didn't. He'd lost most of his mates, he told Michelle, when he broke up with his ex-wife and moved back to Dublin from Sligo; he was having to start all over again.

'That sounds lonely,' she said when he told her.

'I'm used to it. I lost my only sister, Barbara, when I was a kid and I never found it easy to be close to people after that.'

Barbara had drowned the day of her seventeenth birthday. It

was recorded as an accidental death but his parents suspected that it was suicide. They had split up and Luke had been shunted between a broken-hearted father who could hardly bear to look at him and a grieving mother who was terrified to let him out of her sight. He hadn't spoken to either of them in years.

It broke Michelle's heart to think of all that he had lost. It made her want to protect him the way he protected her.

When Michelle got up to go to the loo, Liz got up too. Brian rolled his eyes. 'They've been doing this since they were teenagers,' he told Luke. 'It's like their bladders are synchronised.'

Luke ignored him. 'You want me to order you dessert, sweetheart?'

'No, I'm okay.'

'That's a crème brûlée, then,' he tapped the menu, 'and two spoons.'

Liz grabbed Michelle's arm at the door to the ladies and dragged her on to the end of the corridor and out through a fire exit leading to the small railed-off smoking terrace. She pulled a packet of Marlboros out of her bag.

Michelle raised an eyebrow. 'Is that allowed?'

'Not by Brian, but he's not the one with a black-and-blue ass from hormone injections. You want one?'

Michelle nodded and took a cigarette from the pack. She was still a social smoker but Luke didn't know that.

The first time she had seen him lose his temper was over cigarettes. They had been together for three months and they were having a drink outside a pub in Dalkey when he suddenly pushed his pint away.

'I can't stay here.'

'Why not?' Michelle still had half a glass of red wine in her hand.

'You see that guy?' Luke jerked his head towards a man smoking a cigarette near the door. 'We picked him up after a heart attack at a match in Lansdowne Road last year. We ran a red light in Donnybrook trying to save him. We came this close to being wiped out by a bus.' He slammed a fist on the table. 'I could have been killed. For what? So he can smoke twenty fags a day and give himself another heart attack.'

He was on his feet and off down the street so fast that she had to run to catch up with him.

He arrived at the bookshop the next day with an armful of yellow roses.

'I'm sorry. I didn't mean to spoil your evening. It wasn't your fault.'

He was like that nursery rhyme. 'When he was nice, he was very, very nice.' And when he was not, Michelle remembered the five-year-old who had lost his sister. The small, hurt boy inside the angry man.

'You are so lucky.' Liz cupped a hand around the lighter. 'If some guy threatened to kill me on the way home, Brian would tell him to go right ahead and clean his glasses so he got a better view.' She pressed the burning tip of her cigarette against the railing, shaping the ash into a point. 'We had another massive fight on the way here. You should have heard the things he called me.' She shook her head sadly and let the smoke out in a sigh. 'Luke would never speak to you like that.'

There was a small, awkward pause, as there often was with Liz; an empty space that Michelle would have filled once. But now she just let it pass.

'In fairness,' Liz snorted, 'I did give as good as I got. Warning: IVF might cause you to tell your husband that he's not just a prick, he's a fucking cactus. That's a side-effect they neglect to mention in the patient information pack.' She pulled out a packet of Polo Mints. 'I just hope all this is worth it.'

'You know it is.' Michelle took a last drag on her cigarette then ground it out into the metal bin mounted on the railings. She opened her bag and took out her own packet of mints.

'You come prepared!' Liz said, impressed.

They stood for a minute, sucking their mints, looking at the roofs shimmering in the heat haze, the sunshine flaring in the windows of the cars in the multi-storey car park, the distant purple smudge of the mountains against the flat, heat blasted sky. Dublin looked as tired and burned out as Michelle felt.

'So, are you and Luke going to make one of these any time soon?' Liz patted her tiny bump and gave Michelle a careful, sidelong glance. Liz used to be the queen of the direct question, but she was much more tentative these days, an unspoken acknowledgement that Luke was Michelle's best friend now, as well as her boyfriend.

Michelle transferred the mint from one cheek to the other. 'We're thinking about it,' she said, vaguely. She hadn't told Liz that they had agreed to stop using contraception at Christmas.

'Well, don't leave it too long. Those eggs will be thirty-eight in two weeks. What's Lovely Luke planning for your birthday?'

'Dinner and a night away in a hotel in Wicklow.'

Michelle remembered the wild bashes she used to have when she was with Rob. The session in the snug in Doheny & Nesbitt's when her birthday cake had been a pint of Guinness with a candle that sank into the froth. The Salsa club crawl. The 80s disco in David's old flat that got so rowdy that the neighbours gave in, tired of hammering on the ceiling, and came down to join in. It was on the tip of Michelle's tongue to ask Liz to come along to the dinner in Wicklow. To tell her to bring Brian and Delia and Tom and David and Eamon, but Luke had a romantic evening in mind.

He had seemed to fit in with her friends at the start. He joined the after-work drinks sessions and the pot-luck dinners and karaoke nights. But after a few months, he began to make little comments about them afterwards. 'Liz got very foul-mouthed when she drank, didn't she?', 'Does Brian mind being so hen pecked?', 'Does Delia ever talk about anything other than her cats?', 'David really loves the sound of his own voice, doesn't he?' It made Michelle feel awkward, seeing how nice they were to him, knowing what he was saying about them behind their backs.

'Never had you pegged for one of those women who ditches her friends for the guy,' David said when she turned down another invitation to a weekend in his cottage in Galway. It was said with a smile but he stopped asking her after that.

Liz went back to the table and Michelle went into the ladies. She ran the cold tap and rolled her sleeve up carefully, then held her wrist under the cold stream of water. When Luke flung her hand away it connected with the gearstick. The skin was thin over the bone and it hurt like hell, but there was only a faint red mark. If she was lucky, it wouldn't even bruise.

Luke took her other hand as they walked back to the car in the sunshine. 'We could look into IVF too, you know, if it hasn't happened for us by Christmas.'

'I suppose...' Michelle said.

'Don't worry about the money,' he said, misunderstanding. 'We'll find the money somewhere.'

By Monday, the mark on her wrist had faded but it hurt to take her cardigan off, to type, to tuck a couple of books under her arm. She was distracted and forgot to save her stock take spreadsheet, then she had a crash and lost it. She undercharged one customer and short changed another. She sent back a box of review copies instead of a box of returns.

When the shop was quiet, she Googled IVF clinics in Dublin. She scrolled through pages of airbrushed couples and anatomical drawings of ovaries that looked like orchids. She scanned the Q&As, but she didn't find the answer to the question that had haunted her since Luke had said they should get pregnant. Was it okay for them to have a child?

She hung the 'back in five minutes' sign on the door and found the packet of Marlboro she had hidden in the stationery cupboard inside a fat roll of 'Author Signed' stickers.

It was another sunny afternoon but the tiny yard at the back of the shop was in deep shadow. Michelle tilted her head back and looked up at the cloudless sky. The smoke from her cigarette unfurled like a grey ribbon and she remembered the scarf rising and falling in the window of the gallery, the sound of Luke bringing his fist down on the roof of the little yellow Yaris. For a second, she thought she could hear it again, then she realised that someone was knocking at the door of the shop.

*

She was shaving her legs in the bathroom when Luke came home. It was only eight o'clock; he should have been just starting his shift. She stood with one foot on the side of the bath and listened to his footsteps pass the door. 'Hi!' Nothing. Then the clatter of a beer cap dancing on the kitchen counter. Something was wrong. She felt it with a sickening certainty in her gut. 'Luke?'

When the door opened, his face against the collar of his Hi Vis jacket was white. The knuckles of the hand holding the beer bottle were white too. Michelle's mouth dried up. For a moment, she wondered, stupidly, if he had been to the shop, found her cigarettes.

'I thought you were at work...'

'I was sent home.'

The shaving foam was drying on her shin, pulling the skin tight, making it itch. 'Why?'

He wiped his mouth with the back of his hand. 'Apparently, Mr Yellow Fucking Yaris went to the police. If he decides to press charges, I could be suspended. I could be fired.'

'Don't worry,' she said. 'We'll get through this.'

'We wouldn't have to get through anything,' Luke slammed his foot on the pedal bin and dropped the empty beer bottle in, 'if you hadn't taken your eyes off the road.'

Michelle felt her blood cool. It trickled up the insides of her arms, behind the back of her knees, as if it, too, was looking for somewhere to hide. She needed to take her raised foot off the side of the bath, to stand on two feet, but she is frozen to the spot. Suddenly the bathroom seemed small and claustrophobic. Luke was standing too close, between her and the open door.

'Would we? A simple yes or no answer, Michelle. Would I have been sent home if you had been looking where you were going?'

Words bubbled in her mind but her tongue was too heavy to shape them. She looked at the floor. The line of grouting between the tiles. A drop of foam drying on the bathmat. One of Luke's legs, jiggling. The tip of one of his work boots, thick soled, round toed, huge.

'Speak to me!' he shouted. 'For. Fuck's. Sake. Say. Something!' He grabbed her suddenly, gripped her chin and twisted her head.

His thumb was holding her jaw steady, his fingers were digging into her windpipe. She made a choking sound that was not a word, but it was enough to snap him out of his rage.

He let her go and ran a hand through his hair and stared at her; her own panic was mirrored in his eyes. 'Oh shit!' He picked up a towel and drenched it under the cold tap and pressed it against her neck.

Michelle put her foot on the floor and backed away, but the bathroom was narrow and she couldn't put enough space between them. Her lungs were tight, as if she had been running.

'Shell, I'm sorry, I'm sorry, okay?' He sat down on the lid of the toilet and buried his head in his hands. 'I didn't mean to ... I was just ... I've been dreading this. Feeling sick every day, waiting for the shit to hit the fan. I knew that guy in the Yaris was trouble. I should have done what you said, let it go. But I fucked up. And now I've done it again. I'm going to lose my job and I'm going to lose you. That's what always happens. I love something and then I lose it.'

Tears trickled from between his fingers and down his face. They hung down his jaw and splashed onto the thighs of his trousers. He wrapped his hands around his knees and looked at her. His eyes were frantic. 'I'll never do that again. I swear.' He put his hand out. 'I swear on my sister's grave. You have to believe me.'

The first time it happened, a sixteen-year-old girl had died on Luke's shift. She had been celebrating her Junior Cert results and had taken three tabs of ecstasy and collapsed in a toilet cubicle in a nightclub. Her heart had stopped by the time the ambulance arrived. Luke had broken the door down and they'd managed to resuscitate her, but then had lost her again on the way to the hospital.

When Michelle had come home from work, he'd been sitting on the sofa watching the soccer on TV with the sound turned down. He'd told her what had happened in a mechanical voice without taking his eyes off the screen.

'You did everything you could!' Michelle crouched down beside him and dipped her head so that she could look up into his eyes, but he wouldn't look at her. 'Luke, I know how hard this is for you...'

'Do you? Do you really?' He sprang up and began to pace around the living room.

'You spend your days flogging Peppa Pig and Jane bloody Austen. The most I've ever seen you lose is your gym pass. How could you possibly understand?'

Even as she was flinching at his harsh words, she was telling herself that he was right. He had lost his sister, his parents, and his childhood. She got up and followed him over to the window and put her arms around him.

'Don't!' He pressed his palms against her chest and pushed her away. She threw out her arm to steady herself and knocked a crystal vase off a side table. It came crashing down on her foot.

He picked her up and carried her to the sofa, elevated her foot, ran to kitchen to get the first aid kit and an ice pack. He examined each toe, tenderly. Two of them were badly bruised but nothing was broken.

Afterwards, he was full of remorse. He begged her to forgive him and, of course, she had. It wasn't as if he'd hit her. She had fallen. It was an accident. What was the point of turning it into something else?

The bruises faded. She turned the crystal vase round so that the tiny missing chip on the base couldn't be seen. A few weeks later, she put it in the recycling bin and bought a new one for the flowers Luke gave her. African daisies, parrot tulips, roses. They didn't talk about what had happened but every flower was a small apology. A fragrant promise that it would not happen again.

And, for six months, everything was fine, everything was lovely. Then, one evening, they bumped into David in town and went for a drink that turned into five. David spent the evening telling stories about the awful flat he and Michelle had shared at college. The neighbour who sleepwalked naked. The wild parties. The time a mouse had died under the floorboards of his room and he'd had to sleep in Michelle's bed.

Luke wouldn't look at her in the taxi home. At the apartment, he got out and left the door swinging open. The driver gave her a worried look in the rear-view mirror as she paid the fare. 'You okay, love?'

'Of course,' she said, still on a high from the fun and the wine.

Luke was waiting in the kitchen, his coat still on, his arms folded. 'So I guess it's seven,' he said.

'Seven what?' Michelle leaned in the doorway. She was drunker than she'd realised.

'Seven men you've slept with. You said it was six.'

She smiled, she couldn't help herself. 'I didn't sleep with David. We shared a bed. He's gay, you know that. Even if I got down on my hands and knees, he'd turn me down.'

'And did you?' Luke said, with a sneer. 'Get down on your hands and knees?'

Her smile faded. 'I'm going to bed. I think you should sleep on the sofa.' As she turned to go, he grabbed her sleeve and tried to stop her. She slipped out of her coat and ran down the hall, but part of her could not, would not believe this was happening and she turned around, ready to reason with him, but his face was flushed with anger. He backed her up against the wall. He shouldn't have done it. But she shouldn't have struggled because she wrenched her shoulder as she broke free.

She locked herself in the bedroom. There was silence out in the hall as she began pulling clothes out of the wardrobe and dumping them on the bed. She grabbed shoes from under the bed and threw them on top, then stared at them helplessly through her tears. Her suitcase was in the attic; her sports bag was in the closet in the hall. Helplessness buckled her knees, she sat on the bed. What was she doing? Where was she supposed to go?

She took her phone out of her coat pocket and pulled up Liz's number, then David's, then Liz's again, but she didn't make a call. She lay listening to the slowing of her heartbeat and the sound of Luke's voice, soft and anguished, apologising, promising, pleading to be let in. Eventually, as it was getting light, she opened the door. He wrapped his arms around her and they curled up together on the pile of clothes and hangers and escaped from the reality of what had happened into sleep.

Afterwards, they were too shocked and numb to talk about it. It was another elephant in the corner of another room. Sometimes, the small flat seemed full of them.

Michelle would have Luke for months, the real Luke, gentle, protective, caring, then she'd say the wrong thing or he'd have a bad shift or someone would be rude to him in a shop and his anger would escape, a genie out of a bottle. No, a demon, not a genie.

All the articles she read said that if your partner hit you, you had to leave. To get away and stay away, but Luke never actually hit her. He would pin her down to stop her getting away. He'd grab her arm too hard or twist it. This wasn't like those stories she'd read about domestic violence. He didn't want to hurt her. If she could just stop pushing his buttons, if she could prove to him that she didn't want anyone else, if she could get him to open up about his sister, if there was someone she could talk to, who would tell her what to do, then she could stop it happening.

But she was too ashamed to admit what was happening. A single word to any of her friends would be like pulling the pin out of a grenade. Everything would be blown apart.

She could stand the pain of a bruise, a friction burn, a sore spot on her scalp where he yanked her hair too hard, but what she couldn't stand was the idea that there wouldn't be a future, when she couldn't sleep and Luke would wake up to read to her in a pool of lamplight.

The man in the Yaris accepted Luke's apology and didn't press charges. He got off with an official warning and a referral to a counsellor who specialised in anger issues.

'Maybe it'll help,' Luke said when he rang her to tell her. 'Maybe it's time I talked to someone.'

A weight lifted off her shoulders. It was going to be okay, she could feel it.

'Are you coming down with the flu, love?' the delivery man hesitated before he handed her the docket.

'No.' Michelle took it and, checking off the stock against her list asked, 'Why?'

'It's twenty-five degrees out there and you're wearing a polo neck.'

'Oh,' she felt her face flush. 'It's just a sore throat.'

When she got home, Luke was at work, but he'd left an early birthday present on the bed. A package wrapped in pink tissue paper and tied with a fat pink satin ribbon with an envelope addressed to 'The Birthday Girl'. There was a note inside that said, 'This is really a present for me, because I get to see you wear it on Friday.'

Between the leaves of tissue paper was a beautiful sage-green, chiffon dress with a pattern of tiny grey dots. When she peeled off her clothes, unzipped it and slipped it over her head, it fell around her in an expensive whisper.

She walked over to the mirror and the smile died on her lips. Her hand went to her throat to cover the four bruises Luke's fingers had made on one side of her neck and the larger thumbprint on the other side, just below her ear. They had faded a little, the black turning to purple, the green to yellow, but they would never be gone by tomorrow evening.

She Googled make-up to cover bruises and picked up what she needed on the way to work. The shop was busy all day and it was nearly six by the time she could close up, too late to go home and pick up her overnight bag. She rang Luke and asked him to bring it.

'You're not going to be late, are you?' he sounded tense. 'Dinner's booked for seven-thirty.'

'I'll change here and then get my hair blow dried. I'll be there by seven fifteen, I promise.'

She went into the back room and pulled off her cardigan and jeans and slid on the new dress, then got to work on her make-up. She winced as she pressed the foundation onto the tender skin with her fingers. It took three layers to cover them completely but at last they began to blur and finally, they disappeared.

She slipped out of her Converse and into nude heels, stuffed her credit cards and perfume into her tiny evening bag, then dashed out to her car.

But it was twenty to seven by the time she got to the salon.

Her stomach clenched with anxiety as a solemn trainee slowly washed her hair, but when she explained that she was in a rush, the manageress sent two stylists over to do her blow dry.

They stood on either side of her chair with their round brushes, scorching her scalp and the tips of her ears with the blazing cross draught from their driers.

By ten past seven, they had transformed her thin blonde hair into a shining curtain. She tipped them and hurried back to the car, praying that she could get to the hotel in twenty minutes.

At the traffic lights in Blackrock, she flipped down the rear-view mirror to refresh her lipstick and gaped at her reflection. The heat of the driers had melted the foundation and the bruises stood out, livid, against her pale skin. She upturned her evening bag onto the passenger seat, but she had left the foundation back at the shop. If she went back to get it, she would be an hour late.

She turned away from the mirror in despair and saw where she was. There was the shop she'd seen two weeks ago. And there, in the window, the square of silk, rising and diving behind the glass. A scarf that was, miraculously, exactly the same shade of her dress.

Nora had woken from broken dreams full of jumbled thoughts, her mind somehow trying to wrap itself around the shock of finding her grandmother's travel papers.

She had been to Greece only once, with Liv, seven years ago. They had rented a villa in an exclusive development on Santorini. Liv had lain by the pool and had had massages and manicures, but Nora had wanted to break out of their stylish little cocoon of luxury. She had had a hunger to find out what lay beyond the whitewashed walls; to see the real island.

So, she left early most mornings. Took buses past silver-green olive groves up to remote villages where old people in black sat in the thick shadows of ancient plane trees. She hired a scooter and drove past the fashionable beaches with their bars and sun loungers to tiny, deserted coves where the only shelter was a straggly tamarisk tree.

Liv had fallen in and out of lust a dozen times during that fortnight but Nora had fallen in love only once – with a whole country. Because, in a way she could not fully explain, that island had felt like home.

And now she understood why. It all made sense. Her dark eyes and hair, her olive skin. She was partly Greek.

Why had Lainey hidden this? Why had Hugh helped her to keep her birthplace a secret? Nora had scoured the house, gone through every box of papers in the attic with forensic care, but she had found nothing that cast light on this mystery.

It was yet another tantalising snippet of her grandmother's life. Like the notes she had found. Another tiny glimpse of this woman she had never really known.

Nora had dreamed of Lainey again last night. They were in a boat together. Lainey was wearing her wedding dress and the double string of moonstones around her neck. It was night and a full moon laid a silver path across the sea. There was an island on the horizon that Nora knew, somehow, was Crete.

Nora was trying to row them both back there but the oars were too heavy. The harder she pulled, the further they drifted away, and the boat was letting in water. She handed a bucket to her grandmother.

'You have to help me,' she shouted. 'We have to work together.'

Lainey smiled at her but, instead of bailing out the water, she dipped her hand into the bucket and pulled out a handful of scarves. She let them go and the wind took them. Then, after the scarves, she began to pull out handfuls of torn paper.

And Nora somehow knew they were the pages from Hugh's poetry books. That if she could catch them before they blew away, she would understand everything. But even as she was reaching for them, trying to snatch them out of the air, she woke up.

It had taken her four hours to get a scarf to stay afloat in the window. Three painstaking hours of swapping the pale-pink Chanel for the peacock-pattern Zandra Rhodes square and the yellow Hermes, shifting the three fans a fraction of an inch to try to create a cross-draught.

She was about to give up when she tried the sage-green Pierre Cardin square with the border of tiny grey elephants. It was lighter than all the others. It fluttered for a few moments, like a reluctant kite, then it floated up and stayed up, furling and unfurling lazily, as if it had been made to defy the laws of gravity.

It came down again every time anyone opened the door, so she had to rig up a plywood panel between the shop and the window. She was planning to leave it there for at least another week.

Passers-by were so enchanted by the sight of the scarf turning graceful circles in the window that they came in to ask how it stayed afloat and stayed to browse. Today alone, she had sold a dozen of Lainey's other scarves, six pairs of evening gloves to a stylist, two mirrors to a couple of newly-weds and the polished oak dining table with carved lion's paw feet to an architect looking for a desk.

She was giving the table a last, loving polish with beeswax on Friday evening when a blonde woman in a cream mac tapped on the window of the shop. Nora had closed an hour ago, but she opened up.

The woman looked frantic. 'I know you're closed. I'll only be a minute. I just want to buy the scarf in the window.'

Nora shook her head. 'I'm sorry, I can't let you have that one, but I have plenty of others.' She pointed at the washing line she had run along one wall with another desk fan positioned below it so that the bright silk squares looked like they were fluttering in a garden breeze.

'No,' the woman in the mac was insistent. 'It has to be the one in the window. It's the only one that will match my dress.'

What a princess, Nora thought, folding her arms. 'Do you have the dress with you? If you show it to me, I'm sure we can find another one that works.'

The woman hesitated, then turned down the high collar of her mac and unbuttoned it quickly, covering her neck with her hand but not before Nora glimpsed the bruises and caught her breath. She dropped her eyes to look at the dress, green chiffon with a tiny pattern of grey dots. 'Oh, it's lovely,' she said quietly. 'A really unusual colour, and you're right: I think the Pierre Cardin will be lovely with it. I'll get it so we can see.'

She walked over to the window, her mind racing. What was she supposed to do? Should she ask the woman how she got those marks? If she needed help?

She opened the small, hinged door at the back of the display. The draught from inside the shop shifted the air and the green silk square dived to the floor and lay there trembling, like a dying butterfly. Nora leaned in and picked it up. When she turned, the woman in the mac was behind her.

She took it quickly and turned away, tied it around her neck and shrugged off her coat. She walked over to the gilt-framed mirror on the other wall and stared at her reflection, craning her neck from side to side.

'Isn't that amazing?' Nora said gently. 'It's the exact colour of your dress and the grey elephants match your polka dots.'

'Elephants?' The woman looked startled. She dipped her chin, trying to make them out on the scarf.

'There's a little line of them round the border.' Nora walked over and stood behind her. 'If you take it off, you'll see them.' Maybe she imagined the bruises, she thought, maybe they were not as bad as they looked. If she could see the woman's neck again, she'd know what to do.

The woman adjusted the bow and slipped her arms back into the sleeves of her mac. 'I'll take it,' she said.

'Well,' Nora played for time, 'at least let me wrap it for you.'

The woman shook her head quickly. 'It's okay.'

'Is it?' Nora asked. Their eyes met for a moment in the mirror and the woman flushed. Nora put her hand on her shoulder.

'Is there anything I can help you with?' Nora said softly. 'Anything at all?' For a moment, she thought the woman was going to cry, then she shook her head and managed to smile.

'No, but thank you for this.' She touched the scarf. 'I know you didn't want to take your window apart.' She opened her evening bag and took out her purse. 'You're a lifesaver.'

I wish I was, Nora thought, watching her go. *I hope there is someone in your life who is.*

The moment the silk touched Michelle's neck, the lump of panic at the back of her throat softened. The scarf was like a gentle hand soothing the bruised skin.

She started the car and switched the radio on and Adele's voice poured out of the speakers. The soft summer air blew in through the open window and by the time she was driving along the looping ribbon of road that led to the beach in Killiney, she was counting her blessings. She had a good life. A good job. Good friends. A good man. In a few hours, she would turn thirty-eight, but that was still young. And tomorrow was the beginning of a new year, the year Luke got help so that they could get back to how they were at the start.

Rain started to fall as she turned through the pillars at the gate but she was smiling to herself as she hurried up the stone steps to the door of the hotel, protecting her hair with her hand.

Luke was standing beneath the chandelier in the elegant black-and-white tiled hall and he was another blessing for her to count. This strong, solid, handsome man who belonged to her. Then she saw his face. The drawn-down eyebrows, the clenched jaw, the tight mouth.

'I'm so sorry.' She hurried over, shrugging off her coat. 'I got delayed at the hairdresser and the traffic was hell.'

A waiter appeared to take her coat. 'Your friends are already here,' he said. 'I'll just go and hang this up and bring you to the table.'

'Friends?' She turned to look at the waiter, confused, but he had gone to hang up her coat. She turned back to Luke.

'Surprise!' he said with a bite of sarcasm.

She looked over his shoulder into the brightly lit conservatory dining room and saw Liz's red curls, Brian, looking formal in a jacket and tie, Delia in a yellow dress, David's dark head leaning over to talk to his boyfriend Finn.

'I had no idea you invited them all!' she said to Luke.

'You're not the only one who can keep a secret.' His eyes were cold. 'I had a headache when I got here and I went looking for aspirin. And look what I found.' He slipped his hand into the pocket in his trousers and held up a small plastic disc. The blister pack of contraceptive pills Michelle kept hidden in the zip compartment of her toilet bag.

Panic hit her under the rib cage. He thought she'd stopped taking the pill at Christmas. 'Luke, I can explain.'

'I doubt that, Michelle.' He crushed the blister pack in his hand and put it back into his pocket.

Her throat tightened and the skin on the back of her neck prickled with fear. 'I didn't mean to lie to you...'

'You can save your excuses till later.' He pulled her close, bent down so that their foreheads were almost touching. Anyone seeing them would think it was a romantic moment, but his fingers were digging into the skin on her arm and his voice was hard. 'Right now, there's a table full of people waiting for us. So you can shut up and smile and show them how happy you are. Are we clear?'

She stared at him, then slowly nodded.

The waiter was back. They followed him over to the door but before they go through it, Michelle stopped short. 'I need to go to the ladies,' she said.

'No, you don't.' Luke gave her arm a jerk, but the waiter had already turned around.

'It's just down the corridor on your left, madam,' he said. 'I'll show you to the table, sir.'

'You go on!' Michelle said to Luke. 'I'll be right behind you.'

He was angry but he couldn't show it. He let her go.

At the end of the corridor was a flight of stairs. Michelle ran quickly up the steps past a first, then a second, then a third floor, her heart hammering in her chest, her blood thumping in her ears. She didn't care where she was going, she only knew that she had to get away. The last flight led to a fire door. She pushed through it and out onto the flat roof of the hotel. The rain was heavier now and a gust of wind whipped her carefully dried hair across her face and snatched at the hem of her dress.

She walked to the edge of the roof and looked down at her car parked on the gravel below. She had the keys in her bag.

She could go down and get into it and drive away. But he'd just come after her.

She stepped closer to the parapet and closed her eyes, imagining leaning forward, letting go.

The wind tore at the silk scarf, tugging the bow loose. She opened her eyes and managed to snatch one end of it before it flew away.

She looked down at it. It had seemed so free in the window of the gallery but it had been trapped, caught in a loop of air, rising and falling, never going anywhere.

She was trapped too. She would have to go back down the stairs and pretend, keep up the illusion, smile and laugh and unwrap gifts, clink glasses, blow out candles on a cake. And in a few hours, she would be alone with Luke again. She shivered. *He is going to kill me*, she thought. And a small, scared part of her wondered if it might be really true.

She held the scarf up and the wind filled it like a sail; she could see the elephants now. Trunk to tail, too many to count, marching in a little line around the border. She held her breath deep in her chest, until her lungs began to burn, then she opened her fingers and breathed out.

The scarf took off, a ripple of green unfurling in the light from the car park below. It turned a graceful arc and floated over the tops of a line of chestnut trees, then disappeared.

Michelle turned and walked back across the roof. She went downstairs to the restaurant in her lovely green dress with her neck bare. She was through hiding the bruises and truth. She wanted it to be over now. She wanted to be free.

10

Nine-Carat Yellow Gold Locket

Alanna

The flatbed truck bumped along the uneven track between the paddy fields, jolting every bone in Alanna's body. The others seemed oblivious. Clair and Amelie, the two French women, were fast asleep on one another's shoulders. Dieter, the older Austrian man, was meditating, his back somehow ramrod straight, his face set in a serene half-smile.

The three excitable English gap-year boys were chatting up the two gorgeous American girls who had arrived yesterday. All long limbs and gleaming hair and make-up, they must have been up at 5 a.m. applying it. It made Alanna feel exhausted just thinking about it. She jammed the palm of her hand against her face to try to steady her chin and counted all the things to be grateful for. Another glorious day in Bali. The feathery trees perfectly silhouetted against the dawn sky. The trio of monkeys perched on a wall who turned their heads to watch the truck drive by. The food and cold water in her backpack. Her health. Her beautiful daughter. She felt her mood shift and her heart lift as the truck turned off the track onto the paved road. Dieter, the Austrian guy, had opened his eyes and was rolling a cigarette, his head bent, his hand steady, his thinning blond hair falling into his eyes. He was closer to her age than the others, mid-forties, maybe. Old enough not to make her feel like a complete dinosaur. He wasn't bad-looking and he liked her. And though she had promised herself that she wouldn't get involved with anyone else for a while, she could feel her resolve beginning to weaken. Sometimes her new life felt more like exile than adventure.

Dieter touched her arm and held out the cigarette he'd been

rolling. Alanna smiled her thanks. Another thing to be grateful for. She leaned over to light it then took a drag and settled back to watch the small house compounds and temples slip past. It was almost light now and knots of local women in their bright sarongs and long-sleeved kebayas were coming back from the market. The first heat of the sun slanted through the trees, a burning touch on the back of her bare neck.

Alanna imagined that she was waking up eight thousand miles away, not in the flat in Brixton, that she had shared with Pete, but in the house in Temple Terrace in Dublin.

She closed her eyes and saw the sun spilling through the fanlight window in the hall, warming Houdini's fur. Smelled the sharp, fresh, sappy smell of cut grass, and the salty tang of sea mist in the garden. Even though she hadn't set foot in that house for thirty-five years, some stubborn part of her still thought of it as home.

It would be someone else's home in a month. All those rooms choked with things must be empty now, every trace of her parents' lives swept away. Alanna's father had been dead for nearly a year but she felt his comforting presence close to her. And lately, weirdly, she had felt her mother's presence too. Yesterday, when she was working, she had looked up and thought she'd seen Lainey standing at the edge of the rice field by the stone shrine, watching her, and she had caught her breath before she realised it was just a trick of the light. A tree shadow blurred by the incense smoke. Her overactive imagination. But it was enough to stir up old feelings of anger. If her mother was coming back to say sorry, it was too late. Her father, on the other hand, was welcome to haunt her any time.

She was still aching from the heartbreak of losing him. He had been so much more than a father to her. He'd been a friend and ally and, later, a surrogate father for her daughter. Alanna had imagined that he'd always be there for her but then, suddenly, he was gone and she had done what she always did when things got overwhelming. She had run away.

It had shocked her, how easy it was to do it again. To end another relationship, to leave another flat, to head off into uncertainty again, at fifty-two, carrying her entire life in two suitcases.

And maybe it was because of her grief, but as she was buying her one-way ticket to India, for the first time in her life, she'd felt a disquiet at the thought of moving yet again. Maybe, after this trip was over, it would be time to put down roots. To find a place that would always be there to come back to.

After three months of meditation and yoga at an ashram in Kerala, Alanna was beginning to feel like herself again. Then a message had come from Nora. Her mother was dying. Alanna had expected that it would happen sooner rather than later. What she had not expected was the tiny spark of love for her mother that had survived all the years of their estrangement. Part of her wanted to jump on a plane and dash back to Ireland so that they could make peace with one another. But she knew there was no point. Her mother had never wanted her, that wasn't going to change just because her life was ending.

Those last few days, when she knew that Lainey was dying, Alanna stayed in her bunk bed in the empty dormitory at the ashram, her face turned to the wall. She had waited until she was sure it was too late before she called her daughter. She had not gone back for the funeral; she couldn't face it. She was ashamed now, that she had left Nora to handle everything. Lainey's death, the arrangements, the will, the house. She had done the very thing she blamed her mother for doing. She had been absent when her daughter needed her most.

The truck pulled over and the others climbed out. Dieter jumped down and held out his hand to help Alanna. Maybe all she needed was a fling, Alanna thought, as she watched him climb the terraced field ahead of her. Something different to focus her attention on. Maybe sex and company would drive away all this guilt and regret?

She got to work, weeding a long narrow tier of planted rice. It was backbreaking work. The mud sucked at her feet and her fingertips were puckered from the water. Her arms were aching and her shoulders were beginning to burn, but she wouldn't allow herself to stop for a break. Age was just a number. She had to prove to herself and to everyone else that she was able for this; that she could go on doing it for another fifteen years if she had to.

The pipe dream of having a home in Ireland to go back to had dissolved after Alanna heard about the will. But forty thousand euros was a lot of money out in Asia. She could live well here on half that and put the other half away for Nora so that she could take a few months off at some stage and re-think her career. She had fallen into styling and maybe she was good at it, but it was a hard, cold, shallow world and her daughter was too soft and too easily exploited. Alanna would have loved to see her break away from Liv, strike out on her own and do something creative that came from her heart.

Alanna tugged a stubborn weed out of the water. She was worried about her daughter. Adam was handsome and charming and so good at those grand romantic gestures that women loved, but Alanna had the feeling he cared far more about himself than he did about her daughter. Nora had spent the last two years redecorating that house in Fountain Road, playing house for a man who was hardly ever home.

Alanna felt the first cooling drops of rain on her arms and by the time she had straightened up, it had turned to a wall of water. She gathered her sopping sarong around her ankles and ran for cover beneath a palm tree. The others made a space for her and Alanna passed out a bag of mangosteens from her backpack and they huddled together companionably until the storm had blown over.

'By the way,' Dieter said quietly in his careful English as they climbed back up the sloping field when the rain had passed, 'I've got a bottle of good arak in my shack if you want to come over for a drink before dinner.'

'Oh,' Alanna said, 'that would be lovely.' But she knew, suddenly, that that's all it would be. A lovely brief distraction from the things she didn't want to deal with. Her anger at her mother. Her grief for her father. Her worry about her daughter. She smiled at Dieter. 'But I'm going to skip dinner, thank you. I need to walk into Ubud to check my post.'

He was disappointed. She could see it from the set of his shoulders as he worked beside her in the afternoon and the stiff wave he gave her as the others climbed into the truck to head back to the homestead. Alanna felt a sharp stab of loneliness as they drove away but she fought it off as she turned and set off across the fields towards the village.

The narrow track took her past a homemade tent that a family of migrant workers had pitched beside the storm drains. It wasn't much, a plastic trap rigged up on crossed sticks, but it was home to a couple in their twenties, their toddler, and an older woman who looked after their daughter. The woman was stooped, her skin deeply wrinkled. She had missing teeth at the front of her mouth but she was, Alanna thought, probably younger than her.

Through some signing and pointing, Alanna had found out that she was called Nyoman and that her granddaughter was called Putu.

It always touched Alanna, when she passed, to see all the different ways Nyoman cared for the child. Moving the tarp to keep her in the shade. Giving her rags soaked in water to suck when she was teething. Pulling her into her lap to comb her hair for parasites. When she played, the old woman's eyes were always on her, though her fingers were constantly moving, stringing beads on wire, twisting them deftly to make earrings and bracelets probably intended for the tourist shops in Kuta.

Alanna thought she travelled light but compared to Nyoman, she was as laden down with things as her own mother had been. The tent was open to the world. A heavy woven cloth divided it into separate sleeping quarters. There were folded sarongs for a bed and pillows and a faded plastic laundry basket held stacked pots and plastic plates.

Alanna did not want to offend her by offering money, but she had started bringing small gifts. A packet of cotton bibs for the little girl or a bunch of bananas. When the rainy season had started, she'd brought a mosquito net.

She didn't have anything today, but Nyoman was still pleased to see her. She patted the ground beside her and gave Alanna a gift. A small parcel of rice in a folded leaf, tied with a knotted blade of grass.

Alanna opened it and began to eat and the two women watched the little girl playing happily, tapping on an empty blackened pot with a stick.

Nyoman pointed at the girl and then at Alanna. Alanna understood. She held up one finger to show she had one child and raised her hand to show she was grown up.

Nyoman nodded and pointed at the little girl again and raised her shoulders.

'No.' Alanna shook her head. 'No grandchildren.' She pointed at the watch on her wrist, mimed the hands going round. 'Maybe soon.'

Nyoman beamed.

It was true, Alanna thought. Nora and Adam had bought a house. Any day now, she could be a grandmother. She couldn't wait. Although, she realised with an ache, if she was living on the other side of the world, she would not see much of her grandchild.

She shook the thought away and finished her rice, then wiped her sticky fingers on her sarong and extracted her old Nokia from her backpack. She clicked through until she found a photo of Nora.

Nyoman studied it carefully. She smiled and patted her face, then touched her heart.

'Yes,' Alanna smiled, 'she has a beautiful heart. I'm very lucky to have her.' She joined her palms to show gratitude.

Nyoman joined her own palms to show she was lucky too.

Alanna turned to watch Putu, who was dropping stones into the pot, laughing with delight at their clatter. Where had the last thirty years gone? It seemed like yesterday that her daughter had been that age. Alanna had been so sure that she could give Nora the things every child needed. Love and roots and wings. She had managed the love and the wings, but she'd failed with the roots. Nora had struggled with all the moving around, the changing schools, the different cities. Maybe what she'd really needed was a permanent home, a normal family; routine and security.

Nyoman was looking at her sympathetically. Alanna shook her

head and looked away. 'I wanted to do things differently to my mother, but I now think I might have gone too far the other way.'

Nyoman nodded slowly, as if she understood the sentiment, if not the words. She patted Alanna's hand and then she held it and suddenly the words began to pour out and Alanna found herself telling this stranger who didn't even speak English, all about her childhood.

To anyone looking at it from the outside, that house in Temple Terrace, packed to the ceilings with beautiful things, would have seemed like a kind of paradise compared to the makeshift shack behind her. But it lacked the most important thing of all. A mother.

Alanna could not remember Lainey ever holding her or bathing her or watching over her the way Nyoman was watching over her granddaughter now. Lainey was always too busy. Too lost in the daily ritual of caring for all her precious things: dusting and cleaning the mirrors; rubbing beeswax into the furniture; polishing the silver; refolding the clothes in her wardrobes and drawers; taking out every dish and glass in the huge china cupboard and washing it. A round of tasks that never ended. By the time she was finished, it was time to start all over again.

Her father resigned his high-powered job and went part-time to look after Alanna. He was the one who read her stories and made her meals and walked her to school. And when she skinned her knee or won a prize or needed a hug, it was him she ran to. She didn't have a single memory of her mother ever touching her and yet Alanna's childhood had revolved around her.

She wasn't allowed to have a bike because Lainey was afraid she would fall off. She couldn't cross the road to the library in case she was hit by a car. She couldn't swim on her own in case she drowned. She couldn't play with the kids in the park because they were rough and they might hurt her.

Her father was adamant that her mother loved her but that she just wasn't very good at showing it. She'd had lost touch with her own family during the war.

'Where? How?' Alanna wanted to know.

'It's not my story to tell, sweetheart,' Hugh said. 'Maybe she'll tell you herself, some day.'

But her mother wouldn't talk about her past. She refused to talk about her family. And by the time Alanna was twelve she had figured out why. Lainey cared more about things than she did about people. Family simply didn't matter to her.

Putu came running from where she'd been playing and climbed into her grandmother's lap. The old woman gathered her up in her arms, then pointed at the phone and then at herself and the little girl.

Yes, Alanna nodded, understanding, hoping her clapped-out battery would last. The old woman and the little girl leaned together, the wrinkled cheek pressed against the smooth one and Alanna took their picture.

She turned the phone around to show them the image on the screen.

The little girl crowed with delight and let out a stream of breathless words, touching the screen with a tiny, pudgy fingertip.

'*Matur suksma!*' Nyoman beamed at Nora.

'Thank *you*!' Alanna touched her heart. 'It was so good to talk to you.'

Alanna stayed on the track until she hit the ribbon of dusty road that led into Ubud. The small houses dwindled out and she walked past the walls of hotel compounds, their entrances marked with elaborate carved-stone statues. The road into the village was dotted with restaurants, Internet cafés, tour operators and shops hung with clothes, carvings, souvenirs, fake watches and sarongs. Alanna passed a temple compound where a gamelan orchestra dressed in red-and-gold costumes was rehearsing, eight men filling the air with vibrations of gongs and bells. A small monkey swung by its tail from a sign above a jewellery shop. Two men in an open workshop were putting the finishing touches to an enormous papier mâché bull for a cremation ceremony.

By now, the pavement was crowded. There were ticket sellers and taxi touts on every corner and crowds of tourists, freshly showered and perfumed after a day spent by a pool. Women in high shoes hung on to their men as they picked their way along the broken pavements.

Alanna forced herself to slow down. To look both ways as she crossed the narrow streets where scooters with whole families balanced on the back zipped past. On Sunset Road, she threaded her way through the crowd to the orange-and-black-painted post office. It was the usual chaos inside. When it was her turn at the counter, a tiny, elegant, Balinese woman with a profile as perfect as any film star took her passport, photocopied it and returned with a brown-padded jiffy bag bearing an Irish stamp.

A letter from Nora. Alanna smiled with anticipation as she went outside into the soupy dusk. She headed up a quiet side street, took a table outside a small café and ordered a pineapple juice. Then she tore the seal of the jiffy bag open and shook out the contents. A small roll of bubble wrap and a folded piece of paper. It was a flyleaf torn from a book and it was covered in her mother's handwriting. Alanna flinched at the sight of it. There was no telling what hurt those small, cramped words might contain.

She rolled a cigarette with the last few fragments of tobacco in her pouch, smoked it and finished her sticky pineapple juice before she had the courage to pick the paper up and unfold it.

Alanna's head spun with disbelief as she read the note for the second time:

'I loved her so much but I was terrified that I'd hurt her . . .
I just couldn't look after her . . .
I knew that she would be safer with him. I wasn't a fit mother.'

For a second, Alanna let in the thought that this version of her childhood might be true. Maybe her mother had suffered from some kind of postnatal depression? Maybe that was why she hadn't been able to look after her. But that was wishful thinking.

If Lainey had suffered from depression, then Hugh would have made sure to get her help. She could have taken medication or seen a counsellor.

No. It was lies. She would have remembered if Lainey had ever held her in her arms or nursed her or comforted her. This was an old woman's attempt to justify her coldness and her complete disinterest in being a mother.

Alanna screwed the note up, flicked her lighter and set fire to it. She watched it turn to soft grey ash that lifted and drifted on the warm air. That was what she thought of her mother's attempt to rewrite history.

By the time she was seventeen, Alanna had broken free of her mother's control. She had learned, from her father, how to be open and easy with people. She had a circle of good friends and she shared more with their mothers than she ever could with Lainey. She was a fearless swimmer, nothing scared her. Sometimes, as she leapt off the highest diving board in Killiney, she grinned, imagining the terror on her mother's face if she could see her shooting straight as an arrow into the sea.

She saved her babysitting money for years and, after her exams, she announced that she was going to take a year out to go travelling before going to college. Her father gave her his blessing but her mother locked herself away in her room for days and refused to eat. It was a game, she was trying to get them to feel sorry for her and Alanna didn't back down.

The night before she was due to fly to London, she was woken by a terrible wailing. It was a sound she had never heard before – her mother, crying. Her father was talking to her quietly, trying to console her.

And it occurred to Alanna, just for a moment, that maybe Lainey really did love her. That maybe this wasn't all for show. Maybe she didn't want her to go away because she would really miss her. But, even as tears of sympathy welled behind her eyes, her mother's voice broke through her cries, hoarse and angry and still audible two rooms away.

'I never wanted a child, Hugh. I told you that. You talked me into it. I wish I hadn't listened to you. I wish I'd never had her.'

Alanna didn't cry that night or the next morning when she left. She didn't cry until ten months later when she held her newborn daughter in her arms for the first time and the full weight of her own mother's rejection hit her.

Getting pregnant after a one-night stand at a music festival had not been part of Alanna's plans. It meant that she had to abandon her year out and her chance to go to university. She was on her own, breastfeeding and changing nappies, when all the girls she knew were getting drunk and going clubbing. But Alanna never had a single doubt about what she was doing. From the moment that she saw the faint blue line appearing on her first pregnancy test, she wanted her baby with every fibre in her body.

There was never a chance of finding the father. These were the days before Facebook and mobile phones and all Alanna knew was his first name: Tim. A sweet name for a sweet boy who would never know the part he had played in the best thing that had ever happened to her.

Her father was the first person she told when she found out she was pregnant. She moved back to Dublin so that she could be close to him, but she refused to go back to Temple Terrace. She couldn't bring another child into that suffocating house.

She was only eighteen and she had no idea what she was doing but she muddled along. She waitressed until Nora was born and afterwards she found work she could do without leaving her daughter. She looked after other people's children and walked their dogs and cleaned their houses. Hugh helped out with childcare but she wouldn't let him pay for anything. Sometimes she was late with the rent and sometimes the places where they lived were dingy and damp. But those things didn't matter, what mattered was that she could do this on her own. She could give Nora what every child needed most: a loving mother.

But then when Nora was five, Alanna caught viral pneumonia. She had to spend six weeks in hospital in an isolation ward. She couldn't ask her father to move into her flat so Nora had to go home with him.

By the time Alanna was discharged, Nora had fallen in love with Temple Terrace and Alanna didn't have the heart to take it all away from her. She agreed to let Nora continue to visit the house and sometimes, she even let her stay over. Somehow, her cold, remote mother had wormed her way into her daughter's affections. More than that, Nora loved her, and she could never understand why Alanna didn't. That was why Nora had sent that awful note. She might believe Lainey's lies but Alanna knew better.

The ashes from the burned note were drifting down now, a soft grey snow, settling on the table where the little knot of bubble wrap sat like an unexploded bomb. Alanna pushed it with the tip of her straw, then she picked it up and ripped the tape off.

She had expected some bright glittering trinket of Lainey's but instead, a tarnished locket on a blackened chain clattered out onto the metal table. The one she was supposed to believe she had teethed on when she was a baby. It was even scored by small, deep marks. She tried to prise the two gold circles open but the hinge that joined them had been crushed and it wouldn't open. Alanna dropped it onto the table in disgust.

She wanted to get rid of it. To crush it under her boot or to fling it into the Champuan river. But that would be wasteful. It was gold. It would probably feed a family for a week. She stared at it, resentfully. Then she had an idea. She stuffed the jiffy bag into her backpack and grabbed the locket. She threw down some rupee notes beside her empty glass and set off.

The quickest way to reach her homestay was the paved road, but Alanna took the track across the fields, back the way she had come earlier. It was dark now; there was no moon, just a sprinkle of stars and a few dancing fireflies, but a yellow dot in the distance guided her and as she drew closer, she saw the small fire with three figures gathered around it.

Nyoman was bent over her work, threading beads onto a chain. Her daughter was turning a skewer of meat on a rack over the fire while her husband fanned the flames with a folded piece of cardboard.

In the flickering light, Alanna saw the little girl, cocooned in the mosquito net, sleeping inside the makeshift tent.

The young couple looked up at her curiously, and Nyoman stood up to greet her. Alanna pushed the locket into her hand.

'Please,' she said in English, then in Indonesian. '*Tolong*.' Then, before the old woman could protest or invite her to share her meagre dinner, she turned and walked away quickly.

As the days passed, the terraces of rice that they were weeding were narrower and higher. The work was running out. The gap-year kids were going to Flores to dive. Dieter was heading back to Austria. The two French women had heard about an organic farm in Lombok that needed fruit pickers and Alanna had decided she'd ask if she could join them. She didn't want to spend Christmas alone. She had taken a break to roll a cigarette when she heard someone calling her name from down the hill. She shaded her eyes against the fierce afternoon sun and saw a familiar figure hurrying up the steep terraced field. The woman was nimble and fast, barely out of breath by the time she reached her. Definitely younger, Alanna thought, beaming at Nyoman.

'*Om suastiastu!*' Alanna made a small bow.

Nyoman bowed back and held out a small folded leaf package tied together with knotted grass. It was too small to hold rice. Alanna opened it, expecting to see a piece of durian fruit or a peeled rambutan, but there, instead, was the locket. It had been transformed. The chain glittered; the deep indentations in the gold had been smoothed out.

'No!' She shook her head. 'You don't understand. I didn't want you to fix it. It was a gift. I wanted you to keep it.' She tried to give it back but Nyoman stepped out of reach and pointed at the locket and opened her hands, like a book.

The clasp that had been jammed shut opened with a click. There were two faded, old fashioned black-and-white photographs inside. Inside, there were two tiny black and white photographs set into the oval windows. The faces of two men. One was in his thirties, his chin held high, a heavy moustache above an unsmiling mouth. The other was younger. His eyes had the same proud expression he was smiling. He was so like Nora, he could have been her twin brother.

Alanna knew with certainty that she was looking at her

grandfather and her uncle. The family her mother had never spoken about.

Nyoman said something quietly and reached up with a corner of her sarong and wiped Alanna's face and it was only then that she realised a tear was slipping down her cheek and that it was for her mother. For the first time in her life, she had a sense of what she might have lost.

The internet cafe on the Hanoman Road was packed with people lined up at the banks of computer monitors. The ceiling fan turned slowly above the counter, stirring the humid air that was thick with smoke from the clove cigarettes that all the locals smoked. The man behind the counter had to rummage through a box of jumbled cable leads until he found one that would connect Alanna's ancient Nokia to his computer.

He looked surprised when she told him what she wanted but he didn't ask any questions. He sized the photograph of the old woman and her granddaughter on the screen, then printed it and cut the faces out carefully before fitting them into the round silver locket that Alanna had bought in the jewellery shop on Jalan Raya.

She was heading north today, to another rice plantation in Aceh, but she would stop by the storm drain on her way to the bus station. Nyoman might not have anywhere to put photographs but she could wear the locket around her neck. It would always be with her.

The man did some more rummaging and produced a large blue fake-leather box that had once held a watch. It was far too big for the locket, but it was a kind gesture and Alanna thanked him. He polished the locket, slipped it into the box and handed it over.

When Alanna tried to put the box into the front pocket of her backpack, a ball of crumpled paper blocked it. It was the jiffy bag that Nora had sent her.

She remembered the torn flyleaf covered with her mother's tiny handwriting. She wished now that she hadn't burned it. She wished Lainey was still alive, so she could talk to her. She still did not trust Lainey's version of her own childhood, but she desperately wanted to the boys in the locket. She wanted to know what had happened to them. Why Lainey had never spoken about them. She must have missed them so much, Alanna thought, and she felt a crack in the armour and it occurred to her for the first time that maybe she had judged her mother too harshly. That maybe her mother's coldness and distance was too do with pain, not selfishness. But it was too late to find out now.

As she scrunched up the jiffy bag to throw it away, she realised there was something inside it. She slipped her fingers inside and pulled out the thin white card with gilt edging that had stuck in the lining.

Hi, Mum,
Thanks for your email telling me about your plans to go to Aceh. I'm hoping that you haven't left Ubud yet, otherwise it might be the new year before this gets to you.

I know you said that you didn't want anything from the house on Temple Terrace, but I found this locket among Lainey's things along with the enclosed note and I felt I had to send them both on to you. I know you don't want to go over the past and I'm not sure if reading what she wrote will change anything for you, but I had to send it anyway.

I probably should have told you this in my last email but I didn't want you to worry about me... Something happened between Adam and Liv – an affair or maybe just a fling. I don't want to go into the details now or in an email, but I'll tell you more when I talk to you. It was pretty awful for a while after I found out about it, but I'm doing okay now. Actually, I'm doing really well.

I decided to take six months out in Dublin before I go back to London. I'm staying in Temple Terrace, which is lovely, and I'm keeping busy. I'm sorting slowly through all the stuff in the house and I'm finding out all this stuff I never knew about Hugh and Lainey. And (wait for it!) I've opened up the shop on the ground floor to sell everything off. It makes more sense money-wise and it means I can find new homes for all Lainey's treasures.

I know you probably think I've gone crazy, but I promise,
I haven't. I'm in a good place, despite everything. So please,
don't worry about me. I can tell you all about it all when you
phone me at Christmas. You will phone, won't you? I miss you!
Love,
Nora

Alanna gasped, unable to believe what she was reading. Poor
Nora. The two most important people in her life had betrayed
her. How could she be fine? She must be heartbroken! What was
she doing living on her own in that awful house? And what was
all this stuff about opening a shop?

The shop had a payphone in the corner and Alanna joined the
queue but as she was counting out rupee coins for the call, she
realised that if she called her daughter, Nora would do what she
had tried to do in the note. She would try to convince her that
she was fine.

But Alanna would not be convinced, not until she saw Nora
for herself.

11

Victorian-Era Taj Mahal Bird Cage

Nora

It rained for the seven days straight the week Will was away shooting an ad in Prague. Bitterly cold autumn downpours stripped the leaves from the trees. Low grey clouds rolled in from the Irish Sea, turning the afternoons dark at 4 o'clock. Nora hadn't put a foot outside the door all week. She felt edgy and restless. It wasn't Will she missed, she told herself. It was the fresh air and the exercise. She could have put her coat on and walked the pier on her own, but somehow, she never got around to it.

He'd have landed back in Dublin by now, she thought, locking the shop on Friday evening, but he'd had a week of early morning starts and late night shoots. The last thing he'd feel like was a walk in the lashing rain. She turned out the lights and went upstairs to the kitchen. The table was covered in clutter that she hadn't gotten around to sorting through. She could make a start on it after dinner. She was staring into the fridge, trying to summon up the energy to cook something, when she heard a tap on the front door. Fiona, Nora smiled. And she'd probably have a take-away from the café with her. But when she opened the door, Will was on the doorstep with Mac, holding a tattered golf umbrella.

'It's you!' She sounded more delighted than she'd meant to. 'Both of you!' She bent to pat Mac's drenched ears. 'Are you going down the pier?'

'Apparently I am!' Will said, ruefully. 'This guy hasn't had a proper walk while I've been away. But don't feel under any pressure to come, we'll understand if you want to take a,' he held his hand out from under the umbrella into the stream of water, 'rain check.'

But Nora was already pulling on her coat and stuffing her hair beneath the brim of one of Hugh's hats.

Mac took off along the Monkstown road and they huddled together under the umbrella and trudged after him through a vertical wall of water, Will walking on the outside, so that he was the one who got soaked by waves of water churned up by passing cars. They huddled together beneath the dripping umbrella, careful to keep an inch of air between their shoulders.

Will told her about the shoot, making her laugh with his descriptions of the stand-offs between the client who wanted a bog-standard thirty-second ad and the director who was a budding Quentin Tarantino. Nora filled him in on the week she'd had in the shop, and the theatre set-designer who had bought Lainey's armoire to use as the wardrobe in a production of *The Lion, The Witch and The Wardrobe*.

They were the only two people mad enough to go out in the downpour and they had the pier to themselves. They were surrounded by the sound of water. The crash of the waves on either side of the pier and the drum of the drops on Will's umbrella. But at the very end of the pier, the downpour stopped for a minute and the clouds parted just a fraction, enough to reveal a sliver of navy velvet sky hung with a silver sickle moon. The sight of it stopped them in their tracks. Even Mac looked up from snuffling the wall to take it in.

'This has been the wettest walk of my life,' Will said, 'but it was worth it, just for that.'

He was right, Nora thought. And as the clouds closed over and rain swept in again, she had a fleeting feeling that this was exactly where she was supposed to be, standing here with Will and the dog in this wild, wet place, frozen to the bone, with icy drops trickling down the back of her neck.

'Let's head back, before we drown!' Will said and they turned and began the long trudge back to Temple Terrace.

When Nora opened the front door, Mac pushed past her and trotted, dripping, into the hall.

'Make yourself at home, why don't you?' Will called after him.
'Do you want to come in for a coffee?'

'I won't sleep if I have coffee this late,' Will closed his umbrella,
'but if you had a beer...'

He followed her down the hall.

'The kitchen is a bit of a mess, I'm afraid.' Nora had stacked
the wooden canteens of cutlery and packed the last few dinner
sets and glassware collections carefully into boxes. The table was
covered with mismatched things – plates, tureens, egg cups, bowls
and vases.

Will pulled off his coat and ran his hand through his dark,
drenched hair and laughed. 'If you want to see what a mess is,
you should come home with me'

The rental house he and Alice had moved into in June was
unrecognisable. The kids' things were everywhere. Coats and
jackets in a pile over the bannisters in the hall; shoes abandoned
where Alice, Jake and Froggy had kicked them off; the living-
room floor was a jumble of school bags and books, and toys
and a treacherous tangle of X-Box wires. The sofa where they
squeezed together to play video games was covered in dog hair.
Stephen, in a desperate bid to get Gemma to move home, was
holding back maintenance payments and Gemma wouldn't take
money from Will, she turned the kitchen as a makeshift hair salon
every evening to earn some cash.

When he had come in from the airport earlier, two different
songs were blaring from the speakers in Alice and Jake's rooms
joined by the tinny sound-track of whatever Froggy was playing
on his DS. It felt to Will sometimes, after his quiet, ordered life
in New York, as if he was living in a lunatic asylum.

It was heaven to be in this peaceful, elegant, empty house. Nora
walked to the fridge to get the beers. Her cheeks were flushed
from the walk and her dark curls, wet from the rain, seemed to
have doubled in length.

She twisted the top off a bottle and handed it to him. 'How
did Alice get on while you were away?'

'Pretty good!' Will took a gulp and hoped that she hadn't
noticed him staring at her. 'Gemma told me she got an A in an

art project. I don't want to jinx it but she seems to be settling in to school.'

'She's settling in at the shop too. I don't know what I'd do without her!' Nora tipped her head over and began to rub her hair with a towel. Will was transfixed, for a moment, by the sight of her long, bare neck and he turned away quickly and busied himself looking at the jumble on the table.

He frowned as he spotted a blue-and-white bowl with a lid among the bits of crockery. It couldn't be, he thought, could it? He leaned over and picked it up, turning it in his hands, carefully. The bowl had been broken and put back together again. But instead of glue, the cracks between the pieces had been fixed with veins of gold. 'This is a piece of Kintsukuroi!'

'A what?' Nora looked up from under the towel.

It's the Japanese art of fixing broken things with lacquer dusted with gold.' Will held out the bowl in his hands. The four shards on the lid were held together with glittering threads. 'I went to an exhibition of it once, in New York. It was beautiful. The artists have this philosophy that damage and brokenness can actually make things more beautiful.' He lifted the lid. 'There's something in here. It's a page torn from a book.'

Nora dropped the towel. 'Is there anything written on it?'

'No.' Will said, smoothing the page out carefully. 'It's the lyrics of a Leonard Cohen song. "Anthem." The one about how there's a crack in every single thing, and that that was how the light can get in.'

Will cleared a space on the table for their beers and sat opposite her and Nora told him about the other notes: the shock discovery that her grandmother had been Greek, the dark past that Lainey had hinted at that would probably always be a mystery.

'I'll never know what really happened,' she said. 'Maybe I'm not supposed to. Fiona says that when people want to hide things, it's usually for a good reason.'

'Have you asked your mother about it? She might know what happened.'

Nora sighed. 'She doesn't even know that I found her mum's

passport. They had a huge falling out when she was seventeen. She ran away and they never spoke again, not even once. Which was kind of sad, really, because we're such a tiny family. Neither of my grandparents had siblings so there were no uncles or aunts. It was just my grandparents, my mum and me.'

Will nodded. 'What about your father?'

'My mother met him at a music festival. It was a one night stand. She tried to track him down but it was different back then. No Internet, no social media.'

'Did you ever try to find him?'

Nora shrugged. 'I know it sounds weird, but I never really wanted to. My grandfather was like a surrogate dad. Mum has had boyfriends, but she always takes off when anything gets serious. It's kind of a pattern with her, running away.'

Will was fiddling with the cap of his beer. 'What about you?' he asked without looking up. 'You ever do the whole nine yards?'

They hadn't talked about relationships before. It was as if both of them had an unspoken agreement to avoid it.

Nora took a sip of beer and wiped her mouth. 'No,' she said. 'There was someone in London but...' But he had lied to her. Led her to believe that this was it, then, when she looked away, fallen into bed with her best friend. She fought to keep her face neutral and swallowed hard. 'But it didn't work out.'

'I'm sorry,' Will said. 'I didn't mean to put you on the spot.'

She shook her head. 'It's fine. It's just not something I really want to talk about.'

'Actually, I should probably get going!' Will stood up, knocking his coat off the back of his chair, ducking clumsily to pick it up.

'Okay.' Nora stood up too. She had been about to ask him if he wanted to stay for dinner, before the past had mugged her. Damn Adam and Liv! And damn herself for letting what happened still matter to her. She followed Will out into the hall. Mac was dozing at the bottom of the stairs on Houdini's old spot and he woke up when he heard their footsteps ringing out on the floorboards. All the rugs had been sold now, the console table was gone. The walls were bare.

The rain had stopped completely, Nora saw, as she opened the front door. The clouds had disappeared and the sky above the roof of the library was glittering with stars.

Will had left his umbrella by the door. He picked it up and stepped outside and shook it. 'Thanks,' he said, 'for the walk and the talk and the beer!'

'Thanks for the company,' Nora said. 'I was feeling kind of lonely before you showed up.'

If she'd said that earlier, Will thought, he wouldn't have left. But he couldn't change his mind now. 'Well, goodnight.' As he leaned down to kiss her on the cheek he felt a force, strong and unexpected, to turn his mouth to meet hers. It was an effort to pull himself back, to graze her cheek with his lips.

Jesus! he thought, as he walked away. What was wrong with him? Nora had just practically confessed that she wasn't over some kind of heartbreak and he had sympathised and then he had nearly kissed her. He was praying that she hadn't noticed when he heard her voice.

'Will! Wait!'

He felt a thread of hope pull tight in his ribcage as he turned around, but then he saw Mac standing beside her looking at him reproachfully.

'You forgot the dog.' Nora held out the lead. 'Again.'

The door of the shop was blocked with three bulging plastic bin bags. One of them had split open and spilled out a pile of damp, crumpled clothes. Nora looked up and down the terrace, it was empty. She had put a sign on the door: 'Sorry, we don't take donations,' but that didn't stop them coming.

It had started with one bag, on Monday. A used envelope taped to the side. A note, in spidery writing; an old person's hand: 'These are my late husband's clothes. I couldn't bear to just throw them away so I thought you might be able to use them for your shop.'

The clothes inside were carefully folded, shirts with worn cuffs, a dark suit, shiny at the seams. A zip-up cardigan with leather patches on the elbows. Now there were bags or boxes outside the door almost every day. A cardboard box that contained a dozen wooden carvings of African animals and a note scribbled on the back of a photograph of a couple in 1950s safari suits: 'My uncle and aunt in Kenya, 1953'. A bag of cuddly toys and a box of Monopoly, the paper money leaking from a split in a worn box with a card that said: 'So many happy memories of playing with these, but kids are 40 and 38 now. Maybe someone else's kids can use them.' There was an ivory satin wedding dress that still had its tags. There was no note with it, but Nora could guess the story.

It touched her that The Memory Shop had inspired people like this. She didn't know what she was going to do with all the things they had left yet, but she would figure out a way to find new homes for them.

She was dragging the bags into the shop, water trailing across the floor, when Alice's aunt Gemma drove up to drop her off. Halloween was a week away, but they both looked as if they were going to a fancy-dress party. Gemma was in white wide-legged pants, a striped top and a boxy sailor-style jacket. Alice wore a long, trailing black lace dress and biker boots, her blonde hair backcombed. Her face was white, her mouth painted dark purple. She'd tried so hard to look scary, Nora thought fondly.

She felt slightly awkward as she went outside to say hello to Gemma. Alice had no idea how much time Nora was spending with Will, but his sister must know, must be adding two and two together and getting five. Nora didn't blame her. She had done the same herself the other night. She could have sworn that he was going to kiss her as he was leaving the other night, but after he'd gone, she decided that maybe it had been wishful thinking on her part. A hangover from that magical moment on the end of the pier.

She pushed it out of her mind now and ruffled Alice's hair. 'Hi!' she called out to Gemma. She didn't really know Will's sister at all, but she felt a sense of connection to her. They were on the same path, both walking, as fast as they could, away from the wreckage of infidelity. It cheered Nora on, to see how much lighter and happier Gemma was every time she saw her.

'It's torture not being able to come into your lovely shop to browse!' Gemma said, wistfully. 'But I've got to run. See you later Ali.'

Alice rolled her eyes. 'I'm too old for like, diminutives,' but she allowed Gemma to give her a quick hug and even hugged her back, then she led Nora imperiously into the shop.

'Ugh!' She wrinkled her nose and pointed at the two gaping bags on the floor. 'That's so gross!'

The bags were stuffed with expensive clothes. Crumpled women's coats and sweaters, designer dresses stained at the armpits. A man's tuxedo, some jackets, half a dozen golf jumpers.

They were wet from the rain, but most of them would have to go to the laundry anyway. Luckily, Nora had just done a window for the dry-cleaner a few doors down and he'd been so pleased he'd given her a free pass forever.

'I don't know how you can, like, even touch those,' Alice said, recoiling, as Nora pulled a corduroy jacket out of the bag. 'They stink.'

'It's what happens with old things,' Nora said.

The jacket was soft with leather patches at the elbows. There was a leaf in one pocket. She folded it as carefully as she would have folded it if it had been her grandfather's.

Alice curled her lip and Nora caught a glint of the tongue piercing she was only allowed to wear on weekends. 'The people who owned all these things are probably, like, dead.'

'You're right,' Nora said. 'That's why we have to be extra gentle with their things. If you don't want help me, why don't go upstairs and get on with the birds for our window?'

Alice brightened. 'Okay.'

The window for Lainey's Taj Mahal bird cage might be Nora's last, so she wanted it to be her best. She and Alice had been tracing tiny, brightly coloured birds on postcard-sized sheets of acetate for nearly a week.

Alice had real talent, Nora thought, when she was flicking through the stack of paintings the girl left on her desk, stopping to admire a kingfisher with azure wings and a tiny, bright red cardinal. She was so engrossed that she didn't notice the door opening, but she sensed someone watching her and, when she looked, she recognised the woman immediately as the one who had bought Lainey's green scarf with the border of grey elephants.

'Hi.' The woman was twisting her hands nervously.

'Hello,' Nora stood up. She had thought about this often and wished she had talked to her about that livid bruise she'd seen on her neck.

'I wondered if you could do me a favour.'

'Of course,' Nora said quietly.

'Can you take this for me?' The woman dropped something on the desk between them with a clatter. It was an engagement ring. A diamond solitaire.

'Oh,' Nora said. 'I don't buy things...'

'I know.' The woman smiled. 'Or take donations. I read the notice on the door. But I wondered if you'd make an exception. I tried to give this back but the person who gave it to me wouldn't take it. And I don't want it. I don't want anything of his...' Nora felt a flood of relief. Whoever had hurt her wasn't in her life any more. 'I'm starting again and I want to –' she stared at Nora's drawing – 'I want to draw a line. I can't explain, but I feel like I owe a debt to you. So I want you to take it. I need you to take it. Please.'

She looked at Nora so earnestly that she couldn't say no. She nodded. 'On one condition.'

The woman waited while Nora wrapped the last three of Lainey's silk scarves that she hadn't sold.

A sky-blue square with a pattern of deep pink roses. A pale yellow cubist design. A dramatic op art Zandra Rhodes.

'They're lovely,' the woman said, 'but this isn't necessary.'

But it felt necessary to Nora; necessary and right, like a circle closed.

The first family event after Stephen and Gemma split up was bound to be difficult, so Will decided to hire a bouncy castle for Froggy's eighth birthday. It was an enormous gaudy rubber monstrosity, that, when inflated, looked out of place in the tastefully manicured garden. He liked it, a lot, he thought, getting ready to go down to help his sister. It made the house look like it was lived in by a family which is what they were, for the moment, anyway. Gemma and her boys, he and Alice. And he liked that too.

Gemma had locked herself into the kitchen last night and eventually had appeared at midnight with shoulder-length hair extensions. And when he came downstairs, she was looking as if she had just wandered off the set of *Mad Men* complete with huge Jackie O sunglasses, even though it rained on and off the entire day.

Twenty small boys, high on toasted marshmallows and pizza, rampaged around the garden all afternoon bellowing and roaring and, after they had left, Froggy had unwrapped a small mountain of presents and then promptly vomited spectacularly. Will had cleaned him up and Gemma had carried him upstairs to bed.

By the time she had tucked him in he'd already forgotten that he had just been sick. She kicked off her shoes and lay down beside him.

'I had two birthday parties this year?' he said, solemnly. Stephen had taken him out for pizza Quasar the day before. Gemma had seen the pictures on Facebook.

'Was that a good thing?' Gemma asked, carefully.

'I suppose,' he said, a little sadly. 'But I don't want two Christmases.'

'Right,' Gemma said. 'Well, we'll just have one, then.' Christmas was months away. It was just about conceivable that she and Stephen could manage to be in the same room by then.

'In Wexford?'

Gemma held her breath. Could they manage to be in that house where he'd slept with someone else? She looked into Froggy's eyes. Yes, they could do that for him and for Jake, who was still angry with Stephen. It might do them good to be in the same room too. 'Yes, of course!'

After Froggy had fallen asleep, she went to the window. Alice and Jake had emerged from their bedrooms where they'd hidden most of the day and they were outside now, on the bouncy castle, leaping and shrieking like five-year-olds, daring one another to jump higher. As she watched, Jake flung himself in a series of spectacular belly flops and Alice fell on top of him. He would be okay, she thought, and so would Alice. Teenagers were resilient.

She unzipped her dress and changed into the pink silk kimono she'd seen the very first time she'd been in Nora's shop. She'd decided to buy it to cheer herself up in those first, awful weeks after she's split up with Stephen. She'd asked Nora to put it on hold until she could pay for it. But by the time Gemma picked it up, she wasn't feeling quite so awful any more. And every week that went by now made her feel more and more as if he had done her a favour.

By the time she got back downstairs, the kids had gone inside and Will was alone in the kitchen, making a pot of tea.

'God, I feel about a hundred years old,' she said, pouring a cup.

'I have a cure for that!' He grabbed her hand, dragged her out into the garden and pulled her onto the bouncy castle.

'This is scarier than it looks!' Gemma laughed and lay down on her back. The rubber was slick with drizzle and her dress would get wet but she didn't care. After a minute, Will lay down next to her.

'Was it weird today, without Stephen around?'

Gemma thought for a moment. 'Yes and no. If we were still together, he might not have been around at all. He was just kind of phoning it in the last few years.' She sighed. 'I thought it was my fault, so I kept trying to find ways to fix it, which just kept us stumbling along. Last Christmas,' she leaned up on one elbow to look at Will, 'I was so desperate that I stopped taking the pill. I thought the solution was to have another baby. With my husband, who was having an affair!' She started to laugh at the thought of it. 'I must have gone crazy.'

'You were always pretty crazy,' Will said, affectionately.

'Maybe.' She lay down again and bounced gently. 'This was my worst nightmare, all those years we were together, being all on my own and nearly forty, but I don't know what I was afraid of. This is actually okay. For me anyway. Though maybe not for you. You didn't exactly plan on having me and my kids lumped in on top of you.'

'I like having you here.' Will lay on his side to look at her.

'I've been on my own with Alice for a long time. I like having company. And it's good for her too. I think I was focusing too much attention on her. I'm trying to back off a bit, give her some space and I think it's working. I think she's doing okay.'

Gemma held up crossed fingers. 'So far so good. She seems to be settling in at school. It helps to have Jake in the same year, I suppose. And she's founded a kind of mutual admiration society with Froggy.'

'I know, it makes me feel kind of guilty.' Will sighed. 'It makes me wonder if I should have married again, had more kids. Given her a proper family.'

Gemma wondered whether she should ask him about Nora. 'It's not too late.'

'I don't know.'

'Well, I do.' And she did, suddenly. She knew that there was still time for him, still time for both of them to start again. They had half their lives ahead of them. And that thought made her feel fizzy with possibility.

She bounced up onto her knees and then onto her feet. The rubber was slick beneath her heels. 'Come on! Let's give this thing a try.'

'We're too old, Gems, we might break something!'

She grabbed his hands and pulled him to his feet and they began to bounce slowly at first and then faster, higher and higher, filling the cold, damp dark garden with the sound of laughter.

Alice was up before him, sitting at the table, eating cereal, wearing her school shirt and tie and her pyjama bottoms. Mac was curled over her bare feet, like a blanket.

'What were you and Gemma, like, doing out there last night?'

'Having fun.'

'You woke Froggy up,' she said disapprovingly. 'I had to go in and, like, read him a story.'

'Which one?'

'That *Where the Wild Things Are* one you gave him. I don't think it's right for a seven-year old. Those monster drawings are pretty scary.'

'Right.' Will sat down opposite her and poured the last few drops of milk into his coffee.

There was a long silence.

'If we go back to New York,' Alice said suddenly, 'do we have to go back to the apartment? Can we, like, live in a house, instead? So we can have a dog?'

A year ago, leaving Worth Street would have felt like a betrayal of Julia, but now, Will realised that had all been in his head. She would want him go out there and live, not to shackle himself to the past.

'Sure,' he said. Alice had said 'if' he realised suddenly, not 'when.' 'Do you want to go back to the States?'

She shrugged. 'I don't know.'

'We don't have to decide now, we can talk about it after Christmas.'

'Yeah. Right,' she said cynically.

'I mean that. Where we live is your decision too. I should have realised that when I brought you here. I'm sorry if I made you feel like you had no say.'

Alice studied the ends of her hair. Gemma had dyed the pink ends back to blonde before she started school.

'And another thing,' Will took a breath. 'And I'm sorry if I made you feel you had to live up to some idea of your mom. That was wrong of me. You just have to be yourself, you know that.'

She looked uncomfortable. 'It's okay.'

'I'm proud of you... you know that.'

'Dad!' She winced. 'It's seven in the morning. This is, like, a little bit heavy.'

The bird cage was like a miniature palace, built of gold wire and air, but the base was surprisingly heavy.

'I'm guessing your grandmother didn't keep a bog-standard budgie in this!' Fiona said as she and Nora carried it carefully between them down the narrow corridor to the shop.

Nora didn't know. For as long as she could remember, the cage had been empty.

Fiona held the cage and Alice held the ladder. They fell silent while Nora climbed up to hang the cage in the window. She had already positioned her two desk fans on either side of the window and installed her bird paintings. A hundred or so on clear acetate sheets attached to lengths of fishing line so fine, she hoped it would look invisible.

There were love birds with bright red and aquamarine feathers, scarlet-and-custard cardinals, blue-and-red-spangled cotingas, finches with purple breasts and bright blue heads. She had picked the most exotic ones she could find from Hugh's remaining encyclopaedias. It had been a lot of work.

'Let's hope this works,' she said nervously, folding up the ladder and stepping back.

'Can I switch on the fans?' Alice asked. 'Please?' Fiona threw her eyes up to heaven but Nora nodded and she bent down and flipped the switches.

There was a moment when nothing happened then the acetates began to tremble and shiver in the updraught and it looked as if the cage was at the centre of a flock of hovering birds.

'Tah dah!' Fiona grinned. She checked her watch. 'And you have fifteen minutes before you open. Alice, why don't you run over to the café to get us all three soy chai lattes to celebrate.'

'You go,' Alice said tartly, turning away. 'If you can run in those stupid shoes,' she muttered under her breath.

'Go on, Alice!' Nora took a tenner out of the pocket of her dress.' And get some of those pecan and carob Danishes you like.'

'And keep the change?' Fiona said as the door closed. 'She probably will anyway.'

Nora shrugged.

'You shouldn't trust her with money, Nora. And you shouldn't be paying for things at the café,' Fiona grumbled, but her heart wasn't in it.

Since she and Adonis had become a couple, she was, in her own word, 'like a silly grin on a stick'.

'I know this bubble is probably going to burst but I don't care!' she'd said to Nora a week after the wedding. 'I don't care if he dumps me and high tails it back to Athens. I don't care if the café goes down the tubes and I put on another eight stone. It'll be worth it and it's not just the sex!' Fiona shook her head. 'Well, it *is* the sex, obviously. It's the best sex I've ever had, possibly the best sex anyone has ever had. But I don't have to get to know him now. I already know him. We've been stuck in a tiny hot kitchen for two years. We've prepped food and scrubbed pots and fought about the menu. We like one another. Sometimes I think we might actually have loved one another all the time.'

Nora hid a smile. She had suspected this all along.

'Jesus,' Fiona had clapped a hand to her forehead, 'I sound like a lovesick teenager.'

'You realise,' Nora said to Fiona now, folding up the stepladder and stretching out her aching arms, 'it's been fifty minutes and you haven't said the word "Adonis". I think that might be a record.'

'You're right!' Fiona grinned. 'I'd better make up for it!' She began to dance around the shop in her vertiginous heels, singing, 'Adonis! Adonis!' to the tune of Blondie's 'Denis, Denis'.

Nora waited for her to shimmy past once, so she could put away the stepladder, then again as she tried to get to the desk. 'So everything's good up on that fluffy pink cloud?' she said as she opened her laptop.

'Everything is perfect.' Fiona gave her imaginary tambourine a rattle. 'Except that I'll have to give you free coffee for life now. If you hadn't set up the shop, I wouldn't have found the shrug and I wouldn't have gone to the wedding.' She collapsed onto one of a pair of gilt chairs and kicked off her shoes. 'Enough about me,' Fiona said. 'What about you and Will? What's going on?'

Nora pinched her top lip and scrolled down her spreadsheet, looking for the entry for the bird cage. 'Nothing.'

'Really?' Fiona said, mischievously. 'Then why do I keep seeing the two of you walking past my window with that insane-looking hound?'

'That's all we're doing,' Nora said levelly. 'Walking.'

It wasn't quite true. They'd started going for drives now too. Getting into Hugh's old Merc and heading off into the Wicklow Hills with no clear idea of where they were going, stopping when they felt like it, to admire a waterfall or walk along the ridge of a hill or have a glass of wine in a country pub. And last Sunday afternoon, Nora had driven Will down to Hawk Rock for a swim. Well, he had been swimming. He had picked up the habit from Loughlin. Nora wasn't going to get into the Irish Sea in November. She had spread Lainey's old Foxford rug out on the rocks and opened a book to have something to look at while he undressed. But she looked up when he walked out onto the diving board. He was barely six foot to Adam's six two and more solid, his neck thicker, his arms and thighs heavier, his chest broader. Even at thirty Adam still had a boyish look about him. Will, she thought, as he executed a pretty decent dive, was definitely a man.

He was a good swimmer too, fast and steady and strong. He stayed in so long that Nora had worried about hypothermia, before he emerged spluttering and swearing, laughing through the chatter of his teeth as he pulled himself out of the water.

Adam would never have swum in the Irish Sea in the middle of winter, Nora thought, throwing Will his towel. He wouldn't have swum in it at the height of summer. He would have needed the heated pool of an expensive spa or an exclusive hotel or a Mediterranean beach with a padded sun chair and a fluffy towel and a cocktail waiting for him when he got out.

He wouldn't have come along for those long walks on the pier either, she thought. Well, maybe he would have done it once. But only because he wanted to pose at the end of it for a selfie. And then it would have been on to the next thing. Another place. Another novelty. Everything had to be special with Adam because he was special.

She had spent more downtime with Will in the last few months than she had done with Adam in two years and she had enjoyed it. She liked doing ordinary things, hanging out, just going for a casual bite without having to Google the nearest five star restaurant and dressing up and having a blow dry.

She had been so swept up in the romantic bubble of her relationship with Adam, so pulled along by his plans and his need to achieve the next milestone, that she had never stopped to wonder whether he was right for her. Maybe she would have been happier with someone quieter and more easy going. Someone who didn't have to charm every room when they walked into it. Someone a bit more like Will.

Fiona gave her tambourine a little rattle and when Nora looked up, she was staring at her with those soul scanning green eyes. 'You like him, don't you?' she said softly.

Nora sighed. 'Full disclosure? Yeah, I do. And sometimes I think he likes me, but then the moment passes and I think I might be imagining it. And even if he did like me, it wouldn't work. It's too soon, Fiona, and I'm going back to London in January. And even if I wasn't, I'm not sure Alice would approve.'

Nora wasn't sure if Alice knew how much time she and Will were spending together. The last thing she wanted to do was upset her.

Fiona snorted. 'You're consenting adults, Nora, you don't need your love life rubber stamped by a stroppy Gothy teenager.'

'I know she's spiky but underneath it all, she's actually really sweet. I'm getting to really like her.'

'Good!' Fiona said cheerfully. 'That'll come in very handy if you end up being her step-mother.' Nora shook her head helplessly. 'Never say never!'

'Never,' Nora stood up and, shooing her off the sofa, 'ever come over here again when you are high on love hormones. You're unhinged and I'm trying to run a business here!'

Nora thought that the first cold snap of December would keep people away, but the cage window with the hovering birds worked its magic and the shop was busy all week. By five o'clock on Friday, the steady stream of customers had finally dwindled and the early afternoon drizzle had turned to icy rain.

A woman in her eighties came in from outside, shivering. 'I'm not buying,' she said to Nora. 'But I spent so long looking at your window that I need to warm up.'

'Of course,' Nora looked up from a display of paper fans she was arranging, 'stay as long as you like. It's horrible out there.'

The woman shook a few hailstones off the shoulders of her tweed coat and wandered around, reading the note on a set of china and peering at the shelf of leather gloves.

She stopped to look at some costume jewellery and picked out a diamanté spider brooch. 'I used to have one like this,' she said. 'I haven't seen it for years. I'd forgotten all about it.' She held the brooch over the lapel of her coat and looked at it wistfully. 'My late husband gave it to me as a joke. He was six foot four, a corporal in the army. But he was terrified of spiders; he used to hide in the loo while I got rid of them.'

Nora smiled. This happened all the time. The shop seemed to stir up other people's memories. It was, after the windows, her favourite thing about working here.

'How much is it?' the woman asked.

'Ten euros,' said Nora, knocking fifteen off the price. The woman hesitated. 'Five would do. It's the last one so I need to get rid of it, really.'

'It's lovely,' the woman smiled, 'but I don't really need it. It's not the thing that matters, is it, it's the memory of it. And I have that.'

She was right, Nora thought, locking the door after she had left.

The house was almost empty now. Nora had sold three quarters of the contents and made just over forty five thousand euros for her mother. But the things weren't really gone, not as long as she remembered them.

She was turning the light out when there was a sharp rap on the door. A striking blonde girl in her mid-twenties in a short, belted cream coat and high black boots was scowling at her from behind the glass.

'I'm having the best day ever!' the girl announced as she swept past Nora.

'That's good!' Nora said, then she saw the phone clamped to the girl's ear and realised she was on a call. 'I found an absolutely divine Monique Lhuillier dress in that bridal shop on Drury Street. They're closing down, so it was reduced to two grand. I beat them down to one and a half. They were desperate to sell.' She ran a finger along a rail of Lainey's dresses. The rattle of the wire hangers put Nora's teeth on edge. She began to clear her desk, wishing now that she hadn't opened the door.

The girl moved on to the table of jewellery and upended a glass dish of earrings. 'I'd already paid a five-hundred deposit on a Vera Wang in Bloom in Blackrock and, obviously, I didn't want to lose that. So I had a brainwave! I went in just now and I told them the wedding was off. Turned on the water works. Guilted the owner into giving me my deposit back – in cash!'

Nora gaped at her back in disbelief. Ros, who owned Bloom, had only been open six months. That five hundred euros would have to come out of her own pocket.

The girl wandered over to the wall and examined herself in the long Venetian mirror. 'And it gets even better.' Her pout morphed into a smug smile. 'When I was on my way back to the car, I found this weird little shop opposite the library. And guess what was in the window? The most gorgeous antique bird cage! You know I had to give up on the idea of releasing a dove after the ceremony because I couldn't find the right one? Well, this is perfect! It's totally *Arabian Nights*, so it'll go with the Moroccan theme ... I don't know. I haven't asked. I'll call you back in five.' She slipped her phone into her bag and turned to Nora. 'How much? For the cage?'

'Four hundred euros,' Nora said, this time inflating the price by two hundred euros in the hope that it might put the girl off.

'You're joking!' The girl gave a little snort. 'What is it made of, fourteen-carat gold? Tell you what, I'll give you two hundred, in cash.'

Nora shook her head.

'Come on!' the girl said. 'Four hundred is daylight robbery!'

'Yes,' Nora said, staring her down, hoping it was obvious she'd heard every word of the one-sided conversation, 'it is.'

'Fine.' The girl rolled her eyes. 'Four hundred.' She pulled out her purse. 'But that better include delivery.'

Nora swallowed hard. Four hundred euros was a lot of money but she couldn't sell Lainey's cage to this obnoxious girl. 'Sorry,' she said levelly, 'I forgot. It's actually on hold for someone else.' It was a lie but the girl was a liar herself, so it didn't count.

It was worth every cent she'd lost in the sale to see the look of disbelief on the girl's face.

'You forgot? Seriously?' She frowned, then put her head on one side. 'Look, you obviously don't have a great memory, so I'll tell you what! If you "forget" that you're holding it for someone else and sell it to me,' she smiled conspiratorially, 'I'll slip you an extra hundred euros. You can "forget" to tell your boss about that too.'

'I'm my own boss, actually,' Nora said. And it was true, she realised. She had been a partner in the set design company for over a year, but Liv had always treated her as an employee. 'And so, by the way, is Ros who you "guilted" into giving you back the deposit for your wedding dress. She's put her heart and soul into that shop. You should be ashamed of yourself, ripping her off like that.'

The girl slammed the door so hard that a gust of air blew through the shop, jangling the coat hangers on the clothes rail and rattling the glasses in the display cabinet and rippling through the flock of birds in the window.

Will was back in Prague finishing off the post production of his ad, and there was a taxi strike planned for the day he came back, so Nora texted him and said she'd pick him up.

'You don't have to do that,' Will said. 'It's an hour's round trip. Maybe more if the snow keeps up. I'll hire a car.'

'I have to go to IKEA anyway,' Nora said. 'I need to get some, um–' Some what? 'Some packing boxes.'

'Okay, in that case I'll accept your offer,' Will was smiling, she could hear it in his voice. 'But only if I can buy you dinner on the way back.'

'Oh,' Nora said, 'that sounds –' it sounded almost like a date – 'lovely.'

'You'd be doing me a favour. Gemma is taking the kids to Funderland tomorrow night. I won't have eaten and the house will be empty.'

Not a date, then, Nora thought.

'I owe you a thank you for taking Alice on. And time's going to be tight between now and Christmas.'

He would be spending Christmas Day in Wexford with his sister and her ex-husband. Nora would spend it with Fiona and

Adonis. Gooseberry for all three courses, but it was better than being alone.

'Also –' Will hesitated. 'I have something to tell you. How about we go to that new French place in Donnybrook? Everyone at work is raving about it.'

'Fancy!' Nora said.

'We can be fancy!'

Was he flirting with her? 'Can we?'

After she'd hung up she went over to the half-empty clothes rail that held Lainey's last few dresses. Another three had sold today but the navy silk Schiaparelli was still there. A quintessential fifties frock, full skirted, with a deep V-neck and a belt at the waist. She held it up against her body and walked over to the mirror. No, she thought. Way too much for dinner with Will. Definitely too much for IKEA.

She did need those boxes, actually. She would have to start packing up everything that hadn't sold. The house would have to be cleared when she handed the key over to Loughlin on 3 January, exactly three weeks from now.

'Try it on!' She heard a voice behind her. 'I dare you!'

It was Will's sister, in snow boots and a puffa coat, her blonde hair escaping from under a woolly hat.

'I can't!' Nora put the hanger back. 'I'm supposed to serve customers, not try on the merchandise.'

'I don't think you'll get many today.' Gemma stamped snow off her boots. 'It's like the North Pole out there. But if someone comes, I'll handle it.' She sat behind the desk. 'Go on!'

She grinned as Nora emerged from the dressing room and pointed at the mirror. Nora walked over to it again, the skirt of the dress whispering against her bare legs.

'It'll look even better with your hair up.' Gemma came over. 'Have you got any clips?'

'No!'

'Liar!' Gemma swooped on a bowl of Lainey's diamanté bobby pins that Nora had arranged on a display table. She peeled off her gloves and popped the clips into her mouth, then reached up and began to work on Nora's hair, twisting it and securing it, a strand at a time, leaving a few strands loose to curl around her neck.

It only took a few seconds for her to tame Nora's wild hair into an elegant up-style. 'You're good at this,' Nora said.

'I am,' Gemma said proudly, extracting the last pin from between her teeth. 'It's funny, if you'd asked me six months ago what I was good at, I wouldn't have been able to think of a single thing. But this is easy for me. It doesn't feel like work when you love what you're doing, does it?'

'I guess not.' Nora had been good at styling and set design but this was what she loved, her Memory Shop. Finding a way to shine a light on each of Lainey's lovely things. Losing herself in making a window. Doing something that might make a difference for her mother. She was going to miss it, she realised, all the customers and all the people who had been part of it. Adonis and Ed and Loughlin and Alice. Fiona. Will. A small lump formed in her throat.

'There!' Gemma stood back. 'You look like a sexy Audrey Hepburn. Whoever he is, he won't be able to resist you!'

Nora turned away from the mirror quickly but Gemma put her hand on her arm. 'Can I ask you something?'

'Of course.' Here it came, the probing question about her brother and Nora wasn't going to be able to fend it off.

'I don't know if Alice has mentioned it,' Gemma said, 'but she wants to start working on a portfolio for art college.'

'Oh! Nora said, relieved. 'That's wonderful news.'

'It is!' Gemma looked proud. 'And it's all because of you and this shop. And I was wondering what would be a good present to give her, something to encourage her?'

'How about a stylus?' Nora said. 'She can use it to design on her mobile phone. Or a set of professional pens and some heavy paper. She's always got a graphic novel in her bag. She could start working on her own.'

After Gemma left, Nora couldn't settle. It was hours before she was needed to leave for the airport. She slipped off the dress and laid it carefully over the back of her chair and covered her hair carefully with one of Hugh's hats and locked the shop door behind her.

She walked along the narrow road that led down to the water. The snow had turned the terrace that overlooked the sea into a wedding cake. The pavements had been iced in white along with every railing and moulding, every tree and lamp post.

The sea wall was powdered with snow. Nora leaned on it, smelling the salt and ozone beyond the curtain of fluttering flakes. She let herself imagine that what Gemma had said might be true. That Will might not be able to, might not want to, resist her, then she reminded herself that he had been resisting her pretty much on a daily basis for months now. And that was okay. She would always be grateful that she had met him.

She stuffed her hands into the pocket of her coat and turned to walk back to the house. When she came to Dublin six months ago she had been broken into a hundred pieces, but somehow she had survived. More than that, she had flourished. And Will had been part of that. He had run through her life since they'd met, like a vein of gold, helping to put all the broken pieces back together again.

As she drew level with The Memory Shop, she saw a figure back away from the door. A woman in a cardigan and skirt was holding a bulging black plastic bag to her chest and pulling another one along. For a moment, Nora thought it was one of the mystery donors, then she realised that the bag had been there already. The woman was dragging it away. She was wearing light shoes and was up to her ankles in slush.

'Are you okay?'

'No, I'm not okay,' the woman snapped, hauling the bag through the snow past her. She was panting when she straightened up. She held on to the bag in her arms even more tightly.

'I run the charity shop beside the shopping centre. Every cent I make goes to help prevent suicide. Or it did, until you came along and sucked the life out of it! First you took my customers, then you took my donors. I've had one bag' – she held up a finger and blinked snow out of her eyes – 'one bag donated since the start of December. And every day, I have to watch people walking past my door and leaving their donations here.'

'But I don't want donations!' Nora said. 'Look! I've put a sign on the door!'

'It doesn't stop you taking them in, though, does it? Making up stories about the things people leave and selling them. I've seen your gimmicky windows and your made-up memories and I've had enough. If I don't make enough to cover the rent, I'll lose the shop after Christmas, so I'm taking this back.'

Snow had gathered on the narrow shoulders of her cardigan. She shook it off and bent down to grab the second bag. Nora was worried she might not make it back to the charity shop.

'Can you put those bags down and come inside, just for a minute? I just want to show you something. Then I'll help you to carry the bags to your car.' The woman scowled at her but Nora had seen that look on her grandmother's face many times. She recognised it now for what it was: armour to protect vulnerability.

She took the woman's cold hand and tucked it through the crook of her arm. 'I'm Nora.'

'I know you are!' The woman stiffened but she didn't pull away and after a moment she said, 'I'm Rosemary.'

Nora led Rosemary past the shop and in through the front door of the house, then up the stairs. She opened the door of the first bedroom and showed her the dozens of bags stuffed with clothes. The boxes of toys and board games and glasses. The piles of books. A guitar with all its strings. A buggy with the plastic cover still on it.

'It's all here, everything that was donated,' she said. 'I've been trying to figure out what to do with it, but you can have it for your shop, for the charity along with anything else that comes in before I close. We can load up the car right now, if you like.'

Rosemary's mouth tightened into a tight line and her colour rose. She didn't trust herself to speak but she nodded, quickly.

Nora made tea before they went over, so they could both warm up, and while they drank it, Rosemary told her story. How her daughter Barbara had drowned when she was seventeen, a suspected suicide, and how the loss had broken the orbit of her small family. It had driven her out of her high-powered banking job and into a spiral of depression. It had driven her husband to drink and to an early death. Her younger son, Luke, was only five when it happened. When he finished school, he trained to be a paramedic and, for a while, Rosemary thought he'd be okay. But he'd had anger problems. His marriage in Sligo had ended badly and she hadn't seen him since the break-up. She knew that he still lived in the city, but he wouldn't be home for Christmas. How the shop was the only thing that kept her going, because it was a way that she could do something, anything, to stop this happening to another family.

Nora had planned to take a long bath. To shave her legs and condition her hair and paint her nails. To get ready for tomorrow night with Will. Instead, while Rosemary emptied the shelves and rails in the charity shop ready for the new stock, Nora cleared the junk from the window.

She hung a pair of linen sheets as a backdrop and set up the fans that she had taken from her own window. She polished the glass, then took out a pot of paint and a brush and began to paint the words onto it.

'Gosh,' Rosemary said nervously, coming to take a look. 'This is very exciting. What are you going to put in there?'

Nora had brought along a pair of Lainey's goose-feather pillows. She cut the top off with a pair of scissors and pulled out a handful of feathers. 'Just these.'

It was snowing again when Luke finished his shift. Some of the guys were going across the road for a drink in the Merrion Inn but it had been a long day and they'd lost a patient earlier. A woman in her nineties who had fallen down the stairs in her house had died in the rig, while he held her hand. It was hardly a great tragedy, but it was Christmas and she was someone's mother, someone's sister.

The buses had stopped and he decided to walk home. He'd had the letter in his pocket for a week now but he'd been putting off delivering it to Michelle's shop. He didn't know where she lived now. She hadn't told him and he didn't blame her.

Even after three months of going over and over it with the therapist, he felt sick when he thought of how he'd treated her. He wanted to find her and apologise. To explain what he'd learned, that the grief of losing his sister had broken him, that it was himself he'd wanted to hurt, not her.

But why should she believe him? Why should she listen? Why should she care that he still loved her? She wanted nothing to do with him. He had to accept that. So he'd kept the letter short, like the therapist had suggested. He had said that he didn't expect her to forgive him but that he wanted her to know that he was sorry. That he was on a journey to try to change. That he would not attempt to contact her again but that he hoped she would be happy.

He walked along by Dun Laoghaire, glad that the falling snow blurred his view of the pier where Barbara had lost her life. But still, he knew it was there. He thought of her lying beside his father beneath a blanket of snow in the graveyard in Dean's Grange and the feeling of powerlessness sparked a flare of anger in him. In his pockets, his hands clenched into fists; he felt a rush of heat in his face. He wanted to fight it but he breathed into it the way he'd been taught to. And after a minute, his heart rate slowed and the feeling of rage passed.

But still, it didn't mean that he hated that view any less. He didn't understand how his mother could still live so close to the sea.

He walked on past the piers at Monkstown, glad when a row of houses hid the view of the water. He turned onto Temple Terrace and he recognised the corner where Michelle had jammed on the brakes and he'd jumped out of the car and shouted at that guy in the Toyota and the suspension it had led to. A clammy wave of shame broke over him. He breathed into that too. He'd had to write an apology to that guy too, before he got his job back. But he had been glad to do it.

He walked along the row of closed shops. He crossed the street to avoid the charity shop where his mother still worked, or had two years ago, the last time he'd seen her. Something caught his eye as he passed. For a moment he had thought that it was snowing inside the lit window. He stopped and turned around, blinking to adjust his eyes, and realised that he had been right. He crossed the street again, intrigued. When he got closer, he realised that there were white feathers, not snowflakes, drifting and sifting softly behind the glass. The window was empty, but there was something painted on the window. He backed away to read it: 'We are all as fragile as snowflakes. But we can do amazing things when we stick together.'

Then, in smaller print: 'Please help to support the families of those who take their own lives.'

Luke stood and stared at it. His family had fallen apart after Barbara had died. His father had given up on his life. His mother had never got over the loss. He had done what every child does when scared; he had tried to run away from it. They had all been fragile, in their different ways; maybe if they'd been able to stick together, it would have ended differently.

He thought of the old lady who had slipped away while he held her hand in the rig earlier. And he thought of his mother.

He'd call her, he decided, as he walked on, and ask if he could come over and spend Christmas with her. A flake of snow landed on his cheek and melted. Or maybe it wasn't a snowflake, maybe it was a tear.

Will's flight from Prague was delayed. Nora found a free seat in the crowded rows that faced the arrivals doors, just happy that it had not been cancelled. She felt as if she was in a scene from *Love Actually*.

This was what Christmas was about, she thought, watching a couple in their sixties meet their grandchild for the first time. Two men in their late twenties turned in a slow circle as they hugged. Reunited couples who didn't know whether to laugh or cry did both as they held on to one another. Watching all this outpouring of emotion, Nora wished that her mother was coming home for Christmas.

When Will finally appeared, Nora wanted to slip through the barrier and hug him, but she bottled out. She waved and he waved back and made his way through the crowd to her.

'God! It's good to be home,' he laughed. Home? he thought. Was it possible, when he had spent over half of his life in New York, that Dublin was still home?

'You're not home yet!' Nora warned him. 'It's going to take a while to get across the city. It's pretty bad out there.'

Four inches of snow, he thought, barely a blip in New York or Boston, was a disaster in Dublin. The city had ground to a halt. They were already late for their dinner reservation by the time they got to the first roundabout.

They passed abandoned buses and broken-down coaches. A skidding car sailed out in front of them and turned a full circle gracefully like an ice skater, but Nora was a good driver. She drove the old Merc slowly, her hands at exactly ten to two, her eyes never leaving the road ahead, which allowed Will to take sidelong looks at her.

She always looked good but tonight she looked incredible. She wearing more make-up than she usually did and her dark hair was piled up and a pair of long gold earrings glittered against her bare neck half hidden by a stray curl. He wanted to lean over and tuck the curl behind her ear. He wanted to do a lot more than that, actually. He had to force himself away before he did something stupid.

The Port tunnel was closed. They would never make their dinner reservation now. Will called to cancel but here was no answer. The buses had stopped hours ago. The restaurant had probably closed so that the staff could get home.

The snow was falling so hard now that the wipers could hardly keep the windscreen clear.

'I think we should pull over and wait for a while,' Nora said. She eased the car into a lay-by beside a row of shops, the lit windows all steamed up.

She turned to look at him, her dark eyes glittering behind all that mascara. 'Have you had anything to eat?'

'I had some peanuts on the plane.'

She nodded at the lit window of the Chinese on the street side. 'We could have dinner there.'

The restaurant was tiny and overheated. Apart from two men in Hi Vis jackets, all the tables were empty.

'This is not what I had in mind when I said I'd treat you to dinner.' He looked around at the prints of fat Buddhas and the mural of the Great Wall of China that was so faded, it looked black and white.

A waitress tore herself away from the TV in the corner and showed them to a table by the window and slapped down two plastic menus.

They ordered soup and ribs and crispy duck and pancakes and 'half and half', which the waitress explained was rice and chips. Will picked out the most expensive red from the sauce-stained back page.

'Will I take your coats?' the waitress asked.

Nora hesitated. 'I think what I'm wearing might be a bit much.'

'Me too,' Will said. 'I had to wear a suit for the client meeting. On the count of three?'

Nora shrugged her coat off. She was so lovely in the dark blue dress that Will felt dizzy with longing and he turned away to hang his coat on the back of his chair to stop himself staring at her.

The food arrived quickly to distract him. It was spicy and surprisingly good.

'I forgot to ask, did it all go okay? Did the client approve the final edit?' Nora dipped a chip in the plum sauce that had come with the pancakes.

'Yep. It's done, it's gone, it's on to the next one. What about you? Good week at the shop?'

'Best week yet,' Nora said, 'Fiona helped me to go over the figures last night. I've made, wait for it, sixty-eight thousand euros. If I can persuade my mum to take it, she'll have just over a hundred grand to buy somewhere. But I'm running out of things to sell. The house is nearly empty.'

She wiped her fingers on a paper napkin and he caught a flash of a blue vein beneath olive skin on her wrist. She had beautiful hands, he thought. She had beautiful everything.

'So,' he said, looking back at his plate. 'What's next?'

Nora took a sip of wine and sighed 'Back to London. I've got to find a job and somewhere to live.' She had already sent out some CVs and started looking for a cheap flat-share. 'What about you? Do you think you and Alice will stay in Dublin?'

He leaned back in his chair. 'You know, I think we will. Alice likes it. Not the city, she thinks Dublin is' – he waggled his fingers, making quotation marks in the air – '"the arsehole of nowhere". Jake has finally taught her to say "arsehole" instead of "asshole". I'm not quite sure how I feel about that. But she likes having her cousins around. And Gemma. Coming here has been good for her.' And good for him, he thought. This might possibly be the worst restaurant he had ever eaten in, but there was nowhere else he'd rather be.

Nora wanted to split the bill but Will snatched it away from her. 'Twenty-two euros,' he said. 'I wanted to get you something to thank you for being so good to Alice. This wasn't it, but it will have to do.'

Outside the snow had stopped falling and the traffic had died away. The road was freezing hard and the pavement glittered with a crust of frost. Will took her elbow and they picked their way carefully back to the car.

They were both quiet on the way home. Will wouldn't let her drop him at his house. The suburban roads were too icy, he said. He could walk the rest of the way back from her place.

At Temple Terrace, he got out of the car and walked her to the door.

'Nora,' he said very quietly, as she was putting the key into the lock. 'What is this?

She looked up, thought for a second he was asking about the silver dolphin door-knocker then saw his face.

'I mean us,' he swallowed hard. 'Because, in a couple of weeks, we'll live in different countries, and you're good at letting things go. I wanted to know if this, whatever it is, is one of them.'

'I don't know.' Nora stared at him, her hand was still holding the key in the lock. 'I didn't think you liked me, I mean, not in that way.'

Will threw his head back and laughed, his breath appearing in the frozen air in tiny puffs of cloud. 'You're joking.' He looked down into her dark, serious eyes. Oh my God, he thought. She wasn't joking. 'You have no idea, do you? Nora?' he said. 'At the party, on those walks and those trips in the car. That day when I was swimming, tonight in that Chinese restaurant, it's taken every ounce of my self control not to...' he shook his head.

A moment ago, Nora had been frozen, now she felt a rush of heat rushing up through her feet. It shot through her, like a flame, melting everything in its path. 'Not to what?'

Will's eyes were locked on hers. 'Not to do this.' He put his arms around her and pulled her against him and they rocked together for a moment, as if they were slow dancing out in the snow. 'And this,' he bent down and put his cold lips against her hot mouth and he kissed her.

If anyone had told Alice six months ago that she'd want to spend Christmas in Dublin, she would have thought they were crazy. But now she was kind of looking forward to it. They were spending it in the holiday house in Wexford, where her Uncle Stephen, according to Jake, had been found doing the dirty with some woman who was, like, twenty or so something. Jake didn't want his dad to come, but he was going along with it for Froggy's sake. You would kind of do anything for Froggy, because he was unbelievably cute. He had invented his own name. His actual name was Fergus, but he couldn't say it when he was really little, so he'd told people it was Froggus, and that had stuck.

Christmas Day was going to be deeply weird. But it had been weird back in New York too. Her grandma usually came up for the holidays and they'd go out to some fancy hotel and they'd smile and wear party hats and given one another presents, but they'd be gutted inside, because her mother wasn't there.

It would be different in Ireland and different was not so bad. Different, it turned out, could actually be okay.

Last night had been fun, Alice thought, as she walked to the shop through the empty, snowy streets. Gemma had taken them to a funfair in the snow. Froggy was so small he wasn't allowed to go on the roller coaster, so Alice had stayed behind with him, even though she loved roller coasters. She'd taken him to a stall to get him a hot chocolate to make up for the height thing and while they were waiting, he took her hand and held onto it and she'd thought this must be what it would be like to have a little brother.

Tonight she was invited to a party and a sleepover at the house of one of the girls from school which she didn't think she would be allowed to go to because she was grounded forever. But her dad had called from Prague to say he'd be home late and he'd been in such a good mood that she'd asked him and he'd said okay.

He was probably delighted because if she wasn't around later, he could sneak off and see Nora. They had been hanging out together for months. They weren't dating or anything. Nora wasn't her dad's type. Alice had met four of his girlfriends. They were all blonde, basically clones of her mom.

It was a shame that her dad didn't like Nora because Alice liked her a lot. She could have been totally snotty after she found out that Alice had taken that hairbrush, but she hadn't. She had allowed Alice to help her with the windows and to serve customers and look after the shop. She trusted her so much she'd given her a key.

Alice took it out of her pocket now and slipped it into the lock, then backed up and looked at the window. The birds, her birds, the ones Nora had let her paint and then hang around the bird-cage weren't moving. Maybe Nora had plugged them out, she thought, opening the door. But when she looked into the back of the window, she saw that the fans were gone.

'Is there someone there?' Nora called down from the kitchen

'It's me!' Alice called back. 'I decided to come in early.'

Nora appeared at the door to the house, she looked a complete mess. She was wearing a shirt, a man's one, and her hair was all over the place.

'Where have the fans gone?' Alice pointed at the empty plug board.

'Oh, I gave them to that woman, Rosemary, who runs the charity shop.'

'But you might need them for the next window!'

Nora pulled the shirt tighter around her. She was acting oddly, as if she was embarrassed. 'If the cage doesn't sell before Christmas, it'll be the last window. We'll have to empty it out before the house is sold in the New Year.'

'I know,' Alice sniffed. 'I just thought we might be able to do one more.'

'You know what?' Nora said, backing towards the door, 'we should. It can be your window. You can design the whole thing.'

'Seriously? You'd, like, let me do that?'

Nora nodded. 'Why don't you take a look around at the stuff we still have and have a think about what you might use? I'm just going upstairs to ... to,' she backed towards the door and disappeared without finishing her sentence.

Weird, Alice thought. Then she took off her coat and began to walk around the shop, looking for inspiration.

Will heard the sound of conversation from below in the shop as he crept down the stairs. Nora's soft, low tone. Alice's higher, sweeter voice. He opened the front door and closed it quietly, then hurried quickly down the snow-covered steps.

He was afraid to pass by the window of the shop in case Alice saw him so he turned right, away from the village. He wanted Alice to know about him and Nora, he should have told her weeks ago how close they were getting. But he didn't want her to find out like this.

He walked as fast as he could through the heavy snow. He'd had to leave his shirt behind. Nora had put it on when she went downstairs to make coffee but he'd grabbed one from his cabin bag. He passed a couple walking a dog and they looked at him strangely and he realised that he was grinning. They probably thought he was a lunatic, but he didn't care.

He had spent the night with Nora Malone. He could hardly believe it. She had taken his hand and pulled him up the stairs and they had fallen into the wooden bed in her empty bedroom and this time, there was no talking. They were too busy making up for lost time. He hadn't slept but he felt exhilarated. He could have stayed there for another 24 hours. If Alice wasn't there right now, he would have turned around and gone back.

He didn't want to go back to his own place yet. Gemma and the boys would be there and he didn't want to break the spell of last night just yet. The heat of Nora's mouth and the cool of her fingertips. The long, rambling chats between kisses, the way every time he held her, they seemed to fit together better.

The air was crystalline and the world looked newly made beneath its blanket of snow. Will felt as if he'd woken up from a deep sleep. As if every cobweb had been swept away. He would walk to Dun Laoghaire and buy Nora a Christmas present.

There was a bookshop on the main street called Moby Dickens. A fair-haired woman wrapped in a cardigan looked up from an open book on the counter. 'Good for you for braving the snow.'

'Hi.' He read her name badge. 'Michelle.' It was an American-ism, that habit of over-using a person's name. He could lose it. 'Do you have anything on Greece? Crete particularly.'

'Novels? Travel guides?'

'Either. Both,' Will grinned.

She walked from shelf to shelf confidently and came back with a stack of books. He flipped through them.

The Island by Victoria Hislop. *Zorba The Greek* by Nikos Katzandakis. A Dorling Kindersley guide book to Minoan settlement and a book of photographs of the Cretan landscape. Will paged through it. Mountain ranges and hill-top villages. White-sand beaches. Towering red cliffs. Dusty silver-green groves. Heat seemed to seep out from between the glossy pages.

'I'll take them all,' he said. 'And a map of Crete, if you have one.' Nora had already looked at photographs of the island on the Internet, he knew that. But he wanted to give her something more solid. He imagined the two of them, poring over it together. Maybe they'd go there together. Maybe they'd even take Alice with them.

Every woman he'd introduced to his daughter so far had been intimidated by her, but Nora was different. Without even meeting

Alice, she'd understood her. Will remembered how, that very first day, she had told him that keeping the dog might be a good thing and she had been right.

After a long deliberation, Alice had decided to put the huge fat, bellied copper garden stove into her window and she was Googling how to create a realistic looking fire inside it when the first customer of the day opened the door.

A man in his thirties in skinny jeans and a fur-lined parka. He had a mane of long dark messy hair with too much hair gel in it and, as he pulled off his glove, she saw he had a tattoo on his hand.

'Feel free to look around,' she said in her shop voice, one she had copied from Nora. 'And let me know if I can help you.'

'Hey!' he said. 'I'm looking for Nora Malone.'

Will had been gone when Nora got back upstairs. He must have slipped out when he heard her talking to Alice. Thank goodness, she thought, turning on the shower. Nora had no idea how Alice would have reacted if she'd realised that Will had been here all night.

She pulled off Will's shirt and then held it to her face. It smelled of him. She closed her eyes and buried her face in the cotton folds, and let flashbacks of last night wash over her. It had been like nothing she'd ever experienced. It must have been all those months of delayed gratification but they could not get enough of one another. Her body was still fizzing and her mouth felt bruised from all that kissing, she hadn't slept at all. She shook her head and stepped into the shower. How was she supposed to work today, after that?

She was getting dressed when she heard Alice shouting her name.

'I'm on my way,' she called back. As she hurried down the stairs she remembered stopping to kiss Will on every other step. She was smiling when she walked into the shop, but the smile froze when she saw him.

'Adam! What are you doing here?'

Adam! Alice thought. The boyfriend! The one she'd heard Nora talking to Fiona about.

'Your phone doesn't work,' he said. 'You don't answer my emails. The only way to actually talk to you was to fly over to see you.' He shot a look at Alice. 'Could we get out of here for a bit? Go for a coffee or a walk?'

The last thing in the world Nora wanted to do was go with him, but she couldn't make a scene in front of Alice. She took her coat off the hook. 'I won't be long.'

'I thought I had the wrong address,' Adam said, when they got outside. 'I didn't realise there was a shop as well as a house.'

'Yeah, well,' Nora put up her hood and began to walk. 'Maybe that's because you never bothered to come here.' They had been together two years but Adam had never met Hugh or Lainey or seen Temple Terrace or understood what that had meant to her.

'You're right!' Adam dug his hands in his pockets. 'I should have come, to your grandparents' funerals at least.'

As they passed the café, Nora turned her head away. Will might have gone in there to pick up a coffee on his way home and she didn't want him to see them. She just wanted this over with. She turned to face Adam.

'Why did you come, Adam?'

He looked at her, then looked away quickly. He was so carefully put together, she thought. His hair carefully tousled, his perfectly judged stubble, his long legs in tight jeans, his casual but expensive parka.

'Because there's something you need to know and I wanted to tell you, face-to-face.' He shook his head and swallowed hard. 'This isn't easy.' The snow had started again, a flurry of tiny flakes that floated between them. 'Liv is pregnant.'

Nora almost slipped in the snow. She put a hand on a lamp post to steady herself. 'And you're the father?' she asked.

He nodded. 'I wanted to tell you myself. I didn't want you to find out from her. This was never meant to happen. This was not the plan!' His face was contorted, with anguish and anger, expressions that would have made another person look ugly, but he was still blandly, beautifully handsome. It made Nora sick to look at him. She looked over his shoulder at the wall of a pub where a neon Santa in a sleigh waved his arm over and over.

The lamp post was numbing her fingers, but she held onto it, trying to make sense of all this. 'You and Liv are having a baby.'

'No!' Adam said. 'She's having a baby. I tried to persuade her that it was a mistake to go through with it, but she refused to listen to me. I'm beginning to think she got pregnant deliberately. That she used me. You know what she's like, Nora. And yes, I'm going to do the right thing. I'm going to pay child support but this doesn't change anything, not for me. And it doesn't have to change anything for you either.'

She looked back at him again. 'What do you mean it doesn't change anything for me?'

'I mean, if you want to, we can give this another try. You and me.' He cleared his throat. 'I still love you, Nora. I've missed you so much. The house is so empty without you. I'm finished travelling now, pretty much and I'll be there for you this time, I swear.' Adam's voice was upbeat but his eyes were beseeching. 'What happened has changed me. I'm a better man. Someday, we might look back at this and realise that it made us stronger. You don't have to say "yes" now. You can decide when you get back to London.'

'I'm not going back to London.' The words were out before Nora knew she was going to say them. 'I'm staying here.'

'Here?' Adam, blinked at her in disbelief. 'Why would you do that?' Nora saw the street through his eyes: a suburban seaside village, a handful of hardy Christmas shoppers braving the snow. It was a world away from the buzz and glamour of London, but it was home. It had always been home, really. She turned to go.

'But what about all your things?' he called after her. 'All the stuff you bought for the house? Your clothes?'

'Give them away!' Nora called over her shoulder. 'Give it all away!'

She began to shake as she walked back the way they'd come, not from cold, but from the aftershock of what he'd told her. As she got closer to the shop, she almost collided with a man carrying a large package cocooned in bubble wrap to the open boot of a Mini. A glamorous girl in a short cream coat and high boots, was following him, barking instructions and even through her upset, Nora realised there was something familiar about her.

'I sold her the cage. What's the problem?' Alice said, defensively. 'She held out a handful of notes. 'She paid four hundred euros; she said you told her that was the price. I thought you'd be, like, pleased.'

'I did tell her that ... I didn't want her to have it!' Nora stammered. The thought of that woman having Lainey's cage, made her feel sick. Why did the worst people always get everything they wanted?

'It's just, she's a liar, Alice. She did Ros at the bridal shop out of five hundred euros. She's a thief ...'

'Yeah, well I'm a thief too!' Alice threw down the fan of notes she'd been clutching in her hand. 'So you'd better count that!'

She pushed past Nora, then stopped at the door, her face flushed.

'And she's not the only one who's a liar. I'm not stupid. I know you've been, like, sneaking around with my Dad behind my back. And you probably think he really likes you!' Her eyes were glittering with tears. 'But you're wrong. He's still crazy about my mom. He still has her wedding dress. He keeps it in his bedroom.'

'What?' Nora's head was still reeling from what Adam had told her. She couldn't take this in.

Alice whirled around and then she was gone, the door slamming behind her.

Nora's phone began to ring and she pulled it out of her pocket. Will's number. She couldn't talk to him when she was upset like this. She left it ringing on the desk as she locked the shop and ran through the snow to the café.

Fiona was carrying a tray to a table, but when she saw Nora, she dumped it and came over.

'Jesus! You're white as a ghost. What happened?'

The café was packed. A few curious faces turned to look up and Nora shook her head, not trusting herself to speak.

'Come on,' Fiona said softly, 'let's get out of here.' She put an arm around Nora, and though she was half a foot shorter and twenty kilos lighter, she took her weight. 'I'm going to take you to the pub. It'll be quiet there. You can have a brandy and tell me all about it, okay?'

How long had it been since he'd spent an hour browsing in a bookshop? Will couldn't remember. But it must have been before Julia died. It was something they used to do when they met first, when they were permanently broke. They'd read whole books they couldn't afford to buy, a couple of chapters in each shop.

He'd paid for Nora's books and left them behind the desk while he wandered among the shelves. He had already bought Gemma the Dyson hairdryer she was lusting after and given her money to buy gifts for Alice and Froggy and Jake, but he'd picked up some stocking fillers.

A bestseller on starting your own business for Gemma. A Roddy Doyle called *Rover Saves Christmas* for Froggy. *Into the Wild* for Jake. A graphic novel called *Sheriff Of Babylon* for Alice. A couple of thrillers for Stephen, who was probably going to feel pretty left out this Christmas.

It was snowing again when he left the shop, laden down with his bags. A taxi was passing and he hailed it and got in. He was about to give his home address, then realised how hungry he was. He called Nora to see if she could slip away for half an hour and join him for breakfast, but she didn't pick up.

The café was busy but Will found a free table and dumped his bags, then went up to the counter. 'Where's Fiona?' he asked Adonis.

'With Nora. She was here, maybe five minutes ago. She was very upset, so Fiona took her outside.'

'Nora was upset?' Will felt a wave of protectiveness. 'About what?'

'I don't know. Fiona took her to the bar. At eleven o clock.' He shook his head. 'Crazy!'

Will left his bags and his coat. He tried two pubs before he found the right one. He saw them, through the window, the only customers. They were sitting at the bar with their backs to him. Nora had her head in her hands and Fiona had her arm around her. Will felt a wave of protectiveness. All he wanted to do was look after Nora, to comfort her. But he hesitated, his hand on the door.

Maybe bursting in like this wasn't a good idea. Maybe he'd be interfering. They hadn't noticed him yet. The radio was on, playing Christmas carols, but Nora's voice carried across to him.

'She's pregnant, Fiona. Liv's having his baby. He flew over to tell me. I can't believe it. It was supposed to be me. That was the life I was supposed to have. And he said I could still have it if I wanted it. He wants to try again. He wants me back.'

Will froze. He felt his heart drop like a stone from his chest down into his gut. He had known that Nora had been involved back in London. He had fallen for her so hard that he had persuaded himself it didn't matter. But, apparently, it did, if this guy, whoever he was, had got some other woman pregnant and she was still prepared to go back to him.

The happiness he'd felt earlier crumbled under the weight of defeat. There were some things you could fight, and this was not one of them. He turned and went back out onto the street. Tears welled up behind his eyes. He would have to let her go. He was forty years old. He had kept his broken heart on a shelf since Julia died. And finally he had done the unthinkable: he had taken it down and dusted it off and given it to a woman who couldn't love him. It was his own fault. She hadn't asked for it. He walked back to the café and picked up his coat and his bags and began the walk home.

There was a draught of cold air, as if the door of the pub had opened, but when Nora turned around, the bar was empty. There was nobody there.

'The thing is,' she turned back to Fiona, 'I know I should be angry, but I'm not. I'm relieved. Adam is so deluded, Fiona. He thinks Liv got pregnant on purpose. He wanted her to get rid of the baby and this is her last chance to have a child. This is what she wanted most in the world. And I don't know,' she took a gulp of brandy, 'maybe it's what I wanted too.'

Fiona's green eyes widened. 'You wanted your ex-boyfriend to get your arch-frenemy pregnant?'

'No . . .' Nora said, 'of course not. But I wanted skywriting to tell me what to do next and this is it. I'm not going back to London. Though I have no idea what I'm going to do or where I'm going to live. The shop and the house will be gone on the third of January.'

'You can move into Adonis's place,' Fiona said. 'He's moving in with me.'

'Yay!' Nora grinned.

'Yes,' Fiona's eyes glittered. 'Very yay! Now his place is just a studio. It's tiny and it's in a bit of a state. So we'll have to give it a deep clean first, and give it a coat of paint. But it's incredibly cheap.'

'Sounds exactly like what I need.' Nora nodded. 'It might be a while before I get a job.'

'You already have a job,' Fiona said firmly. 'You'll be doing my windows, and if I put the word out, you'll be doing all the windows in Dun Laoghaire – Rathdown too – and getting paid for it. Okay?'

Nora took a deep breath. 'Okay!'

Fifteen minutes ago, she hadn't been able to imagine a future. Now it was all mapped out. And the best part, the part she hadn't even told Fiona about yet, was that it contained Will.

When Nora got back to the shop, she called Will but he didn't answer. She tried again at lunchtime and in the afternoon, but his mobile was switched off. At first, she thought maybe he'd gone to bed for a couple of hours, but when he hadn't called her by eleven that night, she was starting to feel worried.

It came back to her, what Alice had shouted before she slammed out of the shop. Nora had written it off as a teenage tantrum. But now she wondered if maybe she'd been wrong. She thought about what Alice had said about Will keeping his wife's wedding dress. What if he really was still in love with his wife? What if he had decided that last night was a mistake and this silence was his way of telling her?

In the morning, when she went down to the shop, there was another donation in the doorway. A bag full of books. She carried it in and tipped them out onto the desk. They were all brand new and all about Crete, and there was a note at the bottom of the bag.

Last night was lovely, Nora, but it was probably a mistake.
I'm sorry. I wanted to give you these books myself but I don't feel up to it. I hope you can forgive me.
It was great to meet you and I hope you'll be very happy.
Will.

12

Amber Worry Beads

Nora

Nora wore a red velvet dress of Lainey's and put on a cheerful face when she went along the terrace to Christmas dinner with Fiona and Adonis. The café was strung with fairy lights and lit with candles and four tables had been put together to seat twenty people. Fiona's parents, Loughlin, Ed and his girlfriend Marian, Laura and her little girl and a half a dozen strays from the café who had nobody to spend the day with. Nora pulled crackers and clinked glasses and complimented Adonis's food. Fiona had imposed a 'no presents' policy, but Nora had brought along some thank yous for the people who had been so kind to her over the last six months.

Hugh's blackthorn walking stick for Loughlin. A compass inside a jewelled egg for Fergal, who had admired it the day he'd helped her with the valuation. A pair of silver serving spoons for Adonis. She hadn't been able to carry Fiona's gift – the life-sized brass angel candelabra, so she had made a card with a sketch of it in gold ink.

'But I can't take this. It belonged to your grandmother!' Fiona protested. 'You should keep it.'

'You've been my guardian angel since I got here in June,' Nora said. 'I want you to have it.'

'Well, I'll put her right here in front of the till,' Fiona said. 'So you can see her every day when you come into the café.' She hugged Nora hard. 'I'm so glad you're not going back to London. And I bet I'm not the only one! When's Will coming back from Wexford?'

'He hasn't decided yet,' Nora said vaguely. She hadn't told

Fiona that they'd spent the night together and there was no point in telling her now. She'd just ruin the day.

Every time a shadow passed the window of the café, she hoped it might be him. That he had got into his car in Wexford and driven through the snow to tell her that he had changed his mind. But that wasn't going to happen. He had made his decision and she had to live with it.

She slipped away when the karaoke started and stayed up for a while, hoping that her mum might call to say 'happy Christmas', but by midnight, she gave up and went to bed. She hadn't heard a word since she had sent the locket and the note and she guessed that either Alanna hadn't received it, or that she had and that it had upset her.

Three days after Christmas, Nora dropped Fiona and Adonis to the airport. They were flying back to Athens for his cousin's wedding. She hugged them both at departures and whispered 'good luck' to Adonis. He had bought the diamond solitaire she had put in the charity shop window and was planning to propose in Greece.

Nora thought about Will as she drove back home to Blackrock, remembering how they'd made the journey just a few days ago in a blizzard. That night seemed like part of another life now. And in a way, it was. She felt sad about how things had turned out, but she didn't regret a moment of the time they'd spent together. She was grateful for all the talk and the laughter and for that one blissful night in her room in Temple Terrace. She knew now that the sense of home she'd been searching for all her life wasn't about bricks and mortar and beautiful things. It was the sense of true belonging she had felt lying in the arms of a man she didn't have to impress, who knew the real, ordinary her and still wanted her.

She was grateful for that, she thought as the car sped along the empty motorway. Grateful for the last six months in Dublin. She remembered the day she had arrived, how devastated she'd been. How she'd felt that the life she had wanted so much was over. But really it had just been beginning.

If she hadn't found out that Adam was cheating on her, she would still be working for Liv. She wouldn't have discovered that she had what it took to run her own business.

She wouldn't have opened The Memory Shop or made nearly seventy thousand euros for her mother's fund. She wouldn't have met Fiona or Alice or Adonis or all the customers who had made the shop a success. She wouldn't have found the notes Lainey had written, those tantalising glimpses into her past. She wouldn't have had a chance to design her windows. She thought of all the joyful hours she'd spent sketching and designing and constructing them. And of how happy it made her when people stopped in their tracks to gaze at them.

She remembered something that Will's sister had said to her once. 'It doesn't feel like work, when you're doing something you're passionate about, does it?'

Nora had donated the furniture she couldn't sell along with Hugh's clothes to a homeless men's shelter and boxed up Lainey's novels and driven them to a women's refuge. Hugh's poetry collection had gone to the library. She had been working on the house since Christmas day, clearing and cleaning each room methodically. Packing up her own things to get ready to move into Adonis's old flat. Driving back and forth to the tip with bags of rubbish and moving bits of furniture and boxes of odds and ends that might sell down to the shop. She would keep it open for another day or two, though she wasn't counting on many customers over the holidays.

When she got back from the airport, she made a cup of coffee and went down to the shop to put some order on it. She unpacked boxes and arranged mis-matched china and ornaments and vases as best she could then set about sorting through some boxes of old magazines from Hugh's study. And at the bottom of the last one, beneath a pile of dusty copies of *National Geographic* and the *New Statesman* and *The Economist*, she found one of his books – *The Lyrics of Leonard Cohen*. The page Will had found in the Kintsukuroi bowl had been torn from it.

She could tape it back in, she thought, opening the book and seeing what she had stopped hoping to find. Another one of Lainey's notes.

Japanese pottery bowl, mended with gold.

Hugh collapsed on the last day of December. His heart must have stopped when he was halfway across the hall. He was lying on his back, when I found him, his eyes open, one arm outstretched towards the stairs, as if he had been trying to reach me.

I took his hand and tried to find a pulse but I couldn't. His hand was ice cold. I called 999 and told them it was an emergency. I shouted at him to stay with me. I cried and screamed and then I pleaded with him. I held his cold face in my hands and tried to find a spark of him behind his eyes, but it was gone.

So I lifted up one of his hands and put it on Houdini's head and put the other one inside my nightdress, against my heart. I got down beside him and wrapped my arms around him and tried to pour the warmth of my body into him the way he had poured his warmth into me. He had tried to put the broken pieces of me back together with his love, the way the pieces of the Japanese bowl he had given me for Christmas were held together with gold. And even though my heart was breaking and everything in me was coming apart, I put my mouth against his ear and I began to name all the beautiful things he had given me, one by one, and I thanked him for them.

It was as if Lainey was asking her to make one last window, Nora thought, one about gratitude.

Everyone was still at home or at the sales in shopping malls and in the city. There was no traffic in the village today, no cars to impound, no tickets to write and the clamper in his high vis jacket must have passed half a dozen times while Nora was painting the window. He looked frozen, she thought, and miserable and she was glad to be inside the warm shop, not pounding the slushy pavements on such a frigid day.

He was passing again when she went outside to take a look at the finished window. Fiona would probably kill her, she knew, but Fiona was thousands of miles away.

'Do you want to come inside and warm up?' she asked him.

'Really?' He looked at her, as if he thought this was a trick.

'Just for a minute. It's pretty cold out here.'

'Yeah. If you're sure,' he said nervously. He was the bane of the life of every shopkeeper in Blackrock and she wouldn't have been surprised if he'd had horns and a tail. But up close, he was younger than she'd thought and his eyes were ringed with dark circles. He followed her into the shop and she put away her paints and cleaned her hands on a rag soaked in white spirit while he walked around, leaving a trail of slushy footprints on her polished wooden floor.

'He's a beauty,' he said, and when Nora looked up, she saw that he had squatted down to pat Houdini. His shoulders beneath his high vis jacket started to shake and for a moment, she thought he was laughing, then he sniffed and she realised that he was crying.

'Are you okay?' She asked.

He took a gulp of air and rubbed hard at his eyes with a gloved fist. 'I'm fine. It's just my seven-year-old daughter is in hospital. She's been in and out all year. Cancer. She's been through the wars and she's winning, she's been so brave. They took her in on December 15th for another surgery and I swore to her she'd be home for Christmas and that we'd get her a dog. But they decided to keep her in until the New Year and she's miserable. We have the dog at home and I asked if I could bring him in to cheer her up, but they won't allow animals. Health and safety. They told me to bring in a stuffed toy, but it's not the same, is it?' He wiped his nose on his sleeve and stood up.

'I'm so sorry,' Nora said. Then she looked at Houdini, thoughtfully. 'Do you think he'd pass as a stuffed toy?'

It took the clamper a few seconds to get where she was going.

A smile spread across his exhausted face. 'I don't know. Maybe. It would be worth a try! How much is he?'

'I'm not selling him.' Nora had decided that wherever she was going, Houdini was coming too. 'But you're welcome to borrow him for a couple of nights to keep her company.'

The clamper cleared his throat, then he strode over to her, beaming and for a second Nora thought he might be going to hug her, but he changed his mind and instead he took her hand and gripped it hard and he said the words that Nora had just finished painting on the backdrop. 'Thank you.'

Alice had been allowed to take Mac to Wexford for Christmas. He'd galloped on the beach and gorged himself on leftovers and slept on her bed and she had fooled herself into thinking he belonged to her. But when they got back to Dublin, the couple next door were back from their vacation and her dad said that Mac had to go back. He had gone crazy when he'd seen them and she realised that these people, Caroline and Liam, were his actual family and he must have missed them. They had told Alice she could call over and take him for a walk any time, but it wasn't the same as having him to herself and walking wasn't really her thing anyway.

The house felt weird and empty without him and there was nobody to distract her. Jake had gone to play paintball. Froggy was at a birthday party. Gemma and her friend Des were set up in the kitchen working on a business plan for her mobile hairdressing salon. Her dad hadn't emerged from his room that morning. Her friends were all stuck at home doing Christmassy stuff.

She sat on the sofa in pyjamas and finished a packet of Coco Pops and watched four episodes of *Jessica Jones* back-to-back on Netflix. Then she put on her new coat, with the fur-trimmed hood, and her brand new Doc Martens and walked into the village.

It was only four o'clock but it was already dusk. The snow that had been pretty before Christmas had dissolved into grotty slush. Everything was closed, even the chip shop. It was as if the world was holding its breath, waiting for the old year to end so the new one could start.

She went across the metal footbridge and down the steps and walked out onto the vast rippled crescent of strand that stretched for what seemed like miles to the sea. The sand was puddled with rivulets of water, streaky mirrors that reflected the moving grey clouds. It made Alice dizzy to look down at it. She felt as if she was floating between the beach and the sky. Between New York and Dublin, between whom she had been and who she was becoming.

As she climbed the steps again, she passed a man with a little girl of about two in a bright red coat. She waved her arms imperiously and he lifted her up so she could look at the sea and Alice remembered how close she had been to her Dad when she was small. How she used to leave messages in her diary for him to find. They would never be close like that again because she was grown-up now and she didn't need him to do everything for her. But they were already taking the first steps to a different kind of closeness. They were finding their way.

She walked back along Temple Terrace. She was sure that The Memory Shop would be closed, but she wanted to take one last look at the birds in the window. But the birds were gone and for a second, she thought that the glass had been shattered with a hammer. The window was cracked into hundreds of splinters and running between were gleaming veins of gold. It was a trick, she realised, an incredible optical illusion painted onto the glass. It must have taken Nora hours to make it. She hurried across the street for a closer look and peered between the fragments. The window was empty except for a backdrop that said:

TO EVERYONE WHO HAS HELPED TO MAKE
THE MEMORY SHOP.

THANK YOU.

Nora was in the shop, Alice saw. She was sitting at the desk, her laptop open, her shoulders hunched up, her hands curled around a cup of tea. Alice chewed a flap of skin at the side of her thumbnail. She wasn't going to apologise, she told herself, she just needed to get a few things straight, in case she never saw Nora again.

Nora looked up when the door opened. Her brown eyes were pink rimmed and puffy but her face brightened when she saw Alice. 'Hi!'

'Hi.' Alice looked around the shop. There was hardly anything left for sale. The floating shelf was empty except for a small blue clock. The rail of clothes had only a few hangers. There were two small paintings hanging on one wall and a low table had a pile of mismatched plates. The dressing room she'd helped Nora to put up had been dismantled.

'I like the window,' she said, gruffly.

'Thanks,' Nora said. 'I would have left it for you to do but I didn't think you'd come back after what happened the other day. I shouldn't have shouted at you. I'm sorry.'

Alice swallowed hard. 'Me too.' She bit the inside of her lip and then, before she could change her mind, she unzipped her coat and reached around her neck and unclasped the fine chain with the tiny enamel kingfisher.

The chain was warm from her skin as it puddled in her hand. She held it out and let it fall onto the desk in front of Nora. 'I took it the first week I worked here.'

Nora nodded slowly. 'I know you did. And it's okay. You can keep it.'

'Why would you do that?' Alice frowned. 'Why would you give it to me after I, like, stole it?'

'Because I knew you didn't mean to,' Nora said, 'and because I want to give you something to thank you for all the help you've given me. And it reminds me of all the beautiful birds you painted for the window. Please, I'd love you to have it.'

Alice shrugged. 'Okay,' she said softly. She slipped it into her pocket and bent down to pat Houdini. 'Oh! He's gone! Did you sell him?'

'No.' Nora smiled. 'I just lent him to someone.'

'Mac's gone,' Alice sighed. 'But we think we might get our own dog soon. I asked Dad and he said okay.'

Nora felt her heart clench at the mention of Will. She was trying not to think about him, if she let him into her mind at all, she would not be able to get him out again. 'This tea is cold,' she stood up quickly. 'I'm just going to make some more. Can you mind the shop?'

'Sure.' Alice had just taken her coat off when the door opened and the blonde woman who had bought the cage stalked in, followed by her boyfriend, panting, holding the cage awkwardly cradled in his arms. Alice jumped up and pushed Nora's laptop and her notebooks out of the way so he could put it down on the desk. It was too big and she helped him to manoeuvre it so that it wouldn't fall off.

'Thanks,' he muttered.

'What are you thanking her for?' the blonde woman said sharply. She swivelled round to face Alice. 'We paid four hundred euros for this cage before Christmas! And when we got home, we found one exactly like it on eBay for two hundred and fifty. We want our money back.'

The man didn't look as if he wanted his money back. He looked as if he wanted to be somewhere else.

Alice sauntered slowly around the desk to the cash drawer. She wanted more than anything to get the cage back for Nora, but she didn't want to make it easy for this woman who was what her Aunt Gemma would call 'a bit of a weapon'. But Alice could be a bit of a weapon herself.

She stared down into the drawer. There were at least six hundred euros in there. She remembered what Nora had said about the woman stealing money from the bridal shop. 'Did you say four hundred?' She made a sad face. 'Sorry, we don't have that much.'

'I'll come back for it,' the woman said.

'The shop will probably be gone. We're closing down. I've got three hundred.' She picked at the skin on her thumb. 'You can take it or leave it, it's up to you.'

*

Nora couldn't believe her eyes when she saw the cage.

'Oh my God!' She gasped. 'I was only gone for five minutes! How did you do that? How did you get it back?' She put her tray down on the floor and threw her arms round Alice. 'Thank you!' she said. 'This means so much to me! I couldn't stand to think of that woman having it.'

Alice wriggled out of her embrace and stepped back. 'I only gave her three hundred back. I thought you could give the extra hundred to the woman in the bridal shop.'

'You know that's robbery,' Nora said. 'But it's the good kind. Stealing from the rich to give to the poor.'

Moving the cage was harder than it looked, not just because it was heavy, but because one of the metal supports had been damaged so it was stuck halfway on, halfway off the desk. As Nora rocked it back and forth to free it, Alice lost her grip.

The edge of the base grazed her arm as it fell. She yelped as it hit the ground with a crash.

Nora was already beside her, her mind leaping ahead, figuring out where she'd find an on-call doctor to give Alice a tetanus shot. She tugged Alice's coat off and rolled up the sleeve of her sweatshirt. A fine white line ran from her wrist to the crook of her elbow but the skin was unbroken.

'It's fine, it doesn't hurt.' Alice wriggled away, afraid she might be in for another hug.

'Are you sure?'

Alice nodded and bent to examine the cage. It hadn't escaped so lightly. They lifted it carefully and put it back on the table to examine the damage.

The bars along one side were dented. The dome at the top was flattened and the little crystal water dropper had shattered. The heavy base had come loose, a ragged lip that lifted up in one corner. Nora slipped her hand through the door to press it back into place.

The edge was sharp and the bottom of the cage was dusted with tiny splinters. Something was wedged beneath the base, stopping it from going back into place. She slipped her sleeve over her fingers and pulled the metal lip up to get a better look.

It was half a dozen tightly rolled pages with ragged edges, held together with a rubber band.

Her heart skipped a beat as she pulled it out. These were the missing flyleaves that Lainey had ripped from Hugh's poetry books. She had given up on ever finding them. Her hand shook as she pulled off the rubber band. She turned over the first page and saw her grandmother's small, cramped hand, the lines close together, covering the front and back.

Komboloi, 1941

Every morning, I wake up with new words in the back of my mouth – spiti – house; orea – beautiful; nekros – dead. A language I haven't spoken for over seventy years. Fragments of memory.

Easter in the tiny church of Ayia Irini. The tall, thin candles flickering. The priest chanting. The wreaths of incense smoke setting my head swimming. Papa lifted me up so that I was taller than Nikos, though he was nine years older. I could look down on the glossy coils of my mother's black hair; I could see the gleaming brass sconces and the gold halos of the saints on the altar...

A day in early summer when my mother took me with her to the next village to buy flour. The air vibrating with heat and the rattle of a dozen cicadas. The welcome pool of shadow beneath each mulberry tree...

Following Nikos along the high goat path to the gorge where he kept his beehives. He pulled an orange from his pocket and we sat on a hot stone and ate it together. When it was finished, he put the peel in my hand and told me to stand very still. Silence, the wind, then the chime of bells. From nowhere a few goats come tiptoeing up the vertical cliff to nibble the peel from my hand...

These are the worst memories. These moments from a time before it happened, when my father and my brother were still alive. When we were still a family.

Nora turned to the next torn page but she couldn't read the tiny cramped writing on it or on any of the other pages. Lainey had switched from English to Greek. She needed Adonis to translate this for her but he was in Athens.

'We could photograph the pages,' Alice suggested, 'and Whatsapp them.'

But the pages were written densely and the ink had leaked through from both sides. The text came out indistinct and blurry.

'I'll have to scan them,' Nora bit her lip, 'but the print shop won't be open until the New Year and Hugh's printer is too old to have a scanner.'

'Dad's probably got one in the office.' Alice pulled her phone out of her pocket and began to tap out a message.

Nora shook her head. 'I'm not sure that's a good idea.'

But Alice's phone was already pinging with Will's answer.

Alice checked the screen. 'He's coming over.'

Ten minutes later, Will's car pulled up outside.

Alice stayed to look after the shop and Nora got into the front seat beside Will. He smiled at her awkwardly.

'Hi!'

She folded her arms over her chest. 'Hi.'

'How was Christmas?'

'It was great,' Nora said brightly. 'How about you?'

'Fine. Wexford is lovely. It was a bit tricky for Gemma, with Stephen there, but it was good for the kids and Alice seemed to enjoy it. So...' Will trailed off.

There was a long silence.

'I'm sorry,' Nora said suddenly, 'this wasn't my idea. Alice texted you before I had a chance to stop her.'

'It's not a problem, really,' Will said, politely. 'I've nothing better to be doing anyway.'

The ad agency where Will worked was in a Georgian building on Merrion Square. It had been opened up and extended inside into a vast white atrium hung with a fluorescent-blue chandelier the size of a small car. Will turned on the lights and led Nora up a floating staircase and along a glass-walled corridor past brightly coloured work pods.

His office was surprisingly traditional. A wooden desk, a swivel chair. A wall covered with tacked-up paper layouts. A neatly ordered bookshelf. The desk was neat. A keyboard, two screens, a couple of notebooks. A black-and-white picture in a simple silver frame. Nora wanted – and didn't want – to see his wife, the woman he was still obsessed with. She forced herself to look at the picture. It was of Will, looking ridiculously young, walking hand in hand with a toddler in a red coat. It must have been Alice.

'Okay,' Will said. 'We're good to go.' Nora passed him the first page covered in Greek writing and he smoothed it out carefully and fed it into the printer. The scanner hummed for several minutes as it processed the page. There were another seven to go. This was going to take a while, Nora realised. She shivered in her light coat. The agency had been closed since before Christmas and the air was bone chillingly cold.

'Do you want to make some tea?' Will asked, glancing at her briefly. 'There's a kitchen at the end of the corridor.'

Nora was glad to escape. She dawdled in the small kitchen, washing two mugs out carefully, warming her hands on the steam from the kettle, putting off going back.

Will was still scanning when she returned with the tea. She handed him a mug and went to the window. Beyond her reflection, she could see the jumble and clutter that was hidden at the back of the row of Georgian terraces. The rusting fire escapes, broken brickwork, littered yards with huge metal dumpsters. The secrets that were concealed behind the elegant facades the houses presented to the street.

She wrapped her fingers around the warm mug. Were the pages Will was scanning going to give up Lainey's secret? she wondered. Would she finally discover what had happened to her grandmother?

Will cleared his throat behind her. 'So,' he said, 'not long to go.'

Nora turned, relieved. 'How many pages to go?'

'Oh, two. But I meant that it's not long to go before you go back to London. You said that you had to give the keys of the house back on the third of January.'

'I do,' Nora said, 'but I'm not going back to London. I'm moving into Adonis's place. He's going to live with Fiona.'

'But –' Will looked confused. 'What about your boyfriend? The guy who flew over to ask you to go back with him?'

Nora stared at him. 'How did you know about that?'

'I overheard you talking to Fiona in the pub the morning after we … spent the night together.' Will looked embarrassed. 'Adonis said you were upset and I wanted to find you. But when I heard you talking about him, I realised –' he swallowed hard – 'I realised that you were still involved so I … em, made myself scarce, because I guessed that you thought that you and I were, you know, a mistake.'

Nora put her mug down on the desk with a bang. 'Well, you guessed wrong, Will. I was involved with Adam. We were together for two years but then he slept with my –' the word 'friend' stuck in her throat. She knew what a friend was now. Fiona had taught her. 'With my business partner. He came over to tell me she's pregnant, which is actually fine with me. I'm just glad something good has come out of their affair.'

It was true, she thought. Nora did not forgive Liv for what she had done. But she didn't begrudge her this chance at happiness. She had a feeling that maybe having a baby might be the making of her.

Will put down his mug and walked and stood beside her.

'So you don't regret it,' he said quietly. 'That night at your place that we spent together.'

'Regret it?' She turned to face him. 'Of course I don't. But I've been hurt so badly this year, And I like you. I really, really like you, but I'm not going to set myself up to be hurt again.'

'You like me?' He grinned.

'Yes, but what difference does that make? I know you're still in love with your wife. That your room is,' she looked away, 'full of her things. I know you're still grieving for her. And I understand.'

'No,' Will cut across her, 'you don't. I have been sorting through Julia's things for Alice. I've been doing exactly what you're doing,

I've been letting go of the past so I could move on properly. Finally. Anyway, can we back up here a bit, to the bit where you said you really, really like me? Did you mean that?' He leaned his forehead on hers and looked into her eyes.

Nora shook her head. 'I don't know. Maybe.' She swallowed. 'Yes, in fact I think I do.'

'Good,' he said, wrapping his arms around her. 'Because I really, really like you too.'

They stayed like that, standing very still by the window in the empty building, not moving and Nora felt as if she was falling towards Will. Drifting softly like a snowflake. Landing and sticking and melting into him.

Nora groped for her phone on the bedside table, her fingers closing around handfuls of air. The table was gone, sold last week, with its twin, she remembered, sitting up. She leaned over and retrieved the phone from the floor and put it to her ear.

'Yes?' she whispered.

'It's me, I know it's 6 am. I'm sorry to call so early. We're two hours ahead in Athens.' Fiona's voice sounded husky, as if she had a bad cold.

'Did you get engaged?' Nora asked. 'Did Adonis propose?'

'Yes,' Fiona managed a laugh. 'I did and I'm so happy and I can't wait to tell you all about it but there's something else I need to tell you. Are you on your own?'

Nora glanced at the pillow beside her. Will was asleep on his back, his arms behind his head, as if he was floating in the sea. 'No.'

'Good,' Fiona said. Good? Was that it? Nora wondered. Wasn't Fiona going to ask her who was there and then grill her about Will? Fiona took a deep breath and Nora heard the shake as she let it go and she realised that Fiona didn't have a cold, she'd been crying.

Nora pushed herself up against the pillow. 'What is it? What's wrong?' Will turned towards her, propping himself up on his elbow, his smile fading when he saw her face.

Fiona cleared her throat. 'The email you sent, we got it when we came home from the wedding last night. Adonis translated the pages.'

Nora felt wide awake now. Every nerve ending was alert. 'And?'

'And, he's sent you the translation. But before you read it, you need to know. It's something very sad, Nora. It's something that's going to upset you so. Can you wake Will up?'

She knew Will was here, Nora thought. She'd known all along. 'He's already awake. I'll put the phone on speaker so he can hear.'

'Good,' Fiona said. 'I'll hand over to Adonis.'

His voice came on the line, deeper and slower than usual, his accent heavier.

'Nora, I do not know what you know already about the Greek history.'

'Not very much,' Nora said.

'In the Second World War, in 1941, Crete was taken by the Nazi army but people of this island, they are very fierce, very strong. They very quickly came together to fight and there were many German casualties. And for revenge the German soldiers, they made, I don't know the word –' he said something to Fiona, then came back on the line – 'atrocities. They would come to a village and kill every man. To punish. To warn.' He sighed heavily. 'The village where your grandmother was born, it was one of those places, where this happened.'

'Komboloi,' Nora remembered the word on the first page, the one in English, 'was that what it was called, her village?'

'No,' Adonis said. 'Her village was called Koutonari. Komboloi is the word for what you call worry beads, which all Greek man carry to pass the time.'

Nora remembered the amber-coloured beads on the worn string that Lainey had in her hand when she died.

'But these beads,' Adonis said. 'They are at the centre of your grandmother's story. I will not say more now, but I have sent you an email with my translation of what she says.'

'Thank you, Adonis, and congratulations. I'm so happy for you and Fiona.'

Nora and Will sat up in bed, reading and re-reading the email on Nora's laptop.

My mother had been teasing me, making me guess what it was I would get for my sixth birthday in June. I wanted a gold locket, like the one she wore, if there was enough money. But before my birthday came, it was forgotten about. On May 20th, the German army had invaded Crete. And on June 1st, they reached our village, a convoy of trucks churning up the dust and spitting stones. A pair of soldiers in uniforms walked up and down the narrow streets, shouting an order in German and then in Greek.

All the men were to gather in the platia. It was just an exercise, they said. Nobody would be hurt. My father got ready to go but my mother pleaded with him not to. She was pregnant; her baby was coming any day. She said if he went, she would lose the child. She begged him to take my brother Nikos to the gorge to hide. By the time he agreed, it was too late. When my father and Nikos slipped out, there were already sentries posted at the olive groves around the houses. If they took the mountain track, they would be visible for miles. Instead, they slipped into the small cave in the rock behind the fig tree at the back of the vegetable garden.

They weren't the only men who fled. One by one, as the day got hotter, the German soldiers rounded them up. Pulling old men who could hardly walk from haylofts. Dragging husbands from the arms of their wives. By then, the women knew, this was not an exercise.

My own mother held me close to her. She told me that the soldiers would come to our house. That I must sit quietly and say nothing. That everything would be all right. But she was afraid. I could feel it. When she wasn't looking, I ran outside and across the neat rows of beans and tomatoes my father and Nikos had planted. I squeezed past the branches of the fig tree into the dark, low-roofed space behind it.

They were there, crouched on the dry earth, my father's head in his hands, silent, my brother crying quietly. I began to cry too. My father put his hand over my mouth softly, but I couldn't stop. Nikos took his komboloi, his amber worry beads out of his pocket and handed them to me. He had never let me play with them before but I had watched him closely. I knew what to do. I pulled the beads along the string, counting them, several times, until I had divided them in two. Did I hear voices from outside? I don't remember. But I remember the loud click as I flipped the string and the beads knocked together and my brother

337

and my father gasping. Then I remember the light, suddenly, as the branches of the tree were pulled away. I will never forget the face of the German soldier. His shout to the others. My mother running from the house screaming. I stood, rooted to the spot, the komboloi still in my hand, watching as two soldiers twisted my father's hands behind his back. He kept his eyes on me as he walked away, telling me, without words, not to cry. But my brother fought and struggled. His heavy boots dragging, ploughing up the earth in the vegetable beds as they pulled him away.

They were executed along with nineteen others in an olive grove a few hundred yards from our house. I heard the shots, I tried to go with the women to where the bodies lay, but I was not allowed.

Our house was not burned as others were, but I did not go there again. My mother could not face me after what I had done. I was sent away to the north of the island, to live with an aunt of my father. My things were already there and among them was my mother's locket.

I never saw her again. She could not bear to see me and I understood.

It was my fault, that her husband and her son were executed. That she lost the baby who would have been my younger sister. My aunt tried to be kind to me but I was so ashamed, so guilty about what I had done, that I could not let anyone be close to me.

I heard through a letter, that my mother died just after I left Crete for London and I moved again, as if I putting miles between myself and my country could make any difference.

And for a while, I thought it could. I met Hugh and we married and I had my daughter, my darling child, my beautiful Alanna. But I did not deserve her after what I had done to my own family.

And if I ever forgot that, all I had to was open my locket and look at the faces of my father and Nikos, or hold my brother's worry beads in my hand. And I remember that I am a danger to anyone who loves me.

Will held Nora until her tears had stopped and then they read the note together again, this time more slowly. This was it, the mystery, Nora thought. The dark secret, the terrible thing Lainey had spoken of before she died. A trauma that had happened when she was a little girl, something she could not have prevented. Something she had paid for over and over. A burden of guilt and shame she had carried through her life along with the loss of her mother and her sister and her father and her brother and then her own daughter.

There was a ping as another email arrived from Adonis. This one had an attachment. It was a grainy photograph of a small monument in a small whitewashed square, a dozen names in Greek script carved into a slab of stone, a memorial to the men executed in 1941.

'What was your grandmother's surname?' Will asked.

'Demetriou,' Nora said.

Will opened up a translation site and after a minute, he pointed at the last two names on the list. And there they were, the names of her great grandfather and her great uncle.

'I want to go back,' she said to Will. 'I want to go to Crete, to that village and find their graves and her mother's.'

Will's arm tightened around her. 'And I want to come with you.'

'Okay!' Nora said. 'I'd like that.'

She sat suddenly. 'My mum needs to see this.' She took the laptop from Will and typed Alanna's address into the top of an email. She hadn't even told her mum about finding out that Lainey was Greek or about the other notes she had found. She'd wanted to wait until they were together, but what was in this note of Lainey's had waited seventy years. It couldn't wait a moment longer.

Adonis's flat was two doors down from Loughlin's office. A tiny, L-shaped studio, above a chemist shop, with one tall sash window through which Nora could glimpse a sliver of sea between the buildings opposite. Fiona had already scoured it and Adonis had painted the walls white. There was a bunch of fresh roses in a vase on the draining board and the fridge was filled with food

The clamper, whose name was Joe, had turned up to return Houdini as Will and Nora were loading up the Merc to start moving her things over and he'd insisted on helping and so all the bigger things were delivered, probably illegally, in the back of the clamping van. It had only taken two trips to move the rest over.

It was a random assortment of things she needed, the carry-on bag she'd brought from London, three bags of Lainey's clothes that she'd been wearing over the last six months. The carved wooden bed she'd slept in as a child. The Victorian birdcage. The blue silk curtains from her grandparents' bedroom. A set of antique French bed linen. Some books and boxes of glasses and silver and china including the blue bowl mended with gold. And, of course, Houdini.

'That's it!' Will said, when the last box had been unpacked and they stood back to look at it.

The room was barely big enough to swing a cat, but somehow, Will and Nora managed to fit it all in, though they had to put Houdini under the dining table. And, apart from the cage, none of the things that had been on her list to bring back to London were here. The prayer rug and the temple doors and the swan's back sofa had been sold. But that was okay, Nora thought. She had everything she needed right here. 'I like it,' she said.

'Me too.' Will lay back on the bed. 'We can open the fridge without getting out of bed which is a pretty good thing. You'll have to stand up to put on the kettle though.'

'You want some coffee?'

'Nope.' He held out his hand and she took it and lay down beside him.

He inched down so they were face to face and looked into her eyes. 'Nora Malone,' he caught a spiral of her hair and twisted it around his finger.

'What?'

'Nothing. I just wanted to say your name so many times over the last few months and I couldn't. Now I can. I can also say,' he narrowed his eyes: '"Yassou! Ti kanis". I've been practising my Greek for our trip.' Nora smiled at him, delighted. 'It means "hello, how are you?"'

'Can you say anything else?'

'Se agapo,' he said, tracing the letters on her bare arm.

'Se agapo.' She repeated it after him. 'What does it mean?'

'I'll tell you sometime.' He put his mouth against hers, so she could feel the smile against her lips. 'That you've just told me that you love me.'

'That's not fair...' she began but he cut her off when he kissed her. And it didn't matter, she thought, kissing him back. It was only a matter of time before she said it anyway.

The shop was cleared, the floors scrubbed, the window washed clean, the sign that said *The Memory Shop* painted over. Nora took a last check around the house and sprayed some of Lainey's lemony scent into the air and let a moth that was fluttering in her grandparents' bedroom out of the window into the garden.

There was a knock on the door as she went downstairs and she hurried to answer it, thinking it was Loughlin. He wasn't due to collect the key until tomorrow, but maybe he'd gotten the day wrong and come early.

But it wasn't Loughlin on the doorstep; it was her mum, deeply tanned with bare ankles and soaked sneakers and bare arms underneath one of her trademark silk pashminas.

'Mum!' Nora felt her heart lurch as Alanna put her arms out and she threw herself into them. They stood there, on the wet doorstep, in the biting January wind, holding onto one another, laughing and crying, letting go of one another then embracing again.

'You should have told me you were coming!' Nora said. 'I would have picked you up. When did you get here?'

'I landed an hour ago. My flight was diverted twice because of the weather. It's taken 36 hours to get here, but it's worth every minute to see you.' Alanna put her hand on Nora's shoulders. 'Let me look at you! I've been so worried about you!'

'I'm fine,' Nora laughed. 'I'm good. Do you want to...' she hesitated. Her mum hadn't ever set foot inside Temple Terrace, in her memory. 'Would you like to come inside?'

'Yes. Please!' Alanna shivered. 'It's freezing out there.'

And, to Nora's amazement Alanna stepped across the threshold, shouldered off her rucksack and wrapped her arms around her.

Nora could not believe this was happening. That her mother was home and here, in this house. Then she realised what had brought about this miracle. 'You got my email about Lainey, didn't you?'

Alanna let out a shuddering sigh and nodded.

'I couldn't believe it. It broke my heart, Nora. But it mended it too. I always thought it was me that she rejected, now I see that it was herself she was rejecting all that time. I can't bear to think of all that pain and guilt and shame that must have been bottled up inside her. Why didn't she tell us?'

'I don't think she could tell us while she was alive,' Nora said, 'but she wanted us to know.' She thought about all the other notes that her mum hadn't seen, didn't even know about yet. 'I'm sure of it.'

'Her poor mother and her father and her brother.' Her mum pushed her scarf off her neck. 'I have something to show you.' Nora saw a gleam of gold at her throat. It was the locket she had posted to Bali. Alanna unclasped it and opened it carefully and Nora leaned in to look at the two tiny photographs.

'It's them, isn't it?' she said, softly.

Alanna nodded and Nora studied the faces. The man first and then the boy.

'He's like me,' Alanna said.

She was right, Nora thought. He could have been her younger brother.

'There's a monument,' she said, 'with their names on it, in the village where she grew up.'

Alanna put her hand to her heart. 'Oh that's good. That's something.'

'I'm planning a trip there in February.'

'You and Adam?' Alanna asked carefully.

'No. That's over.' Nora shook her head. 'Oh God! I've so much to tell you.' She didn't know where to start. Will? Lainey's notes? The shop? The money she had made selling everything? But suddenly she remembered that her mum had been travelling for a day and a half.

'You must be tired.'

Alanna yawned. 'Exhausted and incredibly hungry. Is there anything to eat?'

There wasn't even a cup in the house for tea.

'Hang on,' Nora said, grabbing her coat from the hook by the door. 'There's a café a few doors away. I'll be back in two minutes.'

Alanna leaned against the wall after Nora had gone. She had expected to find her daughter heartbroken and upset, but she had never seen her look so relaxed and happy. Whatever she had been doing in Dublin for the last six months, it had done her good. There was a sparkle to her dark eyes and a lightness in her step.

She looked around the empty hall. Thirty-seven years. That's how long it had been since she was last in this house, but she thought she could smell a trace of her mother's perfume still in the air. She followed it from room to room, listening to her footsteps ringing on the bare boards. Seeing the ghosts of all those things that used to be here. The heavy gilt mirrors, the velvet sofas, the cupboards groaning with silver and china and glass The clothes and trinkets and ornaments and artifacts. All those things she had thought her mother cared about more than she cared about people.

Alanna had hated them and she hated her mother, but now, she could see that those things were what stood between Lainey and her pain and her guilt and her shame.

This house looked now the way it must have done the day that her parents moved into it. Her mother, younger than Nora was now, a girl really, trying to escape from the past, trying to heal from a trauma, hoping that maybe, despite what had happened, she could make a happy life. Alanna felt a powerful rush of love for her, as strong and as protective and maternal as the love she felt for Nora.

There were no chairs so Nora and Alanna sat cross-legged on kitchen floor in a square of weak winter sunshine, drinking their coffee. Alanna devouring a pile of the chocolate Florentines that Fiona had told Nora were Hugh's favourites.

'How long are you back for?' Nora asked her.

'Six months at least. I need to take a break from travelling. And I'd like to be near you for a while.' Her mum smiled. 'I've hardly seen you for the last year. I hope you're not about to jump on a plane and go back to London.'

'No,' Nora said. 'I've decided to stay here. I've got a place in the village. A studio. It's tiny but it has everything I need.'

Her mum gave her a long searching look, then she smiled.

'Good. I can't wait to see it!' Her smile broke open into a wide yawn that she tried and failed to stifle.

'Oh God! Sorry Nora! The jet lag is catching up with me. There's so much to talk about but I'm afraid I'm going to have to get some sleep first.'

'Of course!' Nora stood up. 'I can take you back to my place right now.'

'No.' Alanna put a hand on her arm. 'I want to stay here tonight. I left this house in such a hurry and it will be gone tomorrow. I'd like a chance to say a proper goodbye.'

'But there's no bed,' Nora began.

'I have a bedroll in my rucksack,' Alanna said. 'And I've slept in far worse places, Nora, trust me. I'll be fine. Really. You don't have to worry about me.'

They walked arm-in-arm to the front door and then stood for a long time, holding onto one another. Then Alanna leaned back, her arms still around Nora, and looked around the empty hall.

'I feel as if they're still here,' she said softly. 'Hugh and Lainey.'

Nora nodded. She felt it too. She sensed their presence around her, as if they'd come back for one last time to see their house and their daughter.

And Nora smiled as she realised that it had happened. The thing that she had given up on. They were all together, in this house. Her grandparents and her mother. Her broken family, reunited, finally.

It was getting dark as Nora walked out onto Temple Terrace.

She had thought that her heart would break when she closed the door for the last time, when the house had been cleared of

344

all the things she had loved as a child. But she felt a surge of happiness as she turned to look back at it.

At the sign above the darkened window: The Memory Shop. At the shuttered windows and the single light that burned in her mother's old bedroom.

The house wasn't really empty. Her mum was home, properly home, for the first time in thirty-seven years.

And though all the treasures that used to pack the rooms had been scattered, nothing would ever be lost.

Nora had kept a record of everything. There were photographs of all the treasures that Hugh had given Lainey. There were Lainey's notes, the pages she'd scribbled on, carefully pressed and gathered together to make a new story. There were sketches and pictures of every shop window Nora had designed and scraps of stories that her customers had shared with her.

It was the seed of something, all of it. She could feel it. Something alive and brimming with possibility. Some kind of art project about love and remembering.

But Nora didn't have time to think about it now. She was already turning away and walking quickly back to her new flat and to Will. Thinking not of the past, but of the future. Of a new life and her new love and all the memories that were waiting to be made.

Thank You

To my wonderful agent Jonathan Lloyd and to Lucia Walker, Melissa Pimentel, Alice Lutyens, Emma Bailey and everyone at Curtis Brown.

To my brilliant editor Harriet Bourton and to everyone at Orion especially Bethan Jones, Juliet Ewers and Elaine Egan.

To the lovely team at Hachette Ireland. Breda Purdue, Jim Binchy, Ruth Shern and Joanna Smyth.

To my supportive fellow writers, Kate Kerrigan, Cathy Kelly, Marian Keyes and Helen Falconer.

To all the people who have spent time in my corner while I wrote this book. Susan Lamb, Kate Mills, Frances Griffin, Mel Griffin, Bernard Griffin, Danielle Kerins, Doug Lee and Pat Burns.

To my husband Neil, for so many kindnesses it would take another book to name them. And for being part of every single one of my favourite memories.

Read on for an extract from Ella Griffin's
moving and life-affirming novel

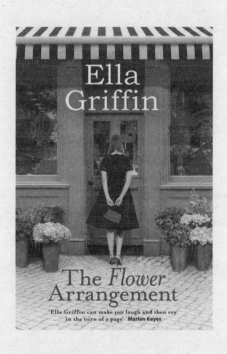

Ivy

Femininity. Tenacity.

Dublin was deserted at 7 a.m. on Saturday morning except for a pair of diehard Friday-night clubbers kissing in the doorway of the antique shop at the corner of Pleasant Street. Three purposeful seagulls flew along the curving line of Camden Street then took a sharp right along Montague Lane. Grey clouds were banked above the rooftops but the heavy rain had thinned out to a fine drizzle and a slant of weak sunshine cut through the gloom and lit a shining path along the drenched pavement ahead of Lara. She stepped into it, luxuriating in the faint prickle of heat on the back of her neck.

This was her favourite time of the year. The madness of Valentine's Day over. Mother's Day still a month away. The wedding season a dot on the horizon. Spring blooms had been coming in from Holland since December but now flowers from Irish growers were arriving. Daffodils with their frilled trumpets and tissue-paper-delicate anemones and the first tulips with sturdy stems and glossy, tightly packed petals.

She made her way past the shuttered shops and the boarded-up stalls, heading for a tall, slim slice of pale pink in the line of red and grey brick facades. Phil, her younger brother, had painted the exterior of Blossom & Grow. The slapdash blobs and trickles he had left in the paint were, she thought, rummaging for her keys, part of the charm, like the swags of realistic-looking painted ivy that seemed to trail up the outside of the three-storey building, curling round the drainpipe and the windowsills. Lara had painted the ivy herself. She had always loved ivy for its tenacity and determination, for the way it pushed through tiny cracks and crevices to reach the light.

She had spent weeks making sketches, teaching herself *trompe l'oeil* techniques, and then conquered her fear of heights to balance on a ladder with her paintbrushes and palette. No two leaves were the same. Even now, five years later, looking up, she felt as if she knew every single one.

She shifted the armful of damp greenery she'd cut from her garden and unlocked the door. The Chubb lock stuck the way it always did. The Yale turned with a soft click and the six Thai temple bells that hung above the door rang out a soft jingle of welcome.

The wild-flower man had already been, she saw. He had his own key and would have driven up from Wicklow before it got light. He had left a huge bucket of narcissi beside the door. The tiny white flowers had been picked before dawn and they glowed as if they had been drenched in moonlight. A second, smaller bucket was packed with bluebells and Lara could smell some hyacinths in there too. She bent down and felt around for the little waxy blossoms and their fragrance rose up to meet her. If perfumes were the feelings of flowers, as her mother used to say, then the hyacinths were as happy to see her as she was to see them.

'You want to open a flower shop?' Her husband's jaw had dropped when she had told him, five years ago. His voice, usually so calm and quiet, had been sharp with anxiety. They had always come to decisions together, careful of one another's needs, but the truth was that deep down they had both wanted the same thing. Then they had lost their baby and instead of turning towards one another they'd turned away.

Lara, who didn't have the energy to shower, who could not find a single reason to get dressed, stayed in bed for weeks. Michael could not sit still. He spent whole days out in the garden bent over his spade, digging beds that didn't need digging, reseeding the lawn, replanting the Chinese camellias he had moved the winter before.

He held Lara when she cried. He reached a hand out to squeeze

2

hers when she lay awake, her knuckles pushed into her mouth to choke back her grief. He told her the pain wouldn't go on for ever; that life would return to the way it had been. But everything had changed, and Lara knew that the only way she could get through it was to change everything.

'Lara, listen to me,' Michael said. 'Floristry is not about floating round arranging flowers. You have no idea what you'd be getting into.'

'I can learn.' She'd hoped he'd be happy for her.

'You don't understand. It's back-breaking work. You'll be on your feet all day, every day, sweeping, cleaning, hauling water around. That's not what you need, not after what you've been through. You need to think about this carefully.'

'All I've been doing is thinking and it's killing me. I thought it would get better when I went back to work, but it hasn't.'

Michael ran his calloused thumb over her palm, following the lines that trailed across it. The head line, the heart line, the health line, the life line.

'Throwing away a career you love is not the answer. Give yourself time. Stay at Green Sea for a few months, then, if you still need a change, set up a design studio at home. Go freelance.'

She shook her head. 'I can't. I've made up my mind about the shop.' She hadn't quite, but she did in that moment.

'Well, you don't need my opinion then.' He let her hand drop. 'But for what it's worth, I think it's a mistake. Retail is tough, and a luxury business in a recession, with unreliable suppliers, difficult customers, perishable stock ... I just hope you're not going to regret it.'

Michael had been trying to protect her, she knew that. He knew what he was talking about. He had run his own landscaping business for eight years. She did trust him, but in some stubborn place deep in her heart, she trusted herself more.

He had been right about some things. It had taken Lara two years to find flower sellers she could trust, and second-guessing how much stock she'd need a week in advance was still a leap of faith. Flowers were expensive and they had a short shelf life. After five years, she had developed better instincts about ordering but

3

there had been disasters along the way. The first Mother's Day she had run out of flowers with half the orders in the book unfilled. Three years ago it had snowed for two weeks before Christmas and she had to throw away over a thousand euros worth of stock. The work was, as Michael had said, back-breaking.

There were late nights, and early starts for weddings, sixteen-hour days in the run-up to Christmas and Valentine's Day. The shop had to be kept cool because the flowers liked it that way, and no matter how many layers she wore, Lara was always cold. Her hands were ruined. Standing all day made her bones ache, and there was a pale blue hashtag in the soft hollow of skin behind her left knee that she thought might be the beginnings of varicose veins.

But Michael had been wrong about the customers. They weren't difficult at all, they were a joy. Lara had known since she was a child that flowers were a language, but what she hadn't realised was that she was a natural translator. That she could help another person to find the flowers that expressed the feelings their words were too flimsy or too worn out to hold. 'I love you' or 'I'm sorry' or 'I'm happy' or 'I'm grateful' or 'I'll never forget you'.

She straightened up and looked around. She loved this small shop, and in a way that she could not explain, it seemed to love her in return. Phil had helped her to strip the walls back to bare brick and to paint the floorboards French grey. They had found the wooden counter in a salvage yard. It had dozens of cubby-holes and drawers for wraps and wire and scissors and ribbon.

The walls behind the counter had deep floor-to-ceiling shelves for vases and jam jars and scented candles, and there was an old wrought-iron revolving stand for cards. But most of the space in the long, narrow shop was taken up with flowers and plants.

Today there were fifty-two kinds of cut blooms, from the tiny cobalt-blue violets that were smaller than Lara's little fingernail to a purple and green frilled brassica that was bigger than her head.

The flowers were set out in gleaming metal buckets and containers of every shape and size. They were lined up on the floor three deep and stacked on the tall three-tier stand in the middle of the shop.

The plants, huge leafy ferns and tiny fleshy succulents, lemon trees and jasmine bushes and freckled orchids, were displayed on floating shelves that were built at various heights all the way up to the ceiling.

Lara had spent weeks getting the lighting right. There were a few soft spotlights above the flower displays and an antique crystal chandelier hung low above the counter. There were strings of fairy lights and dozens of jewel-coloured tea lights and tall, slender lanterns dotted between the buckets. When they were lit, they cast star and crescent moon shapes along the walls and the shop resembled the courtyard of a Moroccan riad – a tiny walled garden right in the middle of the city.

She put her bag and her greenery down on the counter, lit the candles and switched on the fairy lights. Then she took off her coat, pulled her old grey cashmere cardigan off a hook and put it on over the two long-sleeved T-shirts she was already wearing. She went out into the cluttered galley kitchen and filled the kettle. While the water boiled, she rolled forward slowly, loosening up her spine, one vertebra at a time. Her long hair fanned out around her on the worn wooden floorboards. Through a gap in the dark curtain her hair created she spotted a little drift of leaves and petals by the skirting board. No matter how often she cleaned, there was always more to sweep.

She swung her head from side to side to stretch her neck. Then she stood up and spooned loose-leaf peppermint tea into her flask and filled it with boiling water, inhaling the cloud of warm steam.

Opening Blossom & Grow had not been a mistake. No matter how tough it had been, she had only one regret: that she hadn't been able to persuade her husband that it was the right thing to do.

Even now, he didn't seem to understand that the shop had been her lifeline. It had carried her away from the empty space in her own heart and into the lives of thousands of strangers.

When she worked as a graphic designer, the only display of feeling she had seen was when a client who owned a pizza franchise had a meltdown because Lara refused to copy the British Airways corporate identity when designing his logo. Now she

5

was surrounded by feelings every day – joy, sorrow, gratitude, regret, lust, hope. And the one feeling that seemed to underpin them all – love.

She carried her flask and her favourite mug out to the counter, flipped open the fat leather-bound order book and fired up her laptop. She turned on the radio and a Bach cello concerto poured out of the small speakers, the simple, fluid notes weaving around the sounds of the sleepy city waking up outside her window. The rattle of the shutter going up on the betting shop next door. The distant rumble of a Luas train pulling into Harcourt station. The hammering, drilling and whistling from the building site a few doors away. The shouts and laughter from a group of Italian students gathering on the steps of the language school across the street.

A withered petal from the kitchen floor was caught in Lara's hair. She picked it out. It still held its heart shape and an echo of fragrance. She tucked it between the pages of the order book. It was only March but the book was already satisfyingly fat both from daily use and occasional, accidental dousings. The pages were densely covered in a jumble of her assistant Ciara's loopy scrawl and doodles and Lara's copperplate handwriting. Lists of flowers that had been ordered to check off against deliveries. Reminders of the chores that had to be done daily and weekly. Special requests from customers. Bookings that came in on the phone.

Today there were regular orders from two restaurants and a hotel, a dozen small table centrepieces to make up for a charity dinner, and bouquets for the maternity hospital on Holles Street, a house in Kilmacud and an eighteenth birthday party in a tapas bar in Donnybrook. Lara read the message that Ciara had scribbled on a Post-it and stuck crookedly to the page:

It seems like only yesterday that we brought you home, 6 pounds 3 ounces of joy wrapped up in a pink blanket. We felt like the luckiest people alive that day and every day since. Happy 18th birthday to our lovely and amazing daughter Ailish. Love, Mum and Dad.

A thirty-euro bouquet. Lara picked up a biro to start planning it, then gathered up her long dark hair and used the biro instead to fasten a bun at the back of her neck. She rested her chin on her hand. She tried to imagine an eighteen-year-old's cluttered bedroom. The blinds still drawn. A tumble of hair on a pillow. A girl still fast asleep on the day she would take the last few steps across the bridge from childhood to adulthood. She might be given dozens of flowers in her life, Lara guessed, but these might be the very first. And she would remember them twenty, forty, sixty years from now – long after her parents had gone. They would have to be perfect.

By 8.30, Lara had changed the water in every bucket and checked over all her stock, carefully picking out any blooms that wouldn't last for the next seven days. She had trimmed the rejects and popped them into a vase on the counter with a chalkboard sign that said *Please take one home*. She had turned the wild flowers into a dozen ten-euro spring bouquets simply wrapped in brown paper for men who might feel shy about carrying a larger bunch of flowers. She had sterilised the jam jars for the table centre-pieces, made up a rainbow of tissue paper and cellophane wraps, soaked twenty blocks of Oasis and fed the orchids. Ciara had gone away for a romantic weekend with her husband Mort so Lara would be in the shop on her own today. It was a good idea to get a head start.

Mondays were her biggest delivery days. She'd arrive to find huge boxes, fresh off the Dutch transporters that had rolled into Dublin port the night before. She always held her breath as she slit the tape and pulled back the corrugated-cardboard flaps. Ordering online was all about ticking boxes. Species. Colour. Size. Number. Grade of quality. Degree of openness. But there was something miraculous about seeing the flowers she'd imagined brought to life. Roses from Colombia. Chrysanthemums from Ecuador. Orchids from Thailand. Anemones and agapanthus from Spain. Stargazers and parrot tulips from the vast Dutch flower fields.

The shop was usually quiet on Mondays, so she and Ciara could take time to condition everything properly. Stripping leaves, removing thorns, rehydrating the flowers, separating any blooms

7

she'd ordered for weddings or events from the stock for the shop, and filling the tiny cold room.

Tuesdays were catch-up days. Between the phone and walk-in orders, they'd give the shop a proper clean – dusting shelves, polishing vases, replenishing cards and ribbons, tissue paper, cellophane, wire and sterilising fluid.

Midweek there would be a steady flow of customers and some early orders for the weekend. If stock looked as if it was going to run out, there was still time to put in an order.

Fridays were frantic. Men rushing in to buy flowers for their wives and girlfriends. Women looking for last-minute plants to take to dinner parties. Single girls who were going to spend the night in treating themselves to a bouquet on the way home.

Saturday was Lara's favourite day. The shop was busy with strollers and browsers, families out for a walk, loved-up couples in town for brunch, local people who emerged at the weekends to take the streets back for themselves. A Saturday could be even more hectic than a Friday, but it felt more chilled out because everyone had time to stop and, literally, smell the flowers.

Just after nine, the door opened and her first customer came in: a man in his twenties in jeans and a very crumpled shirt carrying two cups of takeaway coffee and a plastic bag full of croissants. He winced when the wind chimes tinkled and Lara turned the radio down in case his hangover was as bad as it looked. 'Good morning.'

'Very good night!' He grinned sheepishly. 'Not sure about the morning yet.'

He rambled around the shop for a while, muttering to himself, apologising to a bucket of stargazers when he bumped into it. Lara asked if he wanted any help, and five minutes later he left with a glorious bunch of white narcissi tucked under his free arm.

A stressed-out woman in her thirties wearing pyjama bottoms under her coat and Velcro rollers in her hair double-parked her Mini on the street right outside and rushed in looking for twelve gifts for a hen party.

'Perfect! Sorted! Done!' She swooped on the line of jam jar arrangements that Lara had just finished. And Lara, who had seen the clamper van go past a minute earlier, didn't have the heart to tell her that the twelve miniature bouquets were meant for the charity dinner.

The shop was busy for the next two hours, then there was a lull. At about twelve, a man in his forties in a light green linen jacket, with thinning hair carefully spiked up to hide a bald patch, ducked in to avoid a sudden shower of hailstones. He cursed under his breath as he shook little nuggets of ice off his shoulders. He looked around at the fairy lights and lanterns and finally at Lara, who was working under a circle of soft light cast from the chandelier.

'It's kind of dark in here.' He sounded disapproving.

'It is.' Lara gave him a quick smile. Choosing flowers, deciding what to write on a card, these were personal things. A little mood lighting didn't hurt.

Hailstones were flinging themselves against the window like handfuls of gravel. 'Bloody typical.' The man rolled his eyes. 'I'm going on a blind date. Better hope she's actually blind if I have to walk to Duke Street in that!'

'Why don't you wait it out?' Lara smiled. 'It won't last long.' She went back to work on a new set of mini bouquets for the charity dinner. She had panicked when she found she didn't have enough jam jars, then decided she could use a dozen mismatched china cups she had picked up in a charity shop at some stage. They were turning out better than she had hoped.

She heard, rather than saw, the man's mood change as he wandered around the shop. He began to whistle, out of tune, to the aria playing on the radio.

The reason why people loved to give and receive flowers, Lara thought for the hundredth time – the truth, the root that ran deep beneath the bouquets for birthdays and anniversaries and births and even deaths – was that human beings were changed by flowers. Even when they were not aware of it, some part of them basked in their beauty. They slowed down. They took deeper breaths. Their faces softened.

'It's stopped.' The man was standing by the counter now. Lara looked up and saw that the sun had come out. The light catching in the drops that clung to the window cast tiny darts of rainbows that danced around them.

'Spring is the sun shining on the rain and the rain falling on the sunshine,' she quoted.

'Seamus Heaney,' the man sighed. 'One of our greatest poets. Hard to believe he's gone. Nobody could say it the way he did.'

'True,' Lara agreed tactfully, although the quote was by Frances Hodgson Burnett, the author of her favourite childhood book, *The Secret Garden*.

The man was staring out of the window. 'I thought I was ready to go out there.' Lara had a feeling he wasn't talking about the weather. 'My girlfriend left me after Christmas,' he said glumly. 'Everyone says I should make an effort to meet someone else, but I haven't been on a date since 1998. I'm not even sure what you're supposed to talk about.' He frowned at the vase of free flowers Lara had left on the counter. 'Isn't that bad for business? Giving flowers away?'

'It's better than throwing them away,' Lara said. 'Help yourself.'

'No, I don't want to look like I'm trying too hard.'

'How about a buttonhole?' she said. 'It'd be something to talk about.'

'Oh go on then!' he sighed. 'Maybe it'll distract her from the fact that I'm not George Clooney.'

Lara picked out a white rosebud. She snipped it below the head, then picked out a stem of *Alchemilla mollis* that was the same colour as his jacket. She twisted it deftly around the bud, secured it with an inch of wire, slipped in a pin and handed it to him. He fixed it on to his lapel.

'What do you think?' she asked him.

He looked down at the flower and then up at her with the beginning of a smile. 'I think I've been very rude and that you've been very kind.' He pointed at the flower. 'What do *you* think?'

'I think you should forget it's a date,' Lara said, 'and just enjoy a nice lunch.'

As she swept the floor for what must have been the tenth time that morning, Lara wondered if she'd see him again. Customers were like flowers: they had their seasons too. Some only appeared once, but there were regulars who came in every other week. Alfredo from Havana, who bought his wife Dominga exotic plants that reminded her of home – succulents and orchids and kumquat trees. Dermot, a perpetually love-struck pensioner who hobbled over from Donnybrook on his Zimmer frame for a single red rose every time a new female guest arrived at his retirement home. Ciaran, who was waving at her through the window right now. He had been coming in to Blossom & Grow with his daughter pretty much every Saturday since the shop had opened.

Lara had met Zoe when she was only five days old – a tiny bundle strapped to her dad's chest in a sling, her face tightly furled, like a rosebud. Zoe had loved flowers when she was still too young to see more than blurs of colour. She would drum her tiny heels in her stroller until her dad took her out and held her up – a flying baby above the buckets of roses and irises and lilies. Once she was old enough to know not to eat it, Lara had given her her own flower to take home every week. A purple iris or a yellow parrot tulip or a bird of paradise cut short and wrapped in cellophane and tissue and tied with a ribbon.

Lara had watched Zoe grow up, week by week, year by year. Seen her take some of her first tottering steps. Now Zoe was the same age as Blossom & Grow. A skinny, long-legged five-year-old in stripy red and black tights and a navy duffle coat. She still had something of a rosebud about her. A saffron-tipped, creamy-centred Leonidas, Lara thought, with her milky skin and her coppery corkscrew curls escaping from under her bunny-ears hat. Seeing her warmed Lara's heart the way the sunshine had warmed the back of her head first thing that morning.

'Well, look who it is!' she said, leaning on her sweeping brush. 'I told the flowers you'd be dropping in this morning.'

'We're late,' Zoe hopped from foot to foot in her scuffed black patent shoes, 'because we had to take a long time feeding the ducks. We have to do everything extra slowly this morning because Mummy needs a long lion.'

'Mummy needs a whole pride of lie-ins.' Her dad yawned and rubbed the coppery stubble on his jaw. 'She was up with Bugs

Bunny here at the crack of dawn. Can you make us up a fifteen-euro bouquet, please, Lara?'

It was what he asked for every week, and Lara had already set the flowers to one side. Three deep-pink anemones with sooty centres, a single full-petalled ballet-slipper-pink Antique rose, half a dozen bluebells, a pale pink hyacinth, a spray of freckly green hellebores.

She made a circle with her thumb and forefinger and began slotting the flowers into it, spiralling the stems so they wouldn't break when she tied them. She watched Zoe out of the corner of her eye. The little girl stopped to gaze up at a bright pink orchid, squatted down to sniff the narcissi and stood on her toes to touch the inside-out trumpet of a calla lily with her red-gloved fingertips.

'Careful there, butterfingers!' her dad warned her.

'It's okay.' Lara smiled. 'She knows not to squeeze them too hard.' She tied the bouquet with a pale green ribbon the same shade as the hellebores.

Ciaran whistled. 'Wow! That is something else. You're a genius, do you know that? It doesn't seem fair that you make that amazing arrangement and I take the credit for it.'

Customers were always telling Lara that she had a gift, that nobody arranged flowers the way she did. Three years of graphic design college and seven years poring over a Pantone colour chart had probably helped. The course she'd taken at the London School of Floristry had taught her the basics of conditioning and arranging. But the truth was that Lara was as amazed as anyone at how instinctive it felt, how easily it all came to her. She rarely had to think about what she was doing. Her eyes and her hands took over, weaving the flowers together, layering colour and texture to create something beautiful and unique every time.

Zoe came over to examine the bouquet. 'How did you know to pick those exact flowers?'

Lara bent down and tucked a curl back under the knitted brim of the little girl's hat. Zoe smelled of outdoors and chocolate cereal. There were breadcrumbs clinging to the front of her coat. Up close, her eyes were the pale green of myrtle leaves.

'You want to know a secret?' Lara whispered. Zoe nodded. 'I don't pick the flowers, they pick me! Now,' she stood up and held out the vase of free flowers, 'let's see which one picks you.'

The small red mitten hovered over the vase and then settled on a bright pink gerbera. Lara folded a sheet of pale pink tissue into a fluffy froth and tied it with a snippet of pink ribbon.

'What's the magic word?' Ciaran asked when she had handed the flower over.

Zoe thought for a moment, then waved the flower like a wand. 'Abracadabra!' she said imperiously.

After they'd gone, Lara stood at the counter for a long time, twisting a stray length of ribbon round one finger while her mind probed nervously at the ache in her heart the way a tongue explores a broken tooth. Seeing Zoe every week was always a blessing, but sometimes it was a cruel reminder too. Five years, she thought, staring down at the ribbon but not really seeing it. Seeing, instead, the life she and Michael could have had if things had turned out differently.

The sadness didn't mug her the way it had in the beginning. Then it had knocked her down every day, worked her over and left her limp and shaking. Now it could leave her alone for a week, then suddenly slide up behind her, pull and prod at her, looking for a way to drag her down.

She forced herself to pick up the phone and make some calls, then check her emails. She swept the floor again. She moved some of the flower buckets around and organised the counter and replaced the till roll. Then, when there was nothing else to do, she dug out the squeegee mop and marched herself outside to clean the already clean window.

One of the girls from the betting shop next door stopped to say hello. A chef from Pizza Heaven who was having a quick smoke by the dumpster bins in the laneway gave her a wave. Ketut, the solemn Balinese man who owned the furniture store two doors down, emerged and asked in his elaborately polite way for Lara's advice about his window display. She spent a few minutes pointing and nodding and shaking her head while he rearranged the gilded Buddhas and the intricate shadow puppets and the brightly painted wooden gods and goddesses who had found their way from Indonesia to keep watch carefully over this tiny corner of Dublin.

As she went back to Blossom & Grow, she glanced over at the Camden Deli across the street and saw the owner behind the gleaming plate-glass window. Glen was fortyish, with a closely shaved head and a mid-Atlantic accent. He had gone to the States on a J-1 Visa when he was twenty and come home a year ago when he'd inherited the café from his mother. He had transformed the place from a greasy spoon to a glossy black-and-white-tiled New York-style deli. Brought in real American bagels and French pastries and Italian espresso and a coffee machine as big and complicated as Lara's brother's motorbike.

Lara raised her squeegee to wave at Glen, but he turned away quickly, in a way that seemed almost deliberate, and ducked out of sight. He used to call over to Blossom & Grow at least once a week, bringing Lara chocolate and raisin twists and cappuccinos with flower designs traced in chocolate dust on the foam. He'd hung around admiring the flowers, complaining good-humouredly about Dublin's lack of decent baristas and gay bars. But it was at least a month now since he'd dropped in. She tried to think back to their last meeting, hoping that she hadn't said anything to offend him.

A flurry of customers arrived, and by the time the shop emptied out again it was after two o'clock and there was still no sign of her brother. She usually liked to do her own deliveries, but today, without Ciara to look after the shop, she'd asked Phil to do the run.

His phone was about to ring out when he picked up. 'What?' He sounded groggy.

'Please tell me you're not still in *bed*.'

'Oh shit! I said I'd come in, didn't I? I forgot to set the clock.' His voice was husky. He'd sounded like this every morning since the age of thirteen, when his voice broke: as if he'd been drinking whiskey and smoking cigarettes in his sleep. 'I decided to take a run down to Kilkee on the bike last night.'

'Why?'

'I don't know. Because it was there. At least I think it was there. It was too dark to see it properly. I could hear the roar of the Atlantic, though.'

'You took a six-hundred-kilometre round trip just to hear the sea?'

'It was only five hundred and eighty-four kilometres,' he yawned. 'And it's an ocean. I'm not sure I'm in a fit state to drive round Dublin.'

'I'll do the deliveries if you look after the shop.'

'Any chance Michael could do it?'

'He's working on a job in Howth all day.'

Michael had started taking on freelance projects after Lara had opened the shop. He worked in his corporate landscaping business Monday to Friday, designing rolling parklands around newly built apartment blocks, dreaming up streams and water-falls to break up the concrete jungles of business parks, colour-coordinating plantings of shrubs and bushes to create pleasing harmonious blurs on the hard shoulders of motorways.

At the weekend, he went back to what he'd been doing when they met – landscaping gardens. Digging out borders, building rockeries and raised beds. Moving earth. Losing himself in activity. Trying to fill the same aching space that she was. She sighed.

'Lara! Stop,' Phil grumbled.

'Stop what?'

'Stop giving me those sad puppy-dog eyes!'

'You can't see my eyes!'

'I don't have to see them to know they're doing that big brown pleading thing. I'll come in for an hour. One hour only, Lara. Then I'm going straight back home to this lovely bed.'

Lara managed to get the delivery bouquets finished between customers. She was about to nip out and load them into the van when she noticed a man in a high-visibility jacket and a hard hat walking purposefully past the window. A moment later, he walked past the other way. Then the door opened a crack.

'Hello,' Lara said.

A head appeared around the door, then the builder edged into the shop in his large dusty boots, looking mortified. He pointed at the flowers in the nearest bucket, some yellow chrysanthemums that Lara kept for funeral wreaths because they were cheerful and because they lasted if not for eternity, at least for a few weeks.

'I'll take ten euro worth of them,' he mumbled.

'They're a lovely colour, aren't they?' She came out from behind the counter. 'But have you seen these?' She pointed at the bucket of sunflowers that blazed in the corner. 'They'll really light up a room.'

He nodded. 'Okay, those then.'

He retreated to the door while she wrapped them, his tattooed arms crossed on his chest, his jaw clenched as if he was waiting for a filling rather than a bunch of flowers.

'Why don't you pick a card to go with them?' she suggested. 'It'll make the flowers last longer.'

His eyebrows, caked in dust, disappeared up under the yellow plastic brim of the hat. 'If she puts the card in the water?'

'If she puts it in a drawer or tucks it into a book.' He looked confused. 'Women don't throw cards away, you know. She'll find it a year, two years, ten years from now, and remember the sunflowers you gave her.'

The builder took a few tentative steps towards the counter and turned the revolving stand slowly, then furtively picked a card and held it out.

'Probably best if you write it.' She slid a biro over to him. It stayed where it was for a long moment, then a huge hand snaked out and took it. The builder hunched over the card, nibbling his knuckles.

'I can't think of anything to say.'

'Just say whatever you'd say in a text.' Lara put the finished bouquet on the counter. 'A romantic one. I just need to pop upstairs for a minute. I'll leave you in peace.'

She went up to the workroom and spent a minute checking over a vase of Memory Lane roses she'd left to open by the window. When she came down again, the builder and the bouquet and the card were gone and there was a pile of change on the counter. She smiled to herself as she put the money away.

*

It had taken careful nurturing and tending and six days of her life every week for two years, but despite the recession and all of Michael's worries, Blossom & Grow had broken even two years ago and had been in profit ever since. Lara was still only earning half the salary she'd made as a graphic designer, but it was enough to cover the mortgage and her share of the bills and to pay back the six thousand euro her father had lent her to start the business, though he always insisted the money was a gift, not a loan.

She and Phil joked that they had to be careful what they said to their father. If Lara mentioned on the phone that she was thinking of repainting her living room, he was quite likely to be at the front door with paint and a ladder before they'd finished the call.

Families fell apart when mothers died, especially when the children were young, but theirs had grown closer, held together by the glue of their father's love and determination. Overnight, his Dick Francis and Stephen King novels had disappeared and been replaced by dozens of books on parenting. He had taken a two-year sabbatical from his marketing job until Phil was old enough to go to school. Walked twelve-year-old Lara down to the local hair salon and asked the hairdresser to teach him how to French-plait her hair. Brought Phil to the toddler playgroup, sat cross-legged on the floor playing clap-handies and singing 'The Wheels on the Bus', not giving a damn that he was the only man there.

He had never missed a school concert or a parent-teacher meeting or a hockey game. He had done the washing and the ironing and the hoovering. Checked their homework every night. Taught both of them to play golf and to fish and to name every plant in the garden. Turned himself, after a rocky start, into a fairly decent cook, though he had never got the hang of baking. Lara remembered coming down in the middle of the night for a drink of water when she was fourteen and finding him in his dressing gown in a blizzard of flour on his third attempt to master a Victoria sponge for her school cake sale.

When Phil arrived, Lara left him propped up at the counter with his leather jacket zipped up, complaining about the cold. She made him a cup of strong coffee and told him to call her if there was anything he couldn't deal with. But her brother was good with flowers, she thought, loading bouquets into the back of her pink van, and with people.

Every light seemed to be green, every loading bay had a free space and she flew through the deliveries to the restaurants and the charity ball. She drove through sun and rain out to Donnybrook to drop off the birthday flowers, making sure that the manager of the restaurant found a champagne bucket to keep them in so they wouldn't wilt before the party started. Then she got into her van again and headed on to Foster Avenue, taking the long way along the Goatstown Road so she could see her favourite tree, a rare magnolia Genie that had taken over the entire garden of a suburban house. The tree was ugly in winter, a tangle of twisting branches like scrawny limbs, but in March it was covered in heart-stoppingly lovely pink and cream flowers the size of teacups.

She had delivered lilies and twisted hazel to that house once, and an elderly woman in a dressing gown with a hot-water bottle tucked under her arm had opened the door and burst into tears when she'd seen the bouquet.

'I'm sorry,' she said, after Lara had found her a tissue and brought her inside into a hallway that felt colder than the doorstep had. 'They're from my son in Sydney. I don't know how to tell him ...' She sat down on the bottom step of the stairs and began to cry again. 'I don't need flowers, I need money to pay the gas bill.'

Lara had given her the money her son had spent on the flowers and left her the bouquet as well. She hadn't told Michael. He had warned her many times that she'd have to separate her heart from the business, but how was she supposed to do that when the flower business was all about heart?

She took a left on to the Kilmacud Road and then another right on to Sweetbriar Grove. She pulled over and opened the back of the van and took out the anniversary flowers. A sullen woman in her thirties with her hair scraped back in a severe ponytail opened the door. 'Can't you read?' she snapped, pointing at a printed sign over the letter box. 'No junk mail, no sales calls, no—' Her eyes widened, her hand floated up to her mouth and here it was, the tiny gap between the moment a woman saw the flowers she'd been sent and the moment when she said 'Ah' or 'Oh' or 'Wow' or, in this case, 'Are they for me?'

And maybe Lara was just imagining it, but it always seemed to her that the relationship between the woman and the person who had sent her flowers fitted into that gap somehow, in all its beauty and complexity, the way the magnolia tree fitted into the tiny suburban garden.

Her heart lifted as she walked back to her van, then sank a little as she began the drive back into town to make the final delivery. The one she had left till last.

Her dad had taken her for an extravagant lunch to celebrate after Lara had paid him back. She had wanted to invite Michael and Phil along but he was having none of it. 'Bring that pair into a Michelin-starred restaurant? Don't be daft. Michael would trample mud all over the carpet and Phil would show up dressed like a bloody Hell's Angel. Anyway, it'll do my street cred some good to be seen out in a posh nosherie with a glamorous woman.'

'Hardly glamorous, Dad,' Lara had sighed, but she had dressed up for the occasion, the way her mother would have. Swapped her shop thermals and jumpers and jeans for an elegant blue jersey dress, worn high shoes.

Afterwards, they walked across Merrion Square to where she'd parked, stopping to admire the flowers in the brightly planted beds. Her dad walked her to the Holles Street gate, then stopped and took her arm and gently turned her around to face him.

For a long time he had looked years younger than he really was. Then, in his mid-sixties, he had started to look his age. Now, every year, her brother looked more like the dashing dark-haired father she remembered from her childhood and her father looked like her grandfather did in photographs. His hair was thinning on top, silvering at the temples. His skin, always tanned from the golf course, was deeply lined. Only his eyes were unchanged. Dark as her own, sparkling now with the wine he'd drunk at lunch and a touch of mock annoyance. He'd been trying to persuade her for most of the afternoon that the money she'd paid back was a gift.

'Make an old man happy.' He put his hands on her shoulders. 'Let me put it into a deposit account with your name on it.'

'We've been through this,' she sighed. 'And you're not old! You're mature.'

'Like a cheese, and you, you're like your mother.' He shook his head. 'You won't do what I want but you give me the brush-off so elegantly that I'm happy anyway. I suppose the money doesn't matter. All that matters is that you're happy. You *are* happy,' he looked at her closely, 'aren't you?'

'Of course I am.' She smiled. 'I wake up wanting to go to work. I think that's about as good as it gets.'

'You've done a great job with the shop. You should be very proud of yourself.' He cleared his throat, a signal that he was straying on to uncomfortable ground but that he was determined to give it to her straight – the way he had when he told her about periods, and later, when he asked her if she needed to go on the pill. He had never shied away from any of the conversations she would have had with her mother, no matter how hard they were for him.

He looked pointedly at the maternity hospital across the street and Lara felt a flutter of anxiety. Please! No! she thought.

'Work is all very well, but it isn't enough. Kids are what give life meaning, Lara. I wouldn't have wanted to go on if it hadn't been for you and Phil. I hope that's not, what do they call it these days, too much information?'

Lara shook her head, hoping that was it, but he went on.

'I know you had your heart broken into a million pieces over there.' He nodded at the hospital. 'I know the last thing you want to do is talk about it. But some women are meant to be mothers, and what happened doesn't change the fact that you're one of them. You know, when your mother and I were dragging our heels about having another baby, you invented an imaginary one of your own.' He looked wistful. 'What did you call her again?'

Lara had called her Lily, but she couldn't say that. If she tried to say anything she would start to cry. She held her breath and managed a jerky shrug.

'Well, I've said my piece.' He tucked a strand of hair behind her ear. 'I'll shut up now and get out of this lovely hair of yours.' He gathered her into a fierce hug. '*Ti amo molto*. You know that don't you?'

He was the straightest talker she knew, but there was one thing he had never been able to say. Phil still teased him about it. 'Come on, Dad, it's three little syllables. You can do it!'

But the words caught in her dad's throat. His face would flush, his hands would flap in frustration. He could say 'I love you' in French or Danish, or Creole or Esperanto. But he couldn't say it in English.

He hailed a passing taxi, and as he opened the door, Lara heard the driver singing along to the radio. George Michael's 'Faith'. She waited until the taxi had disappeared around the curve of Mount Street, then she let her breath out in a little ragged sob and looked up at the elegant facade of the hospital. The red brick glowed in the afternoon sunshine and the windows were full of sky. She wondered which was the room where she and Michael had been told that Ryan was gone.

Faith was not enough: Lara could have told the taxi driver that. She'd had faith through the three years it had taken to get pregnant. Through the false alarms and the dashed hopes and the fear that it was never going to happen. Through those first three months of her pregnancy when she was terrified that she would do something wrong. Through the scare at ten weeks, when she'd had spotting.

She'd still had faith the afternoon of her twenty-four-week scan, when the technician's smile had frozen and she had switched off the machine.

And even after the doctor had told them that she was sorry, really sorry, but there was no foetal heartbeat, Lara had faith. There must be something wrong with the machine, she'd said. She'd felt Ryan moving that morning. Michael was holding one of Lara's hands and the doctor had taken the other one, and she had explained that what Lara had thought was kicking was just a uterine contraction, her body reacting to the loss of her pregnancy. Their baby had been dead for days.

Lara felt then the way she thought people must feel when they realise that the car they are travelling in is about to crash, frozen in the moment between impact and aftermath. Believing, even as the car swerves crazily into the path of the oncoming traffic, that it can somehow be stopped. She turned to Michael, wanting him to tell her that this could not be happening, but all the colour had drained from his face. His mouth above his neatly trimmed dark beard was a thin, shaky line.

She felt as if she was watching herself from a distance as she was admitted to the hospital to be induced. As she had a shower in a tiled communal bathroom, soaping her swollen stomach for the last time. As she lay on a bed in the pre-labour ward hooked up to an IV of Pitocin.

She listened to groans and the restless pacing of the other women on the ward, who were going to deliver live babies. Now she could only remember one of them, a dark-haired girl called Rebecca, very young, very overdue. Sixteen, she heard one of the nurses whisper, unplanned pregnancy, no boyfriend.

Rebecca sobbed all night and Lara was grateful to her for that. She was so stunned by the violence with which her future had been ripped away that she couldn't cry at all. That night, it was as if the girl was crying for both of them.

But in the weeks that followed, all she could do was cry. Everyone said that she would feel better after she went back to work, and she wanted to believe them. But when she finally returned to her office on the top floor of an elegant Georgian house on Leeson Street, Lara felt worse. Everything looked unfamiliar. Her shelves of design books, her framed typography posters, even the weekly work list, written on the whiteboard in her own handwriting. It all belonged to a stranger – the person she had been before she lost her baby. The only things in the room that she felt any connection to were half a dozen flower postcards pinned to the wall above her desk.

The red and white tulip by Judith Leyster. The vase of white lilac by Manet. The bowl of blowsy roses by Henri Fantin-Latour.

The vase of tumbling blooms by Brueghel – lilies and tulips, fritillaries and daffodils, carnations and snowdrops, cornflowers and peonies and anemones. Those flowers had all died four hundred years ago, but that first week back at work, they planted a seed in Lara's heart. Flowers had healed her before, when she was the child who had lost her mother. Maybe they would heal her again now that she was a mother who had lost her child.

'Lara, you do realise,' Michael had said gently, 'that people send flowers to mothers when a baby is born. You'll have to go to maternity wards every other day. You'll have to go back to Holles Street. Have you thought about how hard that will be?' It had been his last attempt to get her to reconsider and the only thing that could have changed her mind, but by the time he said it, it was too late.

She had already resigned. Told her boss, Frank, that afternoon that she was leaving. Blurted it out in a traffic jam on the way home from a meeting because they were friends and because she felt like a fraud taking a brief for an annual report that she was never going to design. He had looked sad and shocked but not surprised.

'When do you want to go?'

'As soon as you can do without me.'

He had helped her clear her desk and driven her home. Her things were still in the boxes, lined up in the room that should have been Ryan's nursery.

Lara parked on Holles Street and unloaded the last delivery of the afternoon, a frothy arrangement of white agapanthus and lisianthus with the faintest blush of pink.

Two overdue women in slippers with fleece dressing gowns pulled around their enormous bumps were smoking on the steps of the maternity hospital. 'Jesus,' one of them said, turning to look at the bouquet as Lara passed, 'I'd have to have triplets before me fella gave me a bunch like that.'

'I'd have to have the winner of the Grand bloody National,' her friend snorted, 'and the Cheltenham Gold Cup.'

Lara was smiling as she crossed the marble floor of the entrance hall, but her throat tightened as she took the stairs to the third floor, where she had given birth to her own baby on a sunny spring morning sixteen weeks before his due date.

The first time she had delivered a bouquet to this hospital she had sat outside for nearly an hour trying to talk herself into getting out of the van. She'd only made it as far as the hall, where she'd dropped the flowers on the porter's desk and bolted back out. But she'd forced herself to keep coming back until she could bring the bouquets all the way up the stairs to the nurses' stations on the maternity wards.

She had learned to distract herself, to fill her mind so there was no room for the memory of the day she'd walked down these same stairs without her baby. Today, she made a mental list of flowers for next week's order, moving on to foliage as she hurried along the corridor, past the closed doors of the private rooms. She handed the bouquet over to the nurse at the desk, then started back the way she'd come.

'Nurse!' A voice called from behind a closed door as she passed.

Lara looked up and down the corridor. It was empty.

'Please?' The woman sounded frantic. 'Could someone help me?'

Lara hesitated, then walked back and opened the door.

A pale, exhausted-looking woman was propped up on the pillows in the bed, a baby in a blue blanket in her arms. 'Please!' she gasped, pointing at a stand near the door. 'Can you get me that bowl?'

Lara picked up the plastic bowl and crossed the room quickly.

'Can you hold him for a second?' The woman held up the bundle. 'I need to be sick.'

Lara froze and looked down at the baby. He could not have been more than a few hours old. 'I can't,' she said. But the woman was already thrusting him into her arms.

Nothing Lara had read in her 'what to expect' books had prepared her for the tiny body of her dead son, so small that he fitted into her cupped hands. He weighed exactly two hundred and forty-one grams. He was the colour of a ripening plum.

She had returned to the hospital and brought Ryan home the night before he was buried. Michael could not bear to look at him but Lara could have looked at him for ever. His eyes sealed closed beneath the finely traced eyebrows. The smooth whorls that would have become his ears, the mouth like a puckered flower. She had sat up all night holding him in her arms, learning him by heart.

'It happened for a reason,' Michael kept saying. But when Lara asked him what that reason was, he couldn't tell her.

The post-mortem showed that their son had died prematurely because of a rare chromosomal problem. The chances of it happening a second time were minimal. The doctor said they could try to get pregnant again whenever they were ready, but a year had gone by, then three, then five, and Lara still felt that having another child would be a betrayal, that they would just be trying to replace Ryan.

Lara braced herself as she took the baby from the woman in the bed. She had not held a baby in her arms since that night she had held Ryan. She waited for the usual tsunami of grief to slam into her, but it didn't come. Instead she was overcome with something that was almost joy. He was small and helpless, but he was so alive. She could feel his warmth through the blanket. He squirmed against her chest and let out a small, scratchy little cry.

The woman finished retching into the basin. 'God! Sorry!' She wiped her mouth with a tissue. 'He was two weeks overdue. They had to induce me last night. The stuff they gave me was awful.' Lara nodded; she remembered it. 'I keep getting these waves of nausea, but it's worth it! I still can't believe he's here!' She held out her arms.

Lara handed the baby over, carefully. 'Does he have a name?'

'My husband thinks he's a Daniel,' the woman settled the baby gently into the crook of her arm, 'but I like Ted.'

'Me too!' Lara smiled. 'It's my dad's name!'

'Seriously?' The woman looked up at her. The colour had come back into her face now. She still looked exhausted, but her eyes were shining with happiness. 'It wasn't just a coincidence that you came to our rescue. It was a sign!'

Lara leaned over and touched the baby's cheek. Felt the velvet of his skin beneath her fingertip, softer than the petal of any flower.

She had the strongest feeling that maybe the woman was right. That maybe this was a sign for her too. She was only just forty; it wasn't too late to try for another child. There was still time.

**Don't miss out on this
captivating tale – order
your copy today!**